The Mind's Door

Cassandra Morphy

Chapter One
The Three

Now

There are many worlds of imagination out there. Neverland, Narnia, Middle Earth. They all have one thing in common, someone had to dream them up. The imagination has spawned more worlds than there are people to live in them. Some of those worlds are closer than you might think. One of those worlds, my world, Desparia, turned out to be more real than I could ever imagine.

I had been coming to the world of Desparia for years before ever meeting the three people who would change my life completely. It started out as an escape from my everyday life and was as easy as simply closing my eyes and imagining myself there. The world of my daydreams started out small and vague and I built it piece by piece as I explored the land that I called Fandor. Little did I know that it would become so much more than just some fickle fantasy.

The day was simple enough. It was raining in the small village that I had been passing through at the time. I was fortunate enough to avoid the worst of it as I dashed for the first shelter that I could find in the middle of the square, the village's one and only tavern. Loud, heavy thunderclaps hit just outside the building and the rain started coming down in earnest just seconds after getting inside.

I waited just inside the door for a few moments while my eyes adjusted to the dim interior light. Even with the downpour and heavy cloud cover outside, the tavern was darker still. The one decent window of the main room was clogged over with gunk that blocked out much of the light. The two old lanterns hanging on the support beams burned low, leaving the dim light streaming in through the door the only source of illumination in the place.

As the room came into focus, I noticed it was a lot emptier than I was expecting. Two of the four round tables that took up most of the room sat empty. Water was leaking down from the roof above, dripping on the two vacant tables and making the room feel as damp and dank as it was outside. Puddles had formed under the tables where the water gradually seeped through the cracks in the floor.

As I made my way over to the empty bar, I stomped out my boots, shaking off my oversized green tunic. I was trying to get what little rain had made its way onto me off, letting the droplets join their friends in the puddles below. Not wanting to venture too far into the place that stank of old beer and sick, I took the first stool at the bar.

"What'll you have?" the bartender asked, barely glancing up from where he was wiping down the bar. The old, dirty rag he was using smelled worse than the rest of the place.

"Just a tankard of mead, thanks," I replied. He simply nodded, before heading off to retrieve it. While I don't get anything from drinking the mead, it would draw too much attention to myself if I didn't have anything. The last thing I wanted to do, in either world, was draw attention to myself.

As I waited for the drink, I looked towards the table in the corner. There were three women sitting there, huddled around something and speaking in low tones. Even with the tavern as deserted as it was, they seemed afraid of the wrong ears hearing what they had to say. I could only see the face of the one in the corner, as the other two faced away from me, the hoods of their cloaks up. She looked prettier than I would expect for someone from a backwater town like that one. Her long black tresses cascading around a face one would not forget easily.

After the bartender slapped the tankard down in front of me, he just stood there looking at me oddly. At first, I was thinking he was about to card me, I was underage after all. But then he just extended his hand. "2 copper," he said in his guttural voice. He rubbed his fingers together after I didn't immediately turn to my purse. This reminded me that there wasn't anything such as a drinking age in this world of mine. The only thing these bartenders cared about was getting paid.

"Right," I said, after getting over the initial shock.

My coin purse hung heavy under my cloak. As usual, it didn't occur to me to consider the origin of my funds. I merely reached in and produced a couple coppers, after fishing around in a large collection of coins of much higher value. The bartender left me alone once he extricated the meager funds for the drink, finishing up his wiping down of the bar.

I looked over towards the only other occupied table, where a man was slumped over, his own tankard held clumsily in his hand. After I took a large sip of my mead, and, more importantly, the bartender headed into the back to get something, I darted a furtive look over at the three women in the corner. They seemed adequately distracted by whatever it was that they were looking at and not likely to notice my own actions. And yet, as I considered what I was about to do, I had an unsettling feeling like I was being watched.

With one last look at the door to the back room, I slipped off my stool and over to the passed out drunk. Feeling a bit braver than usual, I poked at the unconscious man, making sure that he was quite out of it. The man breathed in sharply, causing me to hold my own breath, before he started to snore loudly. I smiled at that, ducking down next to his chair.

By the time the bartender had returned from the back room, I was back in my bar stool, finishing off the tankard. "I'll have another," I said, producing another set of copper coins, this time from my newly acquired coin purse. I'd have to wait until later to properly count out how much I would be adding to my personal funds, though the purse was on the heavier side. I ought to know; I've certainly seen a lot of them in my time there.

After downing the second tankard, I grudgingly headed back out into the rain. I would have liked to stay in there, at least long enough to wait out the rain and get something to eat, but it was too much of a risk to stay any longer. One of the downsides to my way of living is that I really can't overstay my welcome. I did that once and almost lost my hand in the process.

As I headed around the village square, making my way to the road out of town, I noticed that I hadn't gotten out of there as cleanly as I had hoped. I wasn't too sure who my tail was, but as usual, it didn't matter much. Whoever it was, if they caught me... well, let's just say it's a good thing I'm not easy to catch.

The town was small, little more than a farming village. There was only the one road, with what few businesses there were in town all pointed towards it. It didn't provide many options to slipping my tail, but there was a nice alley between the general store and the apothecary. As I headed under the eaves to the apothecary, I resisted the urge to take a peak over my shoulder. To calm my nerves a bit, I started counting the steps as I edged closer to the alley. Once I passed the last pillar, I crossed my fingers and hoped the pillar would block my tail's view of me. I darted around the corner and ran straight into someone standing there, blocking the entrance to the alley.

I fell back into a rather large pile of what I hoped was mud. The rain was coming down too hard for me to smell it if it wasn't. "What the hell," I said angrily, looking up at the person blocking the alley.

"What the 'hell', yourself," she said, though with her accent, she pronounced hell more like heal. It reminded me that they didn't have that word in this world. It was one of those quirks that, no matter how hard I tried to change, my mind would force this world to follow. "You have something that doesn't belong to you."

As she said that, the sky flashed a bit from a lightning strike, lighting up her face almost ominously. It was the first time I had managed to get a decent look at her, the alley being as dark as it had been in the tavern. She was one of the three women at the corner table in the tavern, the one that had been sitting in the corner. I looked over at my tail, who was currently leaning against the pillar that I had ducked behind. When I saw her face, I had to do a double take between the two, as this one had the same exact face as the one blocking the alley.

"What are we going to do with her?" came a voice from behind me. It was a taunting lilt that hinted at more amusement than I had thought the events warranted. Reflexively, I turned my head to look at her. Behind me stood a blond woman, who I took to be the third occupant of the table.

"I guess that would depend," my tail said as her twin stepped out of the alley, into the light streaming from the window of the general store. Their smile echoed the amusement in the voice of their friend. Strapped across the first woman's back was a long quarterstaff, though she never went for it. I noticed the unmistakable bulge of a sword under her sister's cloak as she shifted her weight. She came to a halt on my right flank, her hand unconsciously resting on the hilt of her sword.

"On what?" I asked, recovering my demeanor and plastering a sneer on my lips. "On how close the nearest trooper is?" I gestured towards the sword hilt as I regained my feet, settling my cloak around me and pulling up my hood as I looked around at the three women that had surrounded me. "I'm sure they would be just as happy to take all of your heads for those weapons you so carelessly wear as take my hand for this." I patted the recently acquired coin purse.

"Let's just go," the first woman said, a grimace firmly locked on her face. "The last thing we need right now is to be drumming up trouble."

"Besides," said the blond, the teasing tone gone. "It's not like she'll help us anyway."

This comment took me by surprise. It wasn't often someone actually wanted, let alone needed, my help. I had spent much of my time on that world alone, sticking to myself and the shadows that would protect me while I did my work. If these women were looking for a thief, though, then perhaps this meeting wasn't as bad as I had been originally thinking. "Well, now," I said, in full gloat mode. "I didn't say I wouldn't help. Perhaps we got off on the wrong foot. Hi there, I'm Maya." I held out my hand in greeting.

The twin in the alley stood there, an unsure look on her face, staring at my hand for the longest time.

"Uh, guys," the blond said behind me.

"I don't think we want her help; do we, Tina?" the twin standing by the pillar said, sounding a little worried.

"No, you're right. It was stupid to come out here at all." The twin in front of me sounded almost scared, which surprised me considering they had me outnumbered.

"Uh, guys," the blond said again.

"Let's just get back to the tavern. We'll figure out a plan that doesn't involve people like... her."

"But what about her? I mean she's seen our faces and knows about your swords and--"

"Guys!" shouted the blond.

The twins both jerked their heads over towards her, finally startled out of their diatribe. Their eyes started to bug out a little, as if they had seen something that they weren't expecting. I turned around to see what they were looking at. The blond was wearing some sort of amulet around her neck, the gemstone resting at her cleavage. If I had seen it earlier, I would have figured its sole purpose would have been to draw attention to her breasts, as they were ample and easily the most striking thing about her. However, at this particular moment, the gemstone was glowing brighter than the light streaming through the general store's window.

"I'm guessing that's a bad sign," I said, as I backed away into the newly vacant alleyway as the first twin moved towards the blond. The three girls seemed to have quickly forgotten me in light of the amulet's illumination.

"Run," the blond said, causing the twins to bolt, each in a different direction. I took this as a fine suggestion and followed my own path down the alley. The same path that I had been planning to take only moments prior, before being so rudely interrupted by the three.

On the other side of the alley was a farm, with cornstalks growing well above my head. Whatever the glowing gemstone signified, I imagined the field would be a suitable hiding place. I darted through, trying my best to minimize the disturbance of the corn. Although, no matter how hard I tried, I couldn't stop them from rustling. The sound gave away my position with every step. After a few paces, I stopped and turned around. The path I had taken was hard to distinguish even for me. So, I figured, as long as I wasn't running through the field, I would be easily missed by anyone walking by. I sat down right where I was, the stalks quickly hiding me and blocking most of the rain. Despite any danger that might have been coming from the town, I figured that spot, hidden beneath the corn, was the perfect place to catch a quick nap. The dark of night is usually the best time to head out of town, especially when my exit would be watched for.

Before I could nod off, though, a loud trumpet came from the village square. When I got over the initial shock, I gulped loudly. There was only one group that used a trumpet to announce their presence, and I would do well to avoid them at any cost. Thoughts of a nap quickly forgotten, I stuck to the field as I headed directly away from the square, using the trumpeting sounds that still echoed around me as a guide. They quickly faded as I got deeper into the field, but I managed to keep my bearings and headed straight. With the corn surrounding me and blocking my view of the sky above, I lost track of time and it felt like hours before I finally made it to the other side of the field, coming out into a clearing.

There was an old, worn down farmhouse off to the side of a dirt path. The warped boards showed no sign that they had ever been painted and the thatched roof had a huge hole in it. The road out of town was noticeable down the long path off to my left, a lone figure stumbling up it. When I recognized him from the tavern, I ducked back into the field a bit, hoping he hadn't noticed me. As he approached the house, I heard a squeaking door open.

"Oh, no," a woman's voice said, coming from the house. "Not again. Will you ever go into town without going to that infernal bar?"

"Sorry, Margery, but it is so much worse than that," a dejected voice came from the man. "I... I lost... everything."

"What do you mean?" yelled the woman, as she grabbed the man by the arm and jerked him inside.

I waited a bit, hoping the two would stay inside and not be watching the road. The rain had stopped at some point while I had been wandering through the fields and the clouds in the west had started to part, showing signs of the sun setting over the mountains. I waited in the field until twilight before heading off down the road. The proffered coin purse was left abandoned on the edge of the field where, hopefully, the former owner would find it in the morning. No matter how made up this world was, even I had limits on who to steal from.

Once down the road a bit, I made a broad circle around the town, not wanting to get anywhere near there with the current residents. With the late hour, the troopers were undoubtedly staying the night in the tavern. The officers would take what few rooms were available, expelling and even killing those guests who were stupid enough to refuse to vacate. After all, that was exactly what the Jakala Troopers did, and everyone knows it by now.

It took a good portion of the evening before I made it back to my cache of supplies just outside of town. Pulling on my increasingly heavy pack, I headed down the same road that had taken me to this sorry excuse of a village. I just hoped that I had missed a side road somewhere along the way. It wouldn't do for me to return to the last town that I had visited. After all, it wasn't exactly like I left that one in much better circumstances.

Chapter Two
The Wake-Up Call

Five Years Earlier

A lot of thought went into my escape from the world that I was born to. I didn't give up on life all willy-nilly. There wasn't some overwhelming bully that I had to escape, though there was a bully. No need for adventure more than what life could provide, though there wasn't much on that end either. It was a lot that happened in a very short time that made me give up on the thought of ever finding anything close to peace of mind on Earth. Only then did I forego it for the much more exciting world of Desparia; the world that only existed in my mind. I guess it started my last month of fifth grade.

"Maya, it's time to get up," my mother called from downstairs. As she had every day over the past few years.

I rolled over, dumping The Hobbit onto the bed beside me. I had been reading it, for the fourth time, last night as I was trying to get to sleep. I never managed to go to sleep without a book in my hands. Not since my father used to read to me when I was a child, lulling me to sleep with thoughts of monsters, dragons, treasures, and adventure. That changed when I first went to Desparia, when I started living my own fantasy stories. But I'm getting ahead of myself.

I squealed as I crushed the book beneath me, quickly rolling off of it to prevent further damage. The book was already half destroyed, falling apart at the binding. This was from the time it's spent in my backpack, making its occasional rounds at school. I was in the top track English class, due to my mother's insistence. As none of my friends were in that class, or several others, the open assignment book reports were an excuse to bring my old go to books to school and sneak in a little light reading when surrounded by people that I didn't like.

After flattening the damaged corners of the book as best as I could with my hand, I placed it back with its friends on the large bookshelf that took up an entire wall of my bedroom, right between the LotR box set and the latest book that my father had brought me. This one was a story about a dark elf that wanted to be good, turning from his evil people and their goddess. He promised me the next book in that series when he returned that night, knowing full well that I would have inhaled the first one already. Sure enough, I had gotten through it that first night he was gone this trip, as I always did with the books he brought me.

I hated whenever my father had to go away, but it was important to his job. He was an insurance adjuster and, whenever a large catastrophe happened, he had to go wherever it was and help make things right again. Insurance people tend to get a bad rep, probably from those few bad eggs that are always being depicted as money hungry, greedy swindlers. My dad wasn't like that, though. He only wanted to put people's lives back in order as quickly as possible. No one wants to live in a disaster area.

"Maya," my mom shouted up at me again. Her voice was louder as she shouted directly up the staircase out of the kitchen. "Don't make me come up there."

"I'm coming, Mom," I yelled down to her, as I shook the last of the sleep out of my head and started to get dressed. As usual, I didn't put much thought into what to wear, just grabbing the first thing that I could find in the drawers, and headed down to breakfast. The smell of eggs and bacon greeted me before I got to the stairs. My plate was already full of both, with a glass of orange juice beside it.

"Eat quickly so I can drive you to the bus stop," Mom said, as she fumbled around with the toaster. Her long, wavy, brown hair, which I had inherited from her, was in a high ponytail that day, as it usually was when she had to work. She was a nurse at the hospital just up the road from the schools and had insisted on driving me all the way there until the start of fourth grade, when I insisted on riding the bus with my friends. We had compromised on her driving me to the bus stop, though I was intent on ending that as well soon enough.

"Mom, I'm perfectly capable of walking to the bus stop myself. I'm ten years old, that's double digits. I'm almost eleven. I'm not a little kid anymore."

"Oh, hush. You'll always be my little kid. Now eat."

After wolfing down the food, with my mom egging me on at every step, she grabbed up my backpack and hurried me out the door and into the back seat of her minivan. "I won't always be around to make sure you get up on time," Mom said, as she pulled out of the driveway. "If you want me to treat you like the double-digit person you think you are, maybe you should learn to get up on time by yourself."

"Maybe you can get me an alarm clock," I suggested, as I stared out the window.

She looked at me in the rear-view mirror, a knowing look on her face. "Maybe for your birthday next month."

I just rolled my eyes at that thought. How lame would it be to get something as stupid as an alarm clock for a birthday present, especially since my birthday was right at the beginning of summer, right when I wouldn't need an alarm clock for several months. But that was just the sort of thing for Mom to do.

The bus stop was only down the hill at the end of our street where it meets up with Main Street, but Mom insisted on seeing me there. It always annoyed me how much she babied me. But over the years since then, I had started to feel like I needed it a little more than I admit. She pulled over at the corner, holding my lunch bag over the seat as I got out of the car.

"I have a shift at the hospital, but I will be by to pick you up here after school today."

"Mom, I can walk on my own. You don't have to worry about it."

"I'll always worry," she admitted, giving me one last smile before I closed the door, blocking her from sight.

Less than a minute after she pulled away, heading for work, the bus pulled up. I gave a quick wave to the driver as I climbed up the stairs and headed back to where my friends usually sat. Ashley and Jen lived next door to each other, and three blocks away from me. But Ashley's mom worked as an admin at the same hospital where mine was a nurse, so they threw us all together early and often. We'd been practically inseparable since, though that changed rather quickly after that day.

"Oh, hey, Maya," Ashley said. She straightened her expression as she saw me, trying to hide the fact that she had been laughing before I arrived. She tried to put on her sweet and innocent face, but I had always been able to read right through it. Jen, sitting next to her by the window, looked outside rather than look at me.

"Hey Ashley, Jen," I nodded to each of them before sitting in the seat across the aisle from them. "What's so funny?"

"Nothing," they both said together, which got them laughing again. I shrugged it off, figuring it was some inside joke they had between the two of them, and didn't think much of it until later. We started talking about homework and other boring stuff, which helped to make the time pass less slowly than it would otherwise. School was always so annoying for me, getting in the way of more important things like having fun.

By lunch, all I wanted to do was get home and read, preferably alone. Ashley kept giving me dirty looks all day, as if there was something that she wasn't telling me. Something that she didn't want to tell me but knew that she should. It was getting on my nerves, but I wasn't about to say something. They were my only friends and the last thing I wanted was to lose them over something stupid like that. So, I kept my mouth shut as I started pulling out my lunch.

"Seriously? Peanut butter and jelly again?" Ashley asked, turning her nose up at my sandwich.

"I like PB&J," I said, defending my mom's choice in sandwiches to make for me.

"But every day?" Jen asked. "Don't you ever get tired of it?"

"No," I said, my mouth already half full with my sandwich.

"Lay off her," came a voice from the next table over. "It's not her fault her parents are poor."

Laughter buffeted me from everywhere, like water from a broken dam. Jen ended up with milk coming out of her nose as she and Ashley joined in. I blushed, not used to being the center of attention, and certainly not liking it one bit. I tried to go back to my lunch, ignoring them like I had been taught. But the laughter wouldn't stop, spurred on by jokes here and there about how my clothes were hand-me-downs and that our house was falling apart.

I was a bit confused when they mentioned my clothes. Looking down at the outfit I threw on that morning without looking at it, I only just realized that I was wearing one of my dad's old shirts. It was advertising some old cartoon show that wasn't on anymore, that I had never actually seen. I just wore it because I liked the shirt. I liked that it belonged to my dad, especially when he was out of town. It was like carrying around a memory of him when he wasn't there.

As for the comments on my house, well that made no sense at all. Sure, I didn't live in a mansion or anything. And it hadn't even been built in the last decade. But I liked my house. It had character, as my father would say. And no one who's been inside would think of us as being poor. I looked over to Ashley and Jen, both of whom had been in my house loads of time, only to see them start up a fresh fit of laughter at the look.

I wolfed down the last of my sandwich, glaring over at the people surrounding me. As I grabbed my stuff and burst out of the room, the laughter following my retreat until the door closed behind me. With only a single glance back at the closed cafeteria doors, I headed off to the library. Even before getting there, I pulled my well-worn copy of A Wrinkle in Time, the last book for our English class for the year. I was already ahead of the rest of the class. But, given how quickly my friends had turned on me, I figured I could finish the rest of the book before anyone really wondered where I had disappeared to. If anyone ever did.

I spent the rest of the day hidden away in the back of the library, only reemerging to catch the bus back home.

Chapter Three
Vernala

Now

"I wish you'd stop spending all your time in la la land," Mom said, jarring me out of my daydreams. "You're almost sixteen years old. You need to start living in the real world. Maybe we should do something special for your birthday this year. You know, like a sweet sixteen or something. You haven't had a proper birthday party since..."

"Huh?" I asked, as if her words hadn't registered. Truth was, I never really had trouble remembering what people say to me when I come out of my daydreams, just in focusing on the words enough for them to register consciously.

"I said.... oh, never mind," she said, giving up easily. She had stopped fussing over me lately. I started to wonder if she was hurt that I didn't pay more attention to her. Or if she'd ever give up on trying to break through to me entirely. Or, more importantly, if I would even care if either came to pass.

#

I grudgingly re-entered the good town of Vernala. It took me two days to walk there from the last town. Two long days, in both worlds, which took me a bit by surprise. It used to be that I could just think about being at the new location and I was there, with the suitable travel time taken into consideration. For some reason, though, I had experienced every boring minute of the trip this time around.

There hadn't been any side roads between the two towns. While I had made the trip down that road often enough, in my normal mode of transit, I could have easily missed one. Travelling through the woods could be even more dangerous than the troopers I was leaving behind. I just had to hope that I'd be able to get through town before anyone noticed that I was there. It was a problem that I only seemed to have in Desparia.

Unlike the last town, whose name I never caught, Vernala had five taverns and a good assortment of other businesses across several roads. In a better economy, the place might have even expanded into an actual city. But poor local leadership, the downfall of the last empire, and the taxes stemming from the new one had left it somewhere in the middle.

With a proper disguise, I could manage a day or two there, provided I avoided the three taverns that I had worked in previously. One of the many things I loved about this world was how few people cared when someone walked through town with the hood of their cloak up; it made my job so much easier. My current supplies could last me a few months. So, I could just leave town without spending any time there. But where would the fun be in that?

The Dancing Pony was the tavern in the dead center of town. I had avoided it in my prior visits to this town mostly due to its location. The merchants in the area charged more for their wares, causing their purses to be heavier, but the town guards were also quicker to respond. Basically, it was in the rich part of town, with two of the largest manors in town smack dab in the middle of it. I preferred the slimmer pickings but relative ease of the other, poorer sections of town.

As I entered the tavern, just after sunset, I was reminded of the other reason why I avoided such taverns. The door bumped into a patron, spilling his mead over the table right behind it. I slipped through a small hole that only someone of my dainty physique could manage before the obviously drunk guy could turn around. I'd say the loss of his drink was his own fault for sitting so close, but I was hard pressed to make it even to the bar through the throng of the overcrowded pub. It is rare that I found something in my own world that I'd bring to Desparia given the chance. Occupancy limits due to fire regulations would be one of them. On the other hand, I had managed to procure five decently sized purses along the way to the bar and no one seemed to have noticed.

"What'll it be?" the bartender asked. "First drink is on the man in the corner." He pointed off into the back corner, where there was an elevated section usually reserved for VIPs.

"Well, then, I'll have a..." I began before turning my attention to the direction he pointed in. My face fell. Sitting in the seat of honor was none other than Grandor Fell. Among other things, Grandor was the leader of the thieves' guild in Vernala. My earlier troubles were, in no small part, due to his presence. In towns with no thieves' guild, which were most towns in Fandor, one could steal all they like without repercussions as long as they don't get caught. Here, on the other hand, you could get caught all you like, as long as you had a membership to the guild. It's like your own get out of jail free card, without the card part. I, on the other hand, was not affiliated with the guild. There's a whole thing about dues and giving a cut of your take to the guild, which mostly goes directly into the pockets of Grandor. Plus, they don't like it when you leave town unannounced or work in towns other than Vernala.

And, of course, there's also the fact that I was never invited.

"On second thought," I said, turning back to the bartender. "I'm not that thirsty."

As I turned to leave, my cloak was grabbed from behind by a strong hand on the end of a thickly muscled arm. "Not so fast, little one," came a gruff voice from behind me. "Mr. Fell has requested your presence. It wouldn't be kind to ignore him again."

"What can I say?" I said, as I slipped my club out from its usual hiding place. "I'm not a kind girl."

I didn't have the leverage, or strength for that matter, to make much progress against the meathead that was dragging me through the throng. Instead, I hit someone bigger than him in the shin as we passed by. The bigger man was sitting at one of the few tables the tavern managed to keep in one piece. And from the looks of the guy, it wasn't going to be that way for long. The meathead was trying to get through an overly crowded section of the bar, one right at the steps into the VIP section, when the giant caught up with us.

And by giant, yes, I mean a real giant. Certainly not a full blooded one, as those have been hunted to near extinction by the current empire. But he was close enough. The room had two stories to it, with a balcony over the bar. And yet he still had to crouch to stand.

Maybe it wasn't his shin that I hit with my club. He had looked remarkably smaller when we passed him.

"Uh, hi," I said to the giant, drawing the attention of the meathead to him. The crowd still hadn't parted to let us through, though Grandor had already spotted me and was starting to come my way.

"That hurt," the giant said slowly, as if trying to think of the right words to say. Often common is a giant's second language, so this is very possible. Then again, a giant's blood usually runs out of oxygen before getting to its brain, so it could just be stupid.

"What?" the meathead asked simply. Unlike the patrons that had been blocking our way, the meathead was not smart enough to run from the giant. Unfortunately, I was still stuck there myself. His grip on my cloak was firmer than ever as he stared up at the giant in horror. With the meathead momentarily distracted, I started attacking the knot that kept the cloak in place. If I couldn't dislodge the meathead from the cloak, I'd have to ditch the cloak to save myself. I didn't exactly get that far.

With a grunt of effort, the giant raised his hand, which, sure enough, contained his table. There was no way I was going to get out of there in time, so I simply closed my eyes and waited for the impact. When it came, it wasn't from the direction I was expecting. I expected it to come from straight above, smashing me into the floor. Instead, I was hurtled across the room, sliding on the spilled drinks from patrons running for their lives, and slamming into the wall.

"Ow," I said, as I flopped over onto my back. I never did get a good look at the meathead before this whole thing started. But he wasn't much to look at by this point. Surprisingly, he still seemed to be breathing, though he was flat on his back, half of him up in the VIP section, the other half flattened in the main area. As he sputtered out a breath, the giant slammed his suddenly empty fist back down onto him, the table already in splinters.

I struggled to regain my feet, still dazed from the blow to the head and slipping on the drinks that hadn't soaked into the cracks of the floor. The door wasn't far away, and the tavern was remarkably free of other patrons at the moment. I took to the streets, fleeing as quickly as the other patrons had left, though going much further. Most of the other escapees had only gone a block before turning to their rescued drinks or vomiting up those they already drank. A few even waddled into the equally crowded Horse's Head a couple blocks over. My last visit had ended abruptly in there. So, I headed in the other direction, only slowing once I was able to slip into one of the side alleys.

The only thing that I ever disliked about that world was the tendency for trouble to follow me. A quick check of my supplies made me realize I lost my club and three of the newly retrieved coin purses when the giant had attacked. "I knew I should have just kept going instead of entering that tavern," I said to myself as I made a beeline to the southern gate of the town.

Around the town was a wall. Nothing to write home about, but it was tall enough to make getting in and out of the town without using the gates at least slightly annoying. It extended about a foot over my head in most places, though as it approached the gates it dropped quite a bit, coming to about shoulder height at the gates themselves. There were no trees or buildings within several feet of the wall on either side and the entire length of it was smooth stone, making climbing it without a rope virtually impossible. Oh, and there's patrols along the length of it constantly.

Yea, so, unless I'm literally running for my life, I'm using the stupid gates.

It was late enough in the evening that there was no real traffic at the southern gate. Two guards stood sentry on either side of it, tall bardiches clasped firmly in their calloused hands. No alarms had been sounded in my exodus from the tavern, so I wasn't too worried about leaving town. Even so, I hiked up my hood just to be safe.

As I approached the guards, I gave a subtle nod of my head and kept walking, not expecting much of a response from them. They're no British palace guards, but they are mostly there for the rare case of trouble. I didn't generally look like trouble; I just tended to draw it to me.

So, I was a bit surprised when the guard on my left lowered his bardiche, blocking my way. "One moment please," he said in a low voice.

"Is something wrong?" I asked. I used a deeper than usual voice, in case these two had heard me before. I try not to be memorable, but for some reason it didn't work in this world as easily as it does in the other one. Perhaps my own elevated sense of self-importance was rubbing off on the world around me. After all, this was all happening in my imagination.

"I've just been told not to let anyone through until the captain can check them out. Nothing to worry about."

"This isn't... well, I mean, there was some kind of commotion back there," I pointed back in the direction of the tavern. "Are you sure your friends don't need your help over there?"

This wasn't good. The captain of the guards was well paid, by the thieves' guild, to not do anything. If he was coming there, that meant he was paid a little more to do something. And I had an unsettling feeling that it was specifically to find me.

"You know what?" I said, patting my cloak as if looking for something. "I think I left my keys back at the tavern. If you'll excuse me." I turned to leave, but my way back was blocked by the other guard.

"I don't think so," the first guard continued. "You'll wait right here until he gets here."

Okay, this is very, very not good. I looked around for some kind of an escape route. But the guards were well positioned to block my every move. I took a mental inventory of all my tricks, but none of them seemed up to the task of getting myself out of this. There really was no way out of it.

"Fine," I said, dropping back to my normal voice. My hope was that I could play up my youth. Make it seem like I was no danger to these soldiers. I dropped my hood, revealing my face to them for the first time. If I was stuck there, they were going to see it eventually anyway. Lucky for me, I wasn't actively wanted at the moment.

In either world.

The first guard blinked at me, looking confused by how young I was. While it wasn't unheard of for a sixteen year old to be out in the world on their own, it wasn't common. Certainly, not in Vernala. It was one of the reasons why I always kept my hood up, hiding my identity and my age. As invisible as I was usually, I felt like my youth was a spotlight on me in some places.

However, at that moment, it helped me. Both guards noticeably relaxed, obviously figuring I was no danger to them. But as I moved forward again, they snapped up once more, blocking my way. Not a danger, but not free to go either.

"Will he be long?" I asked, as I took one last step forward. I looked back up the street, drawing the attention of the guards away from me. As soon as their eyes were off of me, and I was close enough to manage it, I kicked my knee right up into the groin of the first guard. His leather armor was little protection against the move, and his bardiche fell to the ground with a loud clang. With the way forward no longer blocked, I made a run for it.

The land outside the south gate was quite hilly. This was useful when under siege, allowing for cover outside of the wall and preventing many siege weapons from coming too close to the gates. It also helped the occasional thief flee from the town without too much trouble. This wasn't one of those times. After the first few hills, I was starting to think I was home free. That was, at least, until an arrow hit the ground right next to me.

I dove off to the side, into a valley deep enough to hide in. Lying down against the steep hill, I looked over it. I was surprised to see not one or two, but five guards hot on my tail. A sixth, the archer, was still at the gates, another arrow notched with two more at the ready. What's worse was that the guard in the lead was none other than the captain himself.

"Well, well, well," the captain said, as they approached my not so good hiding place. "If it isn't Maya San Lukas."

"It isn't," I said, snarkily. "You have the wrong girl."

"Nice try," he said. He grabbed a lantern from one of the other guards and shined it straight in my eyes, momentarily blinding me. "I'd know you anywhere."

"Well, you flatter me sir," I said, sarcastically. "I'm afraid your name has slipped my mind."

"That's fine," the captain said, with a sneer. "I'm sure I'll be having you scream it soon enough. The tone of those screams is up to you." He winked at me, as if I'd ever sink so low as to come anywhere near him willingly. "Take her into custody," he said. He pointed at me, as if they could think he meant someone else. "And make sure not to fall for any of her tricks this time. In fact, all four of you follow her very closely. If any of you even lets her out of your sight for a second, I'll have all of your heads."

The second guard from the entrance, the one I hadn't kicked, reluctantly took out a pair of manacles, looking at me apologetically as he approached. I was starting to regret not kicking that one in the balls when I had the chance. Keeping my head high, under the ever watchful eye of the captain, I presented my wrists, my face as solid as stone.

"So, what's the charge?" I asked, as the four guards led the way back into town. Every few steps, I peeked over my shoulder to see if the captain was still following.

"How about murder, for one," the captain said.

"Murder? Who?" I asked, not needing to feign surprise.

"You know, I didn't actually catch his name myself. Although, you'll probably remember killing him, seeing as how your method of killing was by giant."

"Wouldn't that make the giant responsible for the murder?" I asked. I tried to keep a straight face, but failed miserably. "Not that I'm admitting to knowing anything about what you're talking about."

"Yea, like that would ever hold up in court. It's been a long time since any giant has been incarcerated."

I laughed a little, thinking the recent waves of giantcide had more to do with that than anything else. Well, that and the fact that the judges were scared of the giants themselves.

"Well, there you go then. If a giant can't be held responsible for its own actions, how come you're blaming me for them?"

"When a sword chops off someone's head, do you arrest the sword or the person who swung it?" he asked.

"Now, see, there's where your logic fails. There's no way I would ever be able to lift a giant, let alone swing one."

He didn't seem to think my comment was worth reciprocating, as he merely shook his head and walked off into the night, leaving me to the rest of the guards.

Chapter Four
A Father's Return

Five Years Earlier

I didn't talk to my mom as she drove me back up the street from the bus stop that day. I was so hurt and embarrassed that I headed straight up to bed when I got home. Curling into a ball on my bed, I pulled my book back out, finishing the last chapter in a matter of minutes. Rolling over to stare at my bookcase, filled with books that I had read and reread over the years, I pondered the thought of getting up to get one of them. Instead, I just lay there, staring at the book titles one by one, remembering each story, some in their entirety, without needing to open them at all.

As I went through each plot, I started to mix them up, jumbling the plots and characters in one big mishmash. Suddenly, Frodo and Sam were on the Millennium Falcon, flying through Romulan space to rescue Ender Wiggin from the cylons. At first, I thought about adding myself into the mix, to shoot down the Romulan ships as they wove around the cylon raiders. But I shrugged off the thought, thinking it too egotistical to think I'd ever be able to shoot straight. I've never even held a gun, let alone shot a laser turret.

I was lost in another adventure when a soft knock on the door woke me up, reminding me of the world that still existed around me. "Hey there, little one," Dad said, as he peeked in around the barely open door.

"Dad," I shouted. I jumped up from my bed to run over to him, wrapping my arms around his waist and holding on for dear life. "Never leave me again," I said into his shirt.

"I would if I could," he said, honestly. "But, you know I don't have any control over it. I go where I'm needed." That's one of the things I loved most about my father. He never kept anything from me. Never told me things that I wanted to hear just because I wanted to hear it. He always told the truth, the whole truth, and nothing but the truth. Secrets and lies brought nothing but hardships and heartaches, and I tried to avoid all of that as much as possible.

Of course, being a thief made that a bit hard as of late.

"Fine," I said reluctantly. "Just never leave me for long, okay?"

"You're not losing me that easily. And I didn't come home empty-handed, " he said, as he placed a book onto my head, balancing it there precariously.

I laughed, taking a step back, careful not to dislodge the book. I even stuck my arms out, pretending to balance in place for a few seconds before hopping up so the book would twirl off my head, landing in my outstretched hands. Dad gave a few mock claps as I bowed. "Thanks, Dad," I said. I flipped the book over so I could read the title. "I needed this."

"Run out of books again, have we?"

"Three times over, even the one for school. I was bored out of my mind."

"Ah, so that explains why you were staring off into thin air," he said with a chuckle. "You weren't in your mind."

"Exactly." I placed the book on the edge of my bookshelf, knowing I'd read half of it before falling asleep that night.

Dad sat down on the edge of my bed, patting the space next to him to indicate I should join him. "So, Mom told me you were rather quiet today," he said, as I hopped up next to him. "More so than usual, in fact."

"'S nothing," I mumbled. I looked towards my new book and itched to crack it open. To escape into the world inside.

"It's not nothing," he said, placing a finger on my chin to pull my face around to look at him. "Didn't Ashley and Jen want to come over today? Or were they too busy with homework?"

I just shrugged, looking down at my feet as they dangled above the floor, flipping them back and forth. We sat in a silence that felt like an eternity, his presence there keeping me from drifting back into my dream world. When it became unbearable, I blurted, "I don't think they want to be my friends anymore."

"Now, why would that be?" he asked. "Did you do something?"

"No."

"Did they do something?"

"Not really."

"Maya, I can't help if..."

"The whole school was teasing me today."

"I don't think it was the whole school," he said. "Did you actually see the whole school today? Or did you just hide in the library again?"

"The whole cafeteria at least."

"Did you check everyone there or just the ones near you?"

"Ashley and Jen and a whole other table," I admitted.

"And did Ashley and Jen start it?"

I sat there for a few moments, thinking back to lunch. They had looked down at my sandwich, but it wasn't until the boys at the next table said anything that they started to laugh. "No. But they didn't stop it."

"Were you expecting them to fight your battles for you?" he asked. "Look at these books along the wall here, Maya. Can you point to one where the main character was a helpless kid that let everyone else fight their battles for them?"

"No," I said meekly.

"That's right. The world is your story to write. Make it one worth living."

"Okay," I said, smiling up at him.

"Now, there is someone downstairs in the study that wants to see you."

"Mom?" I asked, knowing that he had played that trick before.

"No, she's in the kitchen making dinner, but she'd like to see you as well. You could pop your head in and say hello on your way over."

"If I have to," I teased, not able to hide my smile. He pushed me towards the door.

The study was a thing to behold. The far wall had every game system ever created, including a couple old Commodore computers, all hooked up to a big screen TV that took center stage. The shelves, built into the back wall, held the systems as well as a bunch of games, with the games next to the system they were designed for. I didn't spend much time in there, other than when I would watch my father play. Usually, that was with a book in hand when the endless slaughter got boring. None of the games held any real draw for me.

As I walked into the room, a scantily dressed woman with bat wings was whomping on a werewolf. His life meter on the top of the screen quickly draining as the woman comboed move after move. I didn't have to look around the couch to know Ashley was sitting there, mashing the buttons in a way that shouldn't have gotten the results being shown on the screen, but somehow worked for her. Without saying a word, I sat next to her on the couch. I refused to lean back and get comfortable as I watched her character slowly kill the werewolf, ripping his heart out of his chest to eat it.

It felt like it was me in there, in the video game, getting my heart ripped out by the girl sitting next to me. I glanced over at her, just out of the corner of my eyes, but she was too intent on the game to even notice that I was there. She didn't move an inch from her place at the edge of the couch until the animation finished and the menu came back up.

"I never understood why you don't play any of these games. They're awesome." She placed the controller back into its usual spot next to the unit, turning it off along with the TV, before walking back to the couch. She somehow managed to do that without looking at me once.

"I still don't understand how you can enjoy that stuff. It's all blood and gore flashing all over the place. Well, except for Tetris, but there's not much else to say about that game."

"Pfft, Tetris, ugh. Anyway, there's more violence in some of those books you read than in most of the games I play. You just don't have the right ones."

"That's all my dad's stuff," I said, shrugging a bit. "It's not like I ask for any games, or even know which to ask for if I did."

"I'll make a list for you," she said, nodding. "Maybe I'll get you one for your birthday. I'm still invited, aren't I?"

"Do you want to be? Are we going to talk about it?" I asked, looking over at her.

"Talk about what?" she asked. Her eyes flicked over to me before quickly returning to the now blank TV in front of us.

"About what happened at lunch today. What was that about?"

"Oh, that was nothing. Don't worry about it."

"It wasn't nothing, Ashley. Not to me at least. The whole cafeteria was laughing at me."

"Not the whole cafeteria," she said, the same argument my father had only just made. "I think the back table--"

"Ashley," I shouted.

"On the bus this morning, before you got on, Jake Donner was saying how everyone in school has had a birthday party where they invite the whole school to come over to their house and how everyone's houses were better than his.

Then he's like 'well, except for Maya, and we all know why'. Then they all went on and on about how your house smells and that it's falling apart and that you're all poor and no one could say otherwise because no one has been in your house. Well, Jen and I had, and we were just about to say something. Well, I was about to say something at least. But then Jake was like 'maybe some people have been in there, but they never come out again'. I stared in shock over at Jen, but she just shook her head. Everyone was laughing on the bus and staring at us, wondering why we weren't laughing too. And then, your mom drove you up to the bus stop and Jake was all 'and that's a creeper van if ever I saw one'. I'm sorry, Maya, even I had to laugh at that one. I'm so--"

"Why didn't you tell me?" I asked, interrupting her diatribe.

"What?"

"Why didn't you tell me about all of this? You could have said something before it got so bad. Before it blew up like that at lunch. We could have, I don't know, stopped the rumors before they got to the rest of the school. Or put out something bigger. Or I could have actually invited people over. I just hate when people keep things from me, especially when they're stupid."

"Hey, I'm not stupid," she snapped.

"No, I mean the secrets are stupid. I mean, seriously? I'm poor because I wear my dad's old t-shirts and I've never had the whole school over to my house? You know I don't like being the center of attention. Besides, my birthday is a good week after school ends and I always found it awkward asking people when they're already heading off on family vacations and stuff like that. I never know if that's the real reason or if they're just saying that because they don't want to come. Anyway, I like my small birthday parties with just the three of us."

"We like them, too," Ashley agreed. "But maybe we should do something different this year."

"Like what?" I asked. I shuddered at the thought of having the whole class in my house. I looked over at the gaming systems, knowing full well that half of them would not survive the encounter.

"How about we have a pool party?" Mom suggested, peeking in around the door frame behind us.

"Paige, leave the kids alone," Dad called from the other room.

"I was just about to tell them that dinner's ready," Mom called back to him. "Anyway, we hardly use the pool and it's getting hot enough for it. How about we celebrate a little earlier? Like the first weekend of the summer, we have all of your class over for a swim. That way no one can say they have vacations to go to. We'll keep everyone in the backyard so that no one 'disappears' or anything." She rolled her eyes as she air quoted the word.

"That could work," Ashley agreed.

"And we can have tours of the mystery house, where one or two of them disappear from the group for an hour or so, convincing them to hide out in the basement for a joke," Mom suggested, wiggling her fingers.

"Or we could just say they can come in here and play video games for a bit," I suggested. "I don't think Dad would want too many people in here at any given time."

"As long as none of the systems get damaged," Dad said, as he came in to see what was taking us so long. "And no one beats my top scores, of course."

"Alright, then," Mom said, nodding. "We have a plan. Ashley, are you staying for dinner?"

Chapter Five
The Jail and Other Realms of Torture

Now

"I'm just worried about you," Mom was saying, though I hadn't even realized she was talking to me until she said it. "I worry that you'll never spend enough time out of that thick head of yours to find love."

"Oh, Mom. I don't need a man to give my life meaning. It has plenty of meaning already, despite my spending so much time in my 'thick head' as you put it."

"I'm not talking about a man, Maya. I'm talking about love. That thing that makes life worth living."

"Funny. I thought the thing that made life worth living was purpose."

#

True to their orders, the four guards didn't leave my side the entire trip to the jail. None of them spoke to me though, leaving me to my thoughts of how simple my life had once been. How much it had changed over the years because of secrets and lies. I know it probably seems a little ironic for a thief to be so hung up on secrets. But, seeing as how I only stole in my own imaginary world, I didn't think it really counted.

I had been past the prison of Vernala several times in my occasional visit to the town, but this had been the first time that I had the pleasure of seeing the inside. Not that I hadn't come close to it over the years. If you ever visit the town of Vernala, I would definitely recommend a tour, preferably one without the restraints. The building was mostly low to the ground, a single story if that, with a tall tower in the middle. The tower was visible from pretty much anywhere in the town, a constant reminder of the strict order the guards and the guild try to impose on the populous. Unlike the town walls, the rough rock of the tower was easily climbable, though for the life of me I don't know why anyone would bother. The tower housed the guard. All prisoners were held underground in the dungeons.

"Over there," one of the guards said.

He pointed towards a low stool in the corner as we came into the main building. The entry room was small, barely large enough to fit the five of us standing. I had to squeeze by a couple of the guards to make it over to the indicated corner. As always, I turned that to my advantage. Once there, I plopped down onto the stool, stretching out my legs in front of me.

"Get up," the guard yelled at me. He grabbed me under the arm and pulled me up to stand on the stool.

The four of them swarmed around me, quickly removing my cloak and taking my growing collection of coin purses. They each pocketed one of the purses, while placing a fifth, the lightest and most recently acquired, on the small table in the opposite corner. None seemed to notice that it had belonged to one of them. The shortest of the four started to try on my cloak, but that didn't sit well with another one of them. I had actually stolen it off a homeless corpse the last time I came to town, though neither seemed to care about that.

As the two of them argued over which would come away with my lovely cloak, the other two started poking and prodding me, trying to find all my hidden gadgets and toys. They managed to find five sets of lockpicks, two knives, three darts, a small bag of marbles, and a large bag of dice. Along the way, they also found three mouse traps, two snares, and several fishhooks... the hard way. Obviously, they weren't happy with me. They all glared at me as they tried to stem the blood flow from the many cuts, with two broken fingers each.

Once they considered themselves finished with the search and seizure section of my processing, they brought me towards the back of the small room. I had to step over the unconscious body of the guard that didn't win the cloak. One of the guards scooped up a lantern that hung against the back wall before leading the way down into the dungeons.

Not many people have been in a working dungeon and lived to tell about it. I will tell you, it stinks, literally. In present day prisons in my own world, there's these things called toilets. They bring all the urine and feces out of the prison and keep the place smelling relatively clean. Dungeons don't have those. If you're lucky, you'll get a hole. If you're really lucky, that hole will lead somewhere. Let's just say, none of the people at that particular dungeon was lucky.

They brought me back to the very furthest reaches of the dungeon, going around several left turns and down so many levels that I quickly lost count. Fortunately, the layout wasn't all that confusing, so my eventual departure wouldn't be slowed by that. There wasn't much to look at on the way down, and only the one lamp to see by. There were doors on either side of the hallway, just barely large enough for the prisoners to crawl in and out of. I was hoping the cells would be more spacious, but with the spacing between them, it wasn't boding well. As we passed a few of the doors, the occupants would bang against them. Perhaps in hopes that the guards hadn't forgotten them. Perhaps in an attempt to scare me. None seemed to be all that successful at either.

By the time we came to my appointed cell, I was half expecting to see the pits of hell ahead of us. Instead, there was just an indication that there was a limit to how far the builders had managed to dig down. The hallway came to a door even smaller than those I had been seeing along the way. One of the guards fumbled around in his pockets for a bit until he found the key. He unlocked the door, holding it open and sweeping his hand towards the portal.

"In you go," he said, a smirk on his face. "I do hope you enjoy the accommodations."

"I'm sure I'll manage," I said, as I bent down and crawled through the small opening. "It's not like I'll be here long anyway."

The two guards laughed at this as they closed the door behind me. I didn't get to see much of my cell before the light from the lamp faded, though it was obviously small. I could just barely sit down, with my back against the wall and my knees against the door. Standing wasn't even an option. The low ceiling overhead smelled of dirt and rotten trash. Thankfully, the stone beneath me didn't suggest many previous occupants to the cell. Unless they cleaned them between residents.

"Oh, yea," I said to myself, after the sounds of the departing guards had faded. "I'm definitely leaving soon. This just won't do."

"I'd like to see that," came a laughing voice from an adjacent cell. "There are people down here that have been here longer than I have."

"Well, how long have you been down here?" I asked.

"I don't know," the voice said, sounding less jovial. "What day is it?"

"The fourteenth of Gafnal, I think. I don't keep track all that well." It's hard enough to keep track of what day it is back home, let alone in this world that I visit so randomly. Not to mention those times when the days would literally fly by here, on those occasions when nothing was happening around me. I didn't want to bank on that happening this time around, already intent on getting out of that cell that night.

"Oh, yes, that doesn't really help much. What year is it?"

"Uh, by the current counting? Sixteen."

"Hmm.... when did they start counting again?"

"So, you've been down here a while, then."

"Oh, yes, a long while."

"Don't let that old bat get you down," said another voice. This one was much closer, sounding like he was in the cell with me, though I knew that was impossible. "He's been here a week."

"Oh, horse snaggle," said the first voice. "It's easily been years."

"No," the second voice argued. "It just feels like that. You came the day after I did."

"Humpf, well, if you say so."

"So, what are you in for?" the second voice asked.

"Murder by giant," I said simply, as if it was as silly as it was. "You?"

"Treason," he replied, equally as jovial. "I wrote a song about the Jakala Empire."

"Ah, you're one of those bards that only sing truths, aren't you?"

"Sing them, say them. I'm not really good at lying, so I try not to. It makes things so much easier."

"I've never been all that fond of them myself. Secrets and lies bring you nothing but trouble and strife. Though, given my current circumstances, the truth didn't seem to help much either. Anyway, I always love a good laugh. Why don't you sing this oh so offensive song?"

"Don't mind if I do," he said, before going through a few voice exercises to warm up with vocal cords.

"Oh, no," came several voices from all around us.

"Stop him."

"My ears, my ears."

"Not again."

It was hard to hear the song over all the voices of complaints. I wasn't really that interested in the song anyway.

I just needed the distraction in case there were guards about. There hadn't been any patrols on the way down, but that didn't mean there wouldn't be any. Or perhaps there would be some guards coming to feed the prisoners. With the distraction firmly in place, I reached into some of my better hidden pockets and produced the set of keys that I had lifted off one of the guards upstairs. It probably would have been a lot harder to lift a set if there had been fewer of them guarding me the whole time. The crowded room had been too good of an opportunity to pass up, and the keys weren't the only items I managed to pilfer.

The main problem was getting my hands through the window in the door. It was small, but not unmanageable. This was one of the times that being small paid off. I had to feel around for a while until I found the keyhole. It was almost too far away to reach, but I had always been rather flexible... at least in this world that is. I just had to believe I could reach it and I, somehow, managed to do it.

Once I found the keyhole, I brought my arm back in so that I could bring out the key. Even being as careful as I could, the keys still rattled way more than I'd like. The clanging echoed down the hallway, even over the sound of complaining prisoners. After I thought I had the key positioned just right, I had to overextend my shoulder to get it into the hole. It hit against wood a couple times before clipping the outside of the hole with enough force that the key slipped from my grasp. "Shit," I cursed, as I fumbled around, catching the ring on the tip of my middle finger.

My arm was practically jammed into the window, giving me almost no leverage and no leeway as I tried to flip the key back up into my hand. Seconds ticked by, feeling like days, my shoulder screaming at me, until I managed to get my hand around the key again. This time around, I managed to get it in the keyhole on the first try. Pins and needles started up my arm as I tried to turn the key. Once I heard the loud click of the door unlocking, I gave out a great sigh of relief, pushing the door open. I still had my arm stuck in the window, but I managed to get out of the cell and find a better position. Once I did, it was just a matter of pulling upwards and free.

"Thank you, thank you. We're here all week," I said, taking a few bows to the fake audience.

"Gee," the second voice said from the door behind me. He had ended his song at some point while I wasn't paying attention, though the cries of complaints still echoed around us. "Do you think you could make a little more noise?"

"Sure," I said. "But where's the fun in that?"

"What the..." he said, noticing that I was suddenly outside his cell. "How the blazes did you get out?"

"It helps to have the key," I said, dangling the keys in front of him.

"How did you..." he began to ask before demanding "Let me out."

"What's the magic words?" I taunted.

"I don't know any magic," he said in all seriousness, sounding a bit stressed out about it for some reason. That saying didn't exist on Desparia, though I would often say it without thinking. "But I can help you get past the guards. I know a few tricks myself."

"I doubt I'll need much help getting past them," I laughed. "They seemed rather oafish to me. I mean, where do you think I got the keys from?"

"Then I'll be a spare distraction, in case you need it. Just, come on. I'll make it worth your while somehow."

I rolled my eyes at the desperation that was coming off of him. "Oh, fine. Prison break for everyone," I called out. I started unlocking cells. A large stampede of fleeing prisoners seemed as good of an exit strategy as any at that point.

My neighbor hung back by me as the others hurtled themselves down the passageway as soon as they were free. It wouldn't work much for a stampede just having one prisoner at a time, so I passed one of the keys from the ring over to my neighbor and he started unlocking the doors on the left while

I tackled the ones on the right. It often took me a while to find the keyholes in the pitch darkness of the dungeons, but after a while I managed to find some decent guide points by feeling around the door. We started getting a decent flow going long before getting to the outside.

As we walked into the entry chamber, I wasn't too surprised to find it deserted. The front door was knocked clean off its hinges and light spilled in from the streetlamp right outside it. Unfortunately, they don't keep the seized items of the prisoners in there and I wasn't about to go looking for my lost items. It was one of the many reasons why I stashed most of my stuff outside the town before entering.

"Shall we?" my neighbor asked, extending his arm towards the gaping maw that used to be the door.

It was the first time I managed to see him. He was relatively clean, given that he claimed to have been down there for a week. His muscled chest gleaming in the light from the lantern drew my attention to the fact that he was shirtless and wore bracers that looked to be designed more to draw attention to his strapping arms than for any amount of protection. His face was free of any facial hair, though he was clearly old enough to grow it. At the time, I hadn't thought to wonder how he maintained it down there. His long blonde hair came down to perfectly frame his face. As he looked back towards the doorway, the light reflected off his stunning green eyes.

"Um, what?" I asked, inarticulately.

He laughed a bit, leading the way out into the world. "I know of a way to get out of the town without being seen. Think that might be worth the inconvenience of letting me out of my cell?"

"I guess it'll do," I said.

I quickly recovered my composure once his back was to me. Not that his back was anything less to look at. I mean dang. Seeing him there, in the low light from the lamp, I was reminded of Mom's words from an hour or so ago of my

inability to find love if I spent so much time in Desparia.
Perhaps this man was my subconscious's answer to that. He
didn't look that much older than me, though anything was
possible on Desparia.

I was half expecting bedlam outside, with the escape of
dozens of prisoners. Instead, all I found was an eerily quiet
and empty street. There was no sign of the passing of the
escapees, or anyone really. It was a normal, pre-dawn street.
The lamps burned low as they expended the last of their daily
supply of oil. The late-night drunkards already returned home.
The early rising merchants were not yet out to greet the day.
It was too normal given the events that had just happened.

I was on edge the entire way as we headed through the
town, jumping at the slightest sound. I felt naked without
most of my gear, the cold night air not helping things. I'd
need to find another cloak, which wasn't easy. Whenever I
tried buying one over the years, they all looked way too nice.
The last thing I need is a cloak that draws attention to me. My
job was best done when nobody saw me. That's kind of the
reason why I picked it.

I wasn't doing all that well in not being seen that night,
though. The streets may be empty of people, but the man
walking beside me seemed way too intent on me for my
liking. He kept darting glances my way, grinning when he
spotted me looking his. Our eyes would lock on each other
for a second before I would turn away, blushing. It was very
distracting and, as we traveled through town, I quickly lost
track of the way we came. I have a terrible sense of direction
even when I'm not so preoccupied with... the scenery.

Every time we passed one of the many street lamps that
were scattered across the town, I was again caught by the
stunning beauty in the man walking beside me. I wondered
what was going on inside that beautiful head of his, and if he
was thinking of me at all. But I knew that I would have been
alone in the attraction. Despite his glances, I knew that I

would be just as invisible to him as I was to everyone, on either world that I lived on.

If only that weren't the case. If only he thought of me in that way. He didn't seem that older than me, perhaps a few years, though he seemed almost ageless in the darkness of the night. With Mom's words on my mind, I suddenly thought that maybe I should ask him out. Perhaps I'd delay my exodus from the town for an hour or so to get some food. Maybe I could even ask him to come with me, to go explore the rest of the world with me. It had been a long time since I had tried to have a traveling companion. Perhaps this would be the perfect time to try. To open myself up to something, even if it was just in my head. Then again, my subconscious often didn't think I deserved to be with people like him. I might just reject myself after all.

He led the way down an alley that, at the time, I thought was a couple blocks over from the Dancing Pony. When I turned into it, I noticed I was completely off. Instead of the expected passageway leading to the town square, I found the entrance to the one and only thieves' guild, complete with half a dozen of those said thieves pointing arrows at me.

"Alright," Grandor said. His voice directed my attention to the back of the alley, where he was leaning on an attractive female thief. Her composite bow didn't waver a hair the entire time it was pointed at me. "Even I am a little impressed by how quickly she made it out of there."

Chapter Six
The Pool Party

Five Years Earlier

Our backyard wasn't large by anyone's standards. In fact, it was the smallest in the neighborhood. I've spent enough time slipping into people's yards, finding all manner of hiding spots for hide and seek. Or just simply hiding from homework. Or exploring the darker side of the neighborhood, looking for elves and pixies in my younger, more innocent years. But the point is, our yard was small. And most of it was taken up by a swimming pool. There's about a three-foot border around the pool that's all cement. Less lawn to mow, as my dad always put it. The rest of the yard was the pool itself.

Now, you might think, what's the point of even having a backyard if you can't play in it? Or don't you feel left out for not having a decent yard to play in? But there's only one thing in this world, or any world for that matter, that I like more than reading. More than exploring a world beyond one's own imagination. That one thing is swimming. So, for my fifth birthday, my parents got me my pool. I would have preferred a heated pool, so I could swim in the winter as well. But it's not like I could tell my parents that. I'm loved, not spoiled.

Anyway, the point of my story is, I love my pool and I spend as much time in it as I can. It always seemed to energize me in some way that I just couldn't put into words.

If I could figure out how to read while swimming, my parents wouldn't be able to get me out of it. So, imagine how conflicted I was when my precious pool was filled with half of all the kids in my class.

Meaning that only half of them came to my party. No one cut any of them in half, though the thought had come to mind.

My dad was in a tall chair at the far corner of the pool, acting as lifeguard. However, we both knew he wasn't the strongest swimmer. Even at eleven I was a stronger swimmer than him. Mom was setting up a table of snacks in the kitchen, with the big sliding glass door wide open to let the kids in and out. There were a few kids standing near the door, wanting the food that was presented but not daring stepping into the dreaded mystery house. Everyone else, including me, was in the pool. It was jam packed with kids, which made it impossible to actually swim. I just sort of bobbed there in place, watching the other kids try to splash each other and wanting them all to just go home.

"Isn't this a fun party?" Jen said. She tried to make it through the crowd towards Ashley and I as we were hanging on the edge of the pool. I barely heard her over the noise from the other kids.

"If you say so," I shouted towards her, giving her the stink eye. She still hadn't apologized for the other day. She had barely even spoken to me since.

"Oh, come on, Maya. It's a great party."

"What's so great about it?"

"Oh, forget you," Jen said. She splashed water at me and hit me right in the eyes. It took me a while to blink the chlorine out of them and, when I had, she had disappeared back into the mosh pit of a party.

"That wasn't nice," Ashley tisked at me. She stared after Jen, trying to find her in the crowd, and generally looked like she wanted to head off to join her. But the bucking kids made movement difficult.

"I'm not quite ready to kiss and make up with her," I said.

"Who's ready for a tour of the spooky house," Mom called out over the noise.

The invitations had promised a haunted house style tour of our home and Mom had spent half the week decorating the basement to "scare the pee out of the kiddies" as she put it. She looked onto the crowd with glee, and a few of the kids climbed out of the pool, eager to see where the people had supposedly disappeared from. They led a shivering, dripping line up to her.

"Perhaps I should have set out a few more towels," Mom said. This caused many of the kids to laugh as they grabbed their towels from the fences that framed our yard.

Even with the departing tour of kids, the pool was still crowded. Ashley spotted Jen in the thinning crowd. After pointing towards her, she took off to join her and a couple guys that she was talking to. It left a decent sized hole of pool for me to reside in. It was enough to make me feel less boxed in, though not big enough to enjoy. I had a permanent sneer on my face as I stared on at the crowd.

"Can you believe this place?" someone said behind me. He sat down next to my arm where it was hooked over the edge of the pool, sticking his legs into the water. "What's the point of having a pool party if no one can do any actual swimming?"

"Maybe I shouldn't have invited this many people. Although, it's not like I had much of a say in it," I told him.

"Oh, this is your party?" he asked. "My mom saw the invitation and made me come. No offense or anything, I'm just not exactly in the partying mood."

"Yea, neither am I," I admitted as I looked up at him. I recognized him from around school, but I couldn't for the life of me remember his name. Not long after that day, I'd never forget it again. "I'd leave but this is my house," I joked.

"I'd join you, but my mom wanted me to do something normal while... well... Anyway, I'm stuck here for at least an hour. Do you have a clock on you?"

My mind went to the watch Mom had gotten me for my birthday, insisting I opened it at breakfast that morning. It was analog, which annoyed me to no end. It was bad enough dealing with analog clocks at school. There was a cookie with a bite taken out of it in the middle of the face and, as the second hand ticked around, the watch sounded like someone nibbling at a cookie. I called it my cookie watch. It was obviously Mom's way of making me stay on time more often. However, there was no alarm on it. Her earlier threat of getting me an alarm clock for my birthday had been forgotten. Not wanting to get it wet and damage it, more for my parents' feelings than any desire to protect it myself, I had left it up in my room.

"No," I said, shaking my head at the boy beside me. "But my mom was planning on the tours taking twenty minutes. Two more and you can leave."

"Works for me. I'm David, by the way. I don't think I caught your name."

"Maya," I introduced myself, climbing out of the pool to sit next to him. My legs dangled in the water, quickly finding the pattern his were making as they kicked through it. "So, why exactly did your mom force you to come? Should I be offended?"

"No, it's nothing like that. I just... I don't really want to talk about it. It kind of makes it real or something, you know?"

"I get that," I said, though I didn't really. Real and I weren't exactly on speaking terms on the best of days, even back then.

"But, no, it wasn't your party more than anyone else's. If Jake Donner had a party today, she would have forced me to go to that one instead, and Jake's a complete jerk."

"Another thing we have in common," I said, smiling. "Maybe we should be friends."

"Ah, a friendship based around no liking the least likable kid in our class and our desire not to be here. What could go wrong with that?" he said, snickering a bit.

Suddenly, a round of screams came from the house. I turned around, looking over my shoulder into the open door. I wondered what was going on, but I didn't want to leave the safety of the poolside. A few seconds later, the kids that had been on the house tour came streaming out of the house, screaming their little heads off. The group came out running, trying to pivot on the other side of the door when they saw the pool in their way. A few of them didn't make it, the others pushing them in their mad attempt to get away from whatever it was inside that they were trying to run from.

Three kids went tumbling into the water, hitting at an odd angle. Before I could think to stand, my classmates that were already in the pool started to help them out, making sure they were alright. All three were looking around, stunned but not hurt by their little spill. As they started to regain their senses, their screams returned as each started trying to scramble out of the pool. One by one, they ran after the other kids, all of whom had disappeared from the backyard. Out through the open gate in the fence that led back around to the front of the house and out to the street beyond. One of the kids started dragging his friends along, pulling them from the pool as he literally screamed in their faces.

"What's that all about?" I asked, looking between the kid who was still scrambling to get away and the open door into the kitchen.

"What's all this yelling?" Mom asked, as she emerged from the house. Her hands were out to the side as she looked on in utter confusion. "It wasn't that scary."

Instead of the yellow sundress that she had on earlier, she was wearing a gray dress that was almost the exact same style. She was wearing some hastily applied white makeup that made her look paler than she had called me more recently. The dress billowed in the light breeze that flowed through the gaps in the fence, making her look like the perfect ghost, which appeared to be the look she was going for.

"What is everyone so afraid of?" she asked, as she looked out at the packed pool. Everyone's gaze was trained on her. Everyone's face was stuck in a shocked expression as they stared at the 'ghost' in their midst.

The scream started close to the door, echoing around the enclosed backyard as it was joined by every kid there. It's not easy to stampede when you're in a crowded pool, but that didn't stop them from trying. The kids started pushing past David and I as we stayed seated on the edge of the pool. They ran straight for the still open gate. I just hunched in on myself, trying to be as small as I could to avoid the rushing kids as they passed. David hunched closer to me, doing his best to protect me from the others as he tried to get out of the way himself.

It felt like minutes passed as the kids scrambled and clawed their way out of the pool, out of the backyard, and away from the party that I didn't want in the first place. Suddenly, my pool was mine once more. Except, I was too scared that I was about to be trampled on to enjoy it. As the screaming faded into the distance, it was replaced by the sound of laughter coming from the lifeguard chair at the other end of the pool. I looked over to it to find Dad lost in hysterics, slapping his hand against his thigh as he tried to catch his breath.

"It's not funny," Mom said. Her fists went to her waist as she gave him the stink eye.

"Mr. and Mrs...," David yelled. He pointed out to the middle of the pool. I looked to where he was pointing and saw someone floating in the water... face down.

Not waiting for my dad to get a hold of himself, I dove into the water, quickly swimming over to the still form. I recognized Ashley long before I got to her. Her hair streamed out around her like a halo. As soon as I got to her, I flipped her over and started pulling her back to the side of the pool, right where David was standing. My mother quickly joined him. Together, the three of us managed to pull her out of the water as Dad rushed around to us.

"Out of the way," Mom said, as she pushed David and me away from Ashley's prone body.

She quickly went into nurse mode, checking her vitals and starting to press down on her chest. David unconsciously wrapped his arm around me as I stared at my friend, lying there on the ground as she gradually turned blue. I was starting to think she was going to die. But then water suddenly spurted up out of her mouth, running down her cheeks and onto the ground next to her. Ashley let off a few rasping coughs as she curled in on herself, rolling onto her side.

"She's going to be alright," Mom said. She looked over to me, scared and helpless as I stood over my friend.

"Thanks to you," I said. "I didn't know what to do. I don't know what would have happened if you weren't here."

"No, Maya," Dad said, as he came up behind me, taking David's place. "Thanks to you. You got her out of the water before I even noticed something was wrong."

"Yea, Maya," David agreed. "You're like a superhero or something."

"I don't know about that," I said, shrugging off the compliment.

"Well, you're at least a better lifeguard than your father," David said, smiling over at me.

I smiled, thinking that wouldn't be a bad thing to try. I gave my mom a questioning look and she just nodded back at me, looking prouder than I had ever seen her look.

Chapter Seven
The Hanging Sword

Now

"Seriously," the captain of the guard said. His voice echoed off the narrow alley filled with thieves and their bows. "I need to beef up the security in there." The man was off to my left, leaning against the alley wall. I was a little surprised to see him. But then I remembered that all the guards were on Grandor's payroll. Grandor barely glanced over at the man who should have been arresting everyone there.

"Well," I said after getting over the shock of seeing my welcome party. "I have you to thank for that." I nodded my head towards the captain. "After all, if you hadn't sent so many idiots to keep an eye on me, I wouldn't have been able to get the keys." I pulled out the set of keys that I still had in my pockets to demonstrate.

"Keys?" Grandor asked, sounding a bit shocked. "You let her get a set of keys? Your guards were supposed to get all her gear off of her, not supply her with more."

"They assured me that they had done a very thorough search. I don't know how they could have missed a set of keys... unless she got them after the search."

"Nope, sorry. Don't take it too hard, though. They also missed two sets of lockpicks and three knives." I would have suggested he switch to a strip search as part of the typical booking process, but I wouldn't want to do his job for him.

Also, I might need to escape from that jail again someday, and I wouldn't have liked to be subjected to a strip search. Not unless the hunk standing next to me was administering it. "So, I'm guessing that whole thing was some kind of test. Did I pass?" I said in a snarky tone.

"Not yet," Grandor said, missing my tone. "You still have to do one last task. Then you get the honor of joining our ranks."

A few of the archers glanced back at Grandor, seeming a bit surprised by this turn of events. One of them even glared at me, edging his bow up a bit more as if he would like nothing more than to shoot an arrow right through my heart. I wasn't quite sure what that was about but guessed he was a friend of the meathead from earlier. Nothing causes hate quite like having a giant squish your friend.

I barely batted an eye at the supposed offer to join the thieves' guild. While I had never been invited before, there really was no draw for me. Nothing to gain and so much more to lose. Not since my first few days in that world had I considered it as something desirable. But it wasn't like I could tell Grandor that.

"Why, I'm just honored to be nominated," I said in a sarcastic tone. "But I'm afraid I really must be going." I turned towards the entrance. My hand slowly moved towards the man I helped escape from the dungeon, meaning to pull him away from the certain death that awaited us there.

"I don't think so," Grandor said, finally catching my tone. "No, I don't think you'll be leaving town anytime soon. See, all the gates will be tightly sealed. The watch on the wall has already been doubled. And," he paused as he took out something from behind him, "I have all your possessions." He spun my pack, the one that I had stashed outside of the city, around a bit with a menacing grin on his face. "You've been allowed to roam freely for way too long, little one. Someone needs to reel you in."

"And you think that someone should be you?" I asked sarcastically, putting as much disgust in my voice as I could manage. "Please. If I had the ambition for it, I could probably replace you."

"My point exactly," he interrupted. "After all, everyone needs a chosen successor."

This revelation seemed to surprise everyone there, most of all me. All of the archers dropped their bows and turned to gawk at their leader. All except the woman that he was leaning on. She hadn't seemed to move a millimeter since setting her sights on me. I wasn't even sure if she was breathing.

"But, in case that's not enough of a motivation," he snapped his fingers, and someone sprang out from the wall. I don't mean someone that was leaning against the wall or anything. Someone actually came out of the wall, as if it had been a hidden doorway. I saw a sparkling glint of something as his arm swung down, hitting me on the wrist.

"All set, master," the guy said. He walked over to stand by Grandor.

I stared at my wrist for the longest time, trying to wrap my mind around what I was seeing. There was an odd, golden bracelet snapped into place on my left wrist. It was right where my cookie watch usually sat, when I was back on Earth and not swimming. On the face of it was an engraving of a small hourglass. As I stared at this, the sand appeared to flow into the bottom half, despite the sand being no more real than the hourglass itself.

"Here's the key," the guy said, drawing my attention over to him and Grandor. He dropped a small, golden key into Grandor's hand, turning around to smile at me.

"A little explanation," Grandor said, with a half-smile on his face. "That bracelet will slowly tick down to zero, exactly two days from now. Once the hourglass runs out of time, your heart will stop. It's as simple as that. The only way to stop it, or to get the bracelet off, is with this key. Zendor here is one of the best mages in the land. There's no point in trying to get someone else to take it off for you. Besides, this task I have for you is rather simple. I just require you to steal one little thing from a manor here in town. Just one little thing. Once you've done that, we'll remove the bracelet and you can join the most prestigious guild in the whole world."

"And what if I don't want to join?" I asked.

"Oh, I'm afraid you don't have much of a choice in that," he laughed. A couple of the others there started to laugh as well. Their laughter sounded rather fake, more to humor their boss than any actual mirth. I was beginning to wonder if they had been promised my blood. "Anyway, time is slipping by us, especially you. So, on to the task at hand. There's a manor not too far from the town square. You've probably seen it often, it's a bit hard to miss."

"You don't mean..." I began. "Please tell me you don't expect me to steal from Sardana Jakala." Certainly, these people weren't crazy enough to have me steal from the emperor's own daughter.

"No!" Grandor shouted. Everyone jumped and started looking around the alley, pointing their bows every which way. "No," Grandor said again, this time quieter. The thieves gradually regained their composure, but most of them still seemed a little on edge. "I want you to steal from her neighbor, the manor next to hers." He stressed the word next, making sure everyone who heard it understood his intention. "There's an object that he keeps in his study. It's a hemisphere of some kind. He usually keeps it in a lead lined crystal case. It's protected by a lot of traps, some of my best work in fact. So, it'll be quite the challenge to get it out. If you can even get to it in the first place."

"Wait a minute," I said, putting up a finger to silence him. "You want me to steal something that you yourself protected?"

"Of course. We can't have anyone thinking they're safe from us. Not without paying for that protection that is."

"But wouldn't stealing this thing, despite the safeguards you put in place, kind of make it seem like your work is, oh I don't know, somehow subpar?"

"My work is flawless!" he shouted in outrage. "No one has ever gotten past my traps, my safeguards."

"And yet you expect me to, as part of this insane test of yours," I yelled back, just as annoyed.

"Well," he said, as he pulled out a thick scroll of paper, "I was going to give you the instructions." He turned to one of the two lamps behind him, tossing the scroll onto the hot sconce. "Perhaps that will teach you not to be insolent to your betters."

"Betters?" I yelled. "The only thing you're better than me at is being a lazy old fool."

Grandor ignored me as he motioned for his people to follow him back into the guild. One by one, they fell into step behind him, turning their backs to me without a second glance. Seemingly almost reluctant about it, the strapping young man that had led me into that alleyway followed behind the others into the guild, giving me a single, solitary glance before heading inside. I was shocked by this, to realize that he had been part of the guild the whole time. That perhaps he was even part of the test that I had been subjected to.

The one woman in the back was the last to drop her bow. She turned on her heels in one fluid motion and followed the others back into the hall. The slamming of the door finally shook me from my petrified state. All the bluster that I had been throwing about was little more than a ruse to hide how scared I really was. I ran for the scroll, hoping it wasn't too damaged by the heat of the lamp.

The sconce was high on the wall. I ran up the stairs that Grandor had been standing on. From the top stair, I jumped backwards and up, landing on the stone railing that ran down next to it. Another backflip took me up against the wall. My foot hit the scroll, knocking it loose from its precarious position. As I came back to my feet on the solid cobblestones of the alleyway, I accidentally hit the bottom stair and stumbled into the railing on the other side. I was reminded of the fact that, had I tried any of that in the real world, I would have fallen flat on my face.

Hell, I would have fallen just running up the stairs.

Once back down on the ground, I examined the damage in the light of the innocent lamp, giving nothing but my backside to the offending one. A whole section of the scroll had been burned away, but most of its surface seemed untouched by the flame. I gave a sigh of relief as I headed away from the dreaded place.

In the east, I saw the first rays of the new day. I wasn't sure how much time I had lost in the dungeons, but now that I had a ticking clock on my life, I couldn't afford to lose any more. Grudgingly, I returned to the Dancing Pony, two blocks over.

Most of its clientele must have returned after the excitement of the night before, as there were quite a few passed out drunk in the main room. There was no sign of the bartender when I first arrived. I grabbed a couple of the heavier purses from the sleepers as I passed through. This was more out of habit and to reassure myself of my own abilities as a thief than any need for the money. While the loss of my main stash was annoying, I was in no danger of starving in that world. Of course, eating wasn't exactly a necessity for me there. Or at least, it hadn't been.

Ignoring the irony, I headed straight over to the VIP section. It was the only area that had escaped the damage of the angry giant. I sat in Grandor's own chair and spread out the scroll across the table. It was going to be a rough night and I would need all the time that I could get to figure out how to manage it.

There were six large manors in the town of Vernala. There was one in each corner of the town where the walls were highest, and the guard patrols the thickest. Two more were dead center in the middle of town. Everyone knew that one of those two in the center belonged to Sardana Jakala, the daughter and heir apparent of the emperor. Her neighbor's identity, however, was somewhat of a mystery and often the subject of gossip. It was popular belief that the manor belonged to a wandering mage and that the entire place was guarded by all sorts of spells. The fact that so few who have been foolish enough to enter the manor had lived to tell about it was all the proof that many needed.

Now, however, I knew that most of those mysterious disappearances were not due to some magical traps, but by traps set by the self-appointed king of thieves. And it was my job to get past all those traps. This fact didn't do much to help my nerves. I'm not one to get drunk often, mostly because the imagined booze of that world didn't seem to affect me in any way. I was very tempted to do so that day. The more I looked at the plans, the less I wanted to venture into that death trap.

Every few minutes, I'd look at the hourglass on my wrist. It seemed like it would make an excellent timepiece... you know, if it wasn't going to kill me. If I had to guess, it probably kept time better than a Swiss watch, though it was a lot harder to translate the flow of sand into an actual time. It made me miss my cookie watch, the one I could see back in reality even as I stared at the new bracelet.

The instructions filled the scroll completely, from beginning to end, top to bottom. The burnt section must have contained a lot more that I could afford to lose, and there didn't seem to be much of a pattern to the parts that I still had. Despite all this, by the time the sun started to set, I thought I had a reasonable plan to get through to the study.

As the darkness set in, I started to feel tired for the first time ever. I never used to feel tired on Desparia, never needed to sleep. It was an imaginary world and, despite eating and drinking, I never really needed to do either of those. I had slept while on that world, but it was mostly to pass the time between jobs. Time would pass as quickly when sleeping as it did when traveling down an empty road, except without needing to actually go anywhere to do it.

And yet, that night I would have liked to have gotten some sleep before heading into the manor. I was feeling very drained, but I didn't know how long it would take me to break in, get through all the traps, find the sphere, and get out. The last thing I needed was to run out of time within sight of the end. Besides, despite feeling tired, my mind was still racing a mile a minute and I didn't think I would get much sleep.

As I sat there thinking about how tired I was, a large group of patrons stormed in, quickly turning the relatively quiet pub into a raucous party. I took that as my cue to leave. With a deep huff to steel my resolve, I rolled up the scroll and headed out. I reminded myself that I had one thing going for me in all this. All the rumors about the manor stated rather plainly that, whoever it was that lived there, they were hardly ever home. In fact, in the weeks that I had spent wandering those streets over the years that I had been traveling to Desparia, I had never so much as once seen even a candle in the windows.

Chapter Eight
The Junior Lifeguard Program

Five Years Earlier

That night, I mentioned the thought of becoming a lifeguard to my parents at dinner. My mom was thrilled. Even back then, I had been spending most of my time alone with my books. Mom had always wanted me to join a group of some kind. This group seemed exactly the kind that she wanted for me. Besides, Dad and I had been so close for so long, with our love of books uniting us. Finally, there was something that I would share with my mom, a passion for saving lives. She managed to pull some strings with a junior lifeguard program that was affiliated with her hospital that was going to be starting up for the summer. Two days later, I found myself waking up at the crack of dawn to make it over to the public pool where the classes were being held.

Dad was still asleep as my Mom drove me over, dropping me off before heading to the hospital to start her shift. I headed in alone, my new gym bag slung over my shoulder, with my suit and towel tucked away along with breakfast. The entry area for the building was empty and I hadn't been there before. So, I had no idea where the locker rooms were. It was a large enough building, with a basketball court and several other large rooms taking up a good portion of it. Even what looked like a ballet studio, which faced the main entrance.

After a little wandering around, I followed the familiar smell of chlorine to find the pool. There was an older boy in a suit sitting on a set of bleachers that overlooked it. When he spotted me, he just glared at me as I walked around the side of the pool to the clearly labeled girls' locker room on the far side of the pool. There were several girls in the locker room, all of a wide range of ages, though all of them were older than me. Many of them were yawning as they donned their swimsuits, though I had been too jazzed for this class to sleep the night before and I was still too energetic.

"Hurry up, ladies," a man's voice came to us through the open door. "We start in five minutes."

I found an empty locker in the back and quickly changed. Just moments after arriving, I was heading back out to the pool area where the older boy was standing in front of the same bleacher. One section of the bleachers was filled with the yawning girls, and several yawning boys, crowded together. As soon as I sat down at the end of one of the rows, the boy started talking.

"Welcome to the junior lifeguard program," he said. His was the voice that had yelled through the doorway. "I see several new faces this year. I'll warn you, this program isn't easy. It's not a place for you to hang out. You'll be learning real lifesaving skills here. Most of you have several years before you can qualify as a lifeguard, as most programs don't let people in until they're sixteen and the rest require you to be older than that. So, don't expect to suddenly become lifeguards after this. Also, being a lifeguard is an important job, not something to make a little extra money over the summer while you read or hang out with your friends. If you're sleeping on the job, people can die."

He stared at each one of us, making sure we were paying attention. I looked around me at the other kids. Most of them were still yawning, looking like they had heard the speech before. I was a bit confused by this, though, as the kid couldn't have been much older than sixteen himself. Were we really going to be learning lifeguarding from someone who barely qualified as one? But none of the other kids thought anything of it. I just shrugged and tried to pay attention as he spelled out the eight-week program. It was going to take up much of my summer plans, but it seemed worth it to me. It would teach me everything that I would need to know to become a lifeguard when I was old enough.

After an hour long lecture on the importance of a lifeguard, which seemed more like the kid gloating about finally becoming one himself, we hit the pool. The instructor jumped in first, leading the laps as the rest of them showed off how strong they were at swimming. I was surprised to find myself keeping up with the older kids who had been going there for years, many of whom had been talking about taking the test at the end of the summer to become lifeguards the next year.

It was exhilarating to swim in such a large pool, easily twice as big as mine, alongside other strong swimmers. Several people were shocked that such a small, young girl could swim better than half the class, watching me soar through the water like it was second nature. And it was, or perhaps even first nature. I always felt more at home in water than in my own skin. At first, I had thought it would have made me one of them. That maybe I'd make some friends there that would make up for the fact that I still hadn't talked with Jen or that I barely got to see Ashley because of it. Instead, when I climbed out of the pool at the end of my laps, it was to hushed words of "freak" and "weirdo". I shrugged it off, insisting to myself that I wasn't there to make friends anyway.

"I'm glad to see that not all of you had been slacking off since last summer," the instructor said, as he glared at those that were still finishing up their laps, lagging far behind the rest of us. "But there's more to being a lifeguard than being a good swimmer."

"It helps though," said one of the other students. He stood next to the instructor, puffing out his chest as he gloated about being the first person out of the pool. No one but he had noticed this, though.

"It also takes quick reflexes and knowing how to react in a crisis. As I said earlier, we'll be going over the first aid requirements in later classes. That will help with how to react. However, quick reflexes aren't something we can train here."

"Sure, it is," someone said. "Think fast."

I wasn't sure who he was talking to, or what thought that person needed to do. The voice had come from right behind me, though, and something flew by my face. I just reacted, taking a step to the side and out of the way of the kid. In the process, I bumped into the bleachers next to me. Confused and overbalanced, I toppled over, coming to sit down hard on the metal bleachers. My legs went up in the air, chopping through the space that the boy had been darting through. My foot hit him on the forehead, knocking him further away from me. The boy barreled past several of the other kids, falling into the pool. The water splashed up, soaking everyone standing next to it.

Before I could get up from my place on the bleachers, the instructor was diving into the water. The other students just stood there, gawking at the boy or complaining about getting wet again. I just shook my head, not understanding why they were complaining. They had all only just got out of the pool minutes earlier. Besides, half the point in going swimming was to get wet.

I was just getting back to my feet as the instructor was pulling the boy back out of the water. The other students quickly clustered around the two of them, blocking my view. I tried to peek around the crowd, but I didn't get any closer to seeing what was happening.

"He'll be alright," the instructor said. "He just needs to go to the hospital to get checked out; he bumped his head pretty badly. I'll need a little help to get him over there, though."

"I'll do it," I said, surprising myself as my hand went up. "I needed to get a ride over there anyway so my mom could drive me home. She works there," I added when people started to look at me funny.

"Fine, whatever. Mostly I just need you to hold open the doors anyway. As for the rest of you... well, class is dismissed obviously. We'll see you all tomorrow at the same time."

With a grunt and a heave, the instructor hauled the kid up off the ground. The kid's eyes were partially open and looking around as if he couldn't quite understand what he was seeing. With a little prodding, the two of them walked through the rest of the class, all of whom were still just standing there, gawking at the injured boy. I began to wonder just how many of those kids would actually make decent lifeguards one day if that was their reaction to someone getting hurt in the pool. I just shook my head as I headed off, stopping just long enough to slip on my flip flops before going over to hold the doors open. Though I was still lost in that building, I did my best to lead the way back out to the front parking lot where I had come in a couple of hours earlier. When we got out there, the instructor pointed over at a black sports car in the corner of the lot, right by a back entrance that probably led right into the boys' locker room.

As I reached for the driver's side door, the car chirped and clunked as it was unlocked remotely. It took a little manipulation to slide the injured boy into the back seat, but I was able to pull him in with me and secured his seat belt around him. We headed over to the hospital, which was only a couple blocks away from the pool, pulling into the emergency room entrance where we were met by a couple people in scrubs who looked better equipped at getting him back out than I would ever be. I just sat back as I watched them work, waiting for the four of them to head off into the building before getting out of the car.

As I came inside, I spotted my mom over with the instructor and the injured student. I waved over at her, but she showed no sign of seeing me as she flurried about, doing her work. Knowing I'd just be in the way around there, I just headed off to the visitors' lounge near the main entrance to the hospital, all the way on the other side of the building.

It was a common thing for me to wander around the hospital on my own. Most days, in the middle of summer, Dad was at work in Portland, Mom was busy, as usual, and I was apparently "too young to be left home alone". I was supposed to head up to the daycare center on the second floor, but I hadn't spent much time there since I turned six. Instead, I'd wander around the hospital, learning every which way there was to get from one end of the building to the other. I even made a game of it sometimes, making it so I couldn't go in any given hallway for more than one turn, always needing to switch between right and left turns, or needing to follow one side of the hall. It was more entertaining than anything they had in the daycare center.

So, I was coming up to a seemingly random blind corner, one of those corners that needs the curved mirror on the ceiling so that no one runs into each other. That was when I spotted a familiar looking boy in the mirror that was hanging there. David was at the elevators just around the corner, pressing the button.

I was rather confused by his being there. Did he know that my mom worked at that hospital and that I sometimes hung out there? Was he there looking for me? But then why would he be using the elevator? A million questions rushed through my head as I stood there, frozen, watching him in the mirror as he walked onto the elevators. By the time I got over the shock of seeing him there and got around the corner, the door to the elevator had already closed and the lights indicated that the elevator had stopped on the third floor.

"Oncology?" I asked myself. I stood there for a moment, wondering if David could have gotten off at a different floor before the elevator continued onward. But I hadn't seen anyone else get on and the elevator stayed on the third floor. Curiosity getting the better of me, I hit the button to call the elevator back down.

I already knew he wouldn't be near the elevator when I got off of it on the third floor. Still, I decided to poke around, figuring I might spot him in one of the rooms around there. The floor nurse barely glanced up from the computer she was using, just long enough to give me a little smile of recognition. All the nurses of the hospital knew me, knew my mom. As long as I wasn't getting in anyone's way, they usually just let me be. I only gave the smallest wave to her as I passed by, not wanting to draw attention to myself or the fact that I was still in my swimsuit. Between the time driving over to the hospital and my explorations below, it had dried up. But I wasn't entirely sure how sanitary it would be, considering the floor I was on. Even at that age, I knew how important that was in Oncology. So, I tried not to draw too much attention to myself as I headed into the main hallway.

Most of the doors on the floor were closed and there was no sign of David in the halls as I walked through them. I was about to give up, to head back down to the ground floor's waiting room where there were some magazines. Briefly, I thought about the books that were still in my bag back in the locker room, cursing myself for not getting them before I left the pool. As I stood there, mentally kicking myself for my forgetfulness, I heard his voice ahead.

"Mom, I don't have anywhere else to be right now," he said. His voice was coming from the door straight ahead, where the hall led off to the left. The door was open just a crack, sunlight streaming through. "I would have thought you'd love to get visits from me."

I snuck forward, trying not to let my flip flops slap too loudly and interrupt the conversation that I knew I shouldn't be listening to. When I got to the door, I slid against the far wall so that I could peek in through the crack. David was sitting in a chair next to the bed where a woman was lying down, coughing into her fist. Plastic tubing was supplying her with oxygen so that her lungs wouldn't need to strain so much. There was a colorful scarf tied around her head, failing to hide the fact that she was bald.

"I... don't want you... to see me waste away like this," she said between coughs. "You should be out with your friends, enjoying being young. You only get to be young once."

"You're still young, Mom," he said, holding her free hand which had another tube sticking out of it. "You'll always be young."

"I will now," she said, smiling at the unintended meaning. "That's the perk of dying young, the only perk I'll get to see. My corpse won't be that beautiful."

"Don't talk like that, Mom," David said. Fresh tears started to flow down his cheeks. "You're not going to die. I won't let you die."

"Oh, honey," she said. Her right hand went to his cheek to comfort him. "There's nothing you can do to stop that. There never was. It's going to happen and it's going to happen soon. I just wish that you didn't have to grow up without a mother. Maybe your father--"

"You're not going to die," David yelled again. "You're going to get better. You have to."

David jumped up out of his seat, losing his grip of his mother's hand as he ran from the room. I wasn't fast enough, still sitting against the wall by the door. He came out into the hall, tripping over my legs and spilling onto the floor.

"David, oh my god, are you okay?" I asked, rushing over to him. It was starting to seem like everyone was tripping or falling around me those days.

"Yea, I'm fine," he said, as he propped himself up. "Maya? What are you doing here?"

"My mom works here," I said. "I saw--"

"Is that Maya from the pool party?" David's mom asked, calling out to us from her bed. "Come on in. Let me get a look at you."

With an apologetic glance back at David, I helped him up off the floor and the two of us headed into her room. His tantrum forgotten, David headed back to the chair that he had only just left, though he wouldn't look his mom in the face. I stood near the door, my hands grasping each other in front of me as I looked everywhere in the room but at her. I was trying not to stare at the pale woman in front of me. I had spent enough time in that hospital to know that her earlier remarks had been right, that she was going to die, and soon.

"So, this is Maya, huh? I approve."

"Mom," David whined.

"Um... what?" I asked, confused.

"Oh, nothing. Just my dying brain playing tricks on me again," David's mom said, waving off my confusion. "Come, come. Sit over here," she said, tapping the chair next to the bed across from David. "So, you know my little Davie?" she asked.

"Mom," David whined again. "I told you to stop calling me that."

"Oh, yes, David. So grown up," she said, reaching over to squeeze his cheek. "He was telling me how great your party was. Very exciting."

"Exciting, right. That's one word for it," I said.

"Now don't sell yourself short," she said.

"I am short."

"And you saved that girl's life."

"I just got her out of the water. My mom saved her life."

"The point is she was saved, and you had a hand in it. You should be proud. We are."

"Mom," David whined again, drawing my attention over to him. He was blushing, which confused me even more. Why would these two, who barely even knew me, or Ashley for that matter, care so much about my saving her?

"Well, you really must come visit me," David's mom insisted. "If you're going to be spending time in the hospital anyway. Your mom works here?"

"She's an ER nurse downstairs," I confirmed.

"Well, then you can come up any time you're here, keep my Davie company. He'll need it, you know, closer to..."

I nodded, knowing all too well to what she was referring. "I have to warn you though," I said as I looked down at my clothes. "I intend to be wearing something a little more than a bathing suit when I come to visit."

She chuckled at that and I even spotted the hint of a smile from David as well.

Chapter Nine
A Little Light Stealing

Now

Mom tossed her fork down on the plate in front of her, jarring me out of my stupor. I glanced around a bit, at a loss for even what day of the week it was, let alone what meal we were eating. "I mean, seriously, Maya. Would it be too much to ask for you to pay attention to me when I'm talking to you?"

"Probably," I mumbled silently. I immediately regretted it as her face instantly changed from frustration to hurt. Still, with the hourglass ticking away on my wrist, I turned back to the two manors in front of me. Mom's head blocked my view of them momentarily as I drifted back to Desparia.

#

It was delicate work maneuvering into position outside of the mystery manor. Sardana Jakala's place was right on the edge of the property, leaving very little room between the buildings. This allowed for easier climbing, but I had to watch for her personal guards, which patrolled the grounds constantly. There was a time when I had considered climbing another side of the manor, but the front and left side were right up against the street, leaving me no shadows to hide in when the city guards came by. The back would have allowed the best protection from being discovered. But, according to the scroll, it was also the most defended by Grandor's traps. No, the side against Sardana's land was the only way in... largely because only an idiot would try that side.

I found a nice post in the alley across the street from the two manors. From there, I watched patiently, trying to predict the patterns of the guards in Sardana's manor. After a while, I started to feel distraught. There didn't seem to be any break in their patrols. No period where their guard was down on any side of that manor. Often, I would shake myself, remembering that it was the other manor that I needed to break into. Even more often, I wished I had access to my gear. There were a few party favors in my pack that would have drawn the attention of the guards. Placed and timed just right, it would have given me the thirty seconds that I would have needed to get inside.

And then I saw it. If I hadn't been sitting there for so long, I would have missed it. One of the guards hadn't turned when he was supposed to. I couldn't see him from where I was, but that was the only sign I needed. He was supposed to be coming along the targeted wall right then, plainly visible from my vantage point.

Crossing my fingers and hoping it wasn't some fluke, I dashed across the road and made for the crevasse between the buildings, scaring a stray cat in the process. I quickly shimmied up between the buildings, using their proximity for leverage like they show on movies sometimes. Trinity and Neo climbing down inside the walls of a rundown building came to mind at that moment, though they were dangerously slow in comparison to my ascent. I scaled the wall in record time. As I flipped over the top, I almost wished I had a stopwatch to keep track of it. But that only reminded me of the ticking clock strapped to my wrist and made me focus on the task before me.

I sat there, my back against the low wall that ran the length of the roof. For the longest time, I just sat there, holding my breath. Waiting to hear a call from the guards across the way. When nothing came, I peeked ever so slightly over the lip of the wall. Whatever had disturbed their pattern seemed to have ended. Their patrols were as thick as they had been a minute earlier. I whispered a silent prayer of thanks to the unnamed goddess of thieves for my luck. She was my patron goddess, in both worlds, though I wasn't so convinced she heard me back in reality.

Staying low and sticking to the shadows, I crept across the roof. There was a small room in the center of the building, designed to give people access to and from there. Remnants of a garden spread out from the door to the room, the plants long dead. They formed something of a pattern that was less recognizable with the flowers gone and the bushes in decay.

Once I was sure I was out of sight of the neighbors, I rushed over to the door, noting a rather large flaw in Grandor's plans. If I had designed the security system, I would have trapped the roof. Trigger plates strategically placed every few feet with a lever near the door to turn them off and on. Instead, I knew from the scroll that the door itself contained the only trap on the roof. It took me a couple seconds to disarm the trip wires around the door, ten more to make sure there weren't any that hadn't made it into the plans, another thirty to pick the lock itself, and I was in.

I had to sidestep a trigger plate that was on the other side of the door, but it was nothing more than a mild inconvenience as I headed down the stairs. My confidence in the plans only grew as I made my way down the stairs. Every third step contained another trigger plate that I had to jump over until I reached step number thirty, then it switched to every forth. I used a spare piece of paper and a piece of charcoal to keep track and I still felt like I needed to recount every five steps. The traps were too dangerous to be wrong about. According to the plans, many of them triggered a series of fireballs that would leave the manor unscathed, but any person inside would end up nothing but ash.

Once I made it to the second floor, the pattern got even more complicated. Often, I would have to pull the scroll back out just to make sure that I remembered it right. I was concentrating so much on the pressure plates that I almost forgot the trip wire halfway down the hallway, right in front of the entrance to the study. I caught myself, my foot in the air a hair's breadth from one of them.

I eased my foot back down to the floor, careful to stay as far away from the trip wires that ran through the area as possible. My goal was already in sight, taunting me right on the other side of the traps. I had to be careful, though, as I started my work, disabling the wires one by one. After clipping the last one, I secured it to the rest of them in a large weave against a neighboring chair. Only after I was certain that they would hold did I step around the corner and into the main study.

That was where I really needed to put my game face on. The trap network was structured to make that room the most fortified room in the world. To make matters worse, the missing part of the plans detailed a good portion of it. I looked around the study, trying to get the scope of its shape and contents and to start figuring out how best to trap it. But when I saw what was in there, my chin dropped practically to the floor. I was surrounded by a splendor that is not often seen in either world, even in museums.

In the corner was a marble carved globe of the world of Desparia that had to be at least three feet in diameter. Unlike most fantasy worlds, with their unrealistic flatness left over from those old days when people thought Earth was like that, Desparia was just as round as Earth. Fandor, the land I spent much of my time in, was pointed towards the door. The rest of the continent took up much of my view of the globe. It stretched towards the north into Norenia and south to the open wilds, where not even the emperor would dare to travel.

The Olorbarak Mountains protruded from the surface on the far left, just barely getting beneath the support that held the globe aloft. The globe was held in an ornately crafted stand that looked to be solid gold.

And that was probably one of the lower worth items I was seeing. The room was full of gemstones as large as fists, marble statues that would put da Vinci to shame, and wall sized paintings that even a luddite like me knew had to be worth a king's ransom. Even what looked like a silvryl dwarven helmet in the corner, what dwarven kings usually wore in place of crowns. Not that I've met many dwarves in my travels.

On top of that were the obviously enchanted items. There was a full length mirror in another corner that didn't reflect the room, instead showing a field somewhere. I wasn't sure if that was a portal or just a scrying device, or perhaps something even more insidious. Either way, I'd be keeping my distance from that section as much as humanly possible. Dead center in the room, on top of a carved marble pillar, was none other than the clovehood diamond. This was rumored to be worn by the ancient empress herself as a magical armor that nothing could penetrate.

Just to the side of the clovehood diamond, suspended from the ceiling in a crystal case, was the target of my search. The metal hemisphere sat on its flat side, showing no real signs that it was anything of importance. From the door, it just looked like an iron ball, about the size of a softball, split in half. I briefly wondered what could have happened to the other half. But it didn't seem all that remarkable, certainly not worthy of being in the vicinity of the other treasures in the room. And yet, I knew that the traps were mostly focused on that as the centerpiece.

"Well, perhaps they're really centered around the clovehood, and the missing notes were the balancing piece of it," I thought to myself.

Knowing it was going to take me a few hours to deactivate all the traps that I already knew of, I got to work. It was a painstaking process, disabling each trap without triggering the rest of them. They were all overlapping each other, making it even harder. A few times I would get halfway through disabling a trap before realizing another one was too close. Half the time I would be holding the ends of two or three other traps as I disable two more. It's very complicated and I won't bore you with the details.

Even having started less than an hour after dark, the eastern sky was lightening before I was within grabbing distance of the sphere. I was standing right next to the clovehood diamond, quite tempted to grab that and run. Maybe it would be enough to protect me from the bracelet. If it hadn't been for the legend of the gem, I might have. It was said to have driven the ancient empress insane long before her fall. And it was no guarantee, while getting the sphere was. Or, at least, I thought it would be at the time.

It took me another hour before I finally landed at the crystal display case. I ended up making another circuit of the room, my path dictated more by the pattern of the traps than any direction on my part. The case itself had a practically audible humming with the enchantments that had been cast on it. Only the most powerful of enchantments vibrated on a level that could be felt, let alone heard.

Magical traps are a lot harder to deal with than mechanical ones. Mechanical traps, like those used by pretty much all thieves that don't also have skills in the arcane arts, are very simple. It's all about trigger and release. To get past it, you have to either trigger it and get out of the way or make it so that the trigger no longer functions. With magical traps, however, the trigger could be anything. Even breathing in the wrong direction could set it off. And when it goes off, and they usually do, the result doesn't even need to be immediate. I could already have a curse running through my system and I wouldn't even know it until I suddenly exploded later, taking my supposed co-conspirators with me. Or it could be subtle, like making it so that I would no longer see the faint lines of a trip wire, resulting in me setting off a bunch of other traps without even noticing them.

No, when it came to magical traps, I usually didn't mess with them, and I really, really, really wished I didn't have to then. Standing below the crystal box, I scanned the area, making sure my exit strategies were in place. Strategies as in plural. You never know from which direction the huge ball of fire is going to come from. Unfortunately, the study was situated in the middle of the building. No windows were in sight, with only the one door in or out. It was quite literally a death trap in there.

I spent a few more minutes clearing out a few more traps, getting it so that I had a direct line out the door. The last thing I needed right then was to have to run around in the spiral back out again if something went wrong. Also, I was procrastinating. I knew next to nothing about magic. All I knew was the general feel of the hum of enchanted objects and that is readily obvious. It's like the hum of a refrigerator but with no obvious signs of electronics.

Once everything was set, or at least as set as I could make them, I walked a circle around the box, trying to gauge if the hum was weaker on one side than the other. After making three loops and not sensing any difference, I settled on the side opposite from the main exit so I wouldn't need to turn around if I had to run.

With a deep breath, I took out a pouch that I had purchased on the way over here, the one essential part of this whole thing. It was a pouch of cancelation powder. If I still had my supplies, I would have had a huge bag of the stuff. It would have been a lot more potent than the crap I had gotten on the street. The problem was that the stuff was expensive, yet absolutely necessary when going up against magical traps if you have no skill at magic yourself.

Holding my breath, I reached into the pouch and took the smallest pinch I could manage. A little goes a long way with cancelation powder, which is a good thing seeing as how too much of it would just trigger the whole thing instead of removing it. As I blew the fine powder against the box, a few sparks shot off every which way. The hum dimmed for a second but then came back up as strong as before.

"Wow," I said to myself. "This stuff really is crap." With a sigh, I decided to go with a less subtle approach, despite my better judgment. I emptied the entire pouch into my hand, getting it into as tight of a wad as I could manage. Reaching my full hand back, I closed my eyes and prayed to the unnamed goddess, before throwing the powder against the box with all my strength. It scattered across the air, clumping a bit towards the center as it usually does, and smacked hard into the side of the crystal box. Sparks shot off again, this time with much more force. I could see in the corner of my eyes a few small fires start up and die off as I stared at the box in the hopes that my luck of the night held.

It didn't.

Chapter Ten
Wasting Away the Summer

Five Years Earlier

I spent the rest of the day hanging out with David in and around his mom's room. She spent a good part of the day sleeping. The nurses kept insisting that this was a good thing. She needed all the strength that she could get to fight the cancer that was slowly eating away at her. David always looked away from the nurses when they said that, no doubt thinking that it was already too late for his mother, just as she had obviously known the truth. Mom stopped by soon after dinner. She had heard that I was there from the floor nurses. After promising that I could come back to "keep David company" as his mom had said, she took me home.

I spent most mornings at the pool in my class, but I'd always return to the hospital to sit with David. Together, we watched his mom slowly waste away with the cancer as he tried to spend as much time with her as possible. I worried some days that David was left alone while I was at my classes, though he never seemed to complain about it when I got there near noon every day. His dad would pop in from time to time as well, but he was busy with his work as a cop. Whenever he was there, though, it wasn't like he was really there. It was like he was trying to deny that his wife was dying. Or perhaps, it was more accurate that it was like he was treating her like she was already dead.

As busy as I was with my newfound friend, the one thing I didn't miss out on was my time with Ashley and Jen. After I had rescued her from the pool and my mom saved her life, Ashley had just taken off, with barely a word of thanks. I hadn't heard from her since, as absent from my life as Jen was. Honestly, I just wrote the both of them off, a loss that would only hit me once school started up again... once David's mom died.

Spending time with David quickly became the new norm. We seemed to talk about everything. About our hobbies. Our dreams for when we grew up. Middle school, which was starting up in just a few weeks. Despite not encountering David in school before, he was in my grade and would be coming with me to the same middle school. It seemed like we had so much in common, and almost like I had been cheated out of something by not having known him sooner. At the time, though, I wasn't quite sure what it was that I was cheated out of.

By the time August rolled around, David's mother, Mrs. Azalea, was starting to look better. She was regaining some of the color in her face and she was spending more time awake, playing cards and talking with us. The nurses seemed to think it was a good sign, though David continued to look over at her out of the corner of his eye as if expecting her good health was just going to go away again. He had been sullen all afternoon for some reason, from the moment that I had gotten there, and it only seemed to get worse when his dad arrived.

"David," Mr. Azalea said, as he stepped into the room. He didn't glance over at his wife right away, just looking to his son. "We should get going. My partner's wife is insisting we come over for dinner. It would be rude to be late."

"Hello, Joe," Mrs. Azalea said, looking up at her husband. "We're almost done with this hand." She held up the two cards that she was still holding to demonstrate.

Mr. Azalea glanced over at her when she said his name, but he turned back to his son almost immediately. It took him a few seconds to dare another glance, his face lighting up when he saw how well she was looking. "You're looking lively today, Greta," Mr. Azalea said, smiling over at her. She smiled back, nodding over at him.

"Okay, ew," David said, as he slapped the two cards down on the table. "I quit. Maya, let's get out of here before they start kissing or something."

I laughed, looking between the two of them, before following David out into the hall. When I got out there, I looked around confused. I had figured that he would have just popped outside the door. That he would have slumped against the wall to wait for his father. Instead, he was halfway down the hall, heading for the nurses' station. "Wait up, David," I called after him, as I rushed to catch up.

He slowed down as he neared the corner towards the nurses' station. But he didn't stop, didn't turn around. "He just doesn't get it," he said, as he punched the wall.

"Doesn't get what?" I asked. I glanced over at where his fist had hit, but the wall seemed undamaged by his assault.

"No matter how good she looks right now, how many jokes she makes, or how many games we get to play with her, she's still going to die," he yelled at the wall. He walked into the corner, standing between the two doors there, and started to pound his fists into the wall. One of the nurses from the station came around to see what was going on and grabbed him up, pulling him into a hug. He resisted it at first but then went slack, standing there in the woman's embrace for a minute until she let go. She gave the boy a half-hearted smile before heading back to the desk. I watched her go, wondering if all nurses had that power or if it was just her and Mom.

"Don't you think they know that?" I asked, once the nurse was out of earshot. I had just stood there as the nurse embraced him, wondering if I should have tried that. Or if I needed a hug myself. "They're just trying to enjoy what little time they have with each other. I thought that was the whole point of this, of you coming to the hospital every day."

"It is," he said, turning back to the wall. "It was."

"Was?"

"I keep thinking 'this is the day she's going to die; this is the day I'm going to lose her forever'. But it doesn't come. And I'm happy it doesn't, I'm happy she's still here. It just..."

"It doesn't seem real," I suggested.

It wasn't until he said that that I realized I had been feeling the same thing. I kept thinking she'd be dead by the time I went up there. It wasn't the same for me, she wasn't my mother. But she was my friend, and I didn't want to lose her. But I knew I would. Not like I lost Jen and Ashley; I still held out hope that we'd make up when school started again. But it felt close to it.

"You'll feel better when school starts," I suggested. "When you have something to do all day besides wait around for her to die. I have that with my lifeguard classes in the morning."

"But she's not your mom," he yelled. "Why do you care so much?"

"I-I don't know," I said, though I knew.

"I don't want you coming here anymore," he said. "I don't want you getting close to my mom. She's my mom, not yours."

"But... but we're friends," I said.

"We're not friends," he spat. "We never will be. Just go away."

"Fine," I shouted at him.

He glanced back at me as I walked off, heading for the elevator. We made eye contact as the doors closed, sealing off that part of my life.

After that day, I didn't go back to the hospital. Instead, I would just head home after my lifeguard lessons. At first, Mom thought that I still went. This gave me more time to myself. More chances to prove that being eleven meant that I was old enough to be on my own. And, once she found out, she reluctantly agreed.

Mom was nice enough to bring me any news of Mrs. Azalea's condition. But as the days passed with no real change, I soon gave up hope of her recovery. As David had feared, her returning color was temporary. By the end of the summer, she was back to where she was when I first walked in on her and David talking. I prayed for her every night, but as her condition worsened, I started to doubt that anyone was listening.

Chapter Eleven
The Mad Dash for the Exit

Now

Mom and I were curled up on the couch, watching the ten o'clock news. It was one of the few rituals we had together where I didn't spend most of my time daydreaming of Desparia. Of course, this time, I wasn't in too much of a hurry to get back there, with the traps going off all around me. Instead, I found myself lost in memories of that fateful year. Before I knew it, the anchors were closing out the news hour and I was heading up to bed, knowing I wouldn't fall asleep anytime soon. My adventurous life awaited me there.

#

When cancelation powder works correctly, the enchanted object sparks for about ten seconds and then the enchantments simply go away, never to return. When it doesn't work, one of three things happens. Either the enchantment fades for a few seconds before snapping back at the same power, the whole thing explodes, or, in the case of the enchantment triggering something, whatever it is set to trigger does. With the pinch of dust, the first had happened. With the whole wad...

Behind me, I heard a hissing, sizzling sound. If a dragon had to inhale through a really small hole before breathing fire, it would make that sound. This was my only indication that it was about to get very hot in there.

"Screw it," I yelled over the cacophony behind me.

I grabbed a large, silver, ornamental sword off its display plaque on my left. It looked to be elven made, second century old reckoning perhaps, and worth a fortune. As everything in that room was. It was also very, very heavy and not very sharp. With all my might, I swung it at the chain that was suspending the crystal box. The sword went through it like it wasn't even there, dropping the box and the hemisphere inside of it. I tossed the sword, grabbed the crystal box up in a football hold, and made a mad dash for the exit.

If you've ever tried to outrun a ball of fire, you know that it's not as easy as it sounds. If you've never tried to outrun a ball of fire, well... don't. As I made it out of the room, less than 5 seconds after the powder failed, almost literally all hell broke loose. It wasn't just the fireball that came from the back of the study, somehow missing every item in there as it invariably sought me out. Fireballs, lightning bolts, and all sorts of offensive spells were flying everywhere. The spells covered the entire area in a destructive chaos that was avoiding everything in the room, outside in the hall, and generally everywhere in that small manor. If people were outside observing the spells that were going off and could see through the walls to what was happening, they would applaud. Although, that would not be at my ability to avoid the spells. That I just put down to blind luck and a small blessing from the unnamed goddess.

I took the corner at speed, grabbing onto the door frame for added leverage. Five paces down the hall, I spotted another fireball coming up the hallway at me from the direction I was going. I made a quick decision that was probably one of the dumbest things I could have done right then. I pivoted and jumped right out the window. Normally, this might be the thing to do, but I was still on the second story... and the window faced the other building.

Had there not been a window on the other side, directly opposite, I would have slammed right into the wall and fell the ten feet straight down, too dazed to land properly. It wouldn't have killed me, but it would have seriously hurt. I would have also been knocked out long enough for some guards to find me and stick me back in jail.

Seconds after jumping out the window, I smashed through a window in the manor across the way. My trained thief reflexes worked to my advantage, and I went into a tumble, coming up on my feet... in the bed chamber of Sardana Jakala... the emperor's daughter... as she was getting up out of bed... completely naked.

"Um... hi." I said, stupidly. Behind me, I felt more than saw the flashing heat of passing fireballs. Do I know how to make an entrance or what?

She grabbed a throwing knife off the bedside table and threw it at my head. Why she would have throwing knives there would be anyone's guess. Reflexively, I used the crystal box as a shield. The knife bounced harmlessly off into the corner. As I held the box there, the crystal started to crack from the force of the throw. Obviously, the knife was enchanted, making me overly thankful for my quick reflexes and the fact that the crystal box made a great shield.

After a few seconds, the crystal shatters. I fumble around with the box a bit, trying to catch the sphere without getting cut on the crystal shards. I only managed the latter. The sphere tumbled down, and I caught it with my foot. I tossed what was left of the box away as I flipped the sphere back up into my hands.

"Thanks for that," I said, tossing the sphere into the air. As I returned my attention to Sardana, I noticed the shocked expression on her face. Her eyes were practically bugging out and her mouth was hanging open. "What?" I asked. "It's not like I'm that impressive."

"Guards!" she yelled.

"I'll take that as my cue to leave," I said. I headed back out the window. This time I was properly situated, and not fleeing from a giant fireball, so I was able to swing downward, landing lightly on my feet.

Not wanting to overstay my welcome, I darted off into the street, where the local merchants were just starting to set up their wares. I was barely a block away when Sardana's guards hit the street. They weren't subtle about it either, pushing their way through the throng. They even went so far as knocking down a few people that didn't move out of their way fast enough. It only took a moment before everyone on the street realized they were there and started to make room for them. This made it even easier for me to duck down one of the alleys and get out of there, hidden by the crowd as they cleared the street.

Once clear of the town square, I looked at my bracelet. More than half of the sand was gone, having spilled into the bottom section of the hourglass. My life was slowly ticking away but I had enough common sense to not head straight for the guild. It had to be one of my messiest departures from a job, but at least the task was completed. I patted one of my deeper pockets, where I had stowed the sphere. It helped to reassure myself that I still had it.

I took a roundabout path back to the guild, in part to avoid any guards that were smart enough to check there for me and in part to make sure I wasn't being followed. I spent most of the time practicing my craft, lifting a few purses off those early bird shoppers and grabbing a lovely cloak from a merchant stall. I later managed to trade the much too nice and new cloak for a panhandler's old one. It only smelled slightly of pee and was considerably more non-descript than anything one can get in a store. The panhandler seemed to think the world of that deal, which probably meant the guy was a recent addition to the role. No one is going to give money to a guy that has a cloak that nice.

That is, of course, assume he could hold onto it. The other beggars were bound to grab it off him and try to pawn it.

Once reasonably sure I was in the clear, which was at about nine in the morning, I headed back over to the guild. Something kept nagging at me the whole way. Some deep part of my psyche that always seemed to be smarter than me. I usually didn't listen to that part; I have way too much fun when I don't. But for some reason I did that day. As I approached the alley that led to the front door of the guild, I pulled up the hood on my recently acquired cloak. It was a quick and easy disguise in case someone was looking for me. I walked right past the alley that held the entrance to the guild on the first approach. This was a very good thing.

The smell was my first hint that something was up, at least that I noticed. From the far side of the alley, I peeked backwards and around the edge of the building on that side, trying to stay as inconspicuous as I could. There was a large object in the middle of the alley, taking up most of the space. It almost looked like a pile of trash and refuse. But it would have taken weeks for it to pile up that badly if everyone in town came down here to drop it off. I hesitantly approached the blob, picking up a stick that I spotted off to the side. Once I was within stick prodding distance, yes, I poked it with a stick. It's stupid, I know, but not as stupid as poking it with a finger first. Skirting around it a bit, I finally managed to figure out what I was looking at. It was a body... specifically the body of the giant from the other day. He, like most of his brethren, was dead.

As I stood there, at a loss for words, the front door to the guild opened up. Reflexively, I ducked behind the body, using it for cover from whatever, or whomever, was coming out. The black uniforms were unmistakable.

"Let's go," said the first Jakala Trooper to exit the building. He was pulling on a rope that extended behind him and into the guild. A long line of troopers came out of the building, all pulling their own ropes, tugging them every few steps. I heard the sounds of hooves hitting the cobblestones out in the road and moved further behind the giant's body, trying to avoid detection by whomever was coming up there. There was a small cubby in the side wall of the alley that was almost completely blocked by the corpse. I only just managed to duck out of sight when a large prison coach fell into position at the mouth of the alley, blocking any exit.

"Come on," the lead trooper said as he approached the coach. He tugged on his rope harder than ever, causing a long line of people to come into my view. They were each tied to the ropes that the troopers were pulling, their ankles similarly tied together, in a long prison-chain-gang style line. Each prisoner had a hood over his head, but it was easy to guess that they were the members of the thieves' guild. Who else would the troopers be dragging out of the guild in such numbers? I just hid there, counting the thieves as they got loaded into the cart.

Halfway through the thieves passing by my little hiding spot, a flash of flesh caught my eye. The man from earlier, who I had rescued from the dungeons, was tied up with the rest of them. Despite his head being hooded, like all of them, I easily recognized him from his muscled chest, gleaming in the dawn's early light. Seeing him so restrained was almost enough of an excuse to jump out. To try to fight the troopers off and rescue the thieves. But I knew that such an action would only get me caught as well.

It felt like forever, waiting in the cubby as I watched the group get carted off. Every once in a while, I would look down at the gold bracelet still attached to my wrist, still ticking down what little time I had left. The best I could hope for right was that Zandar or Grandor had somehow managed to escape the raid. Without either of them, I was going to be dead in a few hours. I had to keep reminding myself that it wasn't really going to kill me. That the bracelet was as imaginary as the rest of the world I was in. In either case, I wasn't about to let the bracelet do whatever it was going to do to me.

I debated whether to follow the troopers and mount a rescue or try to search the guild for the guild leader and mage. If either managed to evade capture, going after the rest of the guild would do me no good. If neither did... well, I decided I couldn't afford to lose track of the group.

When I finished counting the people, there were fifty-three prisoners in four very crowded prison coaches and a good seventy troopers guarding them. Once the troopers started down the road again, I counted off thirty seconds in my head before moving out from behind the giant's corpse. As I peeked out from the alley, off in the distance the caravan turned a corner, heading for the east gate to the city. I followed them, keeping my distance and trying to blend in with the crowd. Once they left the city, it was going to be a lot harder to follow them without being seen. But there was also the added benefit that the area was rather densely wooded, and the carts would need to keep to the road. I debated stealing a horse, but with so many of the troopers walking, I figured that I wouldn't have a problem keeping up.

It took about half an hour for the caravan to get outside the town, heading into the countryside. I actually hadn't been on that road before. So, at first, following them seemed like an excellent excuse to do so. That was, at least, until I came upon the first crossroads, and the sign reminded me why I hadn't been that way before.

The caravan was heading for The Capital.

Chapter Twelve
Middle School Hell

Five Years Earlier

That last week of summer was hell. My junior lifeguard classes had ended a week before school started and, without my visits to the hospital, I didn't have much else to do besides read and daydream. It was almost a relief to go back to school. Ashley and Jen would be there and, hopefully, I'd be able to get them to talk to me. All I could think about was mending our relationship as I walked to the bus stop.

I had finally managed to convince Mom that I didn't need a ride to the stop anymore, though she seemed almost hurt by it for some reason. She didn't say anything, but as I left that first morning, she stared after me as if it was the last time that she'd see me. Like I wasn't going to be returning home after school. Maybe she knew something that I didn't, but I had to shrug that idea off before my imagination took over. It wasn't as easy for my imagination to take over back then as it was lately, but it still happened.

As I walked up the stairs on the bus, nodding to the same driver that drove our elementary school bus, I spotted my friends in the same seat as usual. They hadn't saved me a seat across the aisle from them like they usually did, back in elementary school when we were talking to each other. I didn't think much of it, simply taking a seat closer to the front of the bus and figuring I'd speak to them soon enough.

The middle school was right next to the elementary school and I probably would have gone into the wrong building if the crowd from the bus hadn't led me right to the front door. There was a sign welcoming the new sixth graders, directing us to head to the gym, with friendly arrows along the way. I tried to spot the girls, but I had suddenly become one of the shortest people in my school, no longer towering over the younger kids. All I could see were the chests and bags of the kids around me as I followed along with the flow, hoping it would lead me in the right direction.

By the time that I got to the gym, the first section of the bleachers was already filling up. I spotted Ashley and Jen near the top, but they were talking to some other girl that I didn't recognize. The new girl had short hair, was a bit bulky, and looked really mean. Ashley nodded towards me and I gave a slight wave. As the other girl eyed me, I figured that I was the topic of conversation and that Ashley wasn't actually acknowledging my presence.

The top rows were already filled up with other kids, so I found a spot near the middle. Unfortunately, it wasn't close enough to hear what they were saying. Not over the buzz of conversation that was happening all around me. I just watched the two adults, a man and a woman, dither in place at the front of the section of bleachers.

Just before they started talking, David walked in. He was with two other boys that I didn't recognize, though I figured they were his friends. I wondered briefly why neither of them had visited his mother in the hospital with him. Why it had always been me keeping him company. Why they got a pass. Then I noticed how ragged David looked, almost worse than his mother on her bad days. I figured he must not be sleeping. Suddenly, I was worried about him. When he spotted me in the bleachers, his face lit up with recognition. But he didn't return the wave I gave. Instead, he just headed over into the corner of the bleachers with his friends.

Then, the adults started talking, and my attention was directed towards them. At least at first. My mind kept turning to my friends, both sets of them, as the man introduced himself as the principal. I was barely paying attention as he was talking about new beginnings in the new year and all about making new friends. Meanwhile, I looked between my old friends who all seemed to no longer want to be friends. At least not with me.

As the bell rang for first period, the principal pointed over to the woman, who had been setting up a table off to the side. "You'll find your class schedules on the table," he said. "Please form an orderly line so they can be distributed properly."

Nobody listened to him. Everyone jumped up from the bleachers, pushing past everyone to be the first in line to get their schedules. I lagged behind, hoping to get a word in with Ashley at least. But she, Jen, and the new girl went right past me. The new girl purposely bumped into me as they passed.

"Watch it," she said, as she glared back at me.

I stood there gaping after them as the three of them left the gym together, followed soon after by David and his friends. As I tried to catch up with the rest of my class, I tried to wrack my mind for some reason why they were all snubbing me. Why none of my friends wanted to talk to me. It was like there was some secret that the world knew but I didn't. I hated secrets and silently cursed whatever it was that caused me to lose my friends like that.

At first, I figured it was just the same rumors that were started up at the end of elementary school. About being poor and people disappearing in my house. But I had thought the pool party had fixed that. Or maybe they had caused a whole new set of problems. A new rumor going around about me, perhaps about my freakish mom or something that was as false as the last rumor had been. Whatever it was, I had to do something to undo it. To reverse this plague that had somehow hit me. I had to find out what the rumor was and squash it before it ruined my whole year. Like the last one had ruined the end of fifth grade.

All day long, I tried eavesdropping on everyone in my class, hoping to hear the whispers going around about me. I heard a lot of rumors that day, but none were about me. None gave me any clue as to what it was. I would have asked someone what it was, but my best source of gossip was Ashley and I still couldn't get a word in with her. Whenever I saw her that day, she was cloistered with Jen and the new girl. I managed to find out that her name was Janice but not much else. I only found that out from my eavesdropping. None of the other students would talk to me more than a few words, and mostly those were "go away". Laughter would follow me as I obeyed but no one would talk about it afterwards. At least, not before I had reluctantly left earshot.

By the time lunch came around and I was forced to eat alone at the corner of a half-filled table, I was beginning to regret not bringing a book to read. I had just finished the latest in that same series that Dad had started me on the night before and I was stuck with nothing but reruns again. Figuring I would at least be able to get Ashley to talk to me, I didn't bring anything else to do. No one was assigning homework for the first day of school, so I was left with sitting there daydreaming once more as I slowly ate my lunch.

The daydreaming was starting to become a habit, even then. But it had no focus to it. I kept trying to come up with new settings, new worlds to explore, pulling in the old characters from my old books to fill in the gaps. That day, however, I realized that, no matter which of my old favorites I'd pull into my daydreams, they all did the same thing. They all did what I would do in those situations. They'd go in, guns blazing, swords drawn, arrows at the ready, kill whoever needs killing, rescue whoever needs rescuing, and save whatever needs saving. Even the daydreams were starting to get boring. That was when I realized that I needed a world. A whole, complete world that could stand on its own. One that I could wander through and explore.

The problem was, I didn't know which world to use. The easy answer was to use Earth. To imagine myself exploring the furthest reaches of the planet. But that seemed too boring to me. Reality was boring enough without me having to imagine it too. Conversely, there weren't many fictional worlds that were complete enough to wander through like that, not as far as I knew. I'd need to do some research, build out this dreamworld if I were really going to commit to it. The problem was that would take too much effort for it to be worth it. It took me the rest of the day to realize that, though; I was too intent to escape the dull, boring life that was left to me without my friends.

That's when I heard it. After I had given up trying to find out the secret and started ignoring the world around me. That was when I heard my name and the secret that had been kept from me for the whole day.

"That's Maya?" came a voice from behind me as my math teacher started handing out the topic and test schedule for the year. "She doesn't look that crazy."

"Her whole family is crazy," came the reply. I wanted to look back, to see who it was that was talking about me. But I didn't want to spook them, to let them know I was hearing them. That they were finally revealing the very information that I had needed all along. "Her mom chased some kid into the water, nearly killed her."

"I thought her mom was some nurse at the hospital, though."

"That just makes it worse, doesn't it? That she'd be responsible for people's health."

"Having a crazy mom wouldn't make her crazy, though," said the first voice.

"But stalking a kid all summer? Coming to visit his mom even when he wasn't around? That's a bit much, isn't it?"

I was completely shocked by the accusation. Who was I stalking? Whose mom was I visiting when he wasn't there? David? No, that couldn't have been it. I wasn't stalking David. I never went to see his mom without him, when he wasn't there. Besides, they wanted me there, right? His mom invited me to keep him company. We had talked about everything while I was there. Why would he have talked with me if I had been stalking him? Unless...

That was it, wasn't it. He hadn't really been there. That was always the twist at the end of those books. The main character thinks they're doing one thing and everyone else keeps talking like she was doing something completely different. It turns out that she was crazy the whole time. I had been daydreaming so much lately, perhaps I dreamed the whole thing. Perhaps I had been walking into that poor woman's hospital room and spent the entire time talking to an empty chair as she stared at me in confusion. Maybe I really was crazy. Do crazy people know they're crazy?

Seeing as how I spent the rest of class in a thought spiral around the idea, I had pretty much convinced myself that I needed a straitjacket by the time the final bell rang. Stopping by my locker just long enough to stow all my books away, I left school with a new purpose in mind. I barely glanced towards the bus long enough to spot Jen, Ashley, and Janice. They glanced after me as they laughed to themselves and pointed at me.

The hospital was a little over a mile away from the school. But, after spending the summer in my lifeguard classes, I was in perfect shape and barely noticed the distance. I spent most of the time wondering if they would still let me be a lifeguard if I was crazy. I knew there were medications for some craziness, but would they work for me? For my kind of crazy? It never occurred to me that I might not be. That there might not be anything wrong with me at all.

The psych ward was on the fifth floor of the hospital. I wasn't sure what the protocol was for checking yourself into a mental hospital. But I figured someone there would be able to tell me. Maybe it was something easy, something they could take care of today. Maybe Mom wouldn't even need to find out. Then again, maybe she already had. Maybe that was what was behind the look from that morning. But that would mean that Mom was keeping secrets from me too.

I was still stuck in that thought spiral as I got on the elevator, barely noticing the man in the green scrubs get on with me. When the elevator opened, I got off, thinking I was already on five. I stood there, confused for a moment as I looked around the familiar sight of the oncology floor. The elevator dinged and closed behind me as I gradually came back to reality.

"You can't go down there," came a voice from behind the nurses' station.

I twirled around in startlement before spotting the woman back there. "Oh, hey, Rebecca," I said, recognizing her instantly as she was one of Mrs. Azalea's favorite nurses. She smiled at me as I walked towards her. I figured that I could delay checking myself in for a few minutes as I caught up on Mrs. Azalea's status.

"You can't go down there," she repeated. She must have thought I had come to see Mrs. Azalea rather than just stopping to chat with her.

"Wait, what? Why? Did they ban me from the floor or something?" I asked.

"No," she said.

"Did they put out a restraining order?"

"Why would they do that? No, they moved her."

"Oh," I said, surprised. "Why?"

"Oh, honey, I thought you heard. She took a turn for the worse yesterday. They're moving her into hospice care."

"Oh, god, no," I said, leaning on the desk to avoid falling over.

"Yea, I know. She's just such a nice lady. I'll get you the information for where she is. She'd like to see you."

"Oh, I don't think I should visit her," I said. "David kind of kicked me out last time I was here."

"So that's why you haven't been around?" she asked. "I was wondering. Why would he do that?"

"That's kind of why I'm here. Now, this might come off as a strange question but, when I was here, visiting Mrs. Azalea, had I ever been here when David wasn't?"

"You don't remember?" she asked, looking at me funny. "You're a bit young to be doing drugs."

"Well, if you say the wrong answer, they might just start prescribing them for me."

She stood there for a moment, looking down at me with a look that suggested that I was as crazy as I thought I was. "No," she said. "I don't recall you ever being in there without David. Unless he stepped into the bathroom or something. You two always seemed like you were joined at the hip."

"Then why..." I started to ask, totally at a loss for the rumors that had been spread. "Secrets," I said the word like the curse it is.

"What's that?" she asked.

"Nothing. I'm just... I don't know what's going on."

"Welcome to the world," she said, giving me half a smile. "No one knows what's going on. We all just fake it."

"Did David... Did he ever explain why I stopped coming? Why he asked me to stop coming?"

"No, can't say anything came up. But it's not like he talked all that much even when his mom was doing better. Some kids just take it harder than others."

"I just don't get him."

"What's to get? He's a boy. There's no understanding boys no matter what age you are. And they think we're the big mystery." She snorted at the idea.

"He's been going around telling everyone I've been stalking him all summer. Now no one will talk to me at school."

"Well, you can always come talk to me if you want. Just not right now, I gotta make my rounds." She shooed me away as she got up from her station, heading off down the hall.

I stood there, my thoughts running a million miles an hour. They tumbled all over the place with nowhere to go. I was completely at a loss for why David would have wanted me to stop coming. Why he had gone to such lengths to distance himself from me, taking the rest of the class with him. And the bigger question that started nagging me, even then, was why my life suddenly sucked so much. And yet, I had no idea how much worse it would get before I'd decide to abandon reality all together.

All thoughts of heading up to the psych ward forgotten, I turned around, heading for home.

Chapter Thirteen
Stalking 101

Now

I blinked a few times when I realized I had been staring at David for the past hour as I stalked behind the group of troopers. Shaking my head, I snickered a bit at the thought of me having 'stalked' him five years ago, especially given my current actions back on Desparia.

#

The Jakala Empire spans the majority of the land formerly named Fandor. Most of the locals still call it Fandor, rather than the Jakala Empire. This was largely due to their accents making the name Jakala difficult to pronounce. As empires go, it was fairly young. It had sprung up about sixteen years ago with the formation of The Citadel, the large fortress that overlooked The Capital. The empire's borders have been expanding rather steadily over that time and were threatening to spill over into Norenia, the land to the north. While there are still parts of Fandor not under the control of the empire, they were mostly areas of low population and even lower resources.

One of the reasons why the empire has spread so quickly was the level of fortification they had at home. The Capital stands at the foot of a large mountain. The emperor's fortress was on top of it. All down the mountain's face were ten layers of walls too tall for anyone to scale and too thick for anyone to break. This fortress, known only as The Citadel, can be seen for miles away. I could even make it out on the road out of Vernala. There was only one way to approach the seat of power and the emperor himself, and that was through the large door in the first wall, located at the heart of The Capital. No one gets through that without a proper invitation.

So, when I realized that the caravan was heading there, my heart fell. My only chance at getting to the prisoners would be if the caravan stopped for the night before reaching The Capital. We were far enough from there that it was a possibility, but we were close enough that running the group through the night wouldn't be out of the question. It all depended on what their orders were and how much the emperor wanted the prisoners from the thieves' guild.

It didn't help that I couldn't afford to keep the group in sight. I didn't know what prompted the raid; if it was something about my task from the night prior or if the whole thing was just a coincidence. They might think that they already had the thief in question. Or they may still be looking for me. With how up close and personal I had gotten with Sardana that morning, I doubted they would think I was captured for long. Either way, being seen as a lone figure on the road heading for The Capital not too far behind an official convoy would just be asking for trouble. As the sun set, I started to worry that I might accidentally pass them in the night and miss my chances to get the stupid bracelet off.

It turned out, I didn't have much to worry about on that front. Just before dusk, the familiar trumpet call sounded off in the distance, announcing the presence of the trooper army. When heading up the next hill in the road, I started to see some smoke off in the distance. At the top, a large camp came into view, in a field not too far off. The emperor's flag already hung in strategic positions around the camp, daring anyone stupid enough to go against the emperor to attack the camp. There weren't many such brave fools in the land; and yet, I needed to do just that.

I kept to the edge of the woods as much as possible as I approached the camp. There was a nice vantage point that overlooked the field. From there, I could easily tell that the caravan was a lot larger than I had been expecting. The group that headed out from Vernala must have been joined by another somewhere along the way. There were closer to twenty prison carriages, all just as full as the four that held the thieves from the guild. The troopers seemed to also have had an influx in numbers. It was a bit hard to count them all from where I was, but it looked like there were at least a couple hundred down there.

It was still early. The sun was just starting to set in the west. My guess would be that I had at least eight hours before the bracelet killed me, and the positions of the sands on it seem to confirm that. "Next time I get slapped with a timer bracelet that's going to kill me, I really need to ask them to switch it to digital," I whispered to myself. "Or at the very least analog. This hourglass thingy is really killing me." I cringed at my unintentional pun.

I settled into my chosen post and started studying the camp, relying on the surrounding trees and the blinding light of the sun at my back for cover. There weren't too many guards posted, about four on each side. In the light of day that was enough, especially given how close they were to The Citadel. Its foreboding walls dominated the horizon, declaring for all to see that the area fell under the ever-watchful eye of the emperor. If they didn't increase the guards during the night, I might have a chance at getting in there. The issue would be in getting out with all their prisoners.

A shout off to the side of the camp drew my attention to a group of three troopers heading my way. Each of them carried a bundle in their arms. When one bent down to pick something up, I realized they were collecting firewood. My position suddenly seemed less of a good idea. I abandoned it, heading deeper into the forest to wait out the wood collectors. The possibility of greater danger within the woods was easily forgotten in lieu of the actual dangers outside it. The camp wasn't going anywhere, and I needed to gather a few supplies of my own.

I hadn't eaten all day and had been up for almost 72 hours straight. Imagination or not, it was starting to get to me. My stomach had been growling all day as I followed behind the trooper army. It was almost like this world had become more real somehow. Then again, maybe it's just my imagination. Pun intended.

After setting a few traps, hoping to catch a rabbit or two, I managed to find a few nuts and berries. It wasn't much, but I wouldn't need to light a fire and they'd get me through the night. "Besides," I thought with a wicked grin, "if I'm heading into the camp tonight, I could probably find some leftovers I could pilfer." When finished with my meager dinner, I headed back towards my previous position, hoping enough time had passed that the wood collectors had returned to camp.

I was halfway there when I heard a snapping twig off to my left. Immediately, I dropped down into a crouch, looking around for the source of the sound. After a few more seconds, another twig snapped, followed by a female voice whispering "blast it all to the inferno." The voice sounded familiar, but it was too low for me to place. Not wanting to risk being spotted so close to the camp, I let whoever it was pass by me, even counting off five minutes in my head before continuing on.

By the time I had gotten back to my previous post, night had fallen in full. My heart fell when I noticed that the troopers had, in fact, not only doubled but almost tripled their guard, placing ten guards across each side of their camp. There were several torches lining the way, making it almost impossible to sneak by them. To make matters worse, it looked like they were having quite the party. Drinking songs were clear as they flowed up to me. Several kegs had been lined up around a large bonfire in the center of the camp. Women's cries of passion, adulation, and, in some cases, fear and hatred came up from all over. It looked like the troopers were set on enjoying one last hurrah before once again being subject to the stricter rules of the civilized world. Normally, I'd be elated that a group that I was trying to sneak through were so intent on dulling their senses and giving themselves cause for deep sleeps. However, I was working with a time limit, and I couldn't afford to wait until almost dawn to sneak in. Most of such parties lasted through the night.

It didn't seem like I was alone in this opinion. After hearing another whispered curse off to my left, I could feel the tingling of someone casting a spell. At first, I thought someone had spotted me. That I was the target of the spell. I darted back under cover a bit. When the spell continued to build, I suddenly realized I might actually have an ally in all of this... and that they were about to get themselves caught and killed.

Following the building hum back to its source, I spotted the person in question. Her blond hair gleamed in the moonlight. Slipping up behind her quietly, I put my hand over her mouth to block any screams and pulled her backwards to disturb her concentration. After a few more seconds of the spell building, it eventually shattered as muffled screams came from the mage.

"I'm not a trooper," I whispered into her ear. "I'm trying to get into the camp, same as you. You were about to blow both of our positions. Understand?" I waited patiently for her to nod her head. When no acknowledgement came, I took out my dagger, placing it across her throat, to make myself even more clear. "Understand?" I asked again, finally getting a nod. "Good. I'm going to let you go. Don't do anything stupid like screaming or running off. Got it?" Another nod prompted me to let her go. While I removed my dagger, I kept it out in case I got any more trouble from her.

After I took a couple steps back, she turned around. The moonlight glinted off a few tears that were flowing down her face. Even in the low light of the night, I could tell that it was the blond from the other day, one of the three women who followed me out of the pub. This took me a bit by surprise.

"What the hell are you doing here?" I asked, darting my eyes around looking for the others.

"The troopers got my friends," she said in a hush whisper. It was so quiet that I almost missed it, despite how close we were.

"And, what? You were going to nuke the whole camp or something?"

"Nuke?" she asked.

"Destroy," I explained.

"No, of course not." I just stared at her, waiting for her to explain herself. "Well... not the whole camp anyway. I was going to send a wall of fire at those guards right there," she said, pointing at the closest line of guards.

I looked down there at the unsuspecting guards that I kept from getting broiled. There's usually a lot to say about the direct approach, but in this case, it just wouldn't do. The guards were too spread out to take them all out with a single spell. She might be able to take out one or two of them, but then the entire camp would be up in arms and heading towards us.

"Okay, that might work, if you sent it at the guards on the other side," I pointed out further, at the other side of camp. "The guards might go to where the spell hit to see what's going on. But with the trooper armor protecting them from magic, you'll be hard pressed to do much damage against them one by one. Unless you're going to take out the entire camp all by yourself."

"Well..." she said.

She looked towards the camp in the distance, which stretched across a large space. If I had to guess, it was maybe a quarter of a square mile, all told. And with the prison carts right in the thick of it, her friends were just as likely to be burned with the rest of them.

"No, you're right," she said. "I don't have enough control to not hurt the prisoners in the process."

"Right. Which means we need to slip in and try to rescue them without them knowing we're in there. We'd want them distracted from our approach, not coming to stare at us as we're running in. Besides, the whole camp is still awake. They'll just go on alert and we'd lose the element of surprise."

"What's this 'we' you keep talking about?" she asked. "I didn't invite you on this rescue mission."

"Of course not, I'm just taking it over as it was about to interfere with my own." She stared at me, a startled look on her face. "What?" I asked.

"Who in the world are you trying to rescue and what's in it for you?" she asked.

With a sigh, I sat down a few paces off from where she was. I wasn't quite back at my old vantage point but in one about as good. I looked down at the camp, trying to figure out the best way in, as I explained to her my situation, even going so far as showing her the sphere. She rolled the sphere around in her hands for a while, almost idly, as she thought over my explanation.

"So, I was right about you, then? You wouldn't have helped us unless there was something in it for you?"

"I didn't say that. It's not like you guys explained what it was that you were trying to do. If I think it's a cause worth fighting for, maybe I would."

"Well...," she said. She placed a finger to her lips, which kept moving back and forth, like she was trying to do math in her head. "I'm not quite ready to trust you with that information. Let's just see how things work out with this rescue mission first. Speaking of which, what's the plan?"

"Yes, I've been thinking about that," I said, a malicious grin on my face.

Chapter Fourteen
Things Coming to a Head

Five Years Earlier

Things came to a head at the end of that week. After the
first four days of middle school, no one was talking to me.
Even the seventh or eighth graders were in on it, though it
had been rare for them to talk to sixth graders anyway. I
mean, sure, the teachers talked to me, but most of them were
as ignorant of what was going on as I had once been.
Sometimes, I still wished that I were. Ashley, Jen, and Janice
were still giving me darted looks as they obviously talked
about me, though they were doing less to hide that fact than
they had on Monday. David and his friends started avoiding
me overtly, as if I were some plague or something. And I had
quickly lost track of how much time I had spent, during the
day and even at home, daydreaming the same adventures over
and over again.

By the time lunch on Friday came around, I was just so
tired of the whole thing that I decided to do something about
it. I had decided to confront Ashley and demand that she be
my friend again. Looking back on that idea, it was probably
one of the dumbest things I ever came up with. But it made
perfect sense when I was eleven.

My usual PB&J brown bag lunch was clutched in my fist
as I stood by the door to the lunchroom, waiting for the three
of them to show up. David and his friends, whom I still

hadn't found out the names of, walked past me. They didn't seem to see that I was there until they were already past the first set of tables. When David noticed me, he gave a little jump, twisting around in the air as if he were afraid to turn his back towards me. His friends seemed to think that hilarious, laughing as they imitated him. He chuckled right along with them. However, before heading off to their usual table near the other cool kids, he gave me a sidelong look that was almost apologetic.

My stomach growled as the bell rang to signal the start of the period, with no sign of the three of them. I was about to wander off, giving up on my plan, when they walked past me. They were laughing as they entered the cafeteria a minute late. Janice gave one of the attendants a glare as he got up to tell them off for being late, as if that really mattered for lunch. The teacher decided it wasn't worth it, so he turned around and headed back to his own lunch.

"Ashley, can I talk to you?" I asked, as I eyed the retreating teacher.

"Aren't you busy enough stalking your 'boyfriend'?" Janice asked. She stepped between Ashley and me, pushing me away from my former friend just with her bulk. "Why don't you leave the rest of us sane people alone."

"I wasn't talking to you," I said. I didn't look up at her as she towered over me, standing at least six inches taller than I was. "I was talking to Ashley."

"Well, she doesn't want to talk to you. No one wants to talk to you. Wasn't that obvious all week?"

"The only thing that's obvious to me is that there are people spreading lies about me and all my friends decided to abandon me over them. I just wanted to set the record straight, Ashley. If you don't want to talk to me after that, then fine. I'll make do on my own." I tried to hide the fact that I wasn't sure I could do that. That the seclusion was starting to get to me. But the pre-tears that found their way to the corner of my eyes betrayed my feelings. Still, Ashley turned away from me, hiding her face as she did so. I wasn't sure if she was ashamed of abandoning me or ashamed of the fact that we were ever friends.

"I guess that's your answer," Janice said. She took a step to the side, blocking my view of Ashley. Jen stood on her other flank, staring between Ashley, Janice, and I, almost as if she weren't sure whose side she was supposed to be on. This surprised me a bit, as she had always been more Ashley's friend than mine.

I was about to speak out to her, changing my tactics to capitalize on her display of weakness. But then Janice grabbed my bag, ripping it out of my hands. The sandwich tumbled to the floor as the bag ripped open, part of the paper still held in my fist. I stared down at it in surprise as Janice purposely stomped on it. The plastic bag that contained the sandwich popped open under her weight, the jelly spreading out across the floor and squirting my white sneakers.

"Not just a stalker but clumsy too," Janice said, laughing in my face.

That was the last straw, the sight of my ruined sandwich with her laugh in my ears and her breath on my face. I just snapped. I grabbed up a cupcake off the table that was a couple feet to my right, smashing it into Janice's nose, and smearing it around. Then, as if I weren't in trouble enough, I wiped my hand off on her t-shirt. She stood there, the cake and frosting covering her, as the unobscured portion of her face gradually turned beat red. The frosting was green, which made me think of Christmas. The obligatory call of "food fight" from the guy that I grabbed the cupcake from blocked out my call of "ho ho ho".

A slice of pizza flew right past my head, sailing towards a teacher who was staring out at the mass of kids in utter horror. Before the next barrage could hit him, he jumped up from his seat and ran for the door, no doubt going for backup as the food fight started in full swing.

As usual, with food flying around me, I ducked and covered. I used my backpack as a shield as I dove under the same table that I had taken the cupcake off of. It was almost peaceful under the table as I waited for the food fight to play itself out, for the kids to run out of food, or for the teachers to assimilate and attack to stop the fight. Whichever came first. Ashley and Jen had dived under the table along with me and the three of us were huddled together like during all the food fights that had happened in elementary school. However, neither of them wanted to talk and they couldn't hear me over the screams of glee, pain, and disgust coming from the world above. I was about to pull out my notebook, to write notes to each other like we used to do. But then my legs got pulled out from under me and I was dragged back out into the light, into the storm raging above.

The fluorescent lights momentarily blinded me before Janice's form became silhouetted against them. As her furious face approached me, her fists flew down at my prone body, hitting me in the stomach with enough force to break something. I doubled up on the first punch, trying to protect my injured core. Her third punch hit me in the shoulder before she started kicking me in the back. I lay there, on the cold, food-covered tile floor, trying to stop the beating but not knowing how.

"Enough of this," came a shout from above me. It sounded like the voice of god from on high. The noise quieted instantly, a few last slick thuds resounding off the floor as the food that was already in the air hit its targets. More importantly, the kicks and punches had stopped, though it took a little while for my body to stop anticipating them and for my breathing to normalize. "Who's responsible for this," came the booming voice again.

"That girl instigated it, Principal Snide," came the more familiar voice of the teacher that had run for help. I managed the slightest peek out from the shelter of my arms to see the man pointing down at me.

Me? I thought to myself. What did I do?

"You two," the principal called out again. "Help her up and to my office. The rest of you start cleaning this mess up. We don't hire our cleaning staff to tend to your every whim and clean every mess you decide to make. The mops can be found over there."

Familiar hands gripped me on either side. They hauled me to my feet, which didn't want to move. All I could feel was pain and my body just wanted to crawl under a rock. Jen, on my left, gave me a reassuring smile as she helped me out of the room. Ashley, on the other hand, both literally and figuratively, seemed almost offended by my plight.

As my senses started to return to me, they sat me down in an unfamiliar office. The frowning face of the man that I had only met four days prior, and hadn't seen since, was on the other side of a large desk from me. The desk dominated much of the space that made up his office. It was the first time that I had been to the principal's office, in any school. It wouldn't be the last. My former friends scurried from the room before the man's wrath could be turned to them as well.

"What do you have to say for yourself?" he asked. His voice was barely quieter than it was in the lunchroom.

"Janice started it," I said, childishly.

"I don't care. Mr. Bernstein said you instigated the food fight."

"Nuh-uh," I whined. "Janice smashed my sandwich."

"So, you started throwing food? How did that help anything?"

"I... it..." I stuttered, trying to combat the full set of waterworks that were well on their way.

"Exactly. I'm suspending you for the rest of the day and you'll have one week's worth of detention starting Monday. Sit here and think about what you did while I have the secretary call your parents to come pick you up."

"But..." I started to say, as the man left the room, closing the door behind him.

I just sat there, at a complete loss for what happened. Up until I had walked into that cafeteria, I hadn't thought my life could get any worse. And, yet, in less time than it would have taken me to eat lunch, my whole perspective of worse changed. Completely confused and worried what my parents would say when they heard what happened, I sat there in the office while the bell rang, signaling the end of lunch.

The end of my hope that I'd be able to get my friends back.

Chapter Fifteen
The Daring Rescue

Now

Whenever I think back on that day, it always amazed me that I was so dependent on other people before I found Desparia. The simple fact that I wanted people to sit with at lunch before escaped me as I, as usual, strolled into the lunchroom almost five years after that food fight. I still brought in a PB&J bagged lunch, but never bother to look around for anyone. I was no longer worried if I sat alone or on the edge of a crowded table.

Truth be told, I spend much of my time alone, not just on Earth but on Desparia as well. It just suited me better that way. No one to have to deal with, no one to keep secrets from or who would keep secrets from me.

I barely even look where I'm going as I dip back into my private little world.

#

I left the blond, Heather, back at the edge of the trees. I didn't say it to her, but I figured bringing her with me would make it a lot harder to do what I needed in order to get through the defenses. It was nice having her for the prep part of the plan, but she'd just get in the way otherwise.

I kept to the shadows as best as I could, coming down the hill into the little valley that the camp was in. Unfortunately, that would only get me so far. The torches that were set up around the camp were blocking my access just as much as the guards themselves were. Fortunately for me, I had a mage at my back. And the way that she spoke about firewalls before, I figured that she had a thing for fire.

As I approached the ring of light that stretched out from the torches, I slipped down onto the ground. The grass grew high in the field. At least it did where the troopers hadn't stomped it down. It was enough to keep me hidden from the watchful eyes of the guards on duty. But it also blocked Heather's view of my progress. I had to get into position and just wait. Wait for the appointed time. Wait for some sign that her work had been done.

"Damn it," one of the guards said. "Shoddy workmanship. Hey, Grell. Go get some more torches. These ones are about to die off."

"Get them yourself," Grell called out, from somewhere else on the line of guards.

I smiled as I slipped forward. Hidden there in the tall grass, I couldn't tell that the torch right by me was about to go out. But as I eased out into the flattened area of grass that made up the camp, I looked up to see the torch stand above me. Sure enough, the torch was just flickering out, dropping the area into darkness. The guard that had been posted right in front of me had slipped off, heading for the supply tents in the distance. Using the brief window, the gap in the line of guards, I slipped out from the grass and into the camp.

Once inside the perimeter, I had more freedom than I had outside of it. While under normal circumstances, if I were spotted in a place that I wasn't supposed to be, an alarm would be sounded, and I'd be arrested. However, in a Jakala Trooper camp, it wasn't always easy to know who wasn't supposed to be there. And once I pulled off my tunic and cloak and pulled my rarely used belt around my undershirt, I looked just like all the other party favors that were hanging around. Not as attractive, but at least passable.

The party was still in full swing, showing no signs of fading. If anything, the party had become more raucous as troopers came off their daytime duties. Most of the party was focused on the center of the camp. As with most parties, on both worlds, this was generally where the booze was. I could see five barrels currently in use, with twenty more sitting there waiting to be tapped. The barrels were on a makeshift bench made out of some planks propped up on a few worn-out swords.

Unlike most armies, the Jakala Trooper Corps wasn't in it for king and country. Or emperor and empire as the case may be. The majority of them were little more than mercenaries, working for the emperor largely for the money that he paid. Few of them cared that they were traveling around the countryside, slaughtering mostly innocent people simply because they were different. I never met a single trooper that had anything resembling a conscience. They were basically the high school bullies of my dream world. And, when high school bullies partied, they partied like there was no tomorrow.

So, as usual, the line to get another drink was pretty long. It extended back from the active kegs and wrapped around the tents that had been set up for those of higher rank. And those that were paying to visit some of the occupants back there. Many of the troopers were heading for the back of the line right after getting their refills, knowing it would take them less time to make it back through the line than for them to finish their drinks.

I didn't mind the long line, as I wasn't there to partake. I quickly skirted the edge of this area, doing my best to be as invisible as I always was. My disguise seemed to do the trick. The few troopers that looked my way barely batted an eye at my presence. I looked like all the other camp followers, there to make money off of the mercenaries however I could manage. Fortunately for me, my looks and youth would keep most of the troopers away from me. I just had to make sure that my stealth would help keep me away from the rest of them.

All of the carriages were held at the center of camp, in a cluster that could easily be guarded by a handful of guards. When I got there, there were only two in position. Personally, had I been in charge of guarding the prisoners, I would have had about ten guards in that area, even with the outer ring of guards. But I'm a bit paranoid like that. Considering what I was about to do, though, ten wouldn't have been enough anyway.

There were so many carriages there that it took me awhile to find the right group of them. It didn't help that the four that I was looking for were mixed so thoroughly throughout the area. To make matters worse, the prisoners were all still wearing their hoods and had their hands tied behind their backs, making it impossible for me to recognize the thieves from the rest of the prisoners. What it came down to was actually the model of the carriage.

I've never exactly been a car girl. To me a car is a car and the only way I could tell one car apart from another was the brand symbol. In most cases, carriages are even worse. They usually took on a standard form that simply focused on not falling apart over rough terrain. And yet, the four prison carriages that the thieves had been put in were more enclosed, having smaller sections of bars versus the hardwood that made up the rest of it. The other carriages were all little more than bars between two large plates of wood, the stereotypical prison carts they usually use in cartoons. I couldn't even begin to guess where Heather's friends were in all those other carts. That was the other challenge in all of this.

However, before I could come close enough to the carts to check any of the prisoners, I had to be rid of the two guards standing near them. As I made my inspection of the carts, I kept to the ring of tents that ran around the central area. The two sections of the center of the camp, the prison carts and the booze, were separated by nothing more than a few feet of empty space. It made my search of the carts almost impossible, but it also made the guards' focus diverted. As I made my circuits around them, I could see them eyeing the party. Close enough to see and hear, but not close enough to partake.

As the night went on, the two guards seemed to slacken in their stance. It made me wonder if these two would be relieved at some point, giving them the chance to join in the party. I just had to hope that, if they were relieved before I could make my play, their replacements would be drunk from the party. The problem came from how I was going to get rid of them, though. Imaginary or not, I never liked the idea of killing someone. However, as I spotted the last of the carts from the thieves' guild, I remembered that they didn't have a similar compulsion.

Better than that, this last cart was near the edge of the ring, furthest from the booze table.

With the guards distracted by the promise of booze yet to be drunk, I slipped out towards this nearest cart. I kept my eyes trained on the guards, waiting for some sign that they might turn towards their charges. That they might turn to spot me there in the middle of them. No matter how much I could look like one of the camp followers, I had no right being near the prisoners. If spotted, I was likely to join them.

My lockpicks were already in my hand as I made my way to the door on the cart. I made short work of the lock, pulling the door open. The door creaked in place and I held my breath as I stared daggers over at the guards, expecting them to notice the sound even over the louder sounds coming from the party. Distracted as I was, I didn't notice it when the thieves started pouring out of the cart. They barreled into me, knocking me to the ground as they made their way out into the camp.

Still bound and hooded, the thieves rushed the two guards, knocking them down with barely a sound. Their weapons were quickly scooped up and used to cut the ropes binding them. I just lay there on the ground for a moment as I watched the group slip through the carts. One by one, they freed their fellow thieves before slipping out into the night.

At first, I was shocked. Horrified. The thieves had left me there in the mud, after I had gone through all that trouble to rescue them. None of them had looked to me, barely even noticed I was there let alone recognizing me. They just left me there for dead. And as the hourglass on my bracelet slowly ticked away the last few hours of my life, I figured that they might as well have killed me themselves.

Then, the screaming started.

Two of the camp followers came rushing back out into the center of camp. They were covered in blood, and nothing else. I figured that they had come from the pay tents, probably in the middle of the business that the troopers paid them for. Instead of rushing to their aid, though, the drunk troopers just toasted their arrival. As if seeing blood covered prostitutes was a normal occurrence there. However, the horde that followed them into the clearing was enough to capture their attention.

The entire band of thieves, all fifty or so of them, were suddenly armed and ready for a fight. The troopers, by comparison, weren't. Several lost arms in those first few seconds, their drinks pouring onto the floor at their feet. Those most drunk would stand there for a moment, looking between the stump where their arm had been and the drink on the floor, as if unsure which they would miss more.

I averted my eyes from the gore and blood of the battle as the screams rent the air. Instead, I turned my attention back to the matter at hand. With the guards and troopers properly handled by the thieves, I made my way around the rest of the carts, freeing what prisoners I could. Most of the prisoners stayed in the carts, even after I had freed them.

And, with the sights of the war in the nearby camp, I couldn't say that I blamed them. Those that didn't stay quickly slipped out into the night, running towards the freedom that it offered.

It took awhile for me to find the twins. They had managed to stay together through the whole thing, finding a semi comfortable corner of one of the last few carts to be opened. After they had removed their hoods and saw that their savior was none other than little old me, they stared up at me in complete shock.

"Hi, to you two, too," I said, smiling a bit at the word play.

"Wha... how... where the blazes did you come from?" asked one of them. I had no clue which one it was.

"Oh, relax," I said. "I didn't exactly come for you guys anyway." Reluctantly, I looked over at the thieves, many of whom were covered in blood and... more solid matter. When I looked back at the twins, if anything, their looks were even more incredulous. "It's a long story," I said with a shrug.

Once all the prisoners were released, I stood off to the side with those few prisoners that hadn't run off on their own. A few stragglers could still be seen heading out into the distance. I slowly tapped my feet, trying to be patient for the thieves to finish their carnage. Patience had never been my strong suit.

"What are we waiting for?" one of the twins asked. She followed my line of sight to the mayhem around us.

"Why are we waiting for her?" the other one asked.

"You're not," I said. "Heather should be coming down from the ridge soon."

"Heather? She's here? She's safe?" the two of them asked in unison.

I nodded my head off towards a lone figure, heading towards us in the dark. Even as dark as the area around the camp had become, she seemed to almost glow in the night. No one was left at the edge of the camp to stop her entrance.

She quickly slipped through the tents, making her way towards her friends. The twins gathered Heather up into a huge group hug that seemed like it should have been a more private moment than it was. Averting my eyes from the overt display of friendship, I turned my attention back to the thieves. The mayhem around us seemed to fade as the ferocity of the guild members burned itself out.

"Are you coming with us?" Heather asked, after the three broke their hug. "We still need someone like you, and it's not like we can trust one of their kind." She gestured towards the guild.

"I still have some business with them. When it's resolved, well, my future might not be my own." Without saying anything further, I headed towards the guild members, many of whom had started looting what remained of... well... the remains.

No one seemed to notice my arrival, or my existence in any way. I looked at my bracelet. The few grains left in the top half of the hourglass showed that my death was a lot more imminent than I liked. The sky had started lightening off in the east, seeming to emphasize that my end was nigh. Or it would be if I couldn't find someone to remedy that.

"Hello!" I screamed, trying to draw the attention of the group.

"Hello," someone said. The man didn't even look up from his looting of the corpse that he was standing over.

"Where's Zandar?" I asked, but no one responded. I asked again. "Where's Zandar?" I practically screamed it, but again, no one answered.

I went over to the pile of kegs, which had gone barely noticed in the battle over there. Most of them had been tapped, and drained, by the troopers. I grabbed one of the ones to the side, figuring they would be full of the booze. It was heavy, almost impossible for me to lift. Instead, I set it on its side and rolled it into the fire at the center of the area. The keg just sat there for a moment, the flames licking at its side.

Despite what I wanted to happen, the keg didn't seem to be cooperative.

Heather came up to stand next to me. I could feel her power flowing off of her as she eyed the keg in the fire. With a flick of her wrist, the keg suddenly exploded. Fire soared up into the air in a huge pillar, swirling around in a large conflagration. Those tents that were too close to its side quickly caught alight, though the camp had already been thoroughly destroyed by the thieves.

"Oops," Heather muttered, as she stared at her destructive work. I just smiled over at her, a silent thanks for her efforts, despite how much bigger it had been than it should have.

The explosion drew the attention of everyone around, thief, spectator, and all. In the silence that followed, I yelled my question once more.

"Where's Zandar? Where's Grandor? Where's the key?" I asked, loud as I could.

"You have a lot of nerve asking that," a woman said.

Her face was so covered with blood that it took me a bit to recognize her as the woman archer from the day before. The one that Grandor had been leaning on. In her ire, she was nowhere near as steady as she was at the guild.

"After what you've done, you deserve to die to that thing," she said, gesturing towards my wrist.

"Where are they? Where's Grandor?" I snapped.

"Grandor is dead," she said, a single tear finding its way down her cheek. "They killed him when they attacked the compound, even using his body to trap the rest of us as we came home. And that stupid key is long lost. All because you led the troopers right to us. Right to our home."

"What? How the hell did I do that? By the time I got back to your silly little hideout, the troopers were already there, already ransacking the place."

"Well, who else would it have been?"

"How about your precious pet guard captain? I don't see him captured with the rest of you." I spat at her. This seemed to shut her up, her bluster spent. "Now, where's Zandar?"

Another one of the thieves stepped forward. He was completely covered in blood from head to toe. The gaunt look on his face was one of pity. "You mean you don't know?" he asked. As he came closer, he had his hands in the air as if to comfort me. "He... He's dead. He died in the attack on the guild hall."

Chapter Sixteen
Haven't Hit Bottom Yet

Five Years Ago

After the bell rang to start fifth period, the principal came back into his office and escorted me from the building. He walked me all the way to the curb where the buses were usually waiting after school. Of course, with three more hours left of the school day, the street was empty. The park that ran the length of the street opposite the three schools was in plain view, offering peace and tranquility that was greatly lacking in my life at the moment.

"You are not to set foot on school property until Monday morning," the principal said. "Understand?"

"Yes, sir," I mumbled, completely mollified.

"Now wait here for your father," he said.

I perked up at the mention of my father. I had figured that Mom would have been the one to pick me up as the hospital was so close. It must have been easier for Dad to get away from work, though. That would have worked out well for me. Dad would be more understanding. More ready to hear my side of things. He'd explain it to Mom, make it so that she wasn't mad at me. Things were starting to look up.

Seeing the hopeful expression on my face, the principal sneered down at me before heading back to the school. I watched him walk away, wondering briefly why he hadn't had someone wait with me for a parent to show up. He stopped at the main door, turned around to look at me, and pointed towards the park before heading in. The door slammed resoundingly behind him. Taking his cue, I crossed the street, heading into the park where I could daydream the day away and wait for Dad to come.

Before nodding off to my random daydreams, I did a quick examination of my injuries. My shirt, another one of my dad's old t-shirts, had been torn during the fight, though it was so baggy on me it wasn't noticeable. Bruises were already starting to form around my stomach and chest. No doubt my face didn't look that pretty, either, but I didn't have a mirror on me to look. Perhaps with the added marks, my story would find more sympathy from my parents. It would certainly prove that Janice wasn't without fault in all of this. Trying not to aggravate my injuries, I headed over to the nearest tree. I sat against it as I drifted off to my latest mishmash of old stories and characters.

I was lost in my daydreams for a while, only coming out of them when the sounds of kids celebrating the start of the weekend came to me from the high school. Automatically, I sat bolt upright, my head hitting against the bark of the tree, as I stared over in surprise. The high school was the first to be let out, but that still would have been hours after I had been banished from school grounds. I looked to the cookie watch on my wrist, surprised that it was a quarter to three. With no sign of Dad anywhere.

Briefly, I wondered if he had just missed me. That he wouldn't have thought to look for me in the park before driving past. But he wouldn't have left. He wouldn't have gone home or back to work without knowing where I was. There was no sign of his car along the street. I walked along the entire stretch of the park, trying to peak over at each of the parking lots. But there was still no sign of him. With a final glance over at the elementary school, wondering if he had simply forgotten that I no longer went there, I came to the realization that Dad had simply not come.

"But why?" I asked myself aloud. "Why would he just disappear like that? He wouldn't have abandoned me, too, would he? He's not like my friends. He's nothing like them." I tried to reassure myself that there was some explanation for why he hadn't come. But, for an eleven year old, that wasn't easy.

I glanced over at the buses as the high school students started piling into them. I probably could have gotten a ride from one of them, but I didn't know which would bring me home. Or if there were any high school kids that lived close enough to my house for any of them to head my way. Principal Snide always watched over the middle school kids getting on their buses, and there was no way I'd be able to slip onto one of them when they left half an hour later. For a few minutes, I stood there, looking between the buses and the road that I knew would take me home. It was only a few miles away, not overly hard for me to manage given how in shape I was from my summer lifeguarding classes.

Instead, I turned the other way, heading for the hospital. It was much closer, and I figured that I'd be able to catch a ride with Mom when she headed home after her shift. It would mean dealing with her sooner, and without the buffer that Dad would have provided. But it was better to get it over with rather than prolong the inevitable. I considered leaving word for Dad, in case he ever showed up. But I didn't know who to talk to about it. Something deep within me was telling me that he would have been there already if he was coming.

I tried not to worry as I walked the short way to the hospital. I tried not to keep looking behind me, expecting to see his car just over the hill. He would have come to the school from the opposite direction from the one I was walking, from back towards home. So, if he really was just late, he wouldn't see me. He wouldn't know that I left. I kept telling myself that he had gotten hung up at work. That he couldn't get away, just like Mom couldn't have. Maybe they stuck him with a last minute trip to some other place that got hit by a storm or an earthquake or an asteroid and he wouldn't be home for days.

He wouldn't have just abandoned me without a reason.

But I was eleven, and I didn't believe myself. All I could think was "Dad was supposed to be there for me and he wasn't." No matter how many times I reassured myself that something must have happened, all I could think was "Dad abandoned me like everyone else did." And the tears just wouldn't stop coming.

As the doors of the hospital slid open, I was hit by a wave of sound. Voices overlapped in a cacophony of noise. I had come in through the main entrance, not wanting to see Mom just yet. Wanting to get ahold of my emotions before she just made things worse. People were running all around, ushering several people into the already full waiting room. Everyone there looked worried but unharmed. They were all trying to look around the guards and attendants that were mustering them out of the way, as if they expected to see whoever it was that they were looking for coming around the corner at any minute.

"Maya, not now," Rebecca said, as she came out of the elevator. She talked as she walked down the hallway towards the ER. Obviously, she didn't have the time to stop. "I'm sorry, but you'll need to leave. The waiting room is already at capacity. First a train accident this morning, now a pileup on the highway. I know, God only gives us what we can handle. But I'm starting to think he thinks way too highly of this hospital."

I followed along in her wake until I got a glimpse of the ER around the corner. Mom was running between two patients in the otherwise chaotic room. All the normal beds were taken by people bleeding, crying out in pain. Several other patients were in stretchers out in the hallway. I quickly averted my eyes, though at the time I figured I would have nightmares about that one glance for weeks. Little did I know what I still had in store for me that day.

It was already obvious why Mom couldn't have gotten away. Why she couldn't have come to pick me up even to bring me back to the hospital. She was going to be preoccupied with all of that well into the evening, coming home tired and hungry and too worn out by her job to take care of me. So, I did the only sensible thing. I turned around, retracing my steps back down Main Street, heading towards home.

Backtracking always sucks. It's like you went through all that effort and now you have to do it all over again and start from the beginning. I should have just headed home in the first place. But how was I to know that Mom would be so bogged down? That it would have been impossible for her to get away to drive me home. Had I gone straight there, I would have been home already by the time I made it back to the schools.

Principal Snide was outside the middle school as I passed it, though the busses would still be dropping off the high school kids and not back to pick up the next batch just yet. He pointed towards me, yelling my name, which snapped me out of my daydreams of fighting besides the ninja turtles. The principal pointed down the road, as if to indicate that I should just keep right on walking. That I wouldn't be allowed to get on my bus if I tried. I stared at him for a while as I kept walking, before zoning out once more.

It was dull at home, with nothing to keep my mind off my missing father but my own fantasies. There wasn't anything on the machine to explain Dad's continued absence, which made my worrying more. I just flopped down on the couch in the den, staring up at the blank ceiling where my imagination projected sweeping forest scenes. My fantasies were occasionally interposed by flashes of my father's face, and thoughts of the many things that could have happened to him. The only break in the tedium was when I ordered a pizza, making sure to have plenty left over for Mom and, hopefully, Dad when they got home. Dad was as hopeless in the kitchen as I was. But I would have rather had one of his attempts at cooking, because it would have meant he was home.

It was after eight and I was beginning to wonder if I'd be in bed before anyone came home when the door finally opened. I jumped up from the couch, rushing out into the hall, hoping it was Dad. Mom staggered through the door, exhaustion plain on her face. "Hey, sweetie," she said in a tired voice.

"There's pizza in the kitchen," I said as greeting. "I'll heat some up."

"Dad didn't even try not to burn something this time?" she asked. "Where is he?"

"He never showed up," I called back, as I went to throw a couple slices into the microwave.

"What do you mean?" she grunted. She pulled her sneakers off without unlacing them, a habit Dad had tried to get her to break for years to no avail. "Of course, he showed up. He's your dad. Why wouldn't he show up?"

"I don't know," I mumbled, sitting down at the table. She sort of limped her way into the kitchen, somehow favoring both feet which were sore from walking and standing all day. She plopped down in her usual seat with a loud grunt. "I waited outside the school for hours. He never showed up. There wasn't a message on the machine."

"But... I just talked with him."

"You did?" I perked up. "When."

"It was... is that the time?" she asked, as she stared at the clock on the wall.

"Mom, when did you talk with him?"

"When... I guess it must have been around noon or so. We were just finishing up the patients from the train wreck. An hour later we had... oh god," she said. Her face turned pale in the low glow from the microwave. Neither of us had thought to turn on the overhead kitchen light.

She jumped up from her chair, her sore feet quickly forgotten, as she scooped up the phone and the remote in one quick motion. While dialing the phone, she clicked on the small TV set that was mounted above the stove. As it flickered to life, she started talking into the phone. "Hey, Denise. Were there any... did we get any... John Does from the accident earlier?" I stared at her in confusion, but she didn't supply any answers while she waited for hers. "What about... I mean, I would have heard if... Someone would have told me if my husband had come in, right?"

My eyes went wide as my mind caught up with hers. Robotically, I turned towards the TV, which was showing a commercial for a sports car. It wasn't very helpful, for us or for anyone for that matter. Anyone that wasn't looking to buy a sports car. The beeping from the microwave made me jump. I grabbed Mom's plate out of it. In my hurry, I forgot the oven mitts and nearly dropped the pizza as I hissed in pain.

"Are you sure?" she asked of the phone. "Okay. Call me the moment you hear something, anything... please." The last word came out more heartbroken than I had ever heard my mother speak. It was the moment that I realized that, despite being older than me, and my mother, she was just as human as I was. The phone shook in her hand as she lowered it back onto the cradle. She crumbled against the wall and slid down to the floor.

Picking up an oven mitt from the hooks on the wall, I grabbed her plate again. I placed it on the floor next to her as I sat down on the other side of it. "Eat," I ordered. She complied.

We sat there, staring up at the little TV, for a couple of hours. Neither of us wanted to take our eyes off of it long enough to move into the den. Neither of us cared that we were sitting on a hard, dirty floor as the smell of cold pizza permeated the air. We just continued to stare at the TV, occasionally changing channels, hoping for some news. But then we'd quickly turn back to the original channel, the Fox affiliate that more often reported news of our area.

Every few minutes, Mom would reach up, stretching to grab the phone from its place. She'd call up the hospital again, only to get the same news. No John Does, no news of my father. She'd call the police station as well, even the fire station. But no one had any news about the crash, which was still being cleaned up on the highway. Traffic was backed up in every direction.

"Maybe he missed it," I suggested, after she called the fire station for the second time. "Maybe he just missed it and has been stuck in traffic this entire time."

"Yea," she said, reaching over to pat my head. "Maybe." But she wouldn't volunteer anything more than maybe.

When the TV asked her if she knew where her children were, she hugged me close to her, not wanting to let me go for an instant, as the news started up. "Our top story," the news anchor started. "A train derailment left thirty-one injured and four dead. News van five has the details."

Mom's finger itched towards the fast forward button as we both wished they would hurry up and switch to the car crash. The train derailment had been all but cleaned up, with the authorities waiting on a crane to set the train cars back on their track. They attributed the low casualty count to the good work of the doctors at Mom's hospital and spoke of train schedules for the weekend.

I sat there, completely frozen in my mother's embrace, as we both stared at the warming glow of the TV. It was the only illumination in the entire house. The lights in the other room had turned off from lack of movement. Dad had insisted on the motion detection lights after Mom had left every light on in the house before heading out to a night shift at the hospital. The darkness only made his absence that much more tangible.

"Back to you at the studio," the field reporter said.

Mom cranked the volume as an aerial view of the car crash came onto the screen. "Almost as devastating was the fifteen car pileup on 26 west. It started when a car swerved unexpectedly, sidewinding two others. It is unclear what caused the driver to swerve or the identity of the driver, as he is still pinned under several other cars which piled up on top of his. All the other drivers have been rescued from their cars and sent to St. Michael's as well. All fourteen rescued drivers and four passengers are in stable condition."

Before cutting away from the story, the aerial view cut in on the car that caused the crash. My heart stopped as I recognized my dad's car. It was completely crushed beneath a ford pickup and next to one of those same sports cars that was just being advertised.

Chapter Seventeen
The Sands of Time

Now

The edges of my desk cut into my hands as I clutched at it. It was the only indication I had that I was still at school as my mind was locked in an internal scream of denial.

#

"No," I screamed in denial. "No, no, no, no, no. No, he can't be dead. I'm not... I can't die like this." I didn't just ugly cry, I snot cried. Someone came over and hugged me, but my eyes were too full of tears to see who. All I knew was that their arms were strong and their shoulders wide. I felt comfort in those arms.

Finding out that Zandar and Grandor had both died in the raid on the thieves' guild wasn't as bad as when I found out my father had died. But it came close given the repercussions. I tried to reassure myself that I wasn't really going to die. That this whole thing was some big daydream. But this world, this life, had become so much a part of me that I couldn't bear for it to end. With how real it had become recently, so much more real and so out of my control, I had no idea what would really happen when the last grain fell.

For all I knew, my body on Earth would fall down onto my desk, a completely lifeless husk. My teacher would call the paramedics as my classmates stood over me, gawking. The doctors would have no clue what happened to me. My autopsy would show no signs of anything wrong with my body. Worst of all, my mother would have to attend another funeral.

I remembered my dad's funeral. It was only those five years ago. My mother cried herself to sleep for weeks. His accident was so sudden, and yet it would look like an eternity compared to the warning of my death. She might never survive that.

It took me forever to notice that the chest I was crying into wasn't wearing a shirt. The blood covering it had seemed like one until my tears started to carve a clean path through it. When I did notice, I knew exactly who I was crying on. I looked up at him. I stared into his big green eyes and swallowed the huge lump in my throat. I had forgotten how gorgeous he was after realizing that he was one of them. That he was one of the thieves that had gotten me arrested. That had forced me into stealing that metal sphere. That, now, had slaughtered an entire regiment of troopers.

"Hi," he said, as I tried to back away from him. There was a Maya shaped clean spot on the front of his otherwise blood drenched chest. "We didn't get properly introduced before."

"Yea, after you showed yourself to be a spy for them, I no longer really cared what your story was," I said, once I finally managed to recover my voice. I knew I shouldn't really be mad at him. Sure, he betrayed me and kept a pretty big secret from me. But this whole world was just in my head, as was he. It was more like me keeping a secret from myself. Still, I tried to push myself away from his chest, but his grip on me, both physical and emotional, was far stronger than I was.

"I'm Jason," he said, seeming to ignore my interruption. "It's nice to meet you, Maya."

"I can think of nicer ways. Like ones where I'm not about to die because your friends are assholes." I shoved the bracelet in his face, startling him enough that he let me go.

"Oh, they're no friends of mine," he said, in a whisper. He glanced over his shoulder towards his guildmates, many of whom had returned to rummaging through the odds and ends of body parts, looking for anything of worth. "I'm afraid I'm as trapped as they intended to make you, though they never went as far as putting one of those on me." He tapped my bracelet, as if he could be talking about anything else. He took my hand as he examined my bracelet closer. It all but disappeared in his.

"There's only a few minutes left," I said, trying to fight back the returning tears. "I wish I had gone into the guild and found Grandor and Zandar's bodies. Then at least I would have known there was no point in coming to rescue you people." That's good, I thought to myself, anger, not tears. You're not going to die crying in front of these people.

"But then you never would have rescued us," one of the twins said, as she came up behind me.

"And a bunch of other innocent people who never deserved to be imprisoned," the other twin said, following her sister.

A humming sensation started up towards my right, the unmistakable sensation of a spell being cast. I looked over toward Heather, deep in concentration as she wove a dweomer around herself. Her hands flicked towards my wrist and the bracelet that was there. This worried me. Countering a spell by magic could be just as dangerous as countering it with cancelation powder. Often, it was more dangerous. Using cancelation powder was like dosing a fire with oil-soaked water, a competition between the water killing the fire and the oil stoking it. Using a spell is like adding fuel to a fire in an enclosed space and hoping all the oxygen gets used up before the house burns down.

I cringed away from the spell, holding the bracelet up between Heather and me and as far away from my body as I could while it was still attached. After seeing her work with the fire, I was afraid she'd fry me when trying to help me. Reflexively, I closed my eyes, not even knowing if I would ever open them again. The humming soon became a throbbing, thundering throughout my body as the spell flowed over me. That must have been when I blacked out.

"Maya," someone was calling my name. "Maya," my body was being shaken to the rhythm of my name. "Maya," the person practically shouted.

"What is it?" I asked. "I don't want to go to school today."

There was the sound of snickering and laughter around me, my first indication that I wasn't dead. Most of them were the deep grunts of men, which seemed to indicate that I was still in the world of Desparia. When this realization hit me, I popped up into a sitting position, knocking my head against whoever it was that was shaking me.

"Ow," I said, at the same time as Jason, the shirtless god.

"What just happened?" I asked, rubbing my head with my left hand. When I noticed the bracelet still on my wrist, I gave a sigh. "Well, I didn't really think you'd be able to get it off." I sounded a bit disappointed despite my words.

"Oh, I was never trying to get it off," Heather said. She was standing over me and looking down with a smug look on her face. "Look at the hourglass."

I turned over the bracelet to look at how little time I had left. When I saw the hourglass, I literally did a double take. The top half of the hourglass was full once again, as if someone had flipped it over. "What the..." I began, momentarily at a loss for words.

"Well, I'm nowhere near as powerful as Zandar was with earth magic," Heather admitted, with a small, one shoulder shrug. "Even before he joined up with the thieves' guild, he was a bit of a legend. My teacher... well, he used to tell me stories of Zandar's accomplishments when I was growing up. His favorite story involved a bracelet similar to that one." Heather turned around, trying to hide the fact that she was wiping away a tear. "Anyway," she said after a sniffle. "Bottom line is that I'm not as powerful as he is with earth magic, and I probably never will be. However, I can at least buy you some more time, every couple of days or so, to keep the bracelet from killing you. At least, that is, if you decide to come with us, to help us."

"I still don't trust her," one of the twins whispered to the other.

"Well, we do kind of have her over a barrel now," the other twin whispered back. "It's not like she'd try to run off with that bracelet ticking away."

"I'd like to come too," Jason said. He seemed overly excited, considering neither of us knew what these three were talking about.

"No," the twins said in unison.

"Absolutely not," Heather said.

"I tend to agree with them," I said. I was still unsure where I stood on joining up myself, though the last thing I needed was someone tagging along whom I knew I couldn't trust.

"Why not?" Jason asked. He almost sounded hurt by our rejection. "You freed me from those troopers. I owe you a life debt that I am honor-bound to fulfill."

"Listen, Fabio," I said.

"Jason," he said.

"Whatever. I make it a point not to trust anyone as... well... attractive as you."

"So, you hate me because I'm beautiful?" he asked, oblivious to the old saying.

"No, I don't trust you because you're beautiful." He smiled a huge grin when I said that. "What?" I asked.

"You admitted you think I'm beautiful."

I rolled my eyes. "Quick poll. Who here thinks Jason is beautiful?" I called out into the distance before raising my hand. Heather and the twins quickly raised their own hands. Half of the thieves, still picking over the corpses around us, stopped in their looting long enough to raise their own hands. "See? Everyone here thinks you're beautiful. Don't let my opinion get your hopes up. Besides, you're still one of them, no matter how you came about being involved with them."

"Actually, if you must know, my spying on you fulfilled my debt to them. Whether you let me come with you or not, I'm not going back to that guild."

"He could spy on me any day," one of the twins mumbled.

"I'm right with you on that one, Tina," the other twin mumbled back. "I still don't trust either of them, though."

"Either way," I said. "I don't trust you, and I don't exactly have time for you to earn that trust. I'm living on borrowed time as it is. Besides, it's not like I have much of a say in the matter..."

"She's right about that," Heather agreed.

"... and it's not like I've decided if I'm going myself."

"What?" Heather asked, sounding a bit taken aback.

"I've done enough jumping into situations without knowing anything for one day. I'm not signing up for anything without knowing what I'm getting myself into. Take it or leave it. I have two more days to find another mage that could turn back the sands of time like you just did. I think I can manage."

This, of course, was a total bluff. And from the look on Heather's face, she knew it as much as I did. Mages were pretty high up on the emperor's hit list, right up there with thieves, non-humans, and half breeds. After the troopers' raid on Vernala, I'd be hard pressed to find any of them within a two day's hike. Let alone a mage powerful enough to tamper with Zandar's spell and know how to without killing me in the process.

"Fair enough," Heather said. She nodded her ascent, a faint smile spreading across her face. "We'll have to put some distance between us and them first," she said, pointing off to the looters.

"Amen to that," I said. The four of them gave me confused looks, which I shook off. "Lead the way."

Twin 1, who at the time I thought was called Tina, took point. She led the way back up the ridge into the woods. She had rescued a long sword off one of the troopers and was waving it around a bit, trying to get the feel of the new weapon. Twin 2 took the rear, taking out a knife she had pilfered off one of the troopers. She was looking around for something as we went. Every once in a while, she would head off to the side, only to come back shaking her head. Heather and I walked next to each other in the middle. I wasn't used to going anywhere with other people, in either world. So, every couple of minutes or so I'd get too far ahead of Heather and she'd grab my arm, indicating that I should slow down. This went on for over ten minutes, until we were in the middle of the woods, no longer within sight of the camp ruins. Or much of anything else either. Twin 1 had stopped short, in the middle of a small clearing, and stood over a half rotten stump, its tree lying next to it, rotted through.

"Alright," she said. "This is what you're getting yourself into."

Chapter Eighteen
Numb

Five Years Earlier

I don't remember much of that next week. I know I didn't spend much time daydreaming. Thoughts of such childish things seemed beyond me at that point. I must have suffered the detentions in silence. But there was no further punishment for the food fight, from Mom, from the principal, from anyone, not even Janice. Mom must have figured I'd suffered enough to not do something as stupid as picking a fight with a bully ever again. Or stand up to anyone ever again for that matter.

Janice left me alone for a while. Everyone left me alone after hearing what happened to my dad. The whole school had already been used to ignoring me, they just seemed to go a step further and forget I was even there. That seemed just fine to me, as I didn't want to talk with anyone.

The fog barely lifted long enough for the funeral, which Mom had managed to pull together for a week after the accident. Dad didn't have much family left, but my mom's sister came up from Austin to be with us. Several of the guys from Dad's work showed up to give their respects and a few even spoke. I don't remember a word they said, though. They barely registered at the time. But I imagine they were nice words.

The only thing that broke through the numbness that had become my life was when David and his dad showed up. His dad was in his police uniform, his cruiser parked on the side of the road at the bottom of the hill that my father was to be buried on. The lights bounced off the grey tombstones that would forever mark the area that would be his final home.

David was wearing a suit that seemed to fit him perfectly. I wondered about this for a moment before I realized it was the suit he must have gotten for when his mom died. They were still saying that would be any day. I fidgeted around when I saw him there. His suit reminded me that I was wearing one of my dad's old t-shirts, a black Star Wars shirt with Darth Vader's helmet on it. It seemed more appropriate when I was getting dressed than the black sundress Mom had laid out for me. But standing across from David's snazzy suit was making me rethink things. David gave me the lightest smile as he and his father joined the small crowd staring at the hole in the ground.

I wasn't sure how to feel about him being there. In a way, it was his snubbing of me that had led to my father's death. I could so easily blame him for it. For all the pain that I would be feeling once I started feeling anything again. But, as I tried to get my ire up, all it did was make me see my own hand in it. My own actions that led to my loss, though they had been prompted by his. I didn't want to feel that. So, I turned away from him, looking down towards where my father would arrive.

My dad's old college buddies were carrying the casket up the hill from the hearse. From what Mom said, what was left of Dad when she went to identify the body wasn't pretty. She had opted for the closed casket, wanting to spare me from seeing him that way. It was hard for me to believe that he was in that box. He was never that heavy of a man, but it seemed to take ten of them to carry him up. All of them strained to hold the casket steady and level. After placing it on the green cloth, they backed away from it, each rubbing their sore muscles as they joined the growing numbers.

There was a priest standing by where the gravestone would go once it was done being carved. He spoke a few more words, echoing those he had said in the church, but none of them seemed to reach me. Nothing seemed to reach me... at least, not until they started lowering the casket into the ground.

I stepped forward, feeling like I wanted to throw myself into the hole after him. Like I wanted to be buried with him. Like my life had ended when his did. Before I could do anything, though, Mom stepped up beside me. Her hand grabbed mine, holding me steady on the edge of the hole. I looked up at her, up into her eyes which showed a sorrow deeper than I could ever know.

"It's just you and me now," she whispered to me. "We need to start taking care of each other, okay?"

"Yes, Mom," I said. I looked down at the casket as it reached the bottom of the grave.

Mom reached out, picking up a handful of dirt and sprinkling it over the casket. She sighed then, as if some burden had been lifted. But then she started to cry, kneeling down on the grass, her face in her hands. Aunt Judy came up behind her, placing her hands on her shoulder. She sent her comfort that I couldn't manage to give her, couldn't seem to feel for myself. The numbness roared from beneath me, seeking to swallow me up again. With Mom being the only reason not to, I was tempted to let it.

I grabbed up my own scoop of dirt, sprinkling it over my father. As I watched it hit the wood, I wondered what that was supposed to do. I wondered how I had been expected to feel after I did it. Whenever I tried to feel anything, all I could feel was pain. I was about to succumb to the numbness once more when another hand, a smaller hand, found its way into mine once more.

"I'm so sorry about your father," David said beside me. "It sucks to lose a parent."

"At least you know your mom is going to die. This just took me completely by surprise."

"I don't think it's any better," David said. "I think I'm already feeling some of what you are, just more drawn out, stretched out over months. I keep feeling the loss of her, the absence of the person who was my mom. The person who always took care of me. Who cut the crust off my sandwiches. And then, I'm reminded she's still there, still alive, just not for much longer. She's not that person anymore. It's like she died when we found out it was terminal, but she was still around. I wouldn't want to wish that on anyone, making them watch someone they love wither away, knowing they were going to die and there was nothing you could do about it."

"Was that why?" I asked. My voice was barely a whisper as the tears that I had managed to keep away all week finally found me.

"No," David admitted. "It was something much more stupid than that."

"You were my friend," I said. "And you took everyone away from me. Even my father."

I was shocked that I said it, but I couldn't take it back. I didn't look at David, didn't want to see how those words hurt him. They hurt me to say them. I just dropped his hand and walked, almost robotically, over to the car. The rest of the people had already started to disperse, with talk about heading back to my house, my home, for a wake. A wake where more people would be talking about the man that they didn't know like I knew. I tried to think of a single one of them talking about his love of reading. About how he'd always tuck me in at night when he was home. About how he protected me from the monsters in my closet back when I thought there were some. And yet, I couldn't remember a word anyone had said all day, besides those brief conversations with Mom and David.

I pulled on the car door handle, knowing the car was locked but trying it anyway. When the door refused to open, I turned around, leaning against the car and sliding down to sit in the grass, my butt on the cement curb. I watched the people head for their cars. Aunt Judy was still holding onto Mom as she cried. But no one came over to hold me as I did.

And it was all my fault. Not David's. Not Dad's for not driving more carefully. Not Mom's for scaring everyone away from my party. Not Ashley and Jen's for abandoning me... well, maybe it was a little their fault. David had shown up for the funeral but there was no sign of either of them. No other classmates of mine. But that wasn't a surprise to me. It was just a bunch of strangers, barely sparing a glance for the little girl crying in the dirt.

As I sat there, waiting for Mom and Aunt Judy, watching the people leave, I went back to the old idea. I went back to the thought of creating a dream world of my very own that I could escape to. One that I could help shape and explore the more time I spent there. I had settled on fantasy a while back, settling for magic over spaceships. But I had decided I wanted to start my own world, starting it from scratch. There would have to be some great power that everyone could fight against, though I never wanted to fight him. Perhaps I would make it so that no one would want to go up against him because he was too powerful or too fortified... or both.

The random thoughts flew through my head as the world started to form in my mind, interrupted only when the car behind me clicked open. As I sat in the back of the car, heading away from my father's funeral, I finally figured out what world I wanted to daydream. The world that I wanted to explore. That I wanted to expand on until it was more real than the world that I was meant to suffer the rest of my life in.

The world where my father was still alive.

So, as Aunt Judy drove us back home from the cemetery, I closed my eyes and went there for the first time.

Chapter Nineteen
The Plan

Now

"What do you know about The Citadel?" Heather asked as she pulled a scroll case out of her pack and placed it on the half rotten stump at the center of the clearing.

My face fell when she mentioned the name of the emperor's fortress home. I had only just been thinking of why my fantasy world had a fortified fortress surrounding the eternal evil that ruled it. To think that these three would want to go in there was... unthinkable.

"I'm out of here," I said, walking back the way we had come.

Twin 2 quickly blocked my way with a long branch she must have picked up along the way. There were fresh cuts along the length where she had started carving it, making it into a staff to replace the one that she must have lost. "Not so fast," she said. "Let us explain before you go running off in fear. It's really not as bad as it sounds."

"Oh, please," Heather said. "It's exactly as bad as it sounds."

"No," Twin 1 said, defending her sister. "It's much, much worse than it sounds."

"You guys aren't exactly instilling a sense of confidence in me right now," I said.

"Just answer the question," Heather said, glaring at the twins. "What do you know about The Citadel?"

"Ten impenetrable walls, each more impenetrable than the last, with no way in besides by invitation of the emperor himself," I blurted out. "Same thing everyone else knows about the place."

Heather nodded as she popped the top on the scroll case. She upended it, spilling out a large scroll onto the stump. The twins each brought over a rock, which they placed on either end of the scroll, keeping the parchment flat. The scroll showed a map of the area, centered on the mountain and showing the ten walls of The Citadel. And, more importantly, the location of the door. Correction, the doors, plural, ten of them, one in each of the ten walls, with a long path drawn in a spiral as it passed through each of them in turn.

"Where did you get that?" I asked breathlessly.

"Let's just say that people died in the process," Heather said, as she leaned over the stump. "We're here," she pointed to a location just on the southern edge of the map. "The first door is over here." She pointed towards the indentation in the outer wall in the east, which was surrounded by the town at the foot of the mountain. The Capital. The former seat of power of Fandor.

"And, what? You expect me to pick the lock or something?" I asked. "The front door doesn't have a lock. It doesn't even open as far as I've heard. I imagine the rest of these would be the same. Besides, we'd have to go through The Capital to get to the door. We'd be caught in like three seconds in there."

"Why would we be caught?" one of the twins asked, laughing. "Nobody would ever dream we'd want to break into The Citadel."

"Yes, that's because it's suicide. If it could be done at all, that is. But it can't."

"You only say that because nobody ever has," the other twin said. "There's a first time for everything."

"And a last," I said.

"What if I told you there's a way through the doors?" Heather asked. "What if there was a safeguard built into The Citadel, in case the emperor got locked out and needed to get back inside? And what if I told you that the person who designed it in the first place was the twins' mother?"

That shut me up for a second. It silenced the twins as well. They took a step back from the map, looking over at Heather in surprise.

What if this could really work? What if there really was a way into The Citadel? So what?

"So what?" I asked.

"So what?" the twins said in unison.

"So what if we could get into The Citadel? What if we could go right up to the emperor himself? What exactly do you expect to do in there?"

"We expect to kill him," one of the twins said. "What do you think we're going to do?"

"No, Tina," Heather interrupted, putting up her hand. "It's a fair question. Not all of us have felt the oppression of the emperor equally. I just figured, as a thief, you'd be one of those people who'd want the guy gone."

"Look, I never really wanted to be a thief," I admitted. "It's not like I grew up thinking that taking things from other people would be a great way to make a living. I wanted to be more of an adventurer, you know? See the sights and sounds of the world. Navigate my way through ancient ruins and recover large treasures from dragon's lairs and stuff. Rescuing people and saving villages from invading armies of goblins.

"I became a thief because I was good at it. I kept seeing people walk through lives carrying large purses begging to be taken because they weren't paying attention to them. They were taking their riches for granted, when other people were starving in the streets. Heck, at first I tried to do the whole Robin Hood routine." I got a few confused looks at that comment. "Robbing from the rich to give to the poor. The problem was there were always more poor people than I could ever help, and half the people I did help ended up robbed or killed for what little I gave them. I hate to admit it, but I got a bit jaded.

"Anyway, the point is, I understand where the emperor is coming from in most cases. Thieves are a bit of a plague on the nation right now. There are cities where there are more thieves than people to steal from. I mean, just look at what happened back there." I pointed back towards the remnants of the trooper camp, even though it was well out of sight. "Those thieves just tore up those people when they were too drunk to hold a sword. Don't get me wrong, the troopers are in no way innocent. But not even they deserved that. And those were the more civilized of us. The guild was starting to regulate thieves better than the chaos that came before, controlling who it was that could steal within their influence. There are some theories out there that they were an extension of the empire himself. Now I don't know what to think.

"Besides, it's not like the troopers have been catching many thieves. Those they had caught were the ones worth the extra effort. The ones extorting people or who had taken over towns and living it up in the lap of luxury. Or, of course, those stupid enough to get caught. I spend most of my time just trying to be invisible. It's been a lot easier than I like to admit.

"As for mages, sure, that's mostly because he needs to secure his position. Can't have powerful people walking all over his nation, threatening his powerbase. But, again, there were a lot of mages that had been abusing their powers for years. I've often heard of this mage or that mage terrorizing a village or two into paying them tribute, even burning a few of them to the ground. And don't get me started on the mage wars. There never was any type of guild for mages, any attempt to regulate who learned how to cast spells and what they did with it. Not quite sure why no one tried, but the few mages I've met in my time in this world were even more antisocial than I am. And that's saying a lot.

"Don't get me wrong, I don't agree with the extremes he went to, in any way. There's no reason to go killing all willy-nilly like that. And the specism was absurd. Yes, the goblinoid, giantkin, and trollkin races tended towards violence and the country is, arguably, a safer place without them causing problems. But they were targeted as a whole and killed without a second thought. No one worried if any one of them was worth saving. Not to mention the dwarves, elves, and gnomes they killed right alongside them never did anything to deserve being hunted near extinction.

"So, yes, I understand the desire to 'kill Hitler' as it was," I said, leading towards another round of confused looks. "I just don't see how the job fell to the four of us or how you think we could actually succeed where so many others have failed. Besides, even if we somehow did succeed, what's to stop someone worse from taking over?"

"Huh," Heather said, after a moment of silence. My diatribe seemed to take all three of them a bit by surprise. I felt like it was the most I've ever said in any one stretch, on either world. "I'm sorry," she said, shaking her head. "I just can't believe anyone would actually believe half the stuff you just said."

"I told you she wouldn't help us," one of the twins whispered.

"You know what?" Heather said. "No, I don't believe you. I don't think that the few bad mages would mean that the whole lot of us need to be limited in any way, let alone be killed off all 'willy-nilly' as you put it. Yes, many thieves cause lots of strife in the kingdom, as they steal from hard working people who aren't constantly vigilant when it comes to their money. But there are tons more who work within the law to help protect people's wealth and, yes, recover lost artifacts and treasures from ancient ruins and dragon's lairs and the like. There may not be as many of those ruins and lairs left, after some of the emperor's more benevolent projects. But that's still a rather important role for them, for you, to play. You also come in handy when trying to get into a heavily fortified fortress when a tyrant needs to be eliminated. And yes, it doesn't matter what his reasoning is, there's no excuse for killing anyone when there are other measures that can be utilized. But, when it comes to this emperor, death is too good for him. So, yes, let's go 'kill Hilter', whoever that is."

By the end of that speech, though it was quite shorter than mine, she was getting very loud and animated. In the silence that followed, there was a very loud growling sound coming from the trees around us.

"Um..." I said, eyeing the forest. "Where is the path?" I asked.

"It's over there," Heather said, sounding disinterested. "Why?"

"Can't you hear that?" I asked, edging my way in the direction she indicated.

"It's just a strong wind blowing through the trees. Don't change the subject."

"That's no wind. It's the nightmare."

"Pfft, oh please. Not you too," one of the twins said.

"Yes, I mean, who really believes in the big bad nightmare," the other twin agreed.

"The three of us have been all through these woods and have never seen anything like this stupid, mythical nightmare," Heather said.

The three of them started laughing as I continued to make my way back to the road. "I have," I whispered, just loud enough to be heard over their laughter. This shut them up instantly.

"Um... what?" Heather asked, blinking in surprise.

"It was my first day here. I had... acquired a hefty purse off of a group of thugs," I said, coming up with a believable lie, not wanting to admit to the truth of everything. I wasn't exactly sure how they would handle the idea of them being imaginary. "They chased me into the woods near some mage's tower. The thugs were gaining on me when I heard... that sound. I turned around and this huge black... thing was grabbing them up one by one. The screaming, oh, god the screaming." I couldn't take it anymore. The memory of that day spiked my fear above my caution. I ran, flat out, for the road, hoping to make it there before the nightmare caught up with me. Hoping that getting to the road would be enough.

The growling came closer as the road came into view. I dared a glance behind me and immediately regretted it. The nightmare was hot on our trail, a dark void swallowing up the moonlight behind us and hiding the stars above. Heather was clinging to the map scroll, its ends flapping in the wind. A tear was noticeable down the center where she must have grabbed it too quickly for the stones to let go. The twins each clutched their weapons as they ran, darting glances over their shoulders as if looking for something to hit with them.

I stumbled as I ran onto a small side road, tripping over the wagon rut that was the only sign of its presence. Pausing briefly, I dithered a bit, deciding on whether to keep running or hope that the road was enough to stop it. In all the rumors about the nightmare that had been spreading throughout the region for the past five years, none of them ever spoke about it attacking someone that was traveling on the road. The twins barreled right into me, sweeping me up in their wake. We kept running. Not looking behind us. Not daring to slow down again. Gradually, the growling faded until it was drowned out by the wind. Slowing down to catch my breath, I found a large root sticking out of the ground to sit on. Heather and the twins soon joined me, similarly winded.

"What... in the inferno... was that?" Heather asked between pants.

"Like I told you... It's the nightmare."

"It's real," one of the twins said. Her face was whiter than fresh snow.

"It's really real," the other twin said. She looked similarly pale, though she was hunched over as if she was going to vomit.

"We shouldn't stay here long," I said. "I don't know why it doesn't come onto the roads but, whatever the reason, it might not hold it for long."

"But... how?" the first twin asked, still not able to wrap her head around the myth come to life.

"What was that, really?" the other twin asked. "What is the nightmare?"

"It looked like some kind of... shadow or something," Heather said.

"Sure," the first twin said, nodding her head. "But a shadow of what?"

"No, not a shadow as in the normal sense," Heather said.

"It's still too dark out for a normal shadow that size to be seen anywhere," I said. "No matter how big the source is."

"Right," Heather agreed. "I mean the undead creature known as a shadow." The twins looked at her in utter confusion. "Let's just say, you don't want to be touched by it."

"So... run from the huge dark thing," the second twin said. "Got it." She gave a thumbs up as she got back to her feet.

Heather peeled the map off of her. It was damp with her sweat and clung to her neck and arms. Looking at its sorry state, she shook her head and started to roll it back up, trying to avoid doing any more damage. "Look," she said. "I obviously don't have all the answers. And you're right, whoever replaces the emperor might be worse. But, if we don't stop him now, before his armies reach into the neighboring kingdoms, we'll be at war for decades and he'll be too powerful to stop."

"Besides," the first twin started.

"We owe him a long, agonizing death," the other twin finished.

"What?" I asked, a confused look coming onto my face.

"Yes," Heather said. "Admittedly, I'm the only one here with political reasons for wanting him dead. These two have more personal reasons. It's personal for me too, just also political."

"Now, see, that I could understand," I said, pointing to the twins. "Everyone has their own opinion on politics, but revenge is rather simple. I can get behind revenge."

"Does that..." the first twin said.

"Do you mean..." the second twin said.

"I'm in," I said.

Heather just stood there, her face blank. "Yes," she said after a while. "There really was no way you weren't coming with us, was there?"

I just nodded as I recalled what really happened that day five years earlier. The first time I saw the nightmare. The first time I came to Desparia.

Chapter Twenty
Dipping a Toe

Five Years Earlier

I started small, picturing myself in a forest glade. There was a mage's tower in the distance, dark against the horizon with obsidian spikes pointing out in every direction. Dad would have loved that tower. It was like something out of the Dark Crystal or something. The clopping of horse hooves on a cobblestone road could be heard not too far off, two travelers heading for the tower no doubt. The sky was as blue as on Earth, perhaps bluer, though the cloud cover overhead blocked much of it. It was a startling contrast to the actual sky that I was seeing, and yet not seeing, that had no clouds in sight. Birds called out in the distance, though far away from the sounds of the horses and their riders. The grass beneath my bare feet was tall, reaching to my knees, growing wild with no one to tend it.

My clothing surprised me a little, as if some deep part of my subconscious had brought it out of nowhere. In the car, I was still wearing Dad's old Darth Vader t-shirt. It looked more like a dress on me than a shirt, as it was over a pair of shorts that were mostly hidden beneath the shirt's folds. A well-worn pair of sneakers, the same ones I always wore, completed the outfit. I wiggled my toes in the grass beneath my feet, feeling only the grass and not the socks or the inside of my shoes. Despite my feet being bare in this new world, I was suddenly wearing pants that fell to just above my ankles and a tunic that was the closest item to what I was actually wearing in the car. Both were the grey of undyed wool, suggesting that I was some kind of pauper to this world.

I didn't go towards the tower. I wasn't sure if I was ready to create people yet. Making a character from scratch, even one that had bits and pieces of other characters, was a bit much for my imagination just then. Instead, I headed deeper into the woods, away from where I imagined the road would be. I pushed away the branches that blocked a small deer path that led through the wilderness. The pine trees smelled like Christmas, dangerously close to the subject at hand. But I buried myself in the scents around me, hoping that I could revive some shadow of my father. Even if it was only in this place, this small section of the world that I created around me.

I quickly got lost in the woods, losing track of the glade that I had arrived in. Even the tower disappeared from the horizon, blocked out by the towering trees overhead. I just shrugged, though, figuring that, in my imagination, the tower could just as easily be ahead of me as behind.

Continuing onward, my footsteps started to rustle as leaves started to mix with the pine needles underfoot. A twig snapped and I looked down, surprised as I hadn't felt a stick under my bare foot. I couldn't see one either, no matter how much I searched. Standing there in confusion, another twig snapped off in the distance ahead of me.

"Hello?" I called into the woods, wondering who would have the audacity to encroach on my peaceful daydream.

Stomping, running footsteps quickly approached me through the trees. First one, then another large man ran towards me. They both had swords drawn. When they spotted me, they started screaming, their swords flying wildly. Immediately, I turned and ran, wishing I had imagined myself with boots or sneakers or something proper on my feet. The soft leaves and needles beneath my feet cushioned them better than any shoes would have. But they didn't protect against the rocks that occasionally hit my feet, making them bleed, as I ran from the two men.

That was when I really heard it, running from two men with swords that I had never seen before. I had no idea where they came from or why I imagined them being there. But they were chasing me away from... whatever it was they were chasing me away from. They couldn't have known me any better than I had known them. They couldn't have any reason to hate me. And, yet, they chased me, for no apparent reason, through the forest, when the deep, guttural growl came out of nowhere, scaring me more than the men with swords ever could. It was all the prompting that I needed to put on a little extra speed.

But, yes, the men started screaming again soon after that, this time in fear and pain rather than in shock and anger. I dared to look over my shoulder as the huge, dark... thing grabbed up the man closest to it. He was the one that had come out of the woods second, the slower of the two. Thick tendrils extended out of its dark mass, reaching out seemingly out of nowhere, out of nothing, and wrapped around the man. There was no sign of strain on the monster's part. No grunts of effort. Its form didn't change beyond the tendrils emerging.

I watched in horror as the tendrils drew the screaming man towards a gaping maw. It was something almost cartoonish in its simplicity. Just an extending of part of the bulk in a toothless, almost formless, mouth that opened wider than one would normally think possible. The man's screams continued right up to the point where the maw closed around him, muffling the screams which spiked as a sickening crunching sound echoed around us. Two more crunching sounds and the man's screams were silenced.

My screams joined those of the other man. The dead man's friend. The lone survivor of their group. My panic caused me to dart forward as fast as possible. It was beyond anything that I had ever achieved before. I just focused on the trail ahead of me as I careened through the forest. Somehow, I knew that I would not be able to stay ahead of that thing, no matter how much I tried. I also knew, as the old joke goes, I only needed to be faster than the other man.

At least until the monster grabbed him up too.

Suddenly, the forest opened up. The man shouted in glee, in triumph, as the sun beat down at us. The clouds started to part as if someone on high wanted to show that we were safe there. My legs didn't get the message, though, and I continued to run. I wanted to put as much distance between myself and the monster behind us. And, when the man's gleeful whooping turned to screams of fear, I didn't look back. I didn't want to look back. I knew his fate was sealed the moment that he stopped running. I wouldn't.

Looking around for some form of escape, some source of safety from this abominable creature, I spotted the tower once again, still off in the distance. I would have turned to it, ran for it in hopes that the mage was friendly. And that this creature wasn't their pet. However, the tower, which had been the only sign of civilization in the area, was on fire. The flames roared high into the sky, engulfing the stone in an inferno beyond belief. As the crunching sounds behind me quieted once more, the tower toppled. It shook the ground that I was running on as it crumpled in on itself.

My feet found the road before my brain did. My toe hit a loose cobblestone, tripping me. I tumbled onto the far side of the road on my back. Lying there, I could see the darkness moving towards me, swarming towards my prone body. I closed my eyes, fearing that that moment would be my last...

And bolted straight upright in Mom's car. Blinking around, my mind adjusted back to the reality that was around me.

"What the hell was that?" I mumbled to myself.

"Language," Aunt Judy scolded. She glared back at me in the rearview mirror.

I shook my head, not in denial but to clear the remaining edge of my daydream. That had been more real than I had ever experienced. More substantial than any daydreaming I'd ever thought possible. I could feel the ground beneath my feet. Smell the scents of the forest around me. Hear the bird calls that I would normally have heard in such an area. It was so real that it was almost surreal, though the concept hadn't occurred to me at the time.

But then, what was that whole part about the darkness? The burning tower? Was that some deep part of my psyche bleeding into my imagination? The tower was obviously a representation of my father, with its demise representing me coming to terms with his death. With the fact that I'd never see him again. But was the shadow somehow my gripping depression that was already well on its way?

I still haven't figured out what they meant. Or, more importantly, why my subconscious not only kept the darkness in that world but seemed to integrate it into the legends of the place. A monster that wanders the countryside, catching up people who fail to stay on the path, eating them. A less informed person might have assumed these stories were just a way to keep the wild world wild. But one look at that creature would keep you on the road for the rest of your life. Assuming you survived such an encounter.

At the time, I mostly wrote it off as my imagination running away with me. However, it kept me from returning to that world right away. I didn't want to have that thing spring up again before I was ready to handle it. Before I was ready to get away from it or, more importantly, to get rid of it so that it wouldn't be in my dream world at all.

The only thing that had made sense in my first trip to that world was a feeling that I had while I was there. It was like what I had been seeing, that forest glade and the surrounding woods, was all there was to that dream world. That the world was limited to that small space that I had explored and nothing more. I knew that, if I had walked down the road, a village or a town or a city would have appeared. But it was like no such town existed yet. That my finding it in my imagination would pull it into existence. And that only by exploring it, by meeting the people that lived there, would they be anything more than a background to my world.

As we pulled up in front of my house, I felt a new rush of despair. Looking up at the house, knowing Dad wouldn't be inside. That he'd never be inside again. I didn't want to go inside, where signs of his former presence, and more tangible his current absence, would be everywhere. Where people would be talking about him non-stop. But Mom opened the door, holding out her hand so that we could approach the nightmare together.

Walking up the sidewalk, Mom's hand in mine, I figured my dream world was as appropriate for my current life as any would be. I decided to call it Despairia. Only later did it turn into something more. Something different. Desparia.

Chapter Twenty-One
The Approach

Now

On the way to The Capital, I finally learned how to tell the twins apart... sort of. Tina was the one that carried the staff, and she knew how to use it well. That morning, she took down a buck with a single swing, killing it instantly. I was still gawking at her ability to walk right up to it without as much as startling it. The buck simply turned its head to follow her as it continued to chew the grass that it was eating, right up to the point where she bashed its skull in with a single swing. After the buck died, Tina bent over it and gave a quiet prayer of thanks for its sacrifice.

Serena, the other twin, was the one with the sword. She kept it hidden most of the time, so I usually relied on the absence of the staff. Every once in a while, her hands would inch towards her empty scabbards. It was like an itch that she couldn't scratch at the absence of her own swords. The borrowed sword hung loosely from her belt, tucked under her cloak with only the tip hanging below its edge. I hadn't seen her use it on the trip to the city, but from her stance and the two long, empty scabbards at her side, I figured she was as deadly with it as her sister was with her staff.

We took a few minutes to cook the deer meat, wrapping some of it in the skins for later smoking. As the meat cooked, the twins had drifted off to the side. They seemed lost in thought as they looked to the northwest. Clearly, it was something private that I wasn't allowed to know about. Once our meal was cooked enough, Heather packed up everything in her pack. It was the only pack we had left. The twins worked to clean up the fire, making sure the fire was completely out before leaving our little impromptu campsite. We ate our breakfast as we continued towards The Capital.

It had been a long time since having a proper meal, at least on Desparia. My snares from the previous night were long forgotten, lost in the territory claimed by the nightmare. It was still weird for me, needing to eat in this world that was supposed to be just in my head. I just went with it, a habit I had often taken when my daydreams didn't go exactly as I planned them. From the way the twins were eating, it seemed like the troopers hadn't been feeding their prisoners. They seemed hungrier than I was. Tina even dipped into some of the raw meat once her own portion had been expended.

We traveled mostly in silence, other than the sounds of chewing. After the shadow attack, none of us was tired, despite not having slept the night before. It was decided that we'd continue onward all the way to The Capital that day. We'd need to wait out of sight of the guards for nightfall anyway, as the plan was to slip in under the cover of darkness. We figured it would be better to sleep there than anywhere near the nightmare behind us. Any thoughts we had of planning for the road ahead were quickly forgotten, in light of the shadow's attack.

The sun was just reaching its zenith when we came within sight of The Capital. Even before The Citadel was built right next to it, The Capital had always been a city of splendor. Its tall towers, while never getting close to the skyscrapers back home, were still grand considering the level of technology available. The city walls swept a large swath through the countryside. They were dwarfed only by those of The Citadel itself. The two neighboring walls overlapped in places, but mostly ran separately.

The Citadel had been there since before I started coming to this world. I had always avoided the area, so that was the first time I came there. When I first noticed The Capital, I missed a step, stumbling a bit in surprise. Even though its cityscape was still distant on the horizon to the north, I was overtaken by its beauty. I had heard stories of the city, but seeing it was so much more. Every building was accented in gold, glittering in the distance. It was an irresistible bait to my thieving senses. My pace quickly increased as I was subconsciously drawn towards the sight.

"Hey, wait up," one of the twins said behind me. My attention was too wrapped up in the sight of the city to look behind me and see which.

"Uh oh," Heather said. Her breathing picked up as she sprinted to get ahead of me. "I think she's been gold touched."

This brought me up short, snapping me out of it easier than most who had been similarly affected by their first sight of the city. There had been rumors of people, mostly thieves, who had walked straight into the city, still gawking at the grandeur, right into the waiting arms, and swords, of the city guards. Some stories even told of a few of them managing to get past the guards, only to attempt to peel the gold off the buildings with their bare hands.

"Wow," I said. I shook my head forcefully, trying to clear it. "That was a much stronger compulsion than I was expecting."

Heather came around me, looking deep into my eyes as if trying to find something. "Huh," she said. "I think I can actually see the effect fading in your eyes."

"What?" I asked, surprised. That took me a bit by surprise, that magic would be able to work on my mind so completely. I wondered briefly how something that was supposed to be just in my head would affect me. But then perhaps it being in my head was the whole reason why my mind would be hit so hard by the enchantment.

"Oh, yea. Gold touch was a spell the emperor put in place. All the buildings are enspelled with it. Why do you think he chose this city for the location of his citadel?"

"Hadn't this always been the capital of Fandor?" I asked.

"Well, sure, but he could have built anywhere. The ancient riches of this city were too much even for him to resist. Rumor has it, he was gold touched himself when he first saw the city, back when the term was less literal. In his embarrassment, he cast the spell, making the effect that much more powerful. He liked his work so much that he built The Citadel on the mountain next to the city right after that. In the process, he took the gold mines for himself."

Talk of The Citadel reminded me that it should be in sight as well. In the distances, its towering walls looked like nothing but a backdrop to the glorious sight of The Capital. The Citadel's walls flowed, uninterrupted, unchanging, constantly gray, to the cloud cover of a similar color. It is said that, since the emperor moved into the region, The Capital has not had a single day of sunshine. Even on that day, with the sun shining over the majority of the countryside, there was a large storm cloud brewing over the entire mountain.

"Come on," Serena said, interrupting the history lesson. "There's a small copse of trees over there that should give us some added protection from the view of the city guards. I feel naked out here." She looked around her at the wide open plain we had been walking through since leaving the forest, occasionally giving a shudder.

With a nod and a shrug, I followed behind Serena. Heather and Tina ran ahead to walk side by side with her, their hands clasped together in what seemed like something of a ritual for them. Despite the mood of the day and the seriousness of the task ahead of us, they started to laugh before making a mad dash to the trees. Watching them run as they did, it reminded me that these three girls were probably as young as I was. And yet, they had taken on a responsibility far beyond their years. It warmed my heart to see them enjoying the youth that they had been missing out on.

The copse of trees was more like one large tree with a few bushes surrounding it. The central tree was some form of evergreen. Its bows hung low, a natural ceiling for a nice little cubby. Under the tree we had enough room to stand up, but little more. The ground was covered in a thick layer of needles that looked too comfortable for me to resist. The three days without sleep soon overcame me and I collapsed into unconsciousness, into the first real sleep that I had had on Desparia.

Five seconds later, someone shook me. "Go away, Mom," I said, only half awake. "I don't want to go to school today."

"Maya, it's time to wake up. We're heading into the city now."

"What?" I asked. I stared up at Heather kneeling over me. "The city? Oh, right." I lay back down and almost got back to sleep before Heather started shaking me again. "Right, right. Wake up. I'm awake."

"Did you know that you snored?" Tina asked. She was leaning against her staff. It was holding up the canopy to open a doorway large enough to get through without ducking. "Really loudly, too. It was almost impossible for any of us to get any sleep."

"Sorry," I said. I wiped away the crust that had collected on my chin from the dried drool. Waking up on Desparia was an odd sensation. I wondered briefly if I would ever get used to needing to sleep in both worlds. It helped that I had also been sleeping away back on Earth, passing my lazy weekend time in my usual fashion, between daydreaming and regular dreaming.

"Don't be," Heather said, shaking it off. "It helped some of us stay awake on watch." She glared off into the distance where Serena could be seen on the other side of the ring of bushes.

"Huh?" I asked. I didn't get any further explanations.

Stumbling through the doorway the staff had opened, I followed Heather and Tina out into the night. I looked around, surprised by the change. The sky had gone completely dark. The clouds that hung over The Capital blocked out all the stars. There was a pile of brush off to the side that was still giving off a thick stream of smoke. Serena was standing near it, packing away what was left of the deer meat, now properly smoked into jerky that would last us for days.

"Wow, how long was I out?" I asked. I stood there for a moment, stretching and yawning myself awake.

"Eight hours," Serena said, pointing towards the night sky. "Some of us actually had to stand watch."

"Sorry. It was a while since I managed to sleep last."

"Yes, yes. It's not like the troopers let us sleep either."

"You had hoods on and were in a carriage. How could they tell?"

"They were constantly banging on the bars as we went."

"Guys, can we do this later?" Heather asked. "We still have an hour of walking to do before getting to The Capital gates. At the very least, let's walk while you argue about who is more tired."

"At least we know who's the least tired among us," Tina said under her breath, as she took point. Heather rolled her eyes as she took her usual position in the middle of the group next to me.

The rest of the walk to The Capital was rather uneventful. The twins were more concerned with making sure that the coast was clear than continuing the earlier argument. The moon came up in the east soon after we left the tree. Its light cast our shadows out in front of us before it slipped behind the cloud cover above. It made me uneasy, a constant reminder of the attack from that morning. The Citadel walls off in the distance weren't much better. As we got closer to our goal, they seemed to tower over us even more. They looked all the more formidable. All the more unwelcoming. It was almost as if they knew we were coming to kill their master.

The city gates were firmly sealed by the time we came to them. A long line of torches bordered the road on both sides for the last tenth of a mile up to the gates, bathing the approach in light. There were four guards standing watch outside the gate, two on either side, with several others walking the walls above them. All of the guards were in full metal armor and carried long lances, large rectangular metal shields, and sheathed swords at their side. Even without the extensive training that I knew they had on a daily basis, they already appeared formidable enough to give even the best swordsman in the world pause. None of us came close to that description.

"So, what's the plan to get us in?" I asked. The group ground to a halt on the other side of a large boulder in front of the gates. It was the only cover from the guards in the area.

"That's what you're here for," Tina said, slapping me on the shoulder. "You're our escape artist and infiltration expert. Any ideas?"

I turned around to look at the three of them. They were all staring at me, expectant looks on their faces. "Are you seriously expecting me to get all of us in there?" I asked, pointing over my shoulder. "If you guys had told me sooner that I would be in charge of getting us into the city, I would have told you to go shove it where the sun don't shine... Well, okay maybe not. I would have at least planned it so that we could get in while the gates were still open."

"We were trying to avoid trooper involvement, remember?" Heather pointed out.

"And we could have managed that with disguises and stuff," I said. I turned around, looking back at the high walls of the city. "It's not like they would have recognized us if they had spotted us coming into town anyway."

"They would have recognized us," Heather said. "We're wanted women. Aren't you?"

"No," I said quietly. Her words took on a different connotation for me. I thought that not being wanted was exactly my problem and why I had come to Desparia in the first place.

The city walls easily reached three stories, with no signs of dropping lower. Their hard granite stones did not bode well for easy entry of any form. There weren't any trees or outcroppings anywhere near the walls that would have given us a leg up. I shook my head and turned back around to look at my companions. My mouth was half open, about to state how hopeless slipping in unnoticed that night seemed to be, when three things seemed to happen at once.

The night, which had seemed to be dead silent up until then, somehow seemed to get even quieter. It was as if a humming, so low and so constant that I hadn't noticed it was there, suddenly ended.

The gates behind us creaked open, seeming to be done on their own and certainly taking the guards by surprise.

And an eerily familiar growling sound came towards us over the plains.

Chapter Twenty-Two
The Only Friend Left to Me

Five Years Earlier

By the end of September, I was thoroughly miserable. I was too scared of the shadow monster that had attacked me to try going back to Desparia just yet. I was too afraid that I'd accidentally go there if I tried to daydream at all. So, I was stuck in reality for the entire month, with nothing but a few well-worn books to keep me company. And the thing about reality when you don't have friends is...

"Reality sucks," I said, as I came down to breakfast on the last Saturday of September.

"Wait another decade and it'll start to suck a whole lot more," Mom said, as she put a plate of eggs in front of me. "I know you're lonely since your father... but maybe you can try to make some new friends or something. Ashley and Jen aren't the only girls in your class, are they?"

"Mom, the whole school is still ignoring me. It's kind of hard to make friends when no one will give you the time of day."

"That's why you have your cookie watch, isn't it? Speaking of, where is it?"

"Shoot, I keep forgetting that thing."

"Well, there are other people outside of school, too," Mom put in. "When was the last time you visited Mrs. Azalea? You used to love going over there."

"David banished me back in August," I reminded her. "That's what started this whole thing, or at least this part of it."

"Well, you just have to rise above it," she said. "Go see her in the hospital. If she kicks you out, then fine. But if she doesn't, you still have a friend. Either way, you still have me. You're not getting rid of me that easily."

"She's not in the hospital," I said. I ignored her little comment about not losing her, remembering a similar promise from Dad. "They moved her to hospice a few weeks ago." It was another reason why I hadn't gone to visit her. I didn't want to get attached to her again only to lose her like...

"Well, all the more reason to go then. Even if she's not a friend to you anymore, you're still one to her. I'm sure she'd still like to see you. I'll drive you over there after breakfast."

I nodded as I focused on the food in front of me. I didn't like the prospect of bringing Mrs. Azalea back into my life so close to her leaving it permanently. But Mom seemed adamant about it and I couldn't come up with an excuse not to. Besides, maybe if I could get back in with Mrs. Azalea, she'd guilt David into backing down on everyone ignoring me at school. Or, maybe, at least he might be my friend again.

It had seemed like that was his intent at the funeral, though I was too upset about losing my father to hear it. I figured it would be easier if he wasn't there when I went. But I knew there wasn't anything that I could do about that. While she was at the hospital, he didn't seem to leave her side except when visiting hours ended. But with school in full swing, it could go either way.

With my mind racing through all the possibilities, I didn't realize I had finished my breakfast until my fork couldn't find any food. Still, I stared at my empty plate for a few minutes, not sure what to do. When Mom took the plate away, my mind started to unfreeze, and I got ready to go out.

The hospice was just up the road from the hospital. Though I hadn't been there before that day, I had gone past it too many times to count. I was in a fog while Mom led the way up to Mrs. Azalea's room, showing more familiarity with the way than I would have expected. It wasn't until we came into her room that I realized why.

"Hey, Paige," Mrs. Azalea said, as we entered. Then, when she noticed me next to her, her eyes lit up and she looked happier than I remembered ever seeing her. "Been a long-time Maya. Where the hell have you been?"

"Um... I..." I started. I wasn't sure what to say to her. If I should admit the truth and throw her own son under the bus or take responsibility. But my voice failed me all together when I saw her face. The paleness that had settled in since the last time I saw her. The frailty in her limbs that betrayed just how close she was to death.

"Apparently, your son banished her," Mom explained. She took the empty seat next to the bed. I nodded my agreement, not wanting to keep my own secrets, knowing how I felt about others keeping them from me. Mrs. Azalea seemed shocked by the accusation, but for some reason I couldn't look her in the eye. Instead, I looked all around the room, taking in what would probably be the last room that she ever saw.

The room was smaller than the one that she had at the hospital, with barely enough space for the one chair. David's book bag sat in the corner, which meant he was probably in the building somewhere. There wasn't much else to it, with barely enough room for me to stand in. Machines beeped and hissed as they monitored her, taking up more room than I felt was necessary. The only place I could find that didn't feel claustrophobic was a small corner across from the door. I was standing right next to David's bag and I'd be visible the moment that he came back into the room. I still felt like a caged animal, trapped, about to be caught doing the one thing he didn't want me to do.

"Maya, come over here and sit by me," Mrs. Azalea said. She patted a small space next to her on the bed. "Paige, mind giving us some time?"

"Of course, Greta," Mom said. She nodded as she ducked back out into the hall. I stared after her, pleading silently as she closed the door.

"Come on, Maya," she said again, patting her bed. "I won't bite. I just want to talk, to perhaps explain a few things about my Davie."

"O... kay...," I said reluctantly, edging closer to her. I sat on the bed, but closer to her feet than she had indicated. There was more room there.

"You have to understand; Davie has known I was going to die for almost a year now. To be fair, the doctors only gave me three months. As it is, I'll be lucky to see Halloween. It hasn't set well with him, but I thought he was getting better with you joining him on his visits. It was like you were sharing the burden that he never should have had to bear. He's gotten much worse since you stopped coming."

"But then why?" I asked.

"Well, if I had to guess, it had something to do with his friends coming by. They visited soon after you left the night before your last visit. I think they said something to him that made him feel uncomfortable. That discomfort must have been targeted at you. I'd never seen him so miserable. I think it was just a little too much for him. But, well, it's not like he really tells me anything that's happening in his life. He doesn't want to upset me."

"Secrets," I said, shaking my head. "The plague of my life."

"Secrets aren't all bad; it's how you use them that counts. I wish I could have kept my illness from him. I had when I first found out about it. I wanted to keep him from worrying when he didn't need to be. We first told him when I first went into the hospital. But he's just been so amazing since then. I almost feel bad about keeping it from him for so long. Like I could have spent more time with him if I hadn't been too afraid to let him know. I don't know. I guess I'm a bit ambivalent about the whole thing. Waiting to tell him kept him safe but cost me some time with him, which would have been so precious. You'll understand when you're a parent. But all I really want is for him to be happy. I think you could help with that, but..."

"What's she doing here?" David asked as the door swung wide. He stared daggers at me, as if he were enraged at my audacity to visit his dying mother.

Mom looked startled behind him, staring past him towards me. It was like she didn't know if it was her place to chastise the boy whose mother was about to die. Slowly, I got up from the bed, walking around it towards my ex-friend. "I'm here visiting your mom," I explained. "I missed talking with her, and I won't have many chances to do that anymore."

His ire quickly faded with the reminder of his mother's pending demise. Barely sparing me another glance, he walked around the chair with practiced steps. He sat down and took his mother's hand, almost automatically. His gaze flicked between the machines before settling on Mrs. Azalea's face. "I'm sorry it took me so long," he said in a low voice. It was like he was afraid to wake the dead. Considering where we were, he wasn't too far off.

"Come here," Mrs. Azalea said, looking to me and holding out her free hand to take mine. Eyeing David cautiously, I moved forward, placing my hand in hers as I knelt beside the bed. I seemed to find enough space wedged between the bed and the wall, right next to the machine that was beeping in my ear and across from David, who still darted scathing glances my way. "Now, I don't know what really happened between the two of you--"

"I'd like to know that as well," I interrupted.

"Then don't interrupt me," Mrs. Azalea scolded.

"Sorry," I mumbled.

"Now, as I was saying, I don't know what happened between the two of you, but I'd hate to see it get in the way of your friendship. You both have already been through so much. Too much for your young age. That's going to set you apart from the rest of your class. You should rely on each other to get through these next few months. They'll be some of the hardest of your lives.

"Why don't the two of you head out into the hall and just figure out whatever needs to get figured out. I need to get some rest now."

I gave a half smile as I nodded, thinking over what she was saying. Of course, she knew that my father had recently died, and that she would too soon enough. That would put David and I in a very small group indeed. I looked over at David and nodded towards the still open door to the hall. Mom wasn't out there anymore, but I figured she hadn't gone far, perhaps to give us some space to be alone.

"Look, I'm sorry about everything," David said, after closing the door to his mom's room.

"What exactly happened?" I asked. "What did I do? People at school were saying I was stalking you."

"That's because that's what I told them," he admitted. "I never felt like that. It was just..."

"Just what?" I asked. "Not wanting to be friends with a girl?"

"Actually, yeah," he said.

This surprised the hell out of me and took away quite a lot of my bluster. "Wait, what?"

"Sam saw you leaving the floor in the hospital and was teasing me about you being my girlfriend. I got defensive about it and I just blurted it out. I'm sorry."

"Why didn't you tell me that?" I asked. "I hate secrets. We could have figured something out before I became an outcast at school."

"Like what?" he asked. "Once I told Sam that you were stalking me, he told everyone. That guy can't keep a secret if his life depended on it."

"Then we'd get along perfectly, if things weren't the way they are," I said. "Why didn't he tell me though? Why didn't anyone tell me?"

"He probably thought you knew that you were stalking me," he explained. "I don't know why no one else said anything, though. Maybe you should be yelling at your ex-friends."

"You mean my other ex-friends?"

"I never stopped being your friend," he said. "I just... I didn't know how to be your friend without people knowing about it. Without it getting all crazy."

"You could just admit that you lied," I suggested. "Take it back so people will stop ignoring me."

"That won't help," he said. "It'll just make them hate me too. Besides, after the food fight, that new girl, Janis, has been gunning for you. It was only the stigma over your father's death that kept you safe so far. That'll only last so long. Then she'll be trying to make your life miserable, and anyone else that stands with you."

"And, what? You're afraid to stand up to some bully? Some girl? You can't be friends with one, but you can back down from one?"

"Have you seen that girl?" he asked. "I think the whole school is afraid of her."

"Fine," I said. "Be afraid. Don't come crying to me about it. I'm done being afraid."

With a quick glance towards Mrs. Azalea's closed door, I headed down the hall, looking for Mom. I knew what I'd have to do. It was the one thing that would change everything in my life back to the way it was. Back to the way it was supposed to be. I didn't need to stand up to Janis, that was something David had to do for himself. I had already done that the day of the food fight, the day my father died. If she came after me again, I'd be able to handle it. Nothing she could do to me would compare to me losing him.

No. What I needed to do was stand up to my shadow monster, the embodiment of my loss.

I needed to go back to Desparia.

Chapter Twenty-Three
The Capital

Now

"Run," I yelled. I made a mad dash towards the city gate. The entire way, I darted looks over my shoulder towards my companions, making sure that they were still with me. The twins stood there for a few seconds, looking between the open gates and off towards the wilderness, as if they weren't sure which way to run towards. Heather, on the other hand, was hot on my tail the whole way.

The guards were still scratching their heads about the gates opening on their own. They were too busy with their own concerns to stop us from entering. If the situation weren't so dire, I'd probably be laughing at their confusion. All four of them were on the inside of the doors, trying to pull them closed. I could just see the guards on the wall trying to push on something together. Whatever it was didn't seem to be budging.

"Come on," Heather shouted, as we crossed the threshold into the city. Her call seemed to snap the twins out of their thoughts and they both turned in unison to run towards us.

The shadow could be seen in the distance as an oddly shaped blob flowing in and out of the moonlight. It crossed the road several times as if to show us that it no longer held any sway on it. In the distance, the section of land where the cloud cover hid the moon from sight carved a solid, very noticeable line about half a mile out from the gate. When the shadow got to that line, it dropped out of sight, absorbed by the darkness around it. I had no doubt that it still stalked forward, though we had no further indication of its progress towards us.

Heather and I waited just inside the city gates as the twins ran. Heather started to form a spell in her hands, but as she looked out at the plains beyond, she held the spell. Only after the twins came inside the gates did she throw it. Fire arched out in the space in front of us, obliterating the line of torches and lighting the grass around the road on fire. But the shadow continued on, seeming unperturbed by the fires in front of it.

The guards continued to press against the gates. Their grunts of efforts seemed to echo around the close quarters under the tall city walls. On the other side, the gateway opened up into the city proper beyond. Despite the late hour, there were people walking past us. Some of them seemed to be heading home, but far more were out for a night on the town. None of them seemed to be expecting the shadow charging their way. And if the road outside the city no longer had any sway over it, I doubted a half-open gate would slow it down.

Tina seemed to be of a similar mindset to me. She was staring around at the innocent people heading past, darting glances back at the shadow as it stormed forward. In the distance, the blaze that Heather had set to the grass was slowly turning into darkness. I couldn't tell if it came back on once the shadow had passed. It seemed that our own lights were about to be snuffed out just as easily.

"What do we do?" Tina asked.

"It doesn't look like the road has any sway over that thing anymore," I said. "It's going to come straight at us."

"A wall spell," Heather said. "It's undead, so a holy wall of light would be better than fire. Tina, that's you. Just picture a wall forming across the doorway as you pray."

"Everyone, hold on," Tina said, as she pulled her staff off of her back. She slammed the butt of it into a crack in the cobblestone of the road, pushing it deeper to the dirt beneath it. As she did so, she closed her eyes. Silent words of prayer passed through her lips as I felt the buildup of magic flowing off of her. While she didn't seem to be casting a spell, that seemed to be the effect that her prayer was having.

The shadow came right at us, a stalking predator ready to leap at its prey. It reached out a long tendril towards us. It was significantly darker than the rest of its form, seeming almost to resonate darkness from it. As the tendril snapped at us, I ducked reflexively, hiding my face behind my arms. Just before the tendril hit us, I felt the spell flow out, covering the area. After a few seconds, I realized that I wasn't dead and risked a peek.

The shadow was still coming towards us, more slowly and without any reaching appendages. As it came right up to the door, it seemed to bump into something. The darkness spread out around some form of an invisible wall that ran between the wide-open doors. The guards beside us let out a relieved gasp at this, one that Heather and Serena echoed soon after. I was too intent on the look on Tina's face to feel much relief. She was no longer praying. Instead, she was staring daggers out at the shadow attacking her. The strain it was taking on her was clear on her face. The wall seemed to be keeping the shadow out. The only question is for how long.

"Okay, we need to do something," I said. I was looking between the shadow and Tina. The shadow was stretching upward, trying to reach around the barrier.

"Like what?" one of the guards asked.

"Like... I don't know. What kills a shadow?" I asked.

Seconds after saying that, there was a flash of light coming from the top of the wall. One of the guards up there had thrown something into the shadow. Whatever it was, it disappeared as soon as it entered the monster. Moments after, I could hear shattering glass as the object smashed into the ground. The shadow didn't show any sign of noticing whatever it was as it continued to assault the magical barricade.

"Well, that didn't work. Anyone else have any bright ideas?" I asked, then quickly cringed at the accidental pun.

The shadow didn't seem to like my word play either. It backed up a step... or, you know, whatever it is shadows do when traveling... A glide? Anyway, it stood there, swaying slowly back and forth. A few beads of sweat slowly slid down Tina's face as she relaxed a bit. She mumbled a few more words of prayer and exerted another wave of magic. The barrier briefly lit up in a wave, starting at the center and moving outward. Gradually, as she forced more of her goddess's power into the wall, it started to glow white, lighting up the area better than the torches behind us.

The eight of us, the four guards, my three companions, and myself, stood there, staring at the darkness that was before us. We were each trying to come up with something that would not only stop it from entering the city but cause it to at least give up on the attempts. Or, better yet, to kill it altogether. Heather would occasionally send out another blast of her fire, destroying everything outside of the wall other than the shadow. Meanwhile, the shadow seemed to almost dance, just on the other side of the barrier, neither leaving nor attacking again. A minute that felt like hours passed with neither side making much headway.

And then, the unthinkable happened. Someone actually stepped out of the shadow, as if walking out of a thick fog. The shadow didn't seem to be any less tangible or any smaller in any way. Yet this person, this man, seemed to be almost of the shadow. His eyes were cloudy, dark, and looked around as if trying to see.

"Tina?" he asked. "Serena? Is that really you?"

"P-Papa?" Tina asked.

The hand on her staff seemed to slacken a little, her concentration dipping. The barrier lost some of its light, but I could still see it there. Serena looked pale. Her mouth didn't seem to function at all as it opened and closed around words that refused to come.

"What happened?" Tina asked. "Serena told me you died. You told me he died." She turned around to stare daggers at her sister.

"Uh, guys," I said, as I saw the shadow take a step closer. The specter stepped forward with it, the two coming together as a unit to approach the barrier once more. And with Tina distracted, the barrier was slowly losing its power. It would stand no chance against another barrage from the monster.

"H-he did die," Serena finally managed to get out. "I saw him die. I saw the troopers kill him. I touched his cold body. He... he can't be here."

Heather darted a quick glance towards Serena before stepping forward to stand next to Tina. She placed her hands on Tina's, where they held the staff. The connection to her friend seemed to lend her strength. Heather whispered a few words, too low for me to hear. At first, I thought that she was offering Tina some comfort. But then I felt another blast of magic flowing off the girls. It wasn't as powerful as the one coming from Tina. But I saw a flash of red play out across the surface of the barrier. Together, they seemed to turn the magical wall a strange shade of pink.

"How can he be dead?" Tina asked. Her voice sounded hopeful, as she stared out at the phantom of her father. The barrier seemed to slowly shift from the pink color to a more fiery shade of red as Tina's attention was slowly diverted to her father. "He's right there. You must have seen someone else. The troopers must have killed someone else. He's alive. We need to save Papa. I need to..."

"No," Heather shouted. Tina's hands were slackening, but Heather's held them in place on the wood. "We can't drop the barrier. The shadow will get in. It's too fast."

"But it's Papa," Tina said. She was clearly torn between keeping the shadow away from us and getting her father to the safety of the city. But that was exactly what the shadow wanted. It continued to stalk its way forward, in lock step with the specter.

"Uh, guys," I said again, trying to draw their attention to the looming threat of the shadow.

"It's not Papa," Serena insisted. She held her arms around Tina, hugging her close. In the process, Tina's left hand came off the staff, and the barrier flashed to a much more solid red color.

"Guys!" I shouted, finally managing to get the attention of the group.

"What?" Heather asked.

She focused all of her attention on the barrier in front of her, causing another flash of red to play out across its surface. But I could already see the strain on her. Even without the shadow attacking the barrier, she wouldn't be able to keep it up for long.

"It's trying to distract us so that it can get through the barrier," I said. "Whether or not that is your father is irrelevant. If that barrier falls, we're dead. We're all dead."

I looked behind me, at the audience that had started to form. The people that had been wandering through the main street had heard the commotion near the gates and had come to see what was going on. An audience was forming at the other side of the gateway. No matter what world you're in, there's going to be people who just come to gawk. The barrier was the only thing keeping the shadow from ripping them all apart.

"The entire city is dead," I said in a whisper.

"It's not Papa," Serena said again. "He's dead. The troopers chopped off his head. His blood turned the road red for weeks. You saw that, Tina. You saw the blood."

"But I didn't see him," Tina squealed. "You wouldn't let me see him."

"I saw him enough for the both of us," Serena said.

"Oh, my little angels," the specter of their father said.

He had been standing next to the shadow the entire time, watching the anguish on the twins' faces. But then he started to walk forward alone. The shadow seemed to stare down at it, if such a thing were capable of doing so. Slowly, the specter placed his hands on the barrier. I looked over at Tina and Heather, expecting them to be struggling to keep the barrier up. The expression on Heather's face hadn't changed, and Tina seemed to have lost all control over the spell. Her other hand slipped free of the staff as the twins stepped forward towards their dead father. The barrier flickered for a moment once the connection was lost. The red color faded, dropping the barrier into the more transparent shade that it had when Tina had first created it. Still, Heather strained to keep the spell alive. That seemed to be all that she was capable of.

"I'm so sorry," the specter said again, drawing my attention. Silver tears started to flow freely down his cheeks as he looked at the twins with an undying love that could only belong to a parent looking at his children. "I'm so sorry you had to see that. That you both had to lose me and your mother. I didn't know... I couldn't know..."

The twins were shielding their faces, so neither would have to look upon the reminder that their parents were dead. Their sobs grew louder the more the specter spoke.

"I don't even remember the blow," the specter continued, as he knelt on the other side of the barrier. He pressed his face into it as if trying to come through it to comfort his children. While his efforts didn't seem to tax the barrier, they didn't get through it either. He reached out his arms to hug the wall instead. "If only I could hold you both just one more time," he said, in a voice that would break anyone's heart.

His voice turned to anger as he turned away from his children and towards the monster behind him. The same shadow that had seemed to spawn him.

"But, alas, that can never be. That will never be, as long as that thing still roams this earth." He swung his fists at it, shadow boxing as it were, when the weirdest thing happened... Well, I mean the whole thing was weird, but this was so much weirder. His blows were actually landing.

Roars emanated from the almost shapeless shadow as each punch landed on the insubstantial flesh. The nightmare backed up slowly as the blows continued unendingly. I looked back at the twins again and they were both staring at the specter of their father, hope plain on both of their faces.

"Keep the wall up," I said. "This could still be some kind of trick."

"It's not a trick," Serena whispered. The adoration was almost tangible in her voice. "Only Papa could fight like that."

The shadow continued to back away as the specter's blows blurred with speed. The roars got steadily louder as they slowly turned from sounds of pain to sounds of outrage. The specter seemed to lose a step, overbalancing into a punch. And then it was the shadow moving forward. I felt so helpless just standing there, watching this phantom fighting something that could kill me with a touch. Tendrils again flowed out from the nightmare, this time swinging at the specter. He dodged the first few but took a heavy blow to the side of his head. It knocked him off to the side and out of the way of the shadow's charge.

"Papa, get up," the twins cried together.

The specter shook his head, momentarily dazed, as the shadow passed by him. Before the nightmare could hammer into the barrier once again, the specter came up behind it and threw another punch into its back. This time, as the shadow fled from the blows, it got closer to the barrier, pressing up against it. The instant that the shadow touched the wall, Heather let out a scream of pain. She doubled over, using the staff to hold herself up. Worse, I could see the cracks forming in the barrier where it held off the shadow's bulk.

"Tina," I shouted, hoping she could pull herself together enough to re-enforce the spell.

The specter seemed to have noticed this as well. I could just see him as a darker shade through the bulk of shadow itself. He took several steps away from the shadow monster, giving it the ground that it would need to back away from the barrier. The shadow seemed to take advantage of this, coming forward with another barrage of blows. The specter dodged the blows before coming back with a counter. But he couldn't get around the shadow. He couldn't get position on it to press it away from his daughters.

Tina reluctantly tore herself away from the fight to stand next to Heather. She placed her hands on Heather's, much like Heather had done for her. I could see it when her power flared out through the spell, slamming the wall back in place with the full power of her goddess. It was a bright white, with no sign of Heather's red. Seconds later, the shadow slammed back into the wall. The force of it knocked Heather's hands from the staff, pushing her to the mud behind.

The specter resumed his beating of the shadow, though the shadow didn't seem to be any worse for the wear. The only thing that seemed to have any real impact to it was the barrier keeping it out of the city. Without that, it would sweep through, killing all of us where we stood. Yet, it showed that the shadow wasn't unbeatable. That it could be contained at least. This gave me an idea.

"Tina, can you somehow... invert the wall without dropping it?" I asked. "Make it a dome instead, but with the concave side outward from where it is now."

"Not with them right up against it," she said. "I can't... It's constantly straining my focus. And... Papa..."

"Papa," I yelled out to the spirit, not sure what else to call him. "Stop fighting for a second. Stand down."

The spirit looked towards me but didn't stop his onslaught. He then looked towards his daughters, who nodded their agreement. Closing his eyes, he fell back a step and the shadow capitalized on this. With a snarl, the shadow dove forward, swallowing the spirit where it stood.

"No!" the twins screamed, as they were forced to relive the loss of their father.

"Now!" I screamed at the same time. I wasn't sure that I would be heard over the cries of pain from the twins. But then Tina took up her staff in both hands again, swinging it over her head before slamming it home once more. The barrier glowed as it reshaped itself into a dome, trapping the shadow under it.

"Now what?" Tina screamed through the tears. I couldn't understand how she was still standing under that loss. But her pain seemed to only fuel her anger, her determination to make sure that the shadow suffered.

"Contract the dome," I suggested. "Crush it into the road."

Before Tina could do that, however, the shadow flowed into the road as if being soaked up in a large sponge. Once it disappeared, the road streaked darker into the distance. The fire that still burned in the field beyond slowly came back into view, though it faded soon after as the grass was consumed. The dome stood there, now empty. Tina was holding the spell in place, not quite knowing what happened.

As the low-grade humming returned to the road, the audience that had accumulated behind us started to cheer. "They did it," someone cried. "They destroyed the nightmare."

Chapter Twenty-Four
The Triumphant Return

Five Years Earlier

On the way back home from the hospice, I placed my forehead against the glass of the window, closed my eyes, and went back to Desparia. Given where I had left off, I was surprised, and very much disappointed, to find that the shadow creature was nowhere to be seen. I tried to picture it there, right in front of me, but it wouldn't come. I couldn't even remember what it looked like, besides a formless blob of darkness. Nothing else had changed from the last time I had been there. I was still lying on the side of the road. My head was inches away from the cobblestones. My bare feet were bleeding from the cuts they sustained from running on the rocks.

As I backtracked the path that I took from the woods, I found a splattering of blood in the grass where the second man had been eaten. It was still wet, proving that it had been at most minutes since I had been there last. But there was still no sign of the beast itself. No sign of the creature that had eaten the two men as if they were cocktail wieners on toothpicks. As the memories flooded back, I realized that it was probably a good thing that the creature was gone. As long as it wasn't just over the next hill, lying in wait for me so that it could eat me too.

I remembered the tower, on fire up the road and the destruction of it. But I couldn't remember which way it had been when I was last there. Which way it had stood before it toppled down behind the trees. I figured that would be the best place to head to. It was the reason why I had made up that world to begin with. The world, the tower, that was the best place to find my dad. Or, at least, a reasonable facsimile. An echo of the memory of him.

The only gauge that I had to work with was the road. I knew it was further up the road, with the field that I had first arrived in on my left. The sounds of horses had greeted me that day, which, to that world, had been mere minutes before. So, onward I walked, heading for where I thought the tower would be.

I kept off the road, sticking to the softer grass next to it. The stones hurt my bare, bloodied feet. I took my time, not wanting to step on any more hidden stones. Still, I favored my injured foot. The pain that I felt in it was more real than it should have for my daydreaming. The further I walked, though, the fainter the pain became, until I couldn't feel it anymore. I knew that my foot should still hurt, but it was as imaginary as the rest of the world was. My foot still left droplets of blood in the grass, despite the lessening of my pain.

The forest surrounded the road on both sides, making it hard to see anything that would have signified the presence of the tower. As I headed down the road, I started hearing something off in the distance. It was faint, something that you don't realize you're hearing until you're almost on top of it. A few steps after realizing what I was hearing, the forest dropped away on my left again. The area opened up into another field where the remains of the tower were still burning.

In front of the smoldering ruins, a girl was kneeling. She was so intent on the destroyed tower that she never noticed I was there. The sound I had been hearing was her crying. Her sobs filled the field that the tower had once stood in. The thing that hit me the most about that scene was the fact that the girl looked about the same age as me, perhaps a year or two older. Her hair looked brown where it glistened in the midday light. The fires burning so close to her lifted some of the strands in the air, accenting the curls that I thought belonged only to my mother and me. It was like the girl was some weird representation of myself, an echo of my inner child that was lost with my father. She cried over the ruins of the tower, which easily represented the ruins of my former life. It was the symbol of my father as lost to me as he was. Seeing that there was nothing left of the tower, that there was no sign of my father anywhere there beyond the ruin that his loss had placed in my life, I left the girl to her grief. I left the lingering echo to my grief and continued further down the road.

As I had gotten past her, her sobs faded into the distance. With the empty road as my only companion, my traveling suddenly became like a blur. The empty countryside flew past me as I zoomed towards the next town. As I went, the sun plummeted towards the horizon faster than I had ever seen it move, only to pop up in the east just as quickly. It circled overhead several times as I traveled down the road. I was starting to worry that my imagination was doing something to destroy the world that it had only just started to create. But I soon realized that I wasn't traveling faster than I should have been able to. The road wasn't actually whirling past me faster than my legs should allow. I was experiencing the time differently while nothing was happening. An important fact of traveling through most of these wide-open worlds was long stretches of open land. The days of uninterrupted travel were simply passing me by until I came upon my destination. Or, perhaps, something that would interrupt that travel.

It seemed like no time at all before I was coming up upon a large town. The sun settled in its fast progression through the sky directly overhead, showing that I arrived there at around noon. The sounds and smells of a bazaar assaulted my senses as I passed between a tall stone wall, directly into the town. The two guards standing there barely glanced at me except to note my bare feet, which had turned practically black in my travels. I knew that my first order of business would be to get some decent shoes. No matter how much I tried to imagine some on my feet, they never materialized. I had a feeling that there were several rules that I would need to get used to in that imaginary world of mine.

One good thing about only being there in my imagination was that I didn't have to worry about eating or drinking anything. At least, not in those days, back when such realities didn't plague my travels. The food around me all smelled so good and I hadn't eaten anything while I had been traveling. My stomach should have been rumbling up a storm. But other than a cursory interest in tasting the food, some of which looked really weird, I took little notice of it. Instead, I walked past all the food stalls, intent on my target, the general goods store at the far end of the main square.

The sign hanging down in front of the door showed a backpack and a sack of flour and read, in clear English "Gregor's General Goods". It probably should have seemed odd that the sign would be in English. However, I figured that since I made up the world to begin with, of course my unconscious mind would make everything in English. I didn't even think of the fact that I had yet to speak to anyone in that world, and that I might not be able to understand anyone. Instead, I walked into the store, the bell jingling as I opened the door.

"No shoes, no service," the merchant barked at me the moment I stepped inside. He pointed towards the door behind me.

"I'm here to buy shoes," I said.

"No, you're here to steal shoes," he countered. "Filthy street rat. Out with you." He picked up a broom and started chasing me out of the place as if I were a literal rat living in the streets.

"How rude," I huffed, as the man slammed the door in my face.

"Well, welcome to Vernala," someone said behind me. His voice instantly claimed my attention. I looked up at his smiling face as he stared down at me. "You'll need a beggar's license if you expect to get anything for free. Or you can try for a different kind of license." He winked down at me.

"We're home," Mom said, pulling me out of my daydream.

Stunned, I looked around to find us parked in front of the house. The engine was already off and Mom was staring over at me. Her face was a mix of concern and confusion as I continued to sit there, seeming to be deep in thought.

"Oh," I said, as I came to. "Right. Thanks... for driving me to see Mrs. Azalea. I needed that."

"Anytime sweetie."

Chapter Twenty-Five
The First Door

Now

I don't know what I would do without Mom, if I had lost her too. I probably would never come out of my daydreams. Never leave my wonderful, strange world behind. But what would happen to me then?

Mom placed my dinner in front of me. As she sat across the table, still wearing her scrubs from work, she just focused on her own food. I had a twinge of guilt when I realized that she figured she wouldn't be able to get much out of me. Had she completely given up?

#

The twins collapsed into each other's arms. The shield spell disappeared the moment that Tina's hands left the staff. The staff stood there on its own, embedded in the road where it had stood. The guards were clapping each other on the back, as if their presence made all the difference in the world. The crowd behind us was cheering louder than ever.

I just felt empty as my adrenaline faded. The supposed victory over the shadow had drained me of fervor. I should have felt... victorious... proud... successful... strong... or, at the very least, relieved. Instead, I felt like we had lost somehow and that we just didn't know it yet.

"Come on," Heather said, in a hoarse whisper. She looked down at the twins next to her. After clearing her throat, she tried again. "We need to head to the first door. Let's kill that bastard emperor before he can do this to more families."

Her eyes darted towards the guards near us, and the crowd behind. Their cheers had fortunately drowned out her words, so that it was just the four of us that had heard them. I wasn't sure how the crowd would have reacted to discovering that we were there to kill the emperor, but I wasn't expecting a ticker tape parade and an escort to the front door.

The crowd had seemed to dip into another round of cheers for the supposed demise of the shadow. Several members of the crowd flowed into the gateway, pulling Heather and the twins onward into the city. They tried to grab me as well, but I managed to slink out of their reach, slipping towards the back of the group. I wasn't sure where the crowd was bringing us, but I figured that anywhere was better than the gateway. What with the shadow monster still out there, somewhere, and likely to return despite the celebration.

Every few blocks, a fresh cheer of "they killed the nightmare" sounded out. The shout was followed by a round of cheers. People seemed to join the crowd from all over. Some spilled out of the passing doorways, still carried boxes and bags, obviously returning from the market. A few cheered the crowd on with overflowing mugs of mead and beer. I lagged behind as much as possible, not wanting to get blocked in by the newcomers. In the process, I quickly lost track of Heather and the twins.

As we went further into the town, the low-grade humming flowed through the roads. It was the same hum that I had only started to notice when it suddenly turned off before the nightmare struck. It seemed to grow into a steady crescendo, stronger, and even louder, than any enchantment I had ever felt, including the one around my wrist. Also, the buildings around us got steadily taller. I wasn't sure if those two facts were related.

Ahead of me, another round of cheers struck out. The crowd started to part, flowing outward towards the sides. It was only then that I noticed that we had gotten to the back wall of the city. The tall walls of The Citadel, which had always looked like nothing but a gray backdrop to the cityscape around us, were suddenly right there, their impenetrable heights teasing those foolish enough to try to enter them. And yet, that was exactly why we were there.

As the crowd parted and let me enter the area, I realized that the crowd hadn't brought us to our destination. There was a large city square spreading out around the entrance to The Citadel. A fountain stood in the center, spitting water up into the air. It rained down into several levels of basins, the lowest of which was surrounded by a thick stone bench. The crowd had formed up around the edge of the square, leaving Heather and the twins near the fountain. And yet, they were all staring at the door in front of them.

As Heather stood there in front of the large set of metal doors, she stared at it with a pensive look. The twins stood to her side. While they still clung to each other, their typical composure had returned. Ornate carvings flowed across the front of the doors. Silver and gold were used to color the depicted scene. There were even gemstones embedded strategically where other colors were needed. Emeralds stuck out depicting green eyes and shirts, sapphires spread intermittently across the sky, representing the occasional break in the otherwise silver clouds. As the crowd parted like a curtain, revealing the artwork in its entirety, I stared at a strikingly familiar scene. I looked between the crowd around us, assembled on either side of the road and all along the wall as far as the eye could see, and the crowd depicted on the metal doors, similarly arranged.

"What could it mean?" Heather asked, as I approached them. She didn't seem to acknowledge my arrival as she stared at the carving.

"I'm not sure," I said, tentatively. "Had it always looked like that or did it change on our way here?"

"It had when I saw it last," Heather said. "Just not the coloring. The metals and gemstones. Those are all new. And watch." She pointed towards the door in front of us.

I stared at the picture as more gemstones started popping out before my eyes. I began to wonder where it was that they came from. If the emperor could somehow create gems of such extravagance out of nowhere with just his magic. If that were true, it would be no wonder why he became so powerful... and I suddenly had a renewed interest in getting through to The Citadel. Just thinking of the treasure room of a man that powerful made me drool.

"The picture itself, though," Heather said. "I think... I think it is the same. It's been a while." She looked over at the twins, who both shrugged.

"That scene looks exactly like the celebration around us," I said. "I guess in a city under constant cloud cover and the watchful eye of an emperor, celebrations like this aren't all that common."

"Maybe that was the solution to the first puzzle," suggested Heather.

"Huh," Tina said, thoughtfully. "I guess it was a good thing that the shadow came when he did."

"Probably," Serena reluctantly agreed. She let out a sniffle before continuing. "I just can't stop thinking about Papa. You don't think that was really him, do you? That's he's stuck in that thing somewhere?"

"Heather," I began in a whisper. "How do shadows kill?" When I saw the hurt and pain on the faces of the twins, I almost wished that I hadn't asked.

"No, it's not like that," Heather said. She sounded confident as she answered a different question. "That's not how they kill at all. They're more like vampires, draining their victims until they become one of them. That... well, I don't even know what that was back there. I don't know if it was really your Papa or some trick or something. All I know is that whatever it was, it wasn't the typical victim of a shadow attack."

"But we already knew that, didn't we?" Tina asked. She sounded almost hopeful. "I mean Papa wasn't killed by the shadow."

"No," Serena said between sobs. "He was beheaded by troopers. So were Moma and Toby." She looked up at the door after saying that, a fire in her suddenly rekindled. "And they'll all pay for that."

After she said that, one last gem popped out of the door. It was a large crystal that I would have thought was a diamond, except for the fact that it was as large as a doorknob. It appeared, not in accordance with the picture that the other gems had been coloring in, but right in the middle of the two doors, where a doorknob should be. Without hesitating, Serena stormed right up to the door and grabbed the crystal. After a few seconds of her trying to turn the knob, there was an audible clicking sound. The doors suddenly swung freely, opening into the first area, the first section that spread out between two of the ten walls of The Citadel.

Serena went through the door first, followed closely by Tina and Serena. I took up the rear, my head darting between the town behind us and the doors ahead. As I went through the doors, I had a rather odd thought. This was the first time I went to a town in this world without stealing anything. I glanced behind us towards the cheering crowd and wondered why I hadn't bothered to lift any of their purses as they had swarmed around me.

"I must be getting soft," I said to myself, shaking my head. "Then again, maybe subconsciously I just don't think I'll live to spend the money."

After going through the door, I almost thought we had somehow got turned around. We were on a street that looked exactly like the town we had just left. The streetlamps bordering the roads at regular intervals were all lit, though these were the only signs of people on that side of the wall. The tall towers that had been clustered around the first door were mirrored on the inside, straight down to the facet. I could even feel the same compelling sensation coming off the gilded siding. The only difference, at least as far as I could see, was the lack of an audience. The crowd, obviously, wasn't on this side of the first wall. There was no one here. If it weren't for the cheers still flowing through the still wide-open doors, the place would be dead silent.

I turned around to the doors and tried to close them, in part because I didn't like having that unknown behind me. That possible source of enemies that could just stroll, or, in the case of the shadow, glide, up to us while our backs were turned. Another part of me was curious to see how quiet it really was without those cheering peasants. I still felt like we didn't do anything to deserve the adulation.

"Uh, guys?" I said, as I put my entire weight on the still open doors. "A little help?"

"Woah," Heather said. "It looks like those doors are as stuck open as the gates were."

"Just leave it open," Serena said from down the road. She apparently had no intention of coming back to help with the doors. Or going back for any reason until after either she or the emperor was dead and buried. Tina was stuck between us and her sister, unsure of whose side to take in this.

After a moment of standing there, Tina shrugged as she joined her sister. After a couple of two-person pushes on one of the doors resulted in absolutely nothing, Heather shrugged and headed off after them. I kicked the door, resulting in more damage done to my foot than the door, before following at a limp.

Chapter Twenty-Six
A Strange Encounter

Five Years Earlier

Mom and I spent much of the rest of that Saturday together, playing some old board games and such. It had been the most time we had spent together since before I could remember, at least without Dad. Even during those times when Dad was off on a business trip, we would keep to our own spaces, only coming back together when he returned. But he wasn't going to be returning this time.

It felt weird, like something was missing. Plus, the entire time, she kept giving me odd looks. It was as if she expected me to fade off again like I had in the car. At the time, I figured that I would need to make sure to only dip into my imaginary world when no one was looking. Otherwise, I might find myself forced to explain it to a shrink.

It was long after dinner before I managed to get away to my room. Supposedly, it was to get ready for bed. But my real intent was to head back to that town. The man had called it Vernala. Not exactly the best of names for a town, but what did I expect from my imagination. I'd have to come up with some better names for these places in the future. Maybe I could spend those moments that I was stuck around other people making a list of names that I could use for the places and the people. As I thought of that, I wondered how exactly my mind would insert them into the world.

As I popped back to Desparia for the third time, I was surprised to find the same man staring down at me. I looked around, trying to figure out how much time had passed while I was gone. But the man didn't seem to think anything of my absence, or my sudden popping in and out of that world. Then, I remembered, this was all in my imagination. Of course, the world would just pick up where I last left off.

"I'm sorry, what?" I asked, forgetting what he had last said.

"Oh, come now," he said, waving off my confusion. "Everyone knows this town has the best thieves' guild in the world. There's something about you that makes me think you'd make an excellent thief."

I smiled as I looked up at the man. A thief? It's like one of my father's video games, an NPC asking me if I'd like to join the thieves' guild and gain the thief class. "I don't think so," I snickered. I tried to move around him, ducking beneath his outstretched arm as he tried to block my path.

"Oh, come now, child," he said, as he danced around me.

He flitted in and out of the crowd, passing through it like it wasn't there. He apologized several times as he accidentally bumped into half the people he passed. As I tried to avoid him, he managed to herd me into a blind alley out of the way of the foot traffic. He suddenly grabbed my hand and placed a large ring in it.

"You'd be amazed at what you can find if you look hard enough," he said.

The ruby set in the ring was as large as my thumb, dazzling me as it glittered in the light from the sun overhead. The ring itself was gold and shaped in the form of a dragon tangled around the wearer's finger, with the ruby clutched in its teeth like a meal too big for it to swallow whole. The craftsmanship was amazing, by either world's standards. I doubted it would have been possible at all besides the fact that I was imagining the whole thing.

"It's beautiful, isn't it," he said, as I stared at the ring.

"Who did this belong to?" I asked, half in a daze.

"I don't know," he admitted. "Someone back there had it around their finger, but it was already loose and would have fallen off anyway, had I not--"

"Thief," someone shouted from the crowd behind him. A tall man was looking over the crowd directly at us. My eyes went wide as he started to make his way through the crowd, heading for us.

"Quick, give it back," the thief ordered. He reached for the ring as his eyes darted all over, looking for a way out. He grabbed hold of the gem but for some reason I couldn't let go. My small hand was wrapped firmly around the ring.

"Thief," the tall man called again, as he made it past the last of the crowd and jumped at the thief. The thief lost his grip on the ring as the two of them tumbled to the ground. It took only a few moments for the tall man to grapple the thief into a position that I had seen often on cop dramas and movies. His face was in the dirt with his hands pinned behind his back. "Give me back my ring."

"I don't have your ring," he grunted through a face full of dirt.

"Oh, right, like I'd believe you. If you didn't take my ring, then who did?" The thief grunted in pain as the man pulled his arms.

"The girl."

My eyes felt like they were about to fall out as I backed up against the wall. I hit the brick wall before I had been expecting it, and the ring tumbled from my grasp. It fell to the dirt behind me with a slight tinkling. Shocked by the sudden sensation of pain, with the obvious absence of the pain itself, and quite literally backed into a corner, my hands went out in front of me, palms outward in surrender.

The tall man barely spared me a glance before turning back to the thief beneath him. "How dare you blame a poor street urchin for your crimes. You will return my ring this instant."

"But I don't have it," the thief grunted again.

With a sigh of disgust, the man started patting the thief down, looking for the ring. When he reached into one of the thief's pockets, a loud snapping sound emitted from it. This was followed by a loud yelp as the large man jumped away from the thief, clutching at his hand. A large device not unlike a rat trap was attached to the offended hand. Blood already started to drip from his fingers which were no longer straight.

I ran in fear, not looking back until I was outside the town once more. Only then did I remember that what I was seeing wasn't real. That none of it could affect me in any way. Everything I was seeing was just happening in my imagination. Once I managed to get my nerves in check, I was able to pull myself out of it. I dropped back to my bed in my room, staring up at the dark ceiling above.

My heart was still racing as I threw on my nightgown. While I was heading over to the bathroom to brush my teeth, Mom popped upstairs. She looked tired but almost happy with the time that we had been spending together that day. It took me a few moments to remember what had been happening in the real world before I had managed to escape to my own one.

"Is everything alright?" she asked, as she came over to me. "You've been rather quiet up here for the past hour or so. What have you been doing?"

This took me by surprise. I thought I had been screaming my lungs out for the past few minutes. More importantly, I didn't think I had been gone, lost in my world, for that long. It had felt like only minutes spent in that world. "'M fine," I muttered after a minute of thought. "Just tired. I've... been reading."

"Ah, right," she said, nodding. "I guess we both have our own ways of keeping your father close." She gave me a half smile as she walked around me, heading for her room at the far end of the hall.

"Right," I said to myself as I headed into the bathroom.

Chapter Twenty-Seven
The Empty City

Now

The empty city was eerily quiet. The crackling of the streetlamps' flames were the only sound beyond those we supplied. Our footsteps echoed off the tall walls of the towers, despite our best efforts to be silent. The further we went into the city, the more unnerving the emptiness became.

After a few blocks, the similarities to The Capital ended. Where the towers near the gate were mirror images of their neighbors on the other side of the wall, the ones further in started becoming larger, grander designs. Soon, the soaring buildings seemed like they would fit right at home among the tallest buildings back on Earth. Looking off into the distance, it seemed like they only got taller as the next wall came into view. I began to wonder if we would be seeing a similar city on the other side of that wall as well, with towers extending beyond the heights of the walls themselves. Perhaps we could get above the walls in the towers, somehow bypassing the doors altogether as we jumped from tower to wall and beyond. From what I could see of the buildings in that first section, however, that wasn't going to be an option.

The streetlamps continued on throughout the empty city. Their frequency was the only constant among the ever-changing forms of the buildings. The light they emitted was reflected off the gilt frames of the buildings, bouncing back off each and making the area as bright as day, though it was still early in the night. We had no trouble seeing our way as we traveled through. Our gazes were intent on our next target, the second wall plain as day ahead of us.

The wide-open doors of each of the passing towers called to me to explore their depths. After travelling through the last city without... acquiring anything, I felt the urge to explore in the hopes of finding some forgotten bauble or another. Surely a city this grand could not have remained empty for its entire existence. It made more sense that the boundaries of the original city had been too close to the mountain and the emperor had simply erected his last wall through the city, ignoring the ramifications to the people that lived there. However, as we traveled through the city, there was no sign of any bodies of people stuck within. No signs of trash of any kind that normally accumulated in such cities, whether or not they had been connected to the outside world. The empty city remained just that. Empty... of everything... Well, except buildings, buildings, and more buildings. That was, at least, until I saw something glittering off to the side.

Each building of this empty city was just as gilded as those in the city outside the wall. Even more so in some cases, as their walls became more intricate and demanded more gold to properly ornament them. At the base of one of the more elaborate buildings was a section of gold paneling that had seemed to fall off. It was lying on the ground, bent in an odd shape that reminded me of a Tetris piece. It was huge, longer than my leg and twice as wide, with a bend on the end that was half as long as the rest of it. As it lay there, it looked like an upside-down L.

With a quick glance at my traveling companions to make sure they hadn't left me behind, I took a quick detour over to the gold object. As big as it was, there was no way I would be able to carry it far. Or, at least, that's what I thought at first. I picked it up, doing my best to avoid the edges that could be sharper than they looked. It was light as a feather, hollow on the other side, and quite obviously enchanted. The only thing that would stop me from running off with it would be the general cumbersomeness of it.

"What did you find?" a voice behind me asked.

"Sweet Jesus," I said.

I dropped the paneling down, on my foot no less, to clutch at my chest in a vain attempt to stop my heart from running off on me. I turned around to see Heather standing near where I had cut off from the main road with a curious look plastered on her face.

"Don't ever sneak up on me like that."

"Wow," she said. "I startled our thief. I think we need a new one."

"Hey, don't look at me," I said. "I wasn't the one to choose her."

"Oh, ha ha. What is that?" she asked, again.

"I don't know. It looks like one of the gold panels off the building, but it's lighter than I would have imagined."

"Did you really think they would coat so many buildings in thick layers of gold? It's all papyrus thin, thinner in some places. If it weren't for the enchantments, someone could quite easily peel it off and run away with it."

"Well, this piece is enchanted, but it doesn't look like gold foil or anything. Look." I picked the piece back up, flipping it over to show the hollow underbelly. "Even with how hollow it is, it's lighter than it should be. Also, I may not be an expert in such things like you, but I'm pretty sure it's a different enchantment."

"Oh, I'm no expert," Heather said, shrugging off the compliment. "But... you're right. It is a different enchantment. It doesn't have the same draw as the gold on the buildings do"

"What is?" Tina asked, as she and Serena rejoined us. "Oh, one of those? I think I saw one of those up ahead a bit, but it was shaped differently. It looked more like a T than an L."

"There was a square back there a ways as well," Serena added, pointing back the way we came.

"Okay, this is weird. It's like someone was trying to play a real-world game of Tetris or something." This comment generated three looks of confusion. "Never mind. Let's just find a cart to carry them all in or something. They might come in handy later."

"Or you could sell them when we get out of here," Serena added.

"If we get out of here," I added. I looked around again at the tall walls that surrounded us. They loomed overhead, making me think getting inside their confines was going to be the easy part.

"Oh, please," Tina said, shaking off my fears. "The front door is probably still open. We just have to go back..." She paused, her finger up as if she had meant to point back the way we had come.

We all turned around in the direction we thought we had come. Each of us looked in a different direction. Each direction looked equally wrong. "Um, wasn't the road we were coming down a direct shot from the main doors that way?" I asked, pointing off in the direction down the road I had just stepped off of. That one seemed to go straight for a block before meeting an unexpected tower.

"Direct shot, yes," Heather agreed. "It's just that it was that direction." She pointed off down an alley across the street we had just been walking on, which ended three buildings over from us.

"Woah, this isn't good," Tina said, shaking her head.

"Like I said," I said, with a shrug. "We're all gonna die in here."

"We have enough food to last us a fortnight," Serena said. "Let's wait a week before worrying about dying, okay?"

"Right," Tina said, nodding. "Cart first, worry later."

I picked the L up again, slinging it over my shoulder. As we headed back down the road, I had a compelling feeling to start singing "Hi Ho". I was in a very retro mood that evening. We split up, Heather and I each looking for a cart to stick the Tetris pieces in while the twins headed off to find the ones that they had each spotted. It felt wrong to separate in the confusing city that may or may not be moving around to confuse us more, but I wasn't the leader of this gang. I wasn't used to following someone else's direction, but at least it let me focus on the more important matters. Like finding treasures worth taking.

A couple of blocks later, I found what looked like the remnants of an old market. There were wooden stands and storefronts that, though they looked old and rotten with age, seemed as sturdy as the day they were made. Off in one of the corners, behind one of the larger stands, was a large cart. It had a yolk where an animal would normally be attached to pull the cart, and a seat for the driver. Both of these were as empty as the rest of the city. I slammed my L into the back, half expecting the whole cart to fall apart in front of me. Instead, it just gave a resounding thunk.

I pulled on the yolk experimentally, figuring the whole rig would be too heavy for a lonely human to pull, but it moved smoothly enough. It was a struggle to turn it around corners, but it would work nicely for our needs. It took about ten minutes to get the cart out of the corner, with constant back and forth movements to get it around all of the obstructions. Really, I have no idea how the original owner got it in there to begin with. Once it was clear, I headed back down the street I had just come up. On my way out of the market square, the cart ran a little too close to one of the stalls, tipping it over. The stall fell with a loud thunk that echoed off the surrounding buildings. But there was no sign of any damage to the stall itself, besides the fact that it was now lying on its side. "Sorry," I whispered to whomever it was that originally owned the stall. Whoever that was, they were probably long dead.

A block after heading back down the road, a building that I was very sure wasn't there before suddenly was. Either these buildings were moving, or the roads were. I took a left, hoping I wouldn't get lost as I tried to navigate back through the ever-changing city. At the next block, I turned back to the right, hoping to loop back around the offending building at the earliest opportunity. I soon lost track of my path, with all the back and forth bending, though I was pretty sure I kept running back and forth past the original road. After what felt like the tenth loop, I started to worry that I would never find my way back to the others.

"Hello?" I called out. Anxious to find my way, I started to run. I just wanted to find somewhere, anywhere, that would look at least a bit familiar. My calls echoed back at me from all directions as the overbearing buildings seemed to only get larger the further that I ran. The road only got more bendy and confusing. There was another call of "Hello" coming back from another direction, but it was too difficult to tell if that was another echo or if one of my companions had similarly called out. Either way, I couldn't tell from which direction it came, so I didn't waver in my path.

I took another left, though I had long lost track of the directions I had been going. As I came around the bend, I saw off in the distance what looked like another square. Focusing all my attention on that goal, I ducked my head and ran full out, pushing on the yolk with all my might. The wheels of the cart started to squeak in protest, but I ignored them. I relied on what seemed to be exemplary workmanship of the unknown cartwright. My trust proved sound as the lamp light of a town square once again fell on the cart and myself.

I slowed to a stop in the middle of the square where a large fountain stood. The glittering waters reflecting the sky. Shrugging off the yolk, I stooped down to take a long drink of the warm water, wishing once again that this world had refrigerators. I sat on the edge of the fountain to look around at the square that I had come into. My eyes quickly locked on a familiar sight that shouldn't have been there. Near the entrance that I must have only just walked through, there was an overturned market stall. Looking around the area, I spotted the stall that I had found the cart behind. It was obviously the market that I had only just left.

Chapter Twenty-Eight
Two Returns and a Departure

Five Years Earlier

My trips to Desparia were getting weird. It was almost as if that world was out of my control, despite it being just in my imagination. There were times where I could believe that it was a real place. But how could that be? How could I be traveling to this other world without leaving Mom's car on the way home? It's not like Mom would have missed my disappearance from her side. And whatever was happening there had no impact on the real world. My feet weren't injured by walking on the sharp rocks. No bruises had ever shown anywhere on my body. The place couldn't be real in any real sense.

The next morning, I was thinking of telling Mom about it. But when I looked at her across the breakfast table, I knew she wouldn't react well to my admitting to imagining some other world. Pictures of straitjackets flashed in my head. So, instead, I convinced Mom to drive me back to see Mrs. Azalea, figuring she'd be less likely to overreact. Admittedly, I was also thinking she wouldn't be around much longer. I wouldn't be risking much if she thought less of me. When she was gone, all I'd have is Mom and Desparia. I couldn't afford to lose either to the other.

Even though it had been less than a day since the last time I had been in the hospice building, it felt like weeks had gone by. It was like a part of me had experienced those days of travel on the road in Desparia. Despite the fact that the place didn't look any different, there was a feeling in the air that something really had changed a great deal. It wasn't until we got to Mrs. Azalea's room that I realized just how right I was.

The door was slightly ajar, the sunlight streaming in from the window across from it. I figured Mrs. Azalea must have enjoyed a lovely sunrise until I looked over to where she had been when I saw her last. The bed was empty, the sheets stripped off of it. The machines that had been beeping and hissing were eerily silent, pushed into the far corner, as lost and forgotten as I felt at that moment.

"What's going on?" I asked Mom. That was when I noticed that the name on the door had been removed. The metal slats that held the paper nameplate hung empty. A corner of the paper, ripped off when it was forcefully removed from the door, still hung there as a lingering reminder that there had been someone there the day before.

"I don't... Wait here for a moment, Maya," she said before heading off to look for someone who could explain it.

I stood there, leaning against the wall where I had last talked with David. Where I had last explained how I felt about what he had been doing to me. I had wanted to tell Mrs. Azalea about my travels to Desparia, more so than I would have admitted to myself before that moment. Before I was forced to face the very real possibility that I would never see her again. As I stood there, waiting for Mom to return, waiting to hear the news that I already knew in my heart, I returned to my world. I returned to Desparia, wishing that, somehow, Mrs. Azalea would show up there. Seeing as how I still couldn't make my father appear, though, I didn't hold out much hope.

Suddenly, instead of a wall at my back, I had the gaping maw of the open gate to Vernala. I looked towards the crowd in the distance, looking for signs of the thief or the tall man. Neither were anywhere to be seen, absorbed by the growing miasma of the people wandering the streets. There wasn't any sign of the disturbance from earlier, though I knew it must have been only moments before where that world was concerned.

I glanced over at the two guards flanking the gap in the low stone wall. Neither of them showed any sign of noticing my time away. Or noticing me at all for that matter. With no response forthcoming from them, I walked back into town. I took a roundabout way back to where I had last seen the thief. Back to the alleyway that he had led me to. It took me a few tries to find the right spot. I got turned around in the crowd several times before finally finding the alley that I had only just left a few minutes and several hours earlier. I took one last look around for any signs of the two men. When I didn't see anything, I poked around in the dirt by the wall that I had been standing by, figuring neither would have seen where the ring had fallen. A smile quickly spread across my face as my fingers slid across the golden dragon, the large ruby still clutched in its teeth.

After one last glance around to make sure that no one had noticed me, I tucked the ring into my pocket before darting off through the crowd. I had grown used to being invisible, as I always was at school, in those days and today. It felt somehow right to move through the masses without anyone giving me more than a cursory glance. No one had taken any notice of me, let alone think to stop me. With the words "street rat" flitting through my mind, I walked back into the general store, the bell jingling overhead.

"I thought I told you--" the store merchant began.

"I have payment," I said, slapping the ring down on the counter.

The merchant stopped in mid-sentence. His mouth was frozen between the two words as his eyes bugged out at the sight of the ring. As he came out of his shock, he practically salivated when he picked it up from its place on the counter.

"This is... quite some gem," he said hesitantly. He paused again, as he noticeably tried to get a hold of himself so that he could haggle down the price. He steadied himself, eyeing me and my disheveled state, and seemed to remind himself that I was only a child. His chest puffed out as a smile spread across his face. "I'll give you the boots for it."

"And?" I prompted. I figured that I should just let him outplay his own hand before trying for anything else. It didn't help that I wasn't familiar with the world's money system or the state of its economy. I knew that I was probably going to end up shortchanged in any case.

"And... uh...," he said as he eyed the ring again, hefting it in his hand to test the weight. "Ten apples."

"And?" I asked again. I had no interest in the apples. Apples were easy enough to come by on Earth and it wasn't like I needed to eat on Desparia. At least, not back then.

"And... three loaves of bread?" he more asked than said.

"I'm talking money, moron. I can buy my own food."

He blinked in confusion for a few seconds, thrown by something I said. "Yes, but then you don't have the ring right now, do you?" he asked, flipping the ring in the air. "This is obviously stolen. There's no way some street rat like you holds onto a thing like this for long. I'm giving you a bargain here. A pair of boots, ten apples, three loaves of bread, and I don't call the guards here to have you arrested." He pocketed the ring, leaned forward onto the counter, and glared down at me, a mischievous grin on his face. "Take it or leave it."

I glared back up at him, not sure where I had gone wrong in the negotiation. What I should have done so that I didn't get cheated. I eyed the noticeable bulge in the man's thread thin pocket. The ring's form was easily recognizable there. I tried to figure out how I could get back on proper footing against him, but I saw no way to get the ring back. As he said, it wasn't like I could call the guards on him.

"Fine," I huffed. I figured that I could at least sell the bread and apples for a little money. I needed those boots. My bare feet made me stand out too much, on those rare occasions anyone bothered to look my way at all.

He tossed the boots and a sack containing the food onto the counter then pointed for the door. His eyes went out the window next to it, no doubt expecting the guards to come looking for me any second. I scooped up the boots and sack of food and headed back out into the town, wishing once again that I had managed to get a better deal. As the bell jingled once more, my Mom's voice seemed to come up out of nowhere, pulling me back to Earth. Now that I had the boots and a better understanding of the world, I didn't want to go. I didn't want to return to the real world where I was no doubt going to hear the bad news that I had been dreading.

"I'm so sorry, honey," Mom said, as I blinked the daydream away. "She went last night in her sleep. They said it was very peaceful, especially for these kinds of things."

I nodded, feeling like I had just been cheated all over again. Only instead of losing out on a few coins, I lost my last real friend in the world. In either world for that matter, as I hadn't made any friends in Desparia either. As alone in Desparia as I was on Earth.

That was always the case, until I met those three strange women in the dark, wet tavern

My mind raced with a dozen questions, mostly about what we should be doing for her. And yet, they were all buried deep below the feeling of my own loss. They all amounted to just two words.

"How's David?" I asked in a hushed tone. My throat was closed off from the silent sobs I wouldn't allow out.

"I hadn't asked," Mom said. "I don't think he's here. They already moved the body to the funeral home."

"The body," I repeated. Those words seemed almost alien to me. To that world. A word that seemed much more appropriate for the more primitive world I had been traveling to. Despair in one world, the other Desparia.

"He might be in school tomorrow," she said, as she motioned for us to head back down the hall towards the elevators. "You can ask him how he is then."

"He won't speak to me in school," I reminded her. "No one will. Why would tomorrow be any different?"

"You might be surprised. Anyway, I'm sure they'll let us know when the funeral is. Or if they want us to do anything for it. How about we make them a lasagna platter tonight? I doubt they'll want to cook anytime soon."

"I know how they feel," I said, as I reluctantly followed her away from the last place that I had seen my friend. My last friend. I looked behind me often, to the room that was now empty of everything but the memories, and only so few of them. I felt like I had cheated myself out of so many more of them. If only I had just visited her despite David's words. My thoughts lingered on that room, until I turned the corner where the room, and the memories, were no longer in sight. As we headed back down in the elevator, I retreated from the loss of my friend by heading back to Desparia.

Chapter Twenty-Nine
Circles and Squares

Now

I roared in frustration. The sound echoed around the market square that I had somehow stumbled back to, despite walking what I thought was away from it for the better part of an hour. As I put my head in my hands, my earlier yell of "Hello" seemed to echo back to me once more. This time it was even louder than my original call. I began to wonder if the buildings were so enchanted as to cause anyone who dared step into this empty city to go stark raving mad. In my frustration, I kicked the cart that I had been dragging around in circles for the past hour. It rolled away from me easily, almost as if being pulled by a horse in full gallop. It came to a stop against the same stand that I had pulled it out from behind.

"Hello," I called again, knowing full well it would do me no good and would only cause more of those never-ending echoes that have been plaguing me since I had entered this infernal city. "I knew I should have gone with the thieves' guild," I whispered to myself, despite never having any such intention.

"Oh, come now, you don't mean that," my voice seemed to echo back at me.

"What the..." I began. I spun around in my confusion, trying to find the source of this echo. The twins entered the square from my left, seeming to materialize out of nowhere. I ran to them, pulling them into a huge hug. After a few seconds, they returned the hug hesitantly. "I was beginning to think I'd never see you guys again." I pulled back from the hug, wiping the tears that had begun to leak from my eyes before either could see. "Have you seen Heather?" I asked after I had composed myself.

"Not since we split up," Serena said.

"We had only just found each other again a couple minutes ago," Tina said. She pulled a long, golden T off of her shoulder. "Where's the cart?"

I pointed behind me as I stared at the T. It looked like an actual T. When she had mentioned it, I was picturing the classic Tetris piece that looked like a T with most of its base cut off. This one was as tall as my L piece, with the two sides that flowed outward just as long. So much for the giant game of Tetris idea. Tina headed off to put the T in with the L and Serena pulled the square out from where it was strapped to her back, placing it in as well. The square was a real square, very much like the Tetris piece, and was about as big as the T and L.

"Should we try to look for Heather?" Tina asked as the square clanged against the letters.

"No, I just spent the past hour or so trying to find you guys. I think we should just wait here and hope she shows up like you two did."

"Huh," Serena said. "I would have thought you'd want to find her sooner rather than later."

"Well, it's not like we're going to leave her in this city. We might need her to open the next door anyway. I just think that looking for her in the city would just get us more lost."

"No, I mean because of that," she said, pointing towards the bracelet on my wrist. "Doesn't she need to reset that soon?"

I shook my head while looking at my constant death timer. "Not for another day or so. The hourglass runs for two days and it was only just reset last night."

"I don't know how you can stand that thing constantly threatening your life like that," Tina said. She seemed to scratch at a phantom bracelet on her own wrist. "I think I'd just kill myself, or maybe try cutting my hand off or something, rather than always be waiting for that to go off."

My mind raced at the suggestion of cutting off my hand. I wondered briefly about what affect, if any, that would have on my body back home. But then I pictured having a hook for a left hand. It wouldn't be too helpful when trying to pick a lock or a pocket.

"Well, it is not without its difficulties," I said, as I shook off the suggestion. "With the luck I've been having, cutting my hand off wouldn't help anything. Then I'd be without the hand as well as having this thing still stuck on me. Mostly, I try not to think about it. So, you know, a change of subject would be nice about now."

The twins stared off into the distance in silence for a minute, neither seeming to know what to say. Before long, Tina lifted her finger and turned towards me, as if starting to say something. Before she could say anything, there was a soft rumbling coming from the city behind me. We all turned in the direction it was coming from and I stared in amazement as the buildings started to move. It was the first confirmation that we had that the city was, in fact, shifting around us. I would have been elated except for what the moving buildings eventually revealed. Down the road that I had taken into the square was a large group of men in the unmistakable black uniforms of the Jakala Troopers.

My eyes bugged out of their sockets as I stared at these individuals. They were still several blocks away. They weren't too far from the first wall, which was plainly visible at the end of the restored road. I sat there on the fountain, frozen in place, unsure if they already saw us or if making a run for it would only draw their attention. They were all slowly walking our way. There was no sign of a glint of drawn steel in the lamp light. However, they were still too far away to make much out beyond their uniforms. The twins sat next to me, twitching in similar uncertainty.

"What are you three doing just sitting there?" a voice called from our left. The volume and urgency knocked our senses back into place. "Run," Heather said, as she came into view. She quickly ducked under the yolk of the cart and started pulling it off to our right. It took us another few seconds to react, though a call from the troopers as they started charging at us came soon after.

"Run," I yelled, agreeing with Heather's plan. My own yell seemed to snap the twins, and me, out of our collective stupor. It took only seconds for us to catch up with Heather, restricted as she was by pulling the cart. The cart ran as freely behind her as it did for me, though it seemed to lag a bit more with the added weight of the extra Tetris pieces. I ducked under the yolk and started pulling alongside Heather, as the twins grabbed the sides, pulling with us.

Thinking back, the smarter idea would have been to grab the pieces and run with them. They were easier to carry than the cart was to pull. Although, we had no clue how many of them we would find in the maze that was the empty city, or if they would even come in handy along the way. At the time, all I knew was that the troopers were behind us and that they would not take kindly to us if they were to catch up.

After a couple minutes of running, I dared to look back. I had been expecting the black clothed men to be hot on our tails. Instead, the buildings were once again moving to block our retreat. I wasn't sure whose side the city was on, ours or theirs. Or if it was working to hinder both groups equally. Lost in that uncertainty, I ducked my head once again and put on another boost of speed. My companions, seeing my darted look and added effort, joined me in pulling as hard and as fast as we could.

Ahead of us, I spotted what looked like a palatial stable. Its soaring heights dwarfed the towers in the city outside. But next to the towers in this neighborhood, it looked more like a doghouse than a stable. I pointed in that direction, needing to make no further prodding as the four of us made the slight adjustment in our path. As the ground we were running on turned from cobblestone to hay strewn wood, the others slowed a bit, pulling me up as well.

The stalls on either side of the long aisle were only slightly larger than the average horse stall. However, the main room's ceiling hung so far above our heads, we couldn't even see it in the night's darkness. Lit torches were set in sconces between the stalls, showing several floors of stalls and intersections that would lead to similar sections. There was even an area that seemed specifically designed to store carts, though there were currently none in there. Tall staircases framed individual sections and several pulley-powered cranes that would help to load and unload goods and passengers.

As I stood there, gawking at the monstrosity that was that stable, Tina ran back to close the doors. Serena joined her soon after.

"That was too close," Heather said, as she leaned over to catch her breath.

"Do you think those were part of the group that had nabbed us?" Tina asked.

"I don't think so," I said. "I'm pretty sure none escaped the slaughter."

"It doesn't matter who they are," Heather said. She sat down on the ground next to one of the cart's wheels. The one thing that the stable didn't seem to have was a place to sit down besides the floor. "They know we're in the city now. There's no stopping them from looking for us. We'll need to get to The Citadel's next door before they find us."

"And do what?" I asked. "We couldn't close the first door. That's why they had no trouble getting in here to us."

"No, they had no trouble getting in here to us because they're troopers," Serena said. "They can walk in and out of this place without any problems. They're invited."

"Exactly," I said. "Getting through the next door isn't going to help us any. We need to turn back and regroup."

"You just want us to give up," Heather said. "You never wanted to come on this mission. You'll use any excuse to get us out of here."

"Well, not any excuse. Just the ones that will help us not get killed. But you're right. I didn't want to come on this mission, and I don't think it's worth my life to try and fail to kill the emperor."

"Which is exactly why you'll stick with us and continue inward," Tina said. "I doubt you'll find many mages this close to the emperor's fortress that would be able to reset that hourglass of yours."

"Don't remind me," I said, as I rolled my eyes. "Fine, what's the plan, oh fearless leader."

"We'll hide out in here for a few hours, try to get some sleep, and head out again in the morning," Heather said, without missing a beat.

"Uh, wait a minute," Tina said, holding up a finger. "Who exactly placed you in charge?"

"She was obviously referring to me," Heather said. "I'm not saying I'm in charge of anything."

"Good," Tina said. "Because if anyone is in charge here, it's the two of us. We have the most to lose if this mission fails."

"But, in all reality, it's obvious that Heather's in charge here," I said, suppressing a smirk. "I mean, which of you guys didn't get caught by the troopers."

Tina and Serena started a long babble of words, overlapping each other in a mishmash of sounds that didn't really make much sense. They became very animated and, eventually, very loud. Heather shushed them, and they shut up instantly.

218

"See?" I said. As I pointed towards Heather, I was no longer trying to hide my smile. "She's the leader."

"Oh, shush to you too," Heather said, ignoring the hurt looks on the twins' faces.

"Aye, aye, fearless leader," I said. With a growing smile, I went off to find a stall that didn't smell. Oddly enough, it quickly became clear that, despite the fact that all of the stalls were completely decked out and ready to house any number of horses, not a one smelled like anything other than wood, dirt, and hay. With a shrug, I headed into the third stall on the left, made a nice bed out of straw, and quickly fell asleep.

#

Just in time for my alarm back on Earth to go off. Until then, I hadn't noticed that I had been so intent on the events of my dream world to get any actual sleep in the real one. I groaned as I slapped the snooze button on my little alarm clock.

"This living a literal double life is starting to get to me," I mumbled to myself. Reluctantly, I climbed out of bed and went over to my dresser for a change of clothes before heading into the bathroom. The hope was that a shower would help me stay awake long enough to get to school. Sleep would be more available there.

Chapter Thirty
Theo the Thief

Five Years Earlier

"You know you could have gotten more money for that ring if you traded it in with the guild." The voice seemed to have come out of nowhere, before the world of Desparia had even come into full focus. And yet, I knew instantly that it was the voice of the thief from earlier. Still, I jumped in startlement, dropping my new boots and the sack of food that I had forgotten were still in my hands.

"Don't do that," I scolded the man.

The boots had landed perfectly on their soles, allowing me to simply step into them. They were a little big on me, my feet practically swimming in the loose leather. But I figured that I'd grow into them if I kept coming to that world and grew there as quickly as I was bound to do on Earth.

"And I'm not interested in your guild."

"Oh, it's not my guild," he said. "I'm no Grandor Fell. No, I'm just the lowly Theo, bottom rung of the guild. Unfortunately, I couldn't even get you an invitation if I tried."

"Then why do you keep bringing it up?" I asked. With a darted, sideways look at the annoying thief, I picked up the sack of food and started making my way through the crowd. I had passed several fruit merchants earlier back in the marketplace. The hope was that they'd be interested in taking the apples off my hand. For a steep markup, no doubt, but the coins would be more use to me than the food.

"Pride," he said, as he started following me. "Also, if I manage to bring in a new thief into the guild, one that excels as I'm sure you will, they might move me up a rung or two. I don't intend to stay on the bottom for long."

"And how exactly do you expect to bring me in if you can't even get me an invitation?"

"Well, that's a bit more technical. But basically, you'll need to pull a job for us."

"Look," I said. I stopped suddenly and turned back to the thief. He hadn't been expecting the move and just barely avoided walking into me. I stared up at him, my finger extended, as I tried to remember his name through the long line of drivel that had been spouting out of his mouth.

"Theo," he offered. He took my extended finger in his hand, shaking it as if that was my intent. "And you are?"

"Maya," I said, before reconsidering giving the man my name. "Look, Theo, I never said anything about wanting to be a thief. I do thank you for assisting me before. I'm not sure how I would have gotten the boots without your help. But I'm no thief."

Stealing felt too much like lying to me. Like keeping secrets from everyone around me. At the very least, keeping secrets from the town guards who would want to arrest me if they knew. Even in that imagined world, secrets could kill.

"Not yet, you're not," Theo agreed. "But I know talent when I see it. And that's what you have. It's raw, no doubt, but I can shape you. I can mold you into the best thief this town has ever seen."

"And what would... Grandor you said his name was?"

"Oh, come now. Even Grandor knows you can't stay on top forever. He's more of a bureaucrat these days than a thief, though don't tell him I said that." His eyes darted all over as if he expected Grandor to jump out at any moment. "Anyway, why don't you give it a shot, I'm sure you'll be pleasantly surprised at what you are capable of."

"Look, Theo, I don't know what you see in me, but I have no intention of becoming a--"

"Thief!" The shout came out from right behind me as I was grabbed up around the shoulders. I looked up into the face of the tall man above me. When I looked back over to Theo, he was already running off again.

"Great," I said. I shook my head as I escaped the only way I could, by drifting off back to Earth.

I somehow had managed to get into the car while I was daydreaming about Desparia. This surprised me a bit more than it probably should have. It was like more and more of my life was lived in a daze, drowning out the reality that was going on around me as each of my reasons to pay attention to it were stripped away. Now that Mrs. Azalea wasn't in this world either, what was left to me? Mom and I never got along much over the years, barring those last few days. There wasn't much keeping me there anymore without my friends. Now that I had the option of disappearing into this other world, it was seeming more and more like it was the better option. As long as I didn't do it to the point where people started to think there was something wrong with me.

"You okay over there?" Mom asked. Her eyes stayed on the road as her head turned towards me. "I shouldn't be worried about you, should I?" Her questions echoed my own concerns.

"I'm just thinking," I said, which was true. My daydreams had ended for the moment.

"Well, if you really think David will continue to ignore you, I'll call up Joe when we get home and find out the information for the funeral."

I just shrugged, noncommittally, as I waited for us to get back home before I headed back to Desparia. Despite my desire to escape from the tall man, I knew dipping back to reality wasn't going to do much. No matter how much I tried, my own daydreams didn't obey me like they should. I was getting used to it, though. I was going with the flow of my subconscious. It made for a better story than anything I could come up with on my own. Remembering back to all the previous daydreams that I had thought up, each was more derivative than the last. The whole point of going to Desparia was to get an escape from the world. That was exactly what my subconscious was giving me.

Less than a minute passed after returning from Desparia and we were already turning onto our street, showing just how much time I missed out on by being in Desparia. It was a bit weird how the time I spent there didn't translate equally, or even proportionally, to my time on Earth. At the time, I just thought, "Great. That much less time wasted in the stupid car under my mother's watchful eye. Now to just escape to my room and..."

"Want to go back to the games from yesterday?" Mom asked, interrupting my thoughts.

"I... I kind of want to be alone," I said.

"Oh, yes, of course," she said, nodding. "I understand." She looked over at me again, seeming at a loss for something. I couldn't tell what.

The second she pulled into the driveway, I was out of the car and racing for the door. I didn't so much as look back at Mom to see her hurt expression as I darted up to my room, slamming the door behind me. I jumped towards the bed, not staying in reality long enough to see if I landed properly.

The tall man was already pushing me through the crowd when I got back there. The people parted as they eyed us, glaring openly at me of all people. "Thief," he called again. He patted me on my shoulder to make it clear to the people around us that he was calling me a thief.

"I didn't steal anything," I told him, as a town guard came into view through a tunnel of people.

"Sure, thief," he said, sarcastically. "I believe you. Hey, guard. We have a thief over here."

"Who?" the guard asked. He looked around before his eyes finally landed on me. "Oh, her. Yes, I've been seeing her around all day. Filthy street rat. Well, at least she managed to get some proper shoes on."

"Further proof that she's a thief," the man said. "Take her away."

"She stole the boots?" the guard asked.

"I didn't steal anything," I argued again.

"That's what they all say," the guard said, rolling his eyes. "Come along, little one. We'll get this whole thing sorted out."

The guard grabbed me firmly around the arm. His leather glove squeaked slightly as my wool sleeve bunched up. The tall man made to head off, but then the guard called after him. "You, too, sir. Right now, it's your word against hers. I'm more likely to listen to you at this point. But you'll need to make a statement, or I'll be forced to release the girl."

"Uh, fine," he said, as he reluctantly followed.

I had an odd sense of deja vu as I was pulled towards the guard station. It reminded me of being brought to the principal's office, again for something that I hadn't done. Only, this time, someone had died before it happened, and it seemed like no one was going to die because of it. Remembering the loss of my father once again brought tears to my eyes, though neither of the men took much note of it. They probably figured that it was my reaction to being arrested rather than any real emotional trauma I had gone through.

"I didn't steal anything," I said once more, as I was pulled into a squat, stone building just off the main thoroughfare. I felt like I should duck my head as we entered the low door. There were several steps down from the doorway, into the building. The high windows on the walls looked out at street level, like the windows in my basement back in reality.

The guard threw me down into one of two chairs next to a desk before walking around it to sit in a third chair behind it. The tall man sat in the chair next to mine. His back faced a small cell in the corner of the room. The cell was just large enough for the cot, a little room to stand in, and a hole in the corner that almost made me wish I couldn't smell this fantasy world of mine.

It was the first jail that I had seen in that world, but it wouldn't be my last. Thinking back, it was probably the best one I had seen in that world. Certainly, better than the dungeon several blocks away from there, in the same city, which I had experienced only recently. And yet, I was petrified of being locked inside the cage as I sat there, staring over at the small cot.

"Yes, yes," the guard said. He waved off my pleas as he pulled out a sheet of paper, an ink well, and a quill. "Everyone who comes through here professes their innocence. You're no different. Now, sir, what was it she stole from you?" He dipped the quill a couple times and prepared to write out the report.

"I didn't--" I started to say again. But then the man slapped his ring down on the desk between us. I stared down at the ring for a moment, surprised that the man had been able to get it back from the merchant.

"Gregor recognized my ring immediately and was kind enough to give it back to me. He said she tried to sell it to him for a thousand gold."

"I didn't--" I started to say again, but the guard shushed me.

"We'll need a statement from him as well," the guard said.

"Of course," the tall man nodded.

"I didn't steal anything," I said once more, just managing to get it in before I was shushed again.

"You deny trying to sell the ring?"

"Well... no... but I didn't steal it. I found it."

"Yes, you found it," the man said, nodding. "On my finger." He even stuck up his ring finger to demonstrate what a finger was.

"No, in the dirt," I said. I left off the part where I was the one to have dropped it there in the first place. Or that there was a thief involved that gave me the ring to begin with.

I didn't want to bring Theo into anything. It wasn't like I had any loyalty to the man. He did get me into this mess in the first place. But it wasn't like accusing someone else, who wasn't there to defend themselves, was going to get me out of anything. An inner voice started yelling at me as I was torn between keeping his secret and trying to save my own ass. I hated secrets, but this one seemed like a good one to keep, especially since it might just get me into more trouble if I didn't.

"Look, kid, did you pawn the ring or not?" the guard asked.

"Yes, but--"

"Was the ring yours to pawn?"

"No, but--"

"Then that's that," he said. He started writing on the paper. The quill scraping against the weather-worn wood of the desk seemed to find every ridge there was. It ticked against each in turn. "Trying to sell stolen merchandise. It's as good a crime to stuff you with as any. You'll be my guest for a few weeks. Sorry if the accommodations aren't to your liking." He paused in his scribbling to point towards the cell in the corner with the feather part of his quill. I let out a little squeak, sounding very much like the street rat people kept calling me. "Of course, if you were to give me the name..."

"What name?" I asked. I feared that he was hinting at the very secret that I wasn't trying not to give up. I wasn't sure which would be worse. Telling the guard his name and going free, only to feel the repercussions from the guild he so overtly claimed membership of. Or not telling the guard and staying in that stinking cell for weeks.

"The name of the thief that gave you the ring," he said, confirming my fear. "If you're as innocent as you claim, the ring must have been stolen by someone. Unless you're suggesting that this fine gentleman hid his own ring in the dirt of some alley."

"I should say not," the man said. He literally raised his nose to the thought of going into such a location, despite his current proximity to the hole in the corner.

I looked over to the cramped, confined quarters of the cell, wondering what it would be like to be stuck there for weeks at a time. It wouldn't be pleasant. But I figured there were worse places to be in this world that I had imagined up. Like the actual dungeon of the town where they keep the real criminals. The one I'd be experiencing less than five years after that day.

"So, what's it going to be?" the guard asked, disrupting my inner debate.

Then, I smiled, as I remembered that world really was imaginary. I remembered that, when traveling down the equally empty road on the way to that city, I just breezed through it. I didn't have to witness the endless boredom, pain in my feet, or stretch of time. The 'few weeks' that the guard had mentioned could just as easily last only a few minutes as far as I actually witness it.

I didn't say anything to the guard, I didn't need to, as he took my smile at face value.

Chapter Thirty-One
Giant Discoveries

Now

"Wake up, Ms. San Lucas," my history teacher yelled in my ear. The sudden noise made me jump. My head bumped into his mouth as he didn't back away fast enough. "Now that your snoring isn't interrupting my class, we can go back to discussing the Bill of Rights."

\#

Despite the warmth, comfort, and protection of the stables, we hadn't slept long... Well, I hadn't slept long. A couple hours after I had gone to sleep, about the time my history teacher was waking me up on Earth, Tina woke me up on Desparia and informed me that I would be standing watch for the rest of the night. Apparently, sleeping the whole previous day without standing a watch meant I needed to stand two that night. It was some rule the group had supposedly made ages ago and they expected me to live up to it just like they supposedly did. Really, it was probably just her trying to sound more in charge of the group than she was. Than we both knew that she was. Out of spite, I got everyone moving soon after dawn.

There were no troopers in sight as we left the stables, so we decided to take a more leisurely pace through the city. The streetlamps had been mysteriously lit the whole time that we had been in the city. Their oil chambers were as empty as one would expect for a city that no one had been in for years, yet they managed to burn throughout the night. As we started traveling through the city again, they started to turn themselves off just as mysteriously. One of them turned off just as we passed it and I swore I could hear someone actually blowing it out. I was beginning to think that this giant empty city wasn't so empty. That it was occupied by invisible giants. I kept expecting to run into one of them, literally. It didn't happen, of course, and I felt myself quite silly after a while.

The second wall was only half a mile to the East, but the second door was several miles away on the southern face of the wall. Along the way, we found several more Tetris pieces, none of which even closely resembled actual Tetris pieces. They clanged loudly in the back of the cart when it moved too quickly. This further slowed our pace. With the troopers in the city, and their exact location unknown to us, we wanted to make as little noise as we could. The constant echoes of the tiniest sound didn't help, though the maze that the moving buildings created made tracking those echoes difficult. Either way, we didn't see any sign of the troopers the rest of the morning.

Despite the winding, confusing pathways that the buildings made as we passed them, the way forward was straight as an arrow and quite easy to navigate. Other than a few simple detours we made along the way, mostly to pick up the golden pieces that caught our eyes, it was a simple matter to travel south far enough to get around the corner in the wall and then east until we came to the point where we could find the door.

"One of the many reasons why I hate cities," Serena said, seemingly out of nowhere.

We were just a few blocks away from having turned to the east. She was looking around at the buildings that we were going past as she almost danced while walking down the road.

It made me realize that I had to go to the bathroom as well. That wasn't something that I generally felt on Desparia. I flicked my attention back to the real world for a split second, just to check if it was really in reality that I had to pee. That had been an embarrassing field trip to... somewhere. Thankfully, I did have to go, but it could wait for the period break in three minutes. I was not looking forward to having to go in that weird city.

I stared at my bracelet, which was over halfway through the current sand cycle again. It had become the symbol of everything that I've started to hate about this world. The ticking clock ever threatening to end my adventures. To end my one escape from the boredom that my life on Earth had always been. And would always be as far as I was ever able to determine.

"Let's check out one of these buildings," Heather suggested. "There's bound to at least be a chamber pot in one of them."

"Just go in the street," I suggested with a shudder. "It ends up there anyway."

It always makes me queasy to think of these pre-toilet waste control methods. The smell always permeated the entire area. I had yet been able to turn off my sense of smell, like I could sometimes turn off my pain. The three of them just stared at me like my head had suddenly lit on fire.

"Or, hey, let's check out one of these buildings. Maybe they have something worth stealing while you find your," shudder, "chamber pot."

We stopped at the very next building. The towering doors of the buildings we had been passing had gotten so huge that their tops were no longer visible. As we had seen the night before, the further we traveled into the city, the larger the buildings had become. Along with everything about them. At times, it was apparent that one building or another was a copy of a specific building that we had seen earlier, perhaps even one that exists in the main city outside. The buildings' decorations, when recognizable at all, seemed almost elongated at times, either stretched vertically when the tower was taller, or horizontally when the tower was broader.

The building we were standing in front of didn't have the attached stable. Heather and I pulled the cart over to the side of the road. It felt weird to just leave those golden pieces there, more than just abandoning what could be the only loot I was able to find in the city. And yet, it wasn't like anyone was around to steal it.

"Everyone remember where we parked," I said. No one commented on the weird joke.

It took all four of us just to budge the door open a crack... well, a crack compared to the rest of the door. Given how big the door was, a crack was all we needed. As we slipped into the dark interior, our footsteps echoed louder than outside in the city. Especially those of the twin's as they ran off into the distance in search of their chamber pots.

The interior had an odd assortment of furniture. Just inside the door was a regularly sized coat rack. Its hooks pointed in every direction to accommodate all sorts of attire. Next to the coat rack, on the opposite side of a tall pillar, was a long table. A delicate cloth covered the rich mahogany wood. At first glance, everything looked rather normal, until I realized that the pillar between the two was the leg of a chair. The chair's seat was easily twenty feet in the air, and the back went off into the infinite heights of the room. When I saw the chair, my head tilted back as I tried to see the top

"If you do find a chamber pot, don't fall in," I called after the twins. It was a suggestion so much more applicable to such a house than any other it had ever been made in.

"Is that another one of your ridiculous sayings?" Heather asked. "Or do you anticipate much trouble with falling into a chamber pot ten times larger than we are."

"Well, I imagine it would be rather difficult for them to get out of one that big," I said.

The strange dichotomy in the size of the furniture only increased the further we explored the building. All sorts of furniture could be found. There were even several copies of the same items, right next to each other in places. What made it worse was that the two discrete sizes soon became a mishmash of sizes. They scaled from smaller than normal sizes, some even small enough for us to step on without noticing, to so large that we couldn't even see what it really was.

Near the end of the hallway was some form of dais, the steps too high for us to ever be able to scale without proper climbing gear. There were four large, golden pillars standing up in the middle of it, flowing upward into the infinite. The stone that the dais was made of appeared to be marble, though its black swirls seemed too thick and spaced too far apart to be real. Then again, fake marble would be quite out of the reach of the technology available to this world.

"Could this marble have been created by magic?" I asked Heather. I tried to detect the faint humming that such a creation spell would leave behind, even in an unenchanted object.

"I don't think any of this is real," she said. She stared up at the golden columns. "I think the whole city is just an echo, some sort of distorted mirror image, of the city outside."

"A fun house city," I said, contemplatively.

"Whatever that means," Heather said.

A clattering sound echoed throughout the building as we found our way into the fun house kitchen. "We're okay," one of the twins called out. I just shrugged to myself as I looked around.

If anything, the confusion was even worse in there. The stoves were all sorts of wrong. I even found one stove inside another stove. It must have been too hard to stack them like the furniture outside. The pantry doors, of all shapes and sizes, were right next to each other, each wide open and spilling out food all across the floor.

The food was another story all together. There wasn't anything overly perishable, thankfully. No raw slabs of bacon that were hanging for god only knows how long. Instead, there were dried meats, fruits, grains, even a few wheels of cheese. It was weird, though, seeing grapes the size of horses and watermelons the size of... well... grapes. There didn't seem to be any rhyme or reason to the chaos either. Each door, no matter the size, supplied a random assortment of foods. There was even a grain of wheat the size of an apple stuck inside the smallest doorway.

I picked up one of the more manageable, but still big, grapes. It was the size of my head, and it was weird biting into it. But, oh god, it was the most delicious grape that I had ever tasted. The taste was so much bigger, so much grander, than the outside should have allowed. The juices flowed freely out of the single bite that I took, gushing out like I had turned on a faucet of grape juice.

"This place could literally solve world hunger overnight," I said, between moans of deliciousness. My mouth was still full of grape. Heather stared at me, an incredulous look on her face. I was beginning to think her face didn't have a different look, just boredom and incredulous. "What?" I asked before taking another bite.

"How can you eat that?" she asked. "Do you even know where that's been? Or even how it is? There could be all sorts of enchantments on it. It could be rotten in the center."

"Or it could make me always hungry or never want to eat anything but this for the rest of my life. Or it could fill me up for the rest of my life or just for an hour. We'll never know until we eat it." I took another bite, approaching the center of the grape. My teeth hit something hard and my head jerked back in shock. "Ow." I pulled out a seed the size of an apple and hard as stone. "Oh right, you guys haven't invented seedless grapes yet."

I tossed the seed back into the bedlam of food. As it slipped down and out of sight, I began wondering what would have happened if I planted it. There wouldn't have been much of a point in planting it in the city. The odd echoing properties of the place would have only neutralized whatever traits the final plant would have had. Besides, there weren't many areas of earth to work with. It wouldn't have been until after we left The Citadel that planting such a seed would have made any sense anyway. Our possible departure seemed only less likely the further we traveled. And we still hadn't gotten to the second door.

On that chipper note, I finished the grape, leaving my empty hands stickier than a child's always seemed to be. I looked around for a spicket, finding only those too small or too big for me to use properly. I also didn't find Heather. She had been standing right next to me a second before.

"Heather?" I called out, only to hear a hushed "shhh" from the other side of the food pile. I climbed over to find her staring off into the distance. "What?"

"Look at that," she said. She pointed to a large crack in the wall. It was right next to the largest pantry door. The top of the crack started about ten stories up, though it could start even higher than that and it was only visible at that point. By the time it reached the floor, it was so wide that three semis could drive next to each other and still have room to turn.

"What is it?" I asked.

"It's a mouse hole," she whispered. She sounded more scared than when we encountered the shadow.

Staring at the hole, I half expected to see a set of red, glowing eyes bigger than my entire body. I tried to reassure myself that we hadn't encountered any humans other than the troopers. Animals of any size would be unlikely. Even so, I didn't think it was a good idea to wait around and find out.

"Let's find the twins and get out of here," I suggested, easing back without taking my eyes off the hole. "If there is a mouse in there, he has plenty to eat without bothering with us."

Heather nodded as she followed me. She kept her own eyes on the hole. I almost tripped on an apple that came up to my knee before deciding to turn around and watch where I was going. After putting the biggest mountain of food between me and the mousehole, I picked up a few more of the head sized grapes and started jogging towards the front door. I didn't have to look back to know that Heather was right there with me.

We met up with the twins near the gold pillars on the dais. Tina was staring up at them, while Serena was standing several feet away from her with her hands over her face. At first, I thought she was crying again. Then I got hit by a very foul and very unmistakable smell.

"Oh, what the..." I began.

"Don't say anything," Tina said, interrupting me with her finger up in the air.

"She fell in," Serena mouthed, between stifled snickers.

I tried not to laugh as I handed Serena one of the grapes. Then, I stood in front of Tina, unsure whether or not to offer her one. "Did you at least wash your hands?" I asked. This resulted in a burst of laughter from Heather and Serena.

Chapter Thirty-Two
The End of an Era

Five Years Earlier

That next week was hell on all fronts. Despite my original expectations of how time worked on Desparia, my incarceration did not breeze by. It crawled by in leaps and bounds. Whenever someone was in the room with me, actively claiming my attention or just on the periphery, time would practically stand still. Much like it did when I was stuck in class with nothing to do, no one to talk to, and the assignment too boring and easy to pay attention to. It only sped up when I was alone in the room. The feet walking by the single window flowed past like someone hit fast forward. However, that hardly ever happened. It was only when the guard was called away to tend to justice. The building was constantly manned, even at night. And without the need to sleep in that world, or even the ability in those days, even the nights snailed past.

School hadn't changed one iota, despite my recent loss. No one seemed to think I might miss Mrs. Azalea. They ignored me as they always did, though everyone was giving their condolences to David. I wasn't jealous of him or anything. He lost a parent, and I knew how that felt. But I had still lost a friend and that hurt almost as much. That first day, I tried to find him alone so that I could give my own apologies. But he spent the entire day in the company of his two friends, who had gotten into the habit of glaring at me whenever I came close to him. Considering what they thought of me, I wouldn't be surprised if they were working to get a restraining order out against me. It would have been a bit difficult to enforce it, given the fact that we went to school together and had three of the same classes. David did usually give me an apologetic look whenever he caught his friends glaring my way. I figured that bridge wasn't as burnt as I had previously thought.

Seeing everyone being so considerate of him did remind me of everyone's reaction to me when I lost Dad. It was like I turned from something you scrape off your shoe to someone completely invisible. Every time someone went up to him, to tell them how sorry they were to have heard of his mother's death, it was like a fresh slice of a knife's edge against my heart. It would not only remind me that she was dead but that no one had said one word of condolence to me during my own time of mourning. As I saw David's shoulders sag each time, though, I started to wonder if that had been a good thing. I began to wonder if the condolences were nothing more than salt in the already open and festering wound.

Desparia should have been a better escape for me than it was. Most of the week, I just sat in class, focusing in and out between reality and fantasy, just hoping the clock would tick by in either world so that something more interesting would happen. I figured my time in that cell was a perfect representation of my time in mourning for my friend. I just hoped that it would end when Mrs. Azalea was laid to rest.

Mom had managed to get word from Mr. Azalea that the funeral was that Saturday. He assured us that I would be allowed to attend, no matter David's feelings on the matter. Given the fact that I still couldn't separate him from his friends by the end of the week, I had needed that assurance to get through the time. I felt as trapped at school as I did in the small cell.

The one thing that I had needed more than anything that week was someone to talk to. Someone that I could trust not to send me to a loony bin if I told them what I was doing with my spare time. It was a secret as pervasive and double edged as the one I was keeping in Desparia. Damned if I shared it and trapped if I didn't. Whenever I got to the point where I was about to tell Mom, she just looked at me with more concern than I wanted to ever see from her. And that was without telling her the secret which could just as easily make it worse. No, I was stuck in my own personal prison cell in both worlds, each equally of my making.

It was a relief when the last bell rang on Friday and I could make my final dash to my locker before going to the bus. I hoped that I could make it all the way to my new usual seat behind the driver without seeing any of my former friends. Just the sight of them was a fresh reminder of all that I lost. All due to some stupid secret that never made sense to keep. But, as I closed my locker, David popped into view. The instigator of the secret. The source of all my misery. I tried to remind myself that he wasn't to blame. That he was hurting more than I was at that point. His friends, still by his side, made it difficult.

I watched as the three of them headed down the hall, away from the main entrance and almost directly towards me. As usual, words of condolences followed him down the hall, making him flinch as he went. Just as he passed, the sound of crinkling paper caught me off guard as a folded football hit my thigh. It bounced off and skidded down the hall. I pretended not to notice it, though David never looked back to check.

The paper football was tucked in a corner near the door out to the buses. I just took a darted step to pick it up, which I managed to hide by trying to avoid a group of eighth graders as they headed outside. My name was written on one side. It was the only thing that anyone besides a teacher had addressed to me since the school year started. I waited until I got on the bus to open it up, but it was just a quick note from David informing me of the funeral the next day and his own hopes that I would be able to make it. I quickly crumpled up the note and stuck it in my backpack before anyone else came on the bus. Once it was safely hidden away, I headed back to Desparia.

The low light of the streetlamps outside was the only illumination in the building. The guard had left a moment ago, or at least a moment before I was once again forced to return to reality. It was always hard to tell when time was speeding past at night in the cell, with the limited foot traffic in the street above to mark it. I would have settled for a torch in the room, to be able to note the fast flickering of the flames. But the guards only had candles, which they only used when filling out reports in the middle of the night. Instead, they settled for the light streaming in from outside to see by. It wasn't like they had much to see anyway.

Seeing as how the guard wasn't immediately back, however, I figured time wasn't fast forwarding yet. I had long since lost track of the days that had passed, though with an uncertain sentencing of 'a few weeks', it would have been impossible to gauge how much longer I had to stay in there.

The trays of food were piling up in the corner. The guard that had sentenced me insisting that I was on "some kind of hunger strike". Really, the food didn't appeal to me. It wasn't like I needed to eat in that world. Not in those days anyway. The only problem was it was attracting pests. The trays clattered aside as a large rat jumped up onto them. My own squeak of startlement echoed the one it gave before scampering back into the hole it came out of.

"Ah, there you are, little street rat." The familiar voice came from the window just outside of the cage. "I've been looking all over for you."

"It's not like I've moved in the last few days, Theo. You could have come see me any time."

"Yes, but then you would have just begged for me to let you out." He stared through the bars on the window, his hands clenched around them as if getting ready to pull them free. "I couldn't have done that before today."

Hope swelled before I could bat it down. Perhaps my long imprisonment was soon to be at an end in both worlds. It was almost funny how the two seemed to echo each other, though I figured that was just how my subconscious was working. If only I could find some way to harness that to control this world that had been meant to be an escape.

"You're letting me out?" I whispered. My eyes darted over to the door, where the guard could return at any moment.

"Of course," he said. He kept his voice at a normal level. It made me flinch away from the window, expecting it to draw more attention to me than him. "I wouldn't tease you like that. What kind of person do you take me for?"

"A thief." I said the word like an accusation and a curse.

"Exactly," he said, with a smile. "So, why haven't you yondled on me yet?"

"Yondled?" I asked, confused by the word. I knocked on my skull a couple times, thinking something must have gotten knocked loose at some point.

"Why haven't you told the guard I stole the ring? Surely, he would have let you out by now if you had. Only to replace you by me no doubt."

"Oh, like that would have really helped," I snapped. "He put me in here, without a trial, for trying to pawn a stolen item. He probably would have put me somewhere worse if I admitted to being an accessory to theft. Plus, I'm sure your buddies in the guild would have visited all manner of punishments onto me if I had."

"True, but that hasn't stopped other people from doing it," he said. His smile was only getting bigger. "I guess you passed this test."

"This was a test?" I yelled. I immediately slapped my hand over my mouth when I realized that I had.

"Well, yes and no," he said, shrugging. "A loyalty test is necessary for joining the guild."

"I already told you, I don't want to join your stinking guild," I snapped. "Now are you going to get me out of here or not?"

"I already have," he said. He pointed behind me.

Confused, I turned around to find the door to the cell open a crack. Enough to prove it was unlocked but not enough for me to have noticed it easily. "How did you do that?" I asked.

"I didn't," he said. "The guard left it open before heading off for his 'incident'. There are perks to being in the guild, after all."

I stared at him as what he just said slowly registered in my mind, my confused look still stuck on my face. "You're telling me that the guard just lets you people out of prison because you're in a guild?"

"Not just a guild, the guild. The only guild that matters. And, no, not just because we're in it. Money changes hands, of course, though it's more... wholesale rather than on a case by case basis. So, I was able to pull a few strings. The guild has their eye on you now, so don't let me down."

"Ugh, I keep telling you I don't want to be a thief. Thieves keep secrets by default, and I hate secrets. It's bad enough I keep the fact that I'm here a secret from... well, people back home."

"Oh, come, now, what's wrong with secrets? Secrets can be fun. It's like you're in your own private group among those that know the secret, separated from the rest of the world because they don't know it. We're elite because we know the secret."

"Well, for one thing, secrets got my father killed," I said. "They've pretty much ruined my life back home. And they put me here, in this cell, talking to some thief that can't understand someone not wanting to be a thief."

"But being a thief is so awesome," he said. His voice squeaked in his excitement. "You see something you like, you can just take it. Or, you can go the altruistic route, stealing from those that have too much and giving to those that don't have enough. Provided you keep a little yourself for your own expenses and the kickbacks to the guild. And if secrets really aren't your thing, then don't think of it as a secret. Think of it as an omission. It's only a secret if someone asks, or needs to know, and you don't tell them. Otherwise, it's just you not bragging. It's completely different from a secret."

I wondered at what he was saying, figuring that he was telling me exactly what I needed to hear to ease my conscience about not telling Mom about this place. About spending my time daydreaming about a world that she wasn't in. Perhaps it was just my subconscious giving me an out. A way of looking at my escape as something that no one needs to know, because it doesn't actually affect anyone but me. As long as my going there didn't hurt anyone, why would it matter?

"Fine," I said. I still wasn't sold on becoming a thief, but... "If it'll get me out of this place, I'll do whatever I need to. But--"

"Yes, yes, yes. You're not interested in joining the guild. You will be when I'm done with you. Now pop out of that wide-open door and let's head off to your first job."

"It's not wide open," I mumbled to myself, as I opened the slightly open door and left the cage for the first time in what felt like weeks. I left the door open a crack, the same amount that the guard had left it open. It made me wonder when he opened it and how I hadn't noticed that he did.

I just shook my head as I walked out of the small, squat guard house and out into the night. Then the bus jerked forward as it left one of the stops, knocking me out of my daydream.

I looked around, confused for a moment before I realized that I missed my stop a few stops before. There were only a few kids left on the bus, and they were all snickering to themselves as they looked over at me. I was kicking myself the entire time I was walking home from the last stop, not wanting to admit to anyone, least of all my mom, that my grip on reality was so tenuous that I'd be able to miss something as simple as the bus stop that I had gotten off at for the past couple of years. With my luck, she'd start insisting on driving me to school again. I didn't even think about keeping that secret from her. Maybe that was a sign of some growth on my part, with my subconscious so adamant about those kinds of secrets.

Chapter Thirty-Three
The Second Door

Now

By noon, we found ourselves staring at a hole in the second wall. "What do you think?" I asked.

"I... don't... understand," Heather said. She was turning her map every which way. The tears in the parchment that had ripped open while we were running from the shadow were only getting worse the more that she fiddled with it. "We've been all up and down this section of the wall and this is the only part of it that looks even remotely different. The door is supposed to be right here."

"Well," I said. I put my hands up in a square like movie people have been known to do when they're looking at locations. "If you really look at it, it kind of looks like a doorway. It's about the same size and shape of the first door."

"Yes, but there's no door. And the doorway doesn't lead anywhere. It just seems to go halfway into the wall and is blocked by the rest of it."

"Okay, but maybe this is part of the puzzle. Like, maybe the door is supposed to go here but we need to find it... or something."

"Yea," she said, laughing at that suggestion. "Good luck with that. Finding a door in that city is like trying to find a needle in a hayfield."

"More like trying to find a silver needle in an iron needle factory."

"What's a factory?"

"Never mind," I said, shaking off the question.

"You know, there are times when you just make no sense at all."

"I know." I shook my head, staring at the hole in the wall. "We could always go back. Maybe we missed something."

"Or maybe we need to build the door," Tina suggested. She stood in the alleyway leading back to the main road, halfway between us and her sister.

Serena was standing by the cart over on the road. The main road didn't lead to the hole. Instead, there was just a small alley between two buildings that were, by far, the largest we had seen yet. They were each, easily, a quarter mile in diameter. It was only because of these large buildings blocking our access to the wall that we had found the hole to begin with. With the twins guarding the cart, Heather and I had walked the entire length of both buildings along the wall and the only thing that even came close to marring its perfect form was this one hole.

"Build the door?" Heather asked. "What do you mean?"

"Well, we've been collecting these golden pieces all day," she said. She pointed to the large collection of gold that was practically spilling out of the cart by now. "Maya said something about using these to build a tetric or whatever. Maybe we could put the pieces together and build a door."

"Huh. I don't know. Could it work?" Heather asked me.

"How would I know?"

"You haven't built one of these tetrics before?"

"A tetric? What are you... wait, do you mean Tetris?"

"Yea, one of them," Tina said. "Build a tetric in the doorway and maybe it will become the door."

"You don't build a Tetris. You... oh, never mind. Fine, pass me one of those squares."

Tina headed back over to the cart as Serena climbed up onto it. Serena started fishing around in the mess back there. She eventually came up with one of the large squares that we had found. In the process of pulling it out, she spilled over half the contents of the cart. Tina was coming up next to the cart, and only just managed to avoid the avalanche.

"Hey," Tina shouted up at her sister. "Can we stop seeing how much stuff you could hit me with today? Please?"

"It's not my fault you fell into that chamber pot," Serena said, as she passed down the block. "There were plenty of other pots in that room you could have used."

"Yea, most of them were too small. I can't aim like that like you can."

"Well, it's not my fault that Papa taught me sword fighting instead of you. You just didn't have the dexterity for it."

"Exactly my point," Tina complained, as she passed the piece to Heather.

They continued to bicker as Heather walked the piece back to me. The square was large, but it would only take about a third of the bottom of one of the doors. We had been collecting dozens of those pieces and I had a feeling we might be using every one of them. I slid it into the corner, figuring it was as good of a foundation piece as any. As it slid in, there was an odd clicking noise. It sounded exactly like the sound when a Tetris piece had locked into place. I swear to god.

"Yup, somebody's played way too much Tetris," I said to myself. I was afraid it might have been me.

At the same time, the low humming of the piece seemed to flare up briefly before fading altogether. I figured that was a good sign, though looking back I'm pretty sure it was also a bad one. "Alright, what else do we have?" I asked. "Just keep the pieces coming."

"Ah, so you have built a tetric before," Tina said. The three of them were smiling over at me as they started handing the pieces down in a human chain.

"Oh, yes," I said, going with it. "Many a tetric I have built over the years."

After I stuck the second piece in, the L that I had first found the night before, there was a loud echo that found us. It sounded almost like a squeak of some kind. I looked behind us, figuring the cart had moved or some of the pieces had rubbed up against each other. But the cart was in the same place. In the past, the pieces usually clanged, not squeaked. As Heather handed me another piece, I focused back on my work, figuring whatever it was wouldn't bother us. It wasn't like we had seen anyone in the hours that we had been walking through the city. Nobody since the troopers that had come in through the first door the night before.

I focused on the one side of the doorway, trying to get one of the doors finished so that we could see if it really was working. I had to form something of a staircase along the edge so I could get the last few pieces onto the top. Once the last piece clicked into place, I took a few steps back to look at my work. The pieces had, until recently, seemed completely blank. Their golden facets had shown nothing but a reflection of the world around them. Once they were in place, they were starting to depict a scene, similar to the one that had been shown on the first door. At first, it had looked like the reflection of the road behind us, as the road was easy to see down the alley. The picture seemed like it was from the door's point of view. The only thing was, there was something huge in the road in the picture that wasn't in the real road behind us. I even looked back and forth between the depiction and the real one several times to make sure.

"What is that in the middle there?" Heather asked, pointing at the odd shape.

"I'm not sure," I said. "Whatever it is, it's where the cart is now. Maybe if I start building out from there, we'll be able to see it better."

Another echoing squeak sounded, this time louder and lasting longer. It followed an odd pattern, like it was really made up of several squeaks strung together in a group so thick it was hard to tell them apart. "What is that sound?" I asked, when the squeaks died down again.

"I'm not sure, but I don't want to stick around to find out," Heather said, as she passed me another piece.

I was running out of room left to insert pieces, so I was taking a little more time in planning out each move. I somehow doubted the lines would start moving downward when I completed them, and I couldn't afford to miss any areas. Once I was satisfied that an area would be completed in its entirety, I inserted the section piece by piece. Pieces that I didn't like ended up in a pile off to the side. They would come in handy when I filled in the top part of the door.

Once I filled in the center part of the right door, the picture suddenly became clear. Frighteningly clear.

"What is that?" Heather asked, staring up at it.

"It's the source of the squeaking. It's a giant rat."

"Rat?" Tina said. Her head darted in our direction. When she saw the picture on the door, her face turned white. "Please don't say giant rat. Please, do not tell me we're about to be attacked by giant rats."

"Work faster," Serena screamed in my direction. The twins were suddenly very scared, weapons at the ready, looking around us every which way.

I simply nodded and went back to work, to the almost constant sound of squeaking. It seemed like each time I put in another piece the squeaking only got louder. "I think this is only making things worse," I called, over the almost deafening cacophony.

"No!" one of the twins shrieked, drawing my attention away from my work again.

Darting to the main street, I saw what prompted the shriek. There was a large group of rodents swarming towards us. Not just rats but mice, gerbils, and a few rabbits as well. It would have been just an attack of the cute and furries... except for the weird effects this city had on everything within its walls. They were all the size of cars. It was hard to tell the mice apart from the rats, they were all just so huge. They were only a few blocks away and coming on quickly.

I rushed back to the door. Back to the puzzle. Back to trying to complete the door so that we could open it and escape that terrible place. There was only one section left, one small area two rows high. The problem was, half of both rows were filled in with weird sections from the left door and the row beneath it. There was only room for one more piece... and it wasn't one that I had there. "I need another piece," I called back to the road, as I tried desperately to pull out one of the offending pieces. "I need," I began to say again before I heard another scream.

I darted back to the cart in time to see the flood come on. Tina was standing a few paces in front of the cart. Her staff was held high, facing the swarm of rodents a lot more bravely than her screams would have foretold. Serena stood astride the cart, her borrowed sword at the ready. Heather was standing at the mouth of the alley, blocking my access to the cart. I stood there, trapped, stuck in the alley, knowing full well that there was nothing I could do to help them besides finish the puzzle. And yet, I felt like I had sealed their doom by even starting it. There they were, standing between me and the danger. I felt so helpless, so worthless. Why was it that they even felt like they needed a thief? It seemed like all I ever did was make things worse.

Shaking my head, I reminded myself that I had to get to work. That I had to find that last piece. I was about to yell at Heather to move, as her stance was wide and blocked the entire alley. Her gaze was set on the danger ahead as she focused on drawing in mana for a spell. She threw a fireball at the oncoming swarm and I saw it. I saw the piece reflecting back the light from the fireball.

"There," I shouted, pointing at the one piece that would solve all our problems. "Serena, I need that piece. Throw me it and I can finish the puzzle."

She glanced down at where I was pointing, seeing it easily. The piece was buried beneath three others. She put her sword away, quickly digging through the pieces to get it out. Once it was clear, she tossed the piece to me. It sailed over Heather's head, landing in the alleyway behind with an almost deafening clang. I spun towards the puzzle, scooping it up as I made my way. As I held the piece up, I saw in the reflection as the horde came at Tina. It seemed to part when it got to her, a rock in the oncoming flood, as it flowed onward and up the cart... straight at Serena... who still didn't have her sword out.

As her shrieks turned from fear to pain, I ran for the door.

Chapter Thirty-Four
The Start of Something New

Five Years Earlier

I wasn't looking forward to my first "job" as a thief. At the time I was thinking it would be my last. But I wanted to be there for Mrs. Azalea's funeral, in both mind and body. So, I held off going back to Desparia for a while. Mom had set out the same dress that she had for Dad's funeral, barely three weeks earlier. This time I wore it, rather than an old t-shirt. On the way out of the room, I took one last darted look back at my t-shirt filled dresser. I wondered if Mrs. Azalea would recognize me if she could see her own funeral. She hadn't seen me in anything but my dad's old t-shirts.

"Now that's more like it," Mom said, as she saw me come down the stairs. "Why don't you dress up more often? You look nice. Maybe if you stop dressing like you want to be invisible, people will stop ignoring you at school." I just rolled my eyes at her comment as I grabbed my jacket from beside the door.

It was almost eerie being back at the cemetery so soon. The weather was nice, so they hadn't done any part of the ceremony inside. I figured it was something about the fact that Mrs. Azalea had been stuck indoors for the year before and would want to be under the sun for as long as possible. As Mom and I walked up the hill towards where she was to be buried, with David and his dad standing on the opposite side of the grave from us, the mirror image became complete. David was wearing the same suit he had worn to Dad's funeral. He gave me that same, small smile he had that day, as Mom and I merged with the crowd that surrounded the grave.

David's two friends gave me dirty looks when they noticed me. They were silently questioning how I dared come to such a sacred event as that, as they still thought that I was stalking David. They sat in a couple of the folding chairs directly behind David, the ones that had been mostly empty for my father's funeral. These were full of the family and closest friends of Mrs. Azalea. I felt like I should be over there. I should be sitting right next to David. To be there to comfort him when he needed me. Instead, I just stuck to Mom, holding steady with the former coworkers and other attendants to the funeral.

I stared down at the casket that held my last real friend in that world as the reverend spoke loving words of faith and resurrection. Promises of her being in a better place and that we would all see her again, once we joined her in that place. It reminded me of Desparia, of my original intent of what I wanted that world to be. A way for me to see my father again, even if he was just a dull echo of the man that I knew. I closed my eyes, not to dip back into that world, but to wish that Mrs. Azalea would somehow be there one day. Be in that world that only I could travel to, so that I could see her once more, long before I met her once again in the afterlife. And with that wish, that hope, that prayer, I tumbled backwards, landing back in the world of Desparia, without really meaning to, with Theo's face staring over at me.

"You're going to love who I chose for your first target," Theo said. He was smiling broadly back at me as he led the way down the road. I tried to focus on Desparia rather than Earth, still surprised that I had gone back there without meaning to.

"Um... what?" I asked, as I tried to remember where I had left off. I wondered briefly if I should just pull back out of that world and to the funeral that I had wanted to attend. That I had wanted to be a part of. I pulled back from Desparia just enough to continue to listen to the reverend droll on about the afterlife. That was something that I was starting to believe in less and less, the more that people that I wanted in my life went to it.

"Your first burglary target," he reminded me. "Burglary isn't the same as straight theft. Some think of it as less honorable than stealing from someone right in front of them. But I always find that it's more fun. The fear of being caught at any moment. Looking through a person's personal domain, his own abode that he doesn't expect others to see. It's where a person can be themselves, as perverse as that is sometimes. Plus, the goddess of thieving loves it."

"The goddess of thieving?" I asked, confused. This was the first time I had heard any indication of a religion in that world. It seemed rather appropriate, considering my own crisis of faith that Mrs. Azalea's funeral was stirring up.

"Oh, don't tell me you're one of those Christian people," Theo said. He squared up his face in a look of disgust that almost had me laughing.

"Well, I was raised Catholic," I admitted. "But... well, I guess I'm open to--"

"Perfect." He jumped on my doubt, taking the opportunity as he led me through the town to explain all about the unnamed goddess of thieving. How she worships the power of shadow, which sounded a bit like the monster that I saw that first day I had been there. How most thieves worshiped her, or at least tolerated her, praying to her before any big score. The more he talked, though, the more it sounded like her name wasn't the only thing people didn't know about her.

As he spoke of this religion that he followed so intently, I listened in on the priest's words back on Earth, comparing the two doctrines as they spoke it. Theo never mentioned anything about an afterlife, a point where the lost souls would meet once again. It felt nice to think I'd be able to see Mrs. Azalea again, the real Mrs. Azalea and not some echo of a person that I had hoped I'd be able to find there. But it felt somehow right that there was nothing after. That my friend was really gone, beyond what I could find in my own memories. It was almost like the promise of the afterlife was just a way to hide the secret that there was nothing out there beyond our own senses. That by my being able to trick my own senses by coming to Desparia, I had somehow unlocked a way to something more than the empty promises.

"But, anyway, here we are," Theo said. He ended his lecture, dislodging me from my own internal debate.

"Where are we?" I asked.

"You remember that guy that turned you in before?"

"Gee, let me think," I said, snarkily.

"This is his home. We're going to steal from him. If you come out of this place with his ring, you'll be granted admittance to the thieves' guild."

I just rolled my eyes, knowing he wouldn't listen if I reminded him that I didn't want admission. That all I wanted was to get out of Vernala with no debts owed. Instead, I just stared up at the house in front of me. As I tried to take in the grandeur of the place before me, I could hear the end of the priest's lecture back home. Figuring whatever came after him would be more important than stealing from some imaginary man, I returned to reality and the funeral that I had wanted to attend.

It took me a few moments to shake off the last remnants of Desparia, which seemed to coincide with the reorganization at the funeral. The reverend had stepped back from his place at the head of the grave. He looked towards David and his dad, as if expecting one of them to do something. I looked over to David, sitting there next to his dad. It was obvious that he was trying not to cry. Not to shy away into his father's side and hide from the people looking his way. He looked small, reminding me that he was only eleven, like I was. That he had only seemed older because of what he had gone through, what he had lost. I wondered if I looked that old, given what I had lost. Or did I look older?

David's father whispered something down to him as he placed his arm around his son. David just shook his head, answering some question that I hadn't heard. Mr. Azalea nodded down to him before standing and heading over to the head of the grave. I watched David as the man spoke of his wife, the wife he hadn't seen much of for the past few months. Or at least not while I had been there. He spoke of the woman he married. The mother of his son. The woman I never truly met. It reminded me that I had only known her while she was sick. I knew the woman who was about to die, not the one that had been so full of life that she had given life. David's tears finally broke free, while mine dried up. My loss didn't seem as great as his. My place in the ceremony, or more appropriately my lack of a place, seemed more fitting. My hand found my mother's as I silently sent my strength to David, knowing I wouldn't need it anymore.

The funeral ended soon after, with no one else wanting to speak for her. There was talk of a wake at the Azaleas' house. But due to the limitations of the house, only those that had been in the chairs were invited. I didn't argue as I headed back to the car.

"Wait for me by the car," Mom called after me. "I want to give our condolences to Joe."

I just nodded. I didn't look back to watch Mom head over to Mr. Azalea. I didn't see anything that was happening behind me. I had hoped that she had unlocked the car, figuring I could return to Desparia while I waited. I wasn't that fortunate.

"Why don't you just leave David alone?" came a voice behind me. I jerked around to see David's two best friends making their way around the car to me.

Chapter Thirty-Five
Blood Plain

Now

As soon as I had inserted the piece, the doors swung wide. There were no more video game sounds. At least none that I had heard over the screams and squeaks. I had run back to the road, trying to help, though I had no idea how. It was rather moot by that point. The rodents were in full flight. Tina had already climbed up onto the cart and was cradling Serena's limp form.

"Why?" she was sobbing. "Why her? Why not me? They should have gone after me."

It took several minutes to separate the two so that we could move. Heather and I picked up Serena's body. I was by her head, walking backwards, while Heather had her feet. Tina was too inconsolable to help. She just followed us as if in a daze.

On the other side of the door was a wide open field as far as the eye could see. There were scattered trees lined up along the near wall like in a park or orchard. The far wall was, once again, absorbed in the horizon. The sounds of nature surrounded us, long lost since we had entered the city half a day before. Birds could be heard off in the distance, and even a few locusts tattled on the humidity that was sure to come in the afternoon. Tina seemed to perk up a bit at the sight. But her spirits quickly faded when she looked back to her sister.

"Over here," Heather said. She pointed towards a flat area of grass not too far from the door. Serena's limp form was heavy and awkward to carry, and neither of us was going to be making it far into the field before needing to put her down. As soon as we set her on the ground, Tina knelt down next to her and started mumbling words that were too low for me to hear. Serena's face looked completely shredded. Flaps of skin hung off in pieces. Her left arm was obviously broken in two places and her chainmail armor was in tatters. A slight raising of her chest was the only sign that she was still alive. I knelt down, hoping that my first aid training would help. But Heather just put her arm on my shoulder and indicated that I should follow.

"Leave her to it," she whispered. "She's the only chance Serena has right now."

We got to work collecting firewood and some stones from along the wall to make a proper fire. We stayed close to the door, as neither of us wanted to go far from the twins. Heather pulled a battered old pot out of her pack and started throwing all manner of food into it. I sat there for a while, staring over at Tina. She had started moving her hands up and down Serena's body, smoothing out her clothes.

"What is she doing?" I asked, pointing over towards the twins.

"She's praying to the Great Tree to save her sister."

"The Great Tree?" I asked, sounding skeptical.

"Yes, the source of all life on Desparia. Tina is one of her more devout druids, and Serena herself is much beloved by the goddess. She'll answer this prayer."

"Wait, is it a tree or a goddess?" I asked.

"She's both, actually. You sound like all of this is new to you."

"It is," I admitted. "I've only ever heard of the unnamed goddess of thieves. That was from an old colleague of mine that I had run with a few years back. I never really put much stock in the religions of this world."

"You are a strange one, Maya. You know things about stuff I've never even heard of, but you don't know the first thing about stuff kids learn in school. Why is that?" Heather asked.

I shrugged. "You wouldn't believe me if I told you." I looked back over at the twins. "You're not worried in the least about Serena?"

"Of course, I am. We've been friends for years now. I just trust in Tina and in the goddess." I looked over to find Heather staring at me, an odd smirk on her face. "You care about them, don't you."

This accusation took me by surprise. I had only known the three of them for a couple of days, not including the encounter I had with them by the tavern. In that time, I had been playing the role of the reluctant travelling companion. I was more interested in preserving my tentative connection to the only mage that I knew that could reset the bracelet that continued to threaten my life. But, recently, had it become more? Had it become almost... a friendship? In those five years, I had never had any friends, real or imaginary, in either this world or the real one. And yet, there I was with three of them. Thinking back, I couldn't even begin to guess when it happened. And yet, I was almost certain that it had. I shuddered at the thought that, at sixteen, I had only now developed imaginary friends. And one of them was over there, not ten feet away from me, dying. And there was nothing I could do about it.

"I'm going to go exploring a bit," I said.

I got up from my place on the ground, trying to escape the knowledge that my friend might very well die. I had spent so much of the past five years avoiding connections with people, real or imagined. It was mostly to avoid losing them, like I had lost my father and Mrs. Azalea. Or having them turn on me, like David, Ashley, and Jen. And there I was again, waiting by another death bed. I wiped a pre-tear from my eye, hiding the motion by pushing my hair back a bit. And yet, I couldn't help but hope that this time would be different.

"We don't know how long Serena is going to be out of commission and we can't afford to get too far behind." And I didn't want to wait around, watching her slowly die if Tina's tree doesn't help.

"Don't go too far. I still have to reset your bracelet tonight," Heather reminded me.

"Yup," I said, as I started out.

I didn't get far, couldn't get far. After taking about ten steps, which was about a total of thirty away from the door itself, the whole landscape changed. Up until then, it was all wide open flatlands, barely even a hill in sight. Suddenly, as if triggered by some pressure plate hidden in the grass, massive hedges grew up within seconds, all over the place, blocking my way forward. As I backed away from the hedge, I brushed my offended nose where it had hit the sudden growth.

"Well, that's nice," I said.

Heather was at my side in seconds. "Are you alright?" she asked, sounding almost concerned.

"I'm fine," I assured her. "It's a good thing I'm not allergic to hedges, though."

"Good," she said. "The last thing we need is to have two of us that need healing. Then we'd never get to the center of this place."

"Oh, yes, wouldn't want that," I said to myself. I started heading off towards the west, hoping to find a way past the wall. Given how the last section had acted, though, I was starting to think each area between the ten walls of The Citadel would be some sort of maze.

After a few more paces, I found a large, strong stick and started digging a long groove in the ground as I went. The last thing I needed was to get lost again. The empty city certainly taught me never to underestimate a maze, especially a magically created one.

It took a few minutes for me to find a place where I could turn. There was a small section of the hedge that was missing, about as wide as I was. It turned out to be a simple doorway through the one hedge wall and into an adjacent hallway that flowed east and west, off into the distance.

"Hedge maze," I said, shaking my head. "How cliché." I drew a big X in the ground right where the door was before turning the groove in the ground through it. Three steps into the new passageway and the opening behind me closed up. The hedge grew up where the missing section had been. "Okay, that's a new twist to it at least."

I looked both ways, debating which direction would be more likely to let me back out. Briefly, I considered trying to climb over the hedge. It was only about ten feet tall. Compared to the hundreds of feet tall that The Citadel's walls were, that was nothing. And, as far as I could tell, it should be strong enough to bear my weight. However, with the luck I was having, the hedge would probably just keep growing the higher that I climbed it. With a sigh, I turned back towards the west, hoping a gap had opened up closer to the others after the first one closed. As I retraced my steps, I regretted not having counted my paces as I went.

Forgetting the stick for a bit, I ran part of the ways back, each step showing me nothing but more hedge. It wasn't until after I was almost certain that I had gotten past the little camp that I finally saw another side corridor. The problem was, it was one leading further in.

"Ugh," I yelled in frustration.

I threw my stick up in the air... only for it to be caught... by the hedge itself. A vine seemed to whip out of nowhere, grabbing the stick out of the air. It waved it back and forth a bit before the stick fell back to the ground... in two pieces.

"Okay," I said to myself. "No climbing the hedge. Got it."

I sat down where I stood and listened for a bit. I hoped that I could hear the sound of the crackling fire, or the continued prayers of Tina. Instead, all I heard was a dead silence. There was nothing. Not even the bird songs or the locusts. No crickets coming out early. No rustling of the leaves in the breeze. Just the silence of a grave... My grave if I couldn't find my way out by dawn.

"Hello?" I called out. I hoped that Heather would hear me through the hedge and find me. I wasn't sure how close she needed to be to me in order to reset my bracelet, or if she even needed to be able to see it. The issue was rather moot, however, as there was no answering call from outside the maze.

"Well, at least there's no echo like in the empty city," I said to myself, wondering if that really was a good thing.

"Hello?" I called out again, this time with less volume and less insistence. I figured it would never be answered, anyway. I laid back down onto the ground, looking up at the overcast sky that would probably be the last sky I saw in that world. I wished the clouds would part a little, so I could start trying to find shapes in them. Instead, it was just a blank, gray canvas too far away to paint on.

"Well," I said to myself as I lay there. "At least it's not raining."

Chapter Thirty-Six
Eating Pavement

Five Years Earlier

Sounds from the funeral dispersing came to me from the other side of the car as David's two friends stalked towards me like two hunting cats. The two came around the car towards me, one from each side. When I saw them, I remembered the name Sam from something that David had said about them. I briefly wondered which one was Sam, or what the other boy's name was. But from the looks on their faces, knowing their name would do little to help me with them.

"Why don't you just leave David alone?" the voice said again. It was coming from the thinner of the two, the cheetah to the other's lion. He was coming at me from my left, from the front of the car.

Again, I reached behind me to try the door, and again it was locked. A whimper escaped my lips as I looked between the two. "I'm not stalking him," I insisted. "I was a friend of Mrs. Azalea's."

"Then why weren't you invited to the chairs?" the other boy asked. "If you were so close."

"I-I don't know," I admitted. "I only met her a few months ago, after she was already sick."

"When you started stalking David," the first boy suggested.

"Fine, whatever," I said. I knew they wouldn't believe anything I had to say. "I'm going. You'll never have to see me again."

"That's just it," the second boy said. "We will be seeing you again, every day at school. You'll get it in your head that you can just keep on stalking him, as long as you're in the same school."

"So, we're here to convince you to change schools," the first boy said.

At that point, the two boys were right in front of me, blocking any chance of escape I might have had earlier. They each grabbed me by an arm, slamming me back against the car. I had only been in one other fight in my life before then, that one in the cafeteria against Janis. And she was a girl. One much larger than I was, but still a girl. It felt wrong on so many levels to have these two boys attacking me like that. And we were so close to so many grown-ups that seemed completely ignorant of what was happening just on the other side of that car. That part of the street may as well have been a completely different world to them, as separate from the gravesite as Desparia was from Earth.

Immediately, I tried to escape the only way I knew how, by heading back to Desparia. I momentarily forgot that these boys were in reality. That escaping to my dream world wouldn't remove me from the danger, at least not physically. I just tried to convince myself that Desparia was the only world worth paying attention to.

The large house that was suddenly in front of me again wasn't that big by Earth standards. But it was easily the largest that I had seen since arriving in Desparia. There was a decent sized garden in front. It was fenced off from the road with several "do not enter" signs thrown in for good measure, making it clear that the garden was only for the residents of the house. The windows were all dark and the tall, wooden double doors were closed shut. No doubt they were firmly locked and barred. The place practically screamed at us to keep on walking.

The stone walls of the town were at their tallest in that area. They were maybe a good six or seven feet high. It provided a backdrop for the house, wrapping around it on two sides. There was no sign of a walkway on top of the wall for guards to patrol on and the corner of the wall had no adornments, not even a perch to repel invaders from. The area was so deserted that it was easily the quietest part of the whole town. This was probably the draw to it. Why one of the largest manors in town sat there.

When I first saw the house, I could have sworn it was a dusty shade of brown or gray. But as I looked up at it, the stone took on a redder shade. As if it was painted with blood. It was hard to concentrate, to focus on the world in front of me. I struggled against the draw that I felt from reality, so close to me and yet seeming to get further and further away the longer I stood there. For a second, I panicked, worried that I might lose that tie to reality. That I might become trapped in this world that I had made for myself. But, as Theo started to explain what he had in mind, I started to relax. I started to wonder if losing that tie would be such a bad thing.

"I mean, the man turned you in for stealing some stupid ring," Theo said. He was probably continuing what he had been saying when I had last been there, oblivious as always to the fact that I had left. "We have to teach him a lesson."

"I lost track of all the reasons for this whole field trip of ours," I said. I blinked my eyes several times, trying to clear them, as the house suddenly changed from the red to a darker gray than I had seen before. When the color returned to the dusty gray that I remembered, I could no longer sense what was happening around me in reality. I could no longer feel my body back there. But I tried to put it out of my mind as I focused on what Theo was telling me.

"We try to combine tasks as much as we can," he agreed. "It saves time for drinking and... other activities that you're too young to hear about."

"Some might say I'm too young for this activity," I said. I gestured to the house in front of us.

"Those people would be fools," he said. "It's best to start training people in the thieving arts when they're young. It's a skill, just like any other. You're like my apprentice."

"Does that mean I should start calling you master?" I asked, sarcastically.

"If you'd like," he said, smiling. He obviously liked the title, though I wouldn't be caught dead calling him that.

"Let's just get this over with," I huffed. I wanted to be rid of the man, and that town, as soon as possible.

"Well, we can't just rush in there," he said. "We need to scout around. Find the best way in. Check for traps or alarms that might get us caught."

"Haven't you already done that? What have you been up to while I was stewing away in that jail cell?"

"Like I said, drinking and... other stuff."

I rolled my eyes and headed over to the wall that ran along the left side of the house. The wall was far enough from the side of the house to leave a path twice as wide as the main street. The alley was dark and completely blind, easily the best way to get into the house. Unfortunately, there were also no windows back there. No way to actually get into the house from that side. I continued down the road anyway, walking around to the back of the house, only to find a similar situation back there. However, once I rounded the house, I was immediately spotted by a guard that had been walking up the pathway.

"Halt," the guard called. He pointed at me as he ran in my direction. I looked back, half expecting to find Theo right behind me. The other half wasn't disappointed to see the alley completely empty. "What are you doing back here?"

"I'm... just going for a walk," I said, quickly coming up with what I thought was a halfway decent excuse for being back there. "What are you doing back here?" I threw back at the guard.

"I'm on patrol, as I'm supposed to be. No one is allowed along the walls except guards."

"Oh, I'm sorry... uh... Mr. Guard, sir. I'm new to town."

"That's no excuse," he accused, making me flinch. "Get back to the main road."

"Yes, sir," I said. I gave him a bit of a salute before heading back the way I came. "You know you should put up signs or something if you're gonna go with the 'ignorance is no excuse' crap. I always hate it when people pull that back home. It's like keeping a secret and punishing people for not knowing it."

"Just keep walking," he said. He was walking right behind me until I made it back out in front of the house. "Now shoo. No street rats in this neighborhood."

"I'm not a street rat," I said. I was annoyed by being called that, though everyone in town had been.

"Do you have a home to go back to?" he asked.

"Actually, yes I do," I said.

"Then I suggest you go there before you get into any more trouble."

He shoved me further down the main road before continuing along his route. He followed the wall around past the group of buildings across the street from the manor. I made as if I was going down the road as he demanded, watching behind me for when he passed back out of sight.

Shaking my head, I started to wonder just how much trouble I'd be in if I wasn't able to return home again. If this world became the only world available to me. What would it be like on my world? Would they say I was in a coma? Could I be brain dead, or worse, completely dead without even knowing it? Would I be able to see Dad and Mrs. Azalea as people kept promising... as I kept hoping?

"That was close," Theo said, He came out of the small alley on the house's right side, stretching out between the big house and the smaller houses that made up the rest of the block. "I don't think he would have been so lenient if you weren't a kid, kid."

"Well, isn't that why you want me to help you out?" I asked. "The innocence of youth and all that?"

"Well, sure. Plus, the fact that you seem to have a way to make yourself invisible when you want to. Granted, not as completely as an air mage, but close enough. With a little training, you'll do well in the guild."

"Ugh, I keep telling you--"

"Yes, yes. Steal first, refuse the offer later. Let's just get in there, okay?"

"Fine," I said, huffing. "Any thoughts?"

"Well, you had the right idea by heading for the other sides of the building, but this is the one you'll want to climb up," he said, pointing behind himself.

"But that building only goes up two stories. You're not going to be able to get up to the roof and I doubt there will be a window on that side either."

"You'd be surprised," he said.

Sure enough, there were several windows up along that side of the building. They were at regular intervals, marking each of the three floors of the building plainly. From the way that alley smelled, it was easily obvious why there were windows over there. Fortunately, the alley was slanted, allowing for the rainwater to sweep away the... waste into the street and down the road. Away from the prying noses of the building's occupants and avoiding any buildups of the... stuff. I gagged on the smell anyway, coming close to losing my breakfast. Fortunately, I hadn't brought my breakfast over from reality.

Once I got over the smell, I noticed that the window in the back corner on the second floor was wide open. Drapes were fluttering in and out of it in the wind that flowed down the back walkway and down and around the alley. The wind would waft the smell away from the window, allowing the occupant of the room a light breeze in the otherwise warm weather of the night. Without looking to my companion, I knew that window would be our target. But when looking at both walls of the alley, I couldn't see any way of actually getting up there.

"How do we--" I began to say.

I looked over to Theo, but, once again, he wasn't there. It took a few moments for me to spot him, climbing up the wall in-between the rows of windows. His back was pressed against the low building, with his hands and feet pressed against the large house. I ogled at him as he slowly made his way up, moving one hand or foot at a time.

"There's no way I'm going to be able to do that," I said.

"Shh," he hissed down at me. "I'll lower a rope once I get up there."

Watching him slowly ascend the building, I wondered if I would even be able to climb a rope up. I had never managed to climb a rope in gym class. I could barely make it up the knotted ropes, and only as far as the knots would allow. It was weird to me that I would be as limited physically in that world as I was in reality, given the fact that I was daydreaming the whole thing. I should have been as strong and capable as I could imagine myself being. Then again, I thought, perhaps that's the problem. I can't climb the wall because I don't think I can climb the wall, because I couldn't do such a thing back in reality.

With a renewed sense of determination beyond anything I had ever felt before, I tested the firmness of the two walls. I pressed against them with all my strength, reaching between the two as I straddled the alley. They held firm, but my arms wobbled as I stretched across the narrow alley. Placing my back against the building opposite the large house, as Theo had done, I started trying to walk up the other wall. My arms couldn't quite reach for that added support. I put all my strength into my legs, pressing against the wall as I edged my way upwards. I managed to shift myself up the wall, adjusting my back twice, before my legs gave out and I tumbled back down. In the end, I landed on my butt in the muck that hadn't quite washed away.

"Ew," I shouted in disgust. The grime covered my hands and wrists, as well as my backside.

"Shh," came a hiss from above again.

Theo was already inside. His head popped out the open window as he started to lower the rope. Long before the rope reached me, I noticed that the thin cord, already frayed in several places, was not only not knotted, but a lot thinner than the ropes we used in Gym class. There was no way I was going to be able to climb that. I looked up, meaning to whisper up to him that fact. But the rope was already down, and he was braced against the lip of the window, securing the rope in place with his own weight.

I gripped the rope, meaning to show him just how hopeless it would be for me to try to scale it without help. But as soon as I got a firm grip on it, Theo started to pull the rope up, lifting me easily off the alley floor. I just had to hold on tight and try not to get hit in the head by the edges of the windows as he did all the work. Less than a minute after grabbing the rope, I was already up and into the window, right next to Theo.

With both of us perched on the sill, the window was snug. But I didn't like the idea of going in there alone. The room was dark, and I couldn't make much out. The moon and stars were hidden behind cloud cover and the lamps from the road below didn't stretch up to hit the window. The only illumination was a faint glow coming from under the door in the corner, which would have led out to the hallway beyond. The room was large, taking up half of that side of the building, but it was mostly empty. Right next to the window was a large dresser. Half the drawers were pulled out with clothes sticking out every which way. I pointed at it and looked to Theo questioningly, though he just shook his head and pointed towards the other side of the room.

I followed his finger to see the large, king sized bed that took up much of the far wall. As my eyes adjusted to the low light of the room, I could make out a disheveled tangle of covers over a sleeping form. The comforter had fallen onto the floor in a weird mess, with the blanket just kicked down to the foot of the bed. The sheet was wrapped around the man more like a toga than anything that would protect him from the elements. As I watched him, he gave out a snort and rolled over onto his other side. His hand flopped down over the edge of the bed, the ring catching the light from the door just right to send a glint my way. It was only after I saw that ring that I recognized the tall man from the week before. The man that had me arrested and incarcerated in that jail cell.

"There's your target," Theo whispered to me. "All you have to do is sneak over there and grab the ring off his finger."

"You make it sound easy," I whispered back.

"That's because it is." He smiled encouragingly at me and motioned for me to head over.

I rolled my eyes, knowing that it couldn't be as easy as he said. Knowing that something was going to happen. That I would just get into more trouble by doing this. But I owed him. I owed the guild for getting me out of that jail, despite the fact that it was his fault that I was in there to begin with. The ring that started it all glinted at me as if staring into my soul, pulling me forward with some unknown power.

The hardwood floors of the room creaked as I eased myself down off the windowsill. I hissed in a breath as I darted a glance over at the sleeping man, making sure that he was still asleep. He gave another snort, but then a fresh wave of snores filled the room. Holding my breath, I tried to use the snores to cover the sound of my footsteps and the creaking floorboards. Even with that as cover, it seemed like I stepped on the wrong spot every time I moved. The creaking joined the snores to make an odd chorus that sounded like it was loud enough to wake the neighborhood.

Halfway across the floor, I looked back to Theo on the windowsill. He just gave me a smile and motioned for me to continue. I rolled my eyes at him, figuring the 'expert' should have more instruction than simply "sneak over there and grab it". Turning back to my intended target, I took a few more light steps. I tried to make my steps as far apart as my short legs would allow, trying to cover as much distance as possible using as few steps to limit the noise that I generated. It took me a small eternity to make it to the man's side, but it seemed like he was still asleep when I got there. Still oblivious to the world around him.

The ring was extended up in the air. His arm was flopped over the edge of the bed and hovering over the floor, the hand slack. I figured this would make extracting the ring an easy task, just like Theo had made it out to be. With one last look at the man's face, making sure his eyes were closed tight, I reached down. I took the ring by the oversized gem and slowly started moving it up the man's finger.

I hadn't gotten it past the first knuckle before the ring was pulled from my fingers. The hand it was on flew out at me, gripping me around the wrist. Startled, I practically jumped out of my skin as I sat straight up in bed. My heart was racing a mile a minute as I looked around at the hospital room that I was in.

Chapter Thirty-Seven
When It Rains

Now

I was half asleep on the bus with my head pressed against the glass. It took me a while to figure out that I was heading to school, rather than from it. With how real my dream world was becoming, I found it odd that my real world was starting to become less tangible to me. It was slipping through my fingers like a dream after waking up.

Right before making the turn into the parking lot, the bus driver slammed on the brakes as she swerved. My head bashed against the glass as a man in grey robes darted across the street.

"Ow," I said. As I headed back to Desparia, I wrote off the man as a bleed over from my imagination.

#

Once again, I was being shaken awake. This time, with cold drops of water falling on my face, I wasn't as confused when I woke up. It also helped that whoever was shaking me was also screaming in my ear.

"Wake up, Maya," one of the twins was screaming. Heather and the other twin were pulling on my arms, hoisting me up. "Run," Tina screamed again, as I started coming back to consciousness. If being awake in Desparia could actually be called that.

It was dark out. I noticed this before much else as I ran in the wake of my friends. Heather ran awkwardly beside me as she held a ball of fire in her hand. With the stars and moon above hidden by the cloud cover, the ball of fire was the only light in the area. As my brain started working again, I realized that Serena was running right in front of me, under her own power without needing to be supported. Her armor was still in tatters. It looked more like a chainmail bikini than anything that might actually provide some protection. Her cloak was long gone, having been ripped to shreds by the giant rodents. This left only her underclothes to shield her from the rain and the biting wind. There wasn't much else I could see in the dark with her running in front of me. I was about to voice my elation at her revival. But then I looked behind me and, instead, focused all of my attention on gaining speed.

Behind us was a pack of ten or so troopers. They were barely twenty paces behind us. My friends must have lost valuable distance waking me up and pulling me along. Instead of voicing my concern over their proximity, or my joy of seeing Serena on her feet, I just asked one question between panting breaths as I ran.

"What... happened... to... the maze?"

"It disappeared as soon as they showed up," Tina said. She didn't seem to have much trouble talking as she ran. She was clearly in much better shape than I seemed to be at that moment.

"Let's hope it grows back soon," Heather said. She darted a glance behind us, looking to the troopers hot on our tail. "It might be our only chance to escape from them."

"The buildings moved in their way in the last area," Serena said, sounding hopeful.

"Different... section... different... rules," I gasped. My burst of speed was starting to fail me, and I started to lag behind the others. I didn't even have to look back to know that the troopers were quickly gaining on us. Their own huffing and puffing and the pounding of their feet was only getting louder as they got closer.

"Any ideas, Heather?" Tina yelled, similarly concerned.

"Nothing comes to mind," she yelled back.

"Wait," I said, as an idea came. The problem was finding a way to implement it while still running. Most of my supplies had been lost between the guards' search and the thieves' guild's initiation test. But I did still have a few tricks up my sleeve... quite literally in fact.

I hit the side of my arm, an action that wasn't easily performed considering how much they were flailing around as I ran. It knocked loose the device in question. A simple flicking of my sleeve behind us launched the smoke grenade. It landed right in front of our pursuers. Coughing sounds found us a few seconds later, as the troopers blundered into the large smoke cloud that the grenade created. I crossed my fingers, hoping it would buy us enough time to get away from them. Hoping that distance from them would be enough to make the maze once again block their path towards us.

Ahead of us, the third wall seemed like it was coming on quickly. According to the map, each section was only a half a mile wide. But the sky colored walls were doing weird things with perspectives in there. Behind us, the coughing gradually faded. I was too intent on our destination to risk a glance backwards. We were still several paces from the wall when it felt like I stepped on something. The area had been as flat and level as a track. There wasn't so much as a rock since the area around the second wall. So, with the flat, uninterrupted grasslands, stepping on something was unexpected to say the least. It didn't help when the foot that stepped on it was suddenly thrown upwards, me along with it.

I looked down at the others, several feet below me. Suddenly, they were surrounded on all sides by hedge. The maze had sprung up around us... well, around them. It was more like under me.

"Which means..." I began to think to myself before looking up to the vine that was holding my ankle.

"Crap," I shouted. Although, since the vine decided to start swinging me around right when I started saying it, it probably sounded more like "Cra-uh-aah-uh-ap."

I quickly got dizzy watching the world fly around me. Waiting for the vine to snap my leg in two, like the one that had grabbed my stick. Instead, I just barely missed a long line of fire that seemed to be coming out of nowhere.

"Hey, watch where you're shooting those things," I called down to Heather. I could just see her below me, preparing another flame throwing spell.

"Do you want to die here?" Tina called up to me.

"No, but I'd rather break my leg and fall to my death than be burned alive up here," I called back.

Heather's next shot hit the vine a couple feet below my ankle. It burned up and down the vine like wildfire. The vine had only just swung me back up into the air when it separated from the hedge. My momentum flung me even higher. As I tumbled back down, I got a decent glimpse of the maze. It seemed to only extend a few rows to where the smoke grenade had gone off, leaving the field beyond it wide open. The troopers were starting to regroup near the hedge. But it didn't seem to be interested in retracting again, much like how the buildings in the last area had decided to block their path towards us. This made me smile a bit as I tumbled down to my certain death.

As I approached the ground, a couple rows over from my friends, my descent started to slow. This didn't quite make sense to me until I noticed the faint humming in the air. Heather was casting another spell, this time trying to get me down without me dying. I could see her beneath me, still several rows over from me. Her hand was reaching up in the air, pointed towards me, as she stared at my descending form. She somehow managed to set me down on my feet, despite her view being blocked by the hedge walls. Seconds later, another bout of fire lanced through the hedge a few feet to my left. This left open a gap wide enough to drive an elephant through. Heather and the twins strode through the gap, which continued onwards towards the third wall. I followed behind them, trying not to laugh at their method of traversing hedge mazes. The chainsaw method was probably better, but as I glared back at the vines writhing in pain over the burned hedge, I couldn't hide my smile.

With the immediate threats behind us, I collapsed to the ground as I tried to catch my breath. I remembered being in better shape before meeting these three. At least when it came to my body in Desparia. The longer I spent with them, the more realistic that world was becoming to me and the more my body was taking on the same qualities as the one I had back on Earth. The one I had been mostly ignoring except for the time spent walking home from school or swimming. It was starting to worry me that the bracelet really would be threatening my life in both worlds, not just on Desparia.

"I am not a long-distance runner," I said after I caught my breath, trying to excuse my sudden lack of fitness.

"Well, it's not like that was a long-distance pace we were running," Heather said, seeming to play along.

I laid there for a bit with my eyes closed. I let the rain wash over me, cooling me down and refreshing me like a cool shower after a long hot day in the sun. I half expected the others to join me.

"We should be going. There's no telling how long the maze is going to keep the troopers off our tail."

I looked up and saw Serena for the first time since carrying her through the door. I mean, really saw her. The front of her armor was just as tattered as her back, falling off in places and revealing a white undershirt that was clinging to her skin with sweat and rain. There were bite and claw marks all up her arms, stomach, and chest and all over her face. They all looked weeks old and well on the mend. A few of them even looked like they were nothing but scars that would stay with her for the rest of her days. Those days no longer looked as numbered as they had been before. Fire had once again entered her eyes and she stood straight as an arrow. Her right arm was at her blade, ready to draw it forth.

"Wow," I said, as I begrudgingly got up. "That Great Tree of yours really does good work."

The three of them laughed as they led the way to the west and the third door.

Chapter Thirty-Eight
The Hospital

Five Years Earlier

The room was familiar. It reminded me of Mrs. Azalea's room on the third floor. I didn't think I was in the hospital for cancer, so I doubted I'd be up there. Anything could have happened during my time on Desparia, though. The low light streaming in through the window spoke volumes on the time I was out, making it a few hours at least. How much of that time I spent on Desparia, and how much was I just completely out of it, was anyone's guess.

The tattered remnants of my dress were on the chair to my right. The chair was the echo of the one that I had usually occupied back when I had been visiting Mrs. Azalea in her room. Mom was asleep in the chair on my left. David's chair. I tried not to disturb her as I examined myself, trying to figure out just how bad it was. The hospital gown left my arms bare, though there was only some faint bruising on them where the two boys had grabbed me. A peek down the front of my gown showed a lot more bruising, mostly around my stomach. I was too afraid to reach for the mirror on the rolling table next to me to look at my face.

"Ah, you're awake," said Rebecca, my second favorite nurse in the world, as she peeked into the room. She looked over at Mom, still asleep next to me. "I'll get the doctor," she said, before heading back out into the hall.

David slipped into the room right behind her. His hands were firmly in his pocket and his eyes on the floor. He looked more miserable than I had ever seen him, even at his mother's funeral. To be fair, I hadn't really known him long. Most of that time had been during the worst months of his life. I didn't think for one second that his state had anything to do with me.

"Hey," he muttered to the floor.

"Hi," I whispered. "How long have I been out?"

"It's Sunday morning," he supplied. "You've been here since around noon yesterday. I'm... I'm so sorry, Maya. This was all my fault. I don't know what those two were thinking."

"They were thinking that I was stalking you and that they needed to stop me," I said, knowing full well what they were thinking. "I wonder what gave them that idea."

"I never would have believed they'd take it that far. I told them I didn't want to make an issue of it."

"Perhaps that's why they did it."

"I can't be friends with them anymore. I can't be friends with people who would do... that... to a girl."

"You shouldn't be friends with anyone who'd do this to anyone. But maybe that's just me."

"I should be friends with you, like we were back in the summer. I'll tell everyone at school that this whole thing was just some big misunderstanding or something. I'm sorry. I'll make this right, I promise."

As I looked at him, I suddenly felt so old. Like he was some kid far beneath me, not even worth my attention. He had looked like he was almost an adult, sitting there next to his father at the funeral. Like he had aged decades in the months that I knew him. The thing is, I had gone through the same loss as he. Losing a parent at such a young age. Perhaps I looked as grown up as he. Or maybe the whole thing was just in my head.

"I don't think that's going to work," I told him. "I mean, yes, tell everyone that I hadn't been stalking you all that time.

Maybe people will stop ignoring me then. Or maybe they won't. I certainly know who my friends are now."

I looked over at Mom, still sleeping in the chair. She was the only person who had been by my side that whole time. Always looking out for me. Always trying to make things better. It wasn't my father's fault, or Mrs. Azalea's fault, that they weren't with me anymore. Jen, Ashley, and even David didn't have any such excuse.

"Or, more accurately, who they aren't."

"I'll make it up to you," he said again. "I promise."

"Out," came a voice from the door. Rebecca was back with another woman in scrubs. Hers had animals all up and down them, and a bear clipped onto the end of her stethoscope.

"Family only," the other woman said, as she pointed for the door. David nodded as he retreated from the room. He still hadn't looked up at me the entire time that he was there.

The doctor woke Mom up, then explained how I had a mild concussion from where my head had hit the pavement and some bruising from where the two boys had punched and kicked me. However, with no signs of any swelling and since I was awake, I would be discharged later that day.

"You were very lucky," she said. "You should take it easy for the next week. Avoid any undue stress, both physical and mental. You should make a full recovery with no lingering issues. I'm sure Paige here will be more than capable to help you with that." The doctor flipped my chart closed and handed it over to Rebecca as she headed back out into the hall.

"Of course," Mom said, nodding. "And I'll be talking to that principal of yours tomorrow. Those boys should be expelled."

"Sorry to tell you this, Paige, but since the fighting wasn't at school, you're not going to have any luck in getting the school to punish them," Rebecca told her. "You'd want to go to the police."

"No, Mom, don't," I said. "I don't think it would do any good. Besides, it might get Mr. Azalea in trouble. Funeral or not, he's a cop and he let a kid get beat up just a few feet away from him."

"Maya, they need to be punished somehow, or they'll just do it again. If not to you then to some other kid. I need to do everything I can to protect you." She placed her hand delicately on my arm, lending me comfort. "How about I take it to Joe when he's back at work next week, eh? Let him decide how to handle this, if you're just worried it'll hurt him."

"Sure, Mom," I said, smiling up at her. "I think that'll work fine."

"Good," she said. "I'd hate to think you got over your aversion to secrets."

"Humph. Secrets are a plague on humanity," I said, nodding. "The world would be a better place with fewer secrets in it."

She smiled at me, patted my arm one last time, and stood up. "I'm going to go get something to eat. You rest; I'm sure they'll be bringing in your breakfast shortly." She looked back towards me one last time at the door before heading out into the hall. Rebecca tagged along as they both gave me a little time alone. Before their footsteps faded down the hall, I was already heading back to Desparia, dreading the situation where I left off.

"Come back so soon, little thief?" the man spat in my face, as he gripped tightly to my arm.

I'd laugh at how true his words were, but there wasn't anything funny about the situation. I looked back to the window but was completely unsurprised to find it empty. No Theo in sight.

"I'll make sure they take your hand this time," he said.

He sat up in bed, trying to hold onto my wrist as he did so. I was flailing around, desperately trying to get free of his grasp. As he sat up, I twisted and pulled on my wrist and managed to slip free. Not looking back, I stumbled towards the window. My new boots clomped down on the wood in my haste. Before I could make it out the window, my tunic snagged on something. It pulled me backwards and to the ground, hitting my head against the wood floor.

"I've got you now," the man said.

He was standing over me. His hand released my tunic as he came at me. He reached down, trying to grab hold of me again. But my arms were flailing every which way as I tried to push myself across the floor with my feet. I was still trying to make it to the window. The man grunted as my hand hit his nose. He stumbled backwards, giving me the space that I needed to get back to my feet. I hopped up onto the windowsill, looking down at the ground three stories below. The rope was nowhere to be seen and it was a long way to fall.

"Something wrong, thief?" the man asked behind me, drawing my attention. He was sitting on the edge of his bed. Part of the sheet that was still wrapped around him was in his hand as he used it to stem the flow of blood from his nose. He seemed no longer interested in chasing after me. His left hand, the one with the ring, was held slack against the side of the bed, already forgotten.

"Yea," I said, putting as much bravado into that one word as I could. A smirk found its way across my face as I jumped back down from the windowsill. Brazenly, I stalked back across the room towards him. As I approached, he actually started to squirm away from me, which made my smile bigger than ever. "I forgot to get what I came for."

I grabbed the sheet, pulling it a bit from his hands. As he fumbled to recover it, I managed to slide the ring off his finger. At the same time, I snapped up the comforter off the floor. I ran for the window, dragging the comforter across the floor, intending to use it as a rope to descend out the window. Before I managed to get out, though, the man had grabbed the other end of the comforter. I hadn't expected that. My momentum was already taking me out the window, with no room to stop. I tumbled through the window, falling down into the alleyway. My hands held on tightly to the ring and the comforter. When the comforter went taught, I came to a sudden stop. My back hit the wall of the house. I grunted, trying not to slip from the comforter and fall to my certain death below. At least, that was until the comforter started pulling me upwards back towards the window.

I looked around desperately for an escape, any escape. All I saw was the wall in front of me, for the building across the alley. I didn't think, didn't have time to think, before I let go of the comforter. As I fell, I pushed off the wall behind me as I aimed for the wall opposite. I hit it, hit it hard, and bounced back. As I fell, I flailed around, desperate to find some purchase. Something to hold onto as I made my way to the hard ground below.

Something must have worked in my flailing, because I didn't die when I hit the ground. I fell feet first, my new boots taking the brunt of the force of my fall, before toppling forward into the muck. My previously grey outfit was quite brown afterwards, and I wasn't entirely sure it was all from the alley. Carefully, I got up, first to my knees, then to my feet. My left foot wouldn't take my full weight. I knew it should hurt like hell, but I didn't really feel it much. I was very glad that this was all just happening in my imagination. Calls to the guards rang out from above me as I limped from the alleyway.

I made it another block away before my ankle gave way and I toppled into the next alley over. As I lay there on the floor, I crumpled into a ball and hid there, pretending to sleep as the stomping footsteps of the guards ran past. It occurred to me that this was what Theo had been talking about, my ability to become invisible when I wanted to. Sitting there, in the dark, smelling like an outhouse, I started to laugh a little. I started to think that if I hadn't been so used to being invisible in reality, I wouldn't have been so adept at disappearing from the guards and would have been caught. It didn't occur to me at the time that, had I not been so invisible, I wouldn't have needed to go to Desparia at all.

I waited in that alleyway for dawn. The hours sped by whenever the guards weren't around. I'm sure I would have slept had I been able to do so on Desparia back then. As the sun rose in the distance, the calls for guards and people running past had already stopped. I managed to emerge into the early traffic of the town. It felt like eyes were on me everywhere, though none of the people seemed to notice me besides my smell. Street rat indeed, I thought.

The problem was, I had no idea where to find Theo. He just seemed to always find me. Walking around, with that ring burning a hole in my pocket, was probably the dumbest thing to do after just having stolen it. The only idea I came up with was to find this guild and knock on their door. From how infamous the place was, I figured it wouldn't be out of the question for people to know where it was. The only question was who to ask. Asking the wrong person would just put me back in that jail cell. So, I did what they always did in all those books my dad got me. I walked right into the pub and asked the bartender.

Chapter Thirty-Nine
It Pours

Now

"There's some crazy dude out there with a sword," someone shouted. The shout pulled me back to reality. Everyone in class jumped to their feet, rushing over to the window to look outside. "No, no, no," the guy said. "He was over in the parking lot. Dude tried to steal my car."

"Everyone, calm down," my teacher shouted out, calling the class to order as I headed back to Desparia.

The third door awaited.

#

The third door was just that. A door. Nothing special. It wasn't even that big of a door. It was about ordinary size for a door in either world. There were no markings on it. No scene that needed to take place in the vicinity to unlock the door. It was even made of wood, with a thin layer of stain to help protect against the rain. The rain had become a torrent at about the same time we rounded the southwest corner of the wall. What I wouldn't have given at that moment for a proper umbrella.

"So, what now?" I asked. We just stood there, staring at the locked door as rivulets of rain ran down my face. I shivered as a cool breeze somehow found its way into the protected enclave.

Heather threw her arms back, drawing in mana and shaping it, harnessing it into a strong spell, before throwing forth another lance of fire. The rain hissed as it made contact, quickly turning to a thick wall of steam that blocked our view of the door. Heather kept the fire flowing for almost a minute before breaking off. She rested her hands on her knees and panted to catch her breath. As the steam parted, we all held our breaths, hoping against hope that this door would be so simple.

As the steam parted, I glared at the completely undamaged door. "Well, that didn't work." There wasn't even a sign of singeing. The door was still as light brown as freshly cut wood. "Maybe an unlock spell would work better," I suggested. I didn't really know if such a spell existed, so I laughed a little at my own suggestion.

Tina walked brazenly forward. She grabbed the doorknob and turned it as hard as she could. After a few seconds, she gave up and stepped back next to us. The door was unchanged. "Well, no one else tried it," she said with a shrug.

"Because we knew it was locked," her sister said.

"And an unlock spell wouldn't work," Heather said, dejectedly. "I'd need to be more powerful than the emperor to undo one of his locking spells."

"Well, okay, maybe this is where I come in," I said.

Reaching into one of the deepest folds of my practically bottomless and never-ending collection of pockets, where the guards had failed to properly search, I pulled out one of my two last sets of lockpicks. They weren't my best set. I kept that close to the top of my pockets, so it had been found quickly in the jail. My mind drifted back to them, wishing I had managed to rescue my equipment during the exodus from the dungeons. Even so, this set should have been enough to get the job done.

"If you want something done right," I began, as I stepped up to the door.

I inserted my torsion wrench into the keyhole. It was surprisingly large and reminded me of the locks they usually showed on old western movies that looked like you could reach in and unlock it with a finger. It was a good thing that I hadn't tried doing that, because as soon as I inserted my torsion wrench, the keyhole constricted. The long stretch twirled around the central section as the whole thing collapsed in on itself, taking my wrench with it.

"You were saying something about wanting something done right?" Tina asked in a mocking tone. Serena was laughing almost hysterically behind her.

"My torsion wrench," I whined silently, as I stared at the place the keyhole used to be.

"Come on you guys," Heather said. "Think. We don't have all day. Those troopers are going to get through the maze eventually. I'd like to be well on our way to the next door before they do."

"I'm open to suggestions," I said. I lamented my lost tool as I tucked the remainder of the set back in the same deep pocket that I removed them from.

"Maybe we missed something in the field," Serena said, as her laughing fit subsided. "I mean, we did run through it rather quickly. The solutions to the last two doors were in the area in front of them."

I looked back at the field, which was still completely covered by long, high hedge walls going every which way in several square miles of maze. There was no telling how many days it would take us to do a proper search of the field. The troopers would be on us long before then.

"I don't think so," Tina said. "Those tetric pieces were enchanted to draw our attention. And there were tons of them, probably more than we even found. I imagine there were more than enough pieces to line the whole wall, not just that one door. If the solution was out there, we would have seen it no matter how fast we were running past it."

"You just don't want to have to go back in there," Serena accused.

"Of course, I don't. And you don't either. But if it meant getting to kill the emperor..."

"For our family," Serena agreed with a nod.

"And for all those other families," Tina added.

"Guys, you're not helping," Heather interrupted. "There has to be a solution to this that we're just not seeing."

We stood there for a while, staring at the door that wasn't giving us any clues. We were only getting wetter as the sky grew darker. A distant rumbling of thunder told us that the storm wasn't going to be letting up anytime soon. It would probably last all night. Serena gave a sneeze, startling us out of our thoughts.

"We should try to find shelter," Tina said. "Serena is still weak from the rodent attack this morning. She's bound to catch a cold in this rain."

"Where exactly do you expect to find shelter in here," Serena asked. "We didn't bring tents and what few trees are in this area aren't large enough to give shelter on its own or clustered enough to do us much good. I'll be fine, as long as it doesn't get any worse and we get through this door as fast as we can."

The fading light reminded me of my fading life. I looked down at my bracelet. Most of the sands had already flowed into the bottom half, leaving only a few hours left before my death was once again on the verge of being triggered. "Well, while we ponder on this, would you mind resetting my bracelet again?" I asked Heather. "It's not like we know what to expect on the other side of the door."

"Sure," Heather said. "Maybe you should brace yourself a little this time. We don't need you passing out again."

I thrust my arm out towards her, this time curling away from it and clenching my whole body like a child about to get a shot. As the magic flowed through my body once again, all I felt was a light tickling along my arm and down my back. If the sands hadn't reset themselves, I would have thought the spell had failed. That the rain took most of the power away from her. Instead, the lighter power of the spell gave me an idea.

"Maybe the size of the door is a clue," I suggested. "Like we need to make it bigger somehow."

"Again, I ask with what?" Serena yelled over another rumble of thunder, this one sounding much closer than the last.

"With a spell," I suggested, though it sounded more like a question. "Heather, can you somehow... grow the door to be like the other sets had been?"

"That is the dumbest suggestion I have ever heard," Serena said.

"I can try," Heather said, giving Serena the stink eye. "Let's not crap on every suggestion being made until we really know what we're dealing with here."

Heather faced the door again, this time with her hands balled in fists together in front of her. She mumbled a few words to herself as the spell built in her hands. Then she pulled them towards her body before thrusting them out again. Towards the door and also outward, her hands opening in the process. A ripple flew through the falling rain, knocking several drops off to the side. It spun as it hit the door... and bounced off. It hit the four of us, knocking us to the ground.

"Ow," Serena said, cradling her head as she sat up. "I told you it was a dumb suggestion. The door is protected against magic or something. Nothing is going to get through that thing." Her statement was emphasized by another crackle of thunder.

Heather took something out of her pocket. It was a small ball of light hanging from a string. She let it hang from her hand, using the light to illuminate the area. We all looked over at the offending door. A darkness surrounded it like an aura. Whatever antimagic enchantment was on it blocked out the magical light. "I think she's right," Heather admitted. "We're not getting through that thing with any magic that I know how to wield."

"So, what else do we have to work with?" Tina asked, trying to be helpful. "Maya's tools will just get eaten up by the door itself. Magic isn't going to work. Maybe..." she broke off when an idea came to her.

She stood up, taking a few long strides towards the hedge. She was facing the door with her back to the hedge. I was about to warn her about the murderous vines, but she seemed to be concentrating. She knelt right there, close enough to the hedge to be attacked. The hedge didn't seem to mind her being that close. Her hands pressed together as if she were preparing to pray. Her lips flowed as a long line of words seemed to surge out of her. At first, I wasn't sure what she was trying to do. But then a ripple flowed across the ground. It started at the hedge and headed for the door. Seconds later, several of the vines that had been causing me nothing but trouble suddenly broke out of the ground right in front of the door and started attacking it. As each vine whipped against the door, it shattered into dozens of pieces all the way down to the root. I could almost swear I heard a whimpering sound come from each of the vines as they crept back to the hedge maze to, hopefully, die a slow agonizing death.

"Yea, that's not going to work either," Serena said, as the last vine broke apart. "It was an interesting idea at least, though."

"Well, I don't see you trying anything," I snapped at her. Her pessimism was getting to me.

Serena glared at me, a menacing snarl spreading over her face. She stalked towards me, slowly drawing her sword. When she was right up against me, she leaned into my face. She placed the flat of her blade a hair's breadth away from my neck.

"I fail to see what this would be able to do against that when magic has had no effect. But if you insist..."

She twirled around. The tattered remnants of her chain mail flapped up in my face as she charged the door. After two, halfhearted strikes of her sword against the wood, two loud, hollow bangs, and not much else, she backed away.

"See?"

"Alright, alright, enough of that you two," Heather snapped. She sounded a lot like my aunt when she'd scold my out of control cousins. "There has to be something we're just missing here."

A flash of light struck to our right, startling us. I literally jumped up a few inches in start and my heart felt like it wanted to run away without me. As I landed, something seemed to crumple in my left boot and an amber liquid started flowing out into the small pond that the ground was slowly becoming. "Dang it," I shouted. I took off my boot and opened the hidden compartment in the soul. The broken and expended bottle of lantern oil fell out onto the ground. "So much for my firebomb idea," I said.

"Firebomb?" Heather asked.

"Yea, like one of your fire spells but without magic. It was just an idea I was toying with. A variation on that smoke grenade I used earlier. I never got around to testing it, though." Dejectedly, I reattached the soul and put the boot back on. I hoped that I wouldn't have to walk near an open fire before I had a chance to properly clean out the mess. "I completely forgot it was in there. It seemed like a good place to store it at the time, but I just don't seem to walk as lightly as I used to."

"Ladies, our illustrious thief," Serena snapped at me.

"Enough," Heather shouted again, perfectly timed with another thunderclap.

"Uh, guys, I have a suggestion," Tina said. She was looking off into the field behind us, where a small fire could be seen off in the distance.

"Is that the troopers?" I asked, trying to make out anyone sitting around the fire.

"No," Heather said. "What is that?"

"Well, with Maya's firebomb breaking, it got me thinking that there's more than one way to light a fire," Tina started to explain.

"I only had the one bottle, unfortunately," I said. "I really don't know what's wrong with me these days. I've had that bottle in my boot for weeks and I've never broken it."

"No, I mean the lightning," Tina said.

"What about it?" Serena asked.

"What if the lightning hit the door? It's not magic, so the door wouldn't block it and it might be enough to light the door on fire. We could burn our way through to the next area."

"And how exactly are we going to get the lightning to hit the door?" I asked. "I mean, it's not like we have anything to use as a lightning rod or anything."

"What's a lightning rod?" Heather asked. "Can we use that to control the lightning or something?"

"No, not really. It's just a long metal rod that attracts the lightning so that it won't hit anything more important."

"Will you guys listen to me?" Tina snapped. "I'm saying I can try to call the lightning down to hit the door."

"Well, hell, I can throw lightning at the door," Heather said. "You want to see?"

"No," we all shouted, before she got her spell off. We were all still hurting from the last spell she threw at the door.

"A lightning spell would still be made of magic," Tina said. "I'm talking about calling the lightning that's already there. It's the actual lightning that's been flashing around us for the past few minutes, just directed to a target I give it. However, I don't think we should be standing right next to the target in question when it hits."

I looked over to the door, just a few feet away from me. The ground was covered in a puddle over an inch deep as the already waterlogged ground failed to absorb it. The four of us were already drenched to the bone. If she was able to hit the door, all four of us were bound to be electrocuted in the process. "Yea," I said, exaggerating the word into several syllables. "It might be a good idea for us to move... maybe to even climb up the hedge a bit, if the vines don't attack us while they lick their wounds. This puddle is all over the place and the electricity from the lightning is bound to electrocute the whole area."

"What do you mean?" Tina asked. She sounded confused.

"Lightning tends to travel across water and the whole area is drenched. Calling the lightning down here might kill us even if we back up a quarter of a mile away, and I figure you'd need to be closer than that to aim properly."

"Well, maybe you can make one of those rod thingies," Serena suggested in a snarky tone.

"Like I said, we don't have the material for it. We'd need a long metal rod of some kind, I don't know, like your sword or something."

"Oh, no, you're not taking my sword," Serena snapped. "It's bad enough those mongrels stole my swords and didn't have them with them when we got free. Worse still, they only had one sword among them that was worth taking. You are not taking this one thing away from me. Not without getting me two proper swords in exchange."

"Fine, then what is your suggestion to keep us from being electrocuted?" I yelled back.

"I don't even know what that means," Serena yelled at me.

"Oh, for the goddesses' sake," Heather yelled.

I could feel the buildup of magic flowing into her once more. Her hands shook out next to her several times, her power flowing through them. After a few seconds, her wet dress started to let off a billow of steam. The rain hissed in protest as it hit her, joining in the steam flowing off into the air. As she stood there, continuing to shake her arms, I could feel the heat radiating off of her. Her white dress started to turn almost red from the power of her spell. Slowly the heat expanded, causing the ground around her to sizzle. As the wall of heat approached me, I took a step back, edging away from the power of the spell. But as the wave passed by the twins with no lasting impact, I took a step forward into the heat.

It felt nice to be warm again. To let the spell flow over me and dry out my tunic and pants. I worried a little that the spell would ignite my boot, but it didn't seem to have any effect. As I stared down at my foot, I noticed that the ground around us was dry as well. There was a noticeable circle around us, the limits of the spell, where the puddles from the surrounding area feared to tread. As long as she could hold the spell in place, we would be safe from electrocution.

"Good enough?" she asked. She continued to shake her arms, but she was looking around at her work like it was nothing to maintain the spell.

"Yea," I said breathily. "That... that'll work."

Tina smiled over at Heather before kneeling down next to her, returning to her prayer pose. She started to mumble another prayer to the Great Tree, whose power I would never again question after seeing Tina's use of it. There was another crackle of thunder. This one seemed to be closer than all the other strikes that had come before, but still nowhere near the door.

I was starting to wonder if Tina was getting a busy signal in her prayers when another lightning bolt struck. This time right it was in front of us, right where the door had been. The flash of light blinded me for a moment. I stumbled backwards in shock. Someone grabbed onto the front of my tunic. They pulled me back within the circle of the spell before I got fried by the lightning. As my vision started to clear, I saw Serena take her hand back. I blinked several times as I looked over at where the door had been... and where it still was.

The door was still in place. It looked no worse for the wear of being struck by lightning. The ground around it also showed no sign of being struck. However, the doorway was glowing with an odd power. A golden light flowed up and down the front of the door as the edge glowed brighter and brighter. Before it became as bright as the flash of lightning, a loud clicking sound came from the door and it creaked slowly open. The light faded as it did.

Beyond the door, we could clearly see a large, thick forest that seemed to go on for forever... and behind us the hedge maze slowly retracted once again into the ground.

Chapter Forty
The Bigger Fight

Five Years Earlier

I took the next couple days off from school. It wasn't my idea, but it worked out pretty well. Mom worried about sending me back there with those two kids still going to the same school as I was. True to her word, she didn't go to the cops about them. At least, not right away. Instead, she did something much worse. She went to their parents. By noon on Tuesday, she was completely confident that neither of them would ever be seen in that school again. I didn't get any details beyond that. However, she had another bright idea on how to keep the incident at the funeral from happening again.

"It's these stupid t-shirts," she said.

She pulled all of Dad's old shirts from my drawers, grabbing them with no concern over the destruction she was doing. I was trying to scoop them up as quickly as she was pulling them out. But there were too many of them for my tiny arms to hold. She had a large trash bag that she was dumping them into. It didn't look like it was just a choice for storing them in.

"You look too much like a boy in them and people have been treating you like one. You're not a boy, you're a girl. You should start dressing like the girl you are."

"But, Mom, they're all I have left of Dad," I whined.

"Oh, nonsense," she snapped. "You have all these books. You have the memories that you both shared. You have a large collection of pictures of him. Hell, you have his eyes. You'll see a part of him every time you look in a mirror. You don't need some silly shirts that don't even fit you right to remember him by."

"Please, Mom. Please, don't throw them out. Just... put them in storage or something. I swear I won't wear them anymore. Just, please, don't get rid of them."

It was the most awake, most present I had been in reality for weeks. Since I started going to Desparia on a regular basis. It was freaking me out. It was almost painful. Not just the fear of losing the shirts. Not just the loss I was feeling once more. But the actual paying attention to the world again. I longed for the bubble, the numbness, that my imaginary world provided. But with Dad's shirts on the line, I had to act.

"Alright, fine," she huffed. "But you're going to start dressing like a proper girl your age. We are going to go shopping and you're going to buy everything from the right section of the mall, or these shirts will be thrown out. Deal?"

"Fine," I huffed. I relaxed a little once she promised not to get rid of the shirts.

"Good. Now get your stuff, we're going to head to the mall."

I just nodded, grabbing my book bag and jacket. The jacket was already girly enough, pink and fluffy and it should have been enough to ward off those boys if my clothes really had anything to do with why they went after me. Though, given the original rumors had been regarding my clothes, I figured there was at least a little ringing of truth to her mindset. I knew the mall was over an hour away, in Portland, so I just tucked myself into the car and sunk back into my fantasy world. Back into my comfortable little bubble and away from the bright and painful reality around me.

The bartender I had asked about the thieves' guild that day refused to tell me where the place was. He did manage to get a message to Theo, my only contact at the guild. Two days later, after the heat that had been on me after the break in had died down a little, I was in the back corner of that same tavern, waiting for him to arrive. With my back to the corner and my eyes on the door, I figured there was no way that Theo would be able to sneak up on me.

Still, I jumped as a chair scraped across the floor next to me. Theo sat down, smiling widely. I knew he had done it intentionally, just to startle me.

"Good to see you, kid. Changed your mind about the guild, have you?"

"No," I said. I slapped the ring on the table in front of him. "I just want to get the hell out of this town."

"Good," Theo said, nodding. This took me by surprise, given how adamant he had been about me joining up. I just stared at him in confusion for a few minutes. "You're too green, kid. That's straight from the higher-ups. I'd train you up a little, make you ready for their next test. But you'd need to spend a little time outside the town. The guards are still looking for you, though I'm not too surprised they haven't found you yet."

"Why? Because of my ability to become 'invisible'?"

"No, because you stink so much no one would bother looking twice at you. Seriously, kid, there's such a thing as bathing."

This took me a bit by surprise. Sure, I knew that I still stank from falling in the muck the other day. But I had never thought about bathing in Desparia. I sort of figured it would be like eating, drinking, and sleeping. Something I didn't really need to do, even though everyone else there did. I looked down at my outfit, still brown from the muck that I landed in. Most of it was worked in rather than caked on. A lot of it had flaked off over the course of the two days. But I had been covered by the stuff.

"Here," he said. He slapped down a solid gold coin on the table. "Payment for the ring. It would have been worth more, but, well, I did the scouting and all that. I get my own cut on the job. Look me up if you are ever in the area again and need to offload something. I still see a great future for you kid. In the meantime, get yourself some decent clothes. Something not so crusted in filth. And not so bright either. The brown works better than that bright gray it used to be. Just, use actual dye, not dung, next time."

He snatched up the ring, shaking his head as he headed out the door. I watched him go, having a weird feeling that I would never see him again. That Theo would return to whatever corner of my subconscious he came out of and be reabsorbed with the rest of it. I gave a silent thanks to the weird man, who amounted to my first friend in this much weirder world. My first real friend in years. After he disappeared into the crowd, I scooped up the coin off the table and headed out of the tavern.

"You okay over there?" Mom asked. Her voice pulled me out of my daydream as she turned off the highway and onto the main road that encircled the mall. The names of the familiar shops called out to me from some old memory that didn't feel like it belonged to me as they ran past us.

"Sure," I said. I tried to be subtle as I shook out my sleepiness a bit. "Just thinking."

"You've been doing a lot of that lately. I'm starting to worry about you."

My face went cold as it seemed like my worst fear was about to come true. It was the reason why I never spoke of my time in Desparia to Mom. I was afraid that she'd think I was crazy and commit me to a mental institute. I wondered briefly if I should be committed, though I wasn't sure where the thought came from.

"Don't worry, Mom. I think it's just part of getting used to being alone all the time."

"Well, hopefully after this shopping trip you won't need to be alone all the time. I want you to be happy... or at least as happy as you can be given all that you've been through these past couple of months."

I forced a smile at her, wondering how she'd feel about it if she knew just how much I really had been going through, on both worlds. "Sure," I said, noncommittally.

After pulling into a spot, she hopped out of the car. "Don't forget where we parked," she said, automatically.

"Isn't that your job?" I asked back. It was the usual response for my family. My forced smile turned into one that was more pensive as my thoughts turned to Dad and the incident that spawned the inside joke. The time that we came out the wrong side of the movie theater when I was four. I barely remembered the day, but that moment would be ingrained in my memory forever. This was more due to the repetition of the joke than anything else. It was something for me to treasure among so many fond memories I had of Dad.

Mom dragged me around the entire building. We stopped at each store where she pulled out the most girly stuff she could find. None of it seemed right. None of it seemed like me. Like something I would wear. From my mom's growing frustration over the course of the day, I started to think that was the idea. As we passed through the other parts of the stores, walking past the boys' sections between the door and the intended destinations, I'd see a bunch of old t-shirts that reminded me of the stuff I used to wear. The stuff that I was no longer allowed to wear. The stuff Dad had left to me. I'd stop for a few seconds to look at the graphic t's, mostly those with the cute jokes that no one would get but geeks like Dad.

"Girls' section only," Mom would say, when she spotted me looking at the shirts. She'd pull me away and back on track. "Like we agreed."

It wasn't like there weren't t-shirts in the girls' sections. Most of them were cutesy critters and unicorns. I tried a few of them on, but they all fit me too well. They showed off too much of my figure for my liking. Often, I'd grab a few sizes too big. But even those just didn't feel right. Not to mention that Mom saw me in a changing room as an excuse to get me to try on a few of the dresses that she kept insisting on.

It wasn't until we got halfway through the mall that we passed some weird outlet that had an unfamiliar name. It was one of those non-chain places that would be gone in a month. Only then did I find anything worth getting. The store was called Lumberjanes' Love.

"You are not getting that," Mom said, as soon as I picked up the flannel shirt. It was oversized, coming down to my knees as I held it up to myself.

"Why not?" I asked, disappointed.

"They're boy clothes."

"But, Mom, it's in the girls' section, like you said. That was the deal, right? At least let me try it on, please?"

Mom just rolled her eyes and pointed to the dressing room. I gave out a little yip of glee, which had the overly tattooed cashier smiling my way, before dashing off to try on the new outfit. I even came out to show it off to Mom, twirling around like the flannel shirt and jeans were a ball gown.

"Well, the shirt at least looks a bit like a dress," Mom allowed. Her words practically spat in my good mood. "And, like you said, it's in the right section. I'm still getting you some dresses before we leave here, though."

I smiled, nodded to her to give her her own little fun. As she looked around for something girly enough for her tastes, I dashed back to the display and took every color they had in the same style and size. As we continued in the full circuit of the mall, I started seeing the flannel in those stores too. They were always ostracized to the back corners next to the fire exits or stock rooms. Though there were plenty of jeans in all sizes, none of them were of the same breathy, relaxed fit jeans that could stand up to a beating like the ones I found at Lumberjanes'.

By the end of the day, we headed out of the mall with so many bags that I had lost count. Mom seemed to be overcompensating for giving in to me at the one store. She bought me five girly outfits for each of the flannel shirts. I didn't mind it all that much, as I had never promised to wear any of them. I knew that she wouldn't be able to get me to do so. I was high on life for the first time in what felt like ages as we left the mall parking lot and I was able to dip back into Desparia, where my real life waited for me.

Once I had some money to spend, shopping in Desparia was strikingly similar to shopping in reality, on Earth. I spent only a little time walking through the bazaar, surrounded by the sights and sounds that I was only barely registering consciously. It wasn't too unlike the sights and sounds of the mall that I had been spending the rest of my day in. Quickly realizing that most of the merchants there were selling more perishable goods and small trinkets, I headed to the tailor shop. The familiar sight of Gregor's General Goods made me cautious. But the main tailor shop of the town was right next door.

There was no bell on the door, but that didn't stop the man behind the counter from glaring at me the moment that I set foot in the store. Learning my lesson from my encounter next door, I flashed the gold coin before heading through the shop. The shopkeeper's eyes bulged when he saw the flash of gold. There were a few garments already made and hanging up around the store, even a few that were folded on shelves against the walls. He didn't have nearly the stock that most of the stores at the mall had. But there were a few of the smaller shops that it came close to.

Just like at Lumberjanes', I almost immediately spotted exactly what I was looking for. It would have been rather remarkable how well my imaginary world echoed the real one, except for the very fact that it was imaginary. There was a large tunic hanging from a wooden manikin in the far corner of the shop. It looked a lot like the one I had been wearing since I first came to Desparia, the one that seemed like a part of my subconscious. Instead of wool grey, it was marbled green and brown, like forest camouflage that a soldier would wear.

"Perhaps I might interest you in a newly made dress?" the shopkeeper said, as he came up behind me. "Certainly, a lovely girl like— "

"I'll take this one," I said, interrupting him.

"Ah... Alright then. Perhaps you'd like me to— "

"I'll take it as is," I said.

I knew that the man was thinking it would be huge on me. And it was. The shopkeeper reluctantly placed it over the crud covered tunic. The new one came down almost to my ankles and out well past where my shoulders actually ended. It looked like some old 80's women's blazer. If I knelt down and tucked my head inside, I could completely disappear inside of it like a turtle's shell.

"Perfect," I said, as I looked at myself in the mirror.

"Miss, I would be remiss not to tell you that... you look rather like a street person in that attire, especially with your... current state of... uncleanliness?" He almost said it as a question, as apologetic and sensitive as he was trying to be.

"That's kind of the point," I said, smiling at it. "How much?" I asked. I looked around it for a price tag, finding none.

"It's... three silver, and a promise that you don't tell people I sold it to you. I have a reputation to uphold."

My stomach did a weird dance as I realized I still had no idea how their money system worked. "Can you break a gold?" I asked, thinking it rather funny.

"How many pieces do you want it in?" he asked.

"I don't know. Whatever the change would be after I pay for the tunic."

He stared at me for a few moments, confused by something, before realization hit him. "Oh, you mean convert the gold to silver. Yes, miss, I can do just that. You silly foreigners and your terminologies."

I managed to get a new pair of pants while I was there. They were fashioned in the same style as the tunic. Although, the shopkeeper, who was also the tailor, had to sew them up for me from some leftover material. Altogether, I managed to come away with five silver left over. I still didn't know the conversion rates between the coins, but I didn't feel cheated in the least. Not wanting to waste the few coins that I had left, I just packed up my new purchases and headed off. I hoped to find a pond or lake or river to bathe in and get the foul stench off of me before changing into my new clothes.

As I exited the town, Mom was pulling up into the driveway. All told, despite Mom's attempts to dress me up like a Barbie doll, the day worked out nicely enough. It was one of the last few days that I had spent with someone without trying to leave the whole time. I still felt like I had gotten the better side of our little compromise. I'd miss wearing Dad's old shirts, but I was getting a little old for them. I didn't think the new clothes, even the clothes Mom had picked out for me, would have any bearing on my social status at school. But I was willing enough to humor her. Anything to keep her from leaving me too.

"Grab the mail while I bring these bags in," Mom said, as I hopped out of the car. "I can't believe how much you got today."

"Yea. How much I got," I said, rolling my eyes. I skipped my way back to the end of the sidewalk to the mailbox, feeling like a kid again for the first time in months.

Normally I don't bother to look at the mail. Nothing ever came for me anyway. Even the few items of mail addressed to me that would come over the course of the school year would really be for Mom and... well, only Mom now. However, as the letters came out of the mailbox, Dad's name flashed up to me from the top letter and I, once again, got hit by his loss.

I just stared at the letter as I slowly walked back up the sidewalk. The return address was somewhere in Austin, Texas. For some reason, seeing the city in print reminded me of all the books that he had gotten me over the years. I don't really know why I did it, what got into me at that moment, but I ripped open the envelope. I pulled out the sheet inside. It was a notice for overdue rent for some address down there.

"Why is Dad getting a notice for overdue rent?" I asked.

I hadn't really meant to ask Mom, perhaps more like ask the universe or just ask the question out loud. But Mom had been standing right there. She snatched the notice out of my hand, along with the rest of the mail. She glanced at it just for a moment before crumpling it up and tossing it into the wastebasket by the door.

"Maya, upstairs, now," Mom said, sternly. She pointed towards the large collection of bags that had accumulated at the bottom of the stairs.

"But Mom," I whined.

"Now," she said, the matter obviously closed.

"I hate secrets," I huffed.

I dragged my clothes upstairs. I dumped the dresses that I knew I'd never wear into the bottom of my closet and flopped down on the bed. As I did so, the bed bumped into the bookcase next to it. It knocked a couple of the books down onto the bed, with three more of them falling to the floor. With a huff, I stood back up, picking up each book in turn and placing it back on the shelf.

As I placed each book in their usual spots, I noticed that the price sticker on the back of each book said the name "Austin Books". Frantically, I grabbed each one of the books Dad had gotten me over the years off the shelves, checking each one in turn. He had always told me that his trips out of town were all over the country. He'd even tell me stories of his adventures in his exciting career as an insurance adjuster. And yet, each and every book in that entire bookcase said "Austin Books" on it.

"What the hell?" I asked of the offending books, none of which were telling me anything. "Why would Dad have lied to me all these years? What was he doing with an apartment in Texas? And if he was just going there all the time, instead of going to places for work, why would he have left me? Why didn't he bring me with him?"

Secrets. It always seemed to come down to secrets. Everyone had them. Even I had them, with my time spent on Desparia. And now, even my father, the man I had idolized my whole life, showed me his own little secrets. While this little hint of a secret left me with more questions than answers, I found that I didn't really care for the answers. I'm sure they would have only disappointed me more if I had them.

"Screw it," I said to myself. I scooped up one of the garbage bags that Mom had left behind that morning, when she was packing up the old t-shirts. One by one, I started dumping all the old books into it. They were tainted now, contaminated by my father's secret. I didn't want them in my room. I wasn't quite sure what Mom would have thought about that, I still don't really. But I didn't seem to care anymore. Not about what she thought or what anyone thought.

"Why should I care what other people think? They don't seem to care about me at all," I whined to myself.

As I headed back to Desparia, my thoughts were only on the chance of finding a dragon and stealing half its treasure. I no longer cared if anyone noticed how much time I spent in my head. And I certainly no longer cared if anyone thought I was crazy.

Chapter Forty-One
Where's a Good Maze When You Need One?

Now

None of us needed any prodding in light of the falling hedges. Heather and the twins took off at a decent run. "Not more running," I sighed, as I followed them.

"We have a decent head start over the troopers," Tina said, hearing my complaint. "Also, we finally have some cover with this forest. We don't need to run full out this time, but I wouldn't dawdle if I were you."

They managed to keep the pace bearable enough for me to follow, even with my failing fitness. The woods were eerily silent. At first the only sound besides our hurried footsteps was the soft pattering of the rain on the canopy above. But soon, even the rain stopped. The typical nighttime wilderness noises were noticeably absent. I had the feeling that this wasn't just from our disturbing of the peace within.

The twins led the way, jumping around trees as if they were running on a normal sidewalk. Or, better yet, a perfectly flat track. Heather and I were just struggling to keep up, occasionally tripping on a loose root or getting whacked in the head by a branch. Having Heather struggle as much as I did should have made me feel better. But before meeting these three, I would have been able to make it through that forest with almost as much grace as the twins did.

Every few minutes or so, I'd look behind us, half expecting to see the troopers right on top of us and mostly expecting to see the trees move to block our exit as the buildings and the hedges had done in the past areas. Instead, the trees remained where they were, unmoving, unknowing, uncaring about our passage. I would have felt more comfortable if they had moved.

Needless to say, I was immensely grateful that we were informed the moment the troopers had entered the area. Like before, their entrance caused an immediate change on the landscape. This time, instead of the mazes clearing out, there was a loud trumpeting sound. It was the typical trumpeting sound that the troopers always made whenever they wanted to make their presence known. It always gave me chills when I heard it, making it plainly clear that I had no right being anywhere near where I was at the time. In the absolute quiet of the woods, it was all the more foreboding.

My travelling companions, my friends, had similar reactions. They quickly picked up their pace. When I began to pant loudly, they slowed down a bit. They would glare over at me with looks of disdain, as if my failing fitness was somehow my fault. Granted, I never really cared for my body back on Earth. Not in any intentional way. But then again, I had never expected for it to impact my adventures there. I came to that world to get away from my problems on Earth, not to bring them with me.

To make matters worse, the trumpeting sound was not the only thing that happened upon the troopers' entrance. If I hadn't been so much more clumsy than normal, I might not have noticed it at all. The trees' roots were starting to come out of the ground more, giving me twice as many opportunities to trip and fall. And it seemed like I found every one of them.

It felt like forever before we rounded to the northern side of the wall. I wasn't sure how much further the next door would be, but we would need to keep our lead long enough to solve the new puzzle... and then for six more regions. "This is hopeless," I said. I was almost proud of myself for saying it without a single pant. "Even if we stay ahead of these guys until the door, we're only going to keep losing ground."

"What do you suggest?" Heather asked. "We turn and fight? There's at least ten of them and four of us, and you're not exactly a fighter, Maya. I don't know about those two, but I can't take on three troopers at once. Even one is sometimes a stretch when I'm not properly prepared. And I'm not prepared for a fight right now."

I nodded, putting my head down, and just trying to keep up with them. I just had to hope that we didn't run into another trap, or, better yet, that the troopers did. My heart almost fell when Tina called out ahead of us, until my brain registered what it was that she was saying.

"The door," she called. "I can see the door ahead of us. We're almost there."

The door in the fourth wall was ahead of us, and we would make it before the troopers caught up with us.

But, as I tripped on another root, the bell rang, signaling the end of tenth period and jarring me back to Earth.

Epilogue
The Fourth Door

Heather

The twins were easily staying ahead of Heather. Not that that was their intent. They didn't seem to think anything of the fact that the forest around them was trying to grab hold of them. To hold them in place as it closed in around them. She almost envied their ability to walk through, and up and down, the forest like their own personal playground.

Heather looked back to Maya, who had been having more trouble getting through the forest than she was. She watched as Maya stumbled her way through the forest. Maya used a tree as leverage, before tripping on a root, falling to the ground. Or, at least, she started to fall to the ground. Halfway there, Maya just disappeared.

Heather was distracted momentarily as she stared at the place where Maya disappeared. She expected to find some hidden cavity beneath the leaves that she had fallen into. The forest capitalized off of her distraction. It grabbed hold of her ankles and tripped her up, pulling her to the ground.

"That's it," she huffed.

She turned to her magic, lighting the offending roots and vines on fire so that she could return to her feet. She threw out long lines of flame, twirling around a bit to cover the area in fire.

"Anyone else looking to get burned today?" she asked of the forest.

"Hurry up," Tina called back to her.

When Heather caught up to the twins, they were standing in front of the door. "How did you get it open so quickly?" she asked. She stared through the opening to a weird scene on the other side.

"I didn't," Tina said.

She too stared through at the long stretch of black rock that covered the ground on the other side. A strange, brown building, squat but wide, could be seen past a field on the other side of the patch of rock. People were streaming out of the doors of the building, heading directly towards them. Towards the door.

"It was already open when we got here," Serena confirmed. "Where's Maya?"

"I don't know," Heather said, looking behind her again. "But we can't wait for her. She'll catch up."

"Or she won't," Serena mumbled. She smiled at the prospect of them ditching their thief that never managed to help in their progress through the fortress.

"Either way, we need to get away from those troopers. Let's just head through and hope those people are friendly."

"Why did they hang that towel on top of that pole like that?" Tina asked. She pointed up at the strange red, white, and blue cloth hanging at the top of white pole in the middle of the field as the three girls headed through the door.

###

About the Author

Cassandra Morphy is a Business Data Analyst, working with numbers by day, but words by night. She grew up escaping the world, into the other realities of books, TV shows, and movies, and now she writes about those same worlds. Her only hope in life is to reach one person with her work, the way so many others had reached her. As a TV addict and avid movie goer, her entire life is just one big research project, focused on generating innovative ideas for worlds that don't exist anywhere other than in her sick, twisted mind.

Other books by this author

Please visit your favorite ebook retailer to discover other books by Cassandra Morphy:

Connect with Cassandra Morphy

I really appreciate you reading my book! Here are my social media coordinates:

Find me on Facebook: http://facebook.com/crowbarland
Follow me on Twitter: http://twitter.com/crowbarella
Favorite my Smashwords author page:
https://www.smashwords.com/profile/view
/Crowbarella
Shop me on Amazon: http://Author.to/CassandraMorphy

Made in the USA
Middletown, DE
10 June 2022

66725361R00176